LIAR, DREAMER, THIEF

LIAR, DREAMER, THIEF

MARIA DONG

GRAND
CENTRAL

NEW YORK   BOSTON

Grand Central Publishing
Hachette Book Group
1290 Avenue of the Americas, New York, NY 10104
grandcentralpublishing.com
twitter.com/grandcentralpub

First Edition: January 2023

Grand Central Publishing is a division of Hachette Book Group, Inc. The Grand Central Publishing name and logo is a trademark of Hachette Book Group, Inc.

The publisher is not responsible for websites (or their content) that are not owned by the publisher.

The Hachette Speakers Bureau provides a wide range of authors for speaking events. To find out more, go to www.hachettespeakersbureau.com or call (866) 376-6591.

Library of Congress Cataloging-in-Publication Data

Names: Dong, Maria, author.
Title: Liar, dreamer, thief / Maria Dong.
Description: First edition. | New York : Grand Central Publishing, 2023.
Identifiers: LCCN 2022037054 | ISBN 9781538723562 (hardcover) | ISBN 9781538723494 (ebook)
Subjects: LCGFT: Thrillers (Fiction). | Novels.
Classification: LCC PS3604.O546 L53 2023 | DDC 813/.6—dc23/eng/20220805
LC record available at https://lccn.loc.gov/2022037054

ISBNs: 9781538723562 (hardcover), 9781538723494 (ebook)

Printed in the United States of America

LSC-C

Printing 1, 2022

For Mom, Dad, Tina, and Justin,
who all believed in me
when I couldn't.

For every person who's ever been
forced to hide their truth.

LIAR,
DREAMER,
Thief

I need to make one thing clear before we get started.
I'm not a stalker, no matter what Leoni says.
In this, at least, you cannot trust her.

PROLOGUE

When I was ten, I found a paperback chapter book nestled amongst the tables of the Scholastic Book Fair. Its title was *Mi-Hee and the Mirror-Man*.

Maybe "found" is the wrong word—the cover had a fake mirror made from a reflective foil sticker, and it wasn't until I turned away for another table, eagerly seeking something about stars or animals, that its flash caught my eye.

As soon as I picked it up, I knew it was meant for me. All that delicious alliteration, the symmetrical title—three sets of paired syllables *and* a double hyphen!—but it was Mi-Hee's name that really thrilled me. It was the first time I'd seen a Korean name on a children's book.

In its opening pages, it's revealed that Mi-Hee is eleven years old. Imagine my surprise when I discovered her story was actually much older—because long before my Korean parents immigrated to the United States, both had devoured Mi-Hee's journey into the fantasy world on the other side of her kitchen door. So just like that, before I'd even cracked the cover, *Mi-Hee and the Mirror-Man* had taken on an almost magical significance, a portal into a childhood I couldn't believe my serious parents had ever inhabited.

And though I loved the story, it was Mi-Hee I most identified with, this lonely girl between worlds who couldn't stop compulsively counting the seconds on her fingers, who knew that the sounds of some words made them intrinsically better than others, who received from the wizard a powerful artifact I immediately coveted: a magical spyglass with white jewels along the rim.

Spyglasses are supposed to make faraway things appear closer, but when Mi-Hee put the six-inch telescope to her eye, it revealed invisible layers in the world around her—gods and spirits and monsters, yes, but also the fundamental nature of people. Their souls became little birds that perched on their shoulders, tittering and preening—and the louder the bird, the bigger the ego of the person it belonged to. If two people were deeply connected, glistening strands stretched between them, like brightly colored spiderwebs. Sometimes, a person's greatest fear projected itself in the air above their head, like the flickering images of grainy horses that gallop in old kinetoscopes. The world of Mi-Hee's book was a treacherous one, and the power of the spyglass kept her alive through all 321 pages.

The truth is there's *always* a hidden world under the one we initially perceive, but grasping its nature can be inconvenient, unsettling, even dangerous. It's easier to just pretend we don't see it, like when we tell ourselves the extra slice of cherry cobbler on our plate doesn't count because it's the Fourth of July, or that the company we're temping at will hire us *any day now* so we can muster the energy to drive our clunking Buick into work. We look away from the homeless man on the street, while trying not to think about how long it's been since we last called home.

But there are other times when we really need to see the world clearly—like when we're convinced that the man we follow around the office is aware of our attention, that he returns our glances with his own whenever our back is turned. Belief is a powerful lens; it can shape the whole world to fit.

Like Mi-Hee, I have a way of revealing the true nature of things: for the last three years, I've layered her kitchen-door world over my own, like a colored pane of glass. Most of the time, I know my version of the kitchen-door world isn't real, just like I know some numbers aren't better or worse than others, that drawing my special sigil on doors with my finger can't actually protect me from dangers I can't identify or predict. That the Cayatoga Bridge is just a structure in Grand Station, Illinois, and not a place of supernatural power, and I don't really have a special connection to my mysterious and furtively private coworker Kurt.

But knowing isn't enough. Knowledge alone doesn't keep anyone safe.

FIRST
STELLATION

Endekagram (noun): An endekagram (also hendecagram or endeca-gram) is a star polygon with eleven vertices, or points. As each internal angle ends with a repeating decimal, endekagrams cannot be constructed with a regular compass and straightedge, though one theoretically could be constructed by folding strips of paper.

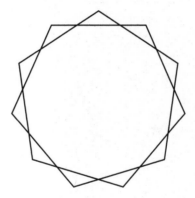

Fig 1. The Small Hendecagram, created by taking the first stellation of an eleven-sided hendecagon polygon. It can be described by the notation {11/2}, where the number after the slash indicates the number of steps between pairs of points that are connected by edges; in an {11/2} shape, a line segment connects every second point. An illustration of this symbol in popular usage is the blue Instagram verified logo.

—The Magical World of Geometry

"And Mi-Hee—it'll be a long, hard road. You'll have to cross the Beaches Strange and Wild, and trek through the mushroom-studded Enchanted Forest That Shimmers as It Sings, where a thousand travelers sleep, trapped after laying their heads down to the cursed lullaby of its trees. In the Vicious Valley, you'll parley with the most fearsome of beasts, the unicorns—and be careful, Mi-Hee, because a unicorn will broker no lies, and if she senses in you the slightest hint of deception, she'll tear you from limb to limb.

"If you answer the unicorn's riddles correctly, she'll give you the secrets you need to climb the Mountain of Cloudy Head and Underground Heart. At the top is a small cottage with an opening in the floor. Journey down it into the Heart: a small room of mirrors that thrums from the power of one world touching the next. Summon the Mirror-Man with his forgotten name, and he will appear. Best him, and he will open the door you need."

Mi-Hee backed away from the wizard. In her pocket, she touched her fingers together, counting the seconds since he'd finished speaking. It was only when she got to seven that she felt brave enough to answer. "I don't want to trek through the Enchanted Forest That Shimmers as It Sings, or meet the unicorns, or fight the Mirror-Man. I just want to go home."

And then she heard a terrible thud, and she knew before she turned around that the door back to her kitchen had closed.

"Don't you understand? Even if you could go back, your house would still be on fire." The Wizard took a long puff of his pipe, and the air around them filled with a soft, purple smoke. "If you don't stop him, he'll take over this entire realm, and end life here as we know it. Sometimes, the only way out is through."

CHAPTER 1

This Is Your Stop

I am on the phone with Leoni, who is *technically* my roommate, though she's out of town for months at a time due to her career as a traveling occupational therapist—mostly working in nursing homes, helping people relearn how to get dressed and bathe and put on hellaciously compressive stockings.

Her absence suits me just fine. The long stretches between our actual cohabitations are probably also our salvation, because even though there's no reason for us *not* to get along, I have a tendency to hate people I spend too much time with, and I've been told I'm not a very good friend, despite my best efforts.

I guess I'm saying I have a habit of getting on everyone's nerves— which is why I'm desperately fighting the urge to tell Leoni about my coworker Kurt's new book. My fascination with Kurt is her biggest pet peeve, and she's put me on notice more than once.

Kurt never takes his lunch in the break room. Instead, no matter how cold it is, he grabs his briefcase and his latest incredibly-expensive-looking phone and walks to his car in the company parking structure. Sometimes, I follow him at a distance, trying to catch a glimpse, but I usually use the opportunity to stroll by his desk and look for clues as to what makes him tick. He always keeps his current book in the second drawer from the bottom, and if he's in a hurry, he doesn't shut it all the way, which is how I've learned that he mostly reads history books: military strategy, secret orders, codes, mythical creatures. He never talks about history, though, and he's never seemed like the kind of person who would buy into conspiracy theories.

If I can get the title of the book and the author's name without attracting the attention of any neighboring coworkers, I write it on a yellow sticky note to look up when I get home—reviews, articles, Goodreads listings—collecting tasty facts with which I can engineer a greater understanding of the man known as Kurt Smith.

Leoni hates my interest in Kurt, which is why I try not to bring it up. But she's been droning on about how the pregnant woman she was temporarily hired to replace might come back early, and how much she dreads talking to her recruiter at the staffing company.

"I swear to god, if I have to call him again about my stipend and hear porn in the background, I'm going to switch companies—"

Normally, I'm grateful for Leoni's ability to keep a conversation going by herself, but on the phone, it's hard to stay in the moment. And when I get bored, I lose sight of what's around me, like the water-stained walls of my apartment or the half-closed, weeks-old pizza box on the coffee table I can't seem to manage to throw out.

Instead, I'm tempted to peer into my version of the kitchen-door world—to watch the sands shift on the *Beaches Strange and Wild*, to immerse myself in the songs of the *Enchanted Forest That Shimmers as It Sings*, to witness the spectacle of hundreds of anthropomorphic once-travelers slumbering on moss as dragonflies wind their way through the breathy, fluting strains of music I've only heard in my mind.

My favorite thing to do, though, is to look for people's

analogues—to observe how my mind represents *real* people from my life in the kitchen-door world.

Not every person or place has an analogue, but important ones do, and they never change. Our apartment, for example, transforms into the hut Mi-Hee found when she first made it across the *Beaches Strange and Wild*: a stinking, one-room hovel with a leaky, thatched roof and crumbling walls covered in mold. It looked abandoned, and Mi-Hee needed a place to hide from the weather.

It wasn't until the middle of the night that she realized it was full of ghosts.

The surrounding apartments in my building are also huts, though they are better maintained, save for our neighbor Mrs. Marple's. I usually imagine her analogue as a robed grim reaper with a scythe, and her army of cats as a flock of tiny demons, each begging for tributes of human flesh. Grim reapers aren't canonical to Mi-Hee's kitchen-door world, so I'm not sure how they ended up in mine—although ever since I realized the book I read was a bad translation, I've wondered how much my kitchen-door world actually reflects Mi-Hee's.

Leoni's always a unicorn, which makes her analogue a shape-shifter, though she's not nearly as brutal as the unicorns in the *Vicious Valley*, which spear liars and evildoers through the heart with their horns before ripping their bodies apart. When I imagine Leoni in her equine version, she's the color of a pearl, with a long, flowing mane. Her human form in the kitchen-door world just looks like herself: a white girl just a bit taller and slimmer than average, with the kind of bleached pixie cut I wish I could pull off. She says it's for her job, that long hair can get caught or pulled when you're transferring patients, but I can't help but think it makes her look like an early-aughts pop star.

Kitchen-door analogues always feel random, at first, but once I get to know the person or place better, I always learn there's something that connects them to their analogue. Leoni's temperament is a lot like the unicorns Mi-Hee encountered, which have a dual personality: so soft and kind they float across the grass without bending it, but carnivorous and bloodthirsty when threatened.

In a way, it's always made me trust Leoni more. She's unpredictable, until you understand her analogue.

I resolved a few days ago to no longer give in to the temptation of the kitchen-door world, even if my visits make me feel like I understand my own life better. I've known all along that carrying around an imaginary realm as a grown woman isn't *healthy*, but it used to seem innocuous and fun—like scoping out an ex's social media.

The strength of the visualizations has grown over time, though, as has my need to indulge in them whenever I'm stressed, bored, or just curious. Lately, it's become compulsive and frantic—like finding out the ex you're still in love with is dating someone new, and if you don't figure out how this person stole them away from you, you'll be doomed to an aching loneliness for the rest of your life.

It doesn't matter that it's bad for me, that the short-lived relief from the kitchen-door world can't compete with the shame of needing it in the first place. It doesn't even matter that I'm not always in control—that the kitchen-door world can overtake me through no choice of my own, that I can't always tell what's real and what isn't. No matter what, I'm always just a breath away from slipping beneath its surface, from seeing and hearing the fantastic overlaid on everything around me.

The urge builds. If I looked into the kitchen-door world right now, Leoni would probably be in her human form—the swoops of her somehow always perfect eyeliner, a puckered red scar on her forehead to replace her horn. Before long, whispers trickle into the corners of my hearing, the rustle of a soft wind that hums with the wings of dragonflies.

There are too many things I want right now—to see her analogue, to tell her about Kurt, to hang up the phone—and the pressure of these desires is like the stretching over a pimple, the tension of an overflowing cup. Something has to give.

I blurt it out before I can stop myself. "Kurt's reading a new book. One about medieval demons."

"That's fucking weird," she snaps. It's almost cruel, the way she says it, like a child's condemnation on the playground.

"It's not that weird." I somehow don't sound as defensive as I feel. "People have lots of interests—"

"You know what I mean. You need to stop doing that." I can hear something in the background, a soft, mechanical hum like a fan, only more rhythmic. An air conditioner? Road noise? Or is it the music that emanates from the *Enchanted Forest That Shimmers as It Sings*?

"It was funny, at first. But you're really becoming a stalker."

As wounds go, this one's deep. "I'm not a stalker." It's an amazing lie, because I believe it, despite knowing most people would disagree. The truth is that I *do* follow Kurt around, and I pay attention—I can tell you the books he reads, the music he listens to, that he has arugula-filled salads for lunch four days a week and treats himself to a sub sandwich on Fridays. That he always answers the phone with "Go for Kurt" and not "Hello"; that on summer weekends he takes his boat out on the water and forgets to put sunscreen on the tip of his nose, which burns so much faster than the rest of him; that his hair always smells faintly of pears. That sometimes, when he thinks nobody is looking, his face changes, the expressions melting off like wax, revealing something as hard and unreadable as concrete, like there's an entirely different man under his skin. It reminds me of those white Greco-Roman statues, the way archaeologists recently discovered they were all once covered in garish paints—a secret, unless you know where to look.

I haven't been able to figure out where Kurt lives yet, because like I said, I'm not *really* a stalker. I don't break a bunch of laws in my quest to discover new things—but I've assembled enough clues in three years of following him around to know a *lot* about his inner world.

Like his deepest secret. I know *that* because it's hidden in a box on my shelf.

"I'm not here to judge," Leoni says. I have no idea how much time has passed since I last spoke. The hum gets louder.

"It's just because it's boring at Advancex." This is another lie-not-lie. Yes, work is boring, but that's not why I can't stop seeking out Kurt.

I don't know why I can't stop.

"I know. But still, you could get in trouble. And he's not really that interesting, anyways. I'd rather just hear about *you*. How are things at Advance-*sex*?" She makes her voice light, leaning on the pun that's sent us giggling on quite a few wine nights—how, *how* could a Fortune 500 company not realize customers would see "Advancex" and think *Advance-sex* instead of *Advance-ex*?

"They're okay." I know I'm supposed to elaborate, but no matter how much I flail, there's nothing else I can tell her—nothing happening in my life that isn't related to Kurt or the kitchen-door world.

She clears her throat. "Listen...I'm starting to worry about you, you know."

"There's nothing to worry—"

"It's not just this Kurt business, although that's part of it. How has...have you still been seeing things?"

My throat closes up, but I manage to give her my best approximation of an exasperated sigh. "*God*, Leoni. We were both drunk. I was *making it up*—"

"I've seen you, though. At least with the numbers. Counting your steps, that kind of thing. Do you think—"

"There's nothing wrong with me!" It's sharp enough that I can hear her pull the phone away from her ear, and I take a deep breath. "I don't think I'm Jesus, or that I can fly. I'm not washing my hands until they bleed. And nobody sends me secret messages over the radio." All lame jokes, and I can tell from the silence between us that they land like frying pans.

Another pause. "Maybe you're right, and you confessing to seeing a fantasy world around you—that you *sometimes* can't tell what's imaginary—maybe that was all drunk talk. Or maybe, you should consider seeing someone. Really, it couldn't hurt."

"Right," I say, though she's wrong. It *can* hurt. Therapy isn't magic, and the wrong therapist can do more harm than good. "I'll think it over, okay?" The edges of the world around me are starting to feel wavery, a sign of the kitchen-door world pressing in. This conversation is making me too upset. I have to get off the phone.

"Either way, you should stay away from Kurt. You don't really *know* him, not the way you think you do—"

"Hey, someone's calling. I've got to go." I hang up before she can answer, but it's too late. When I turn around, there's a miniature forest of enchanted mushrooms growing in my kitchen, populated by dragonflies that dart back and forth, their bellies shining with the lights of the tiny fairy lanterns they carry. The entire room is cast in a soft purple glow, which I know is actually white and emanating from the hood lamp over the stove—but my eyes don't see it, and after a few moments, I'm no longer sure. Is the light purple or white? Am I in my kitchen, the *Enchanted Forest That Shimmers as It Sings*—or both?

I close my eyes hard and count to eleven, focusing on the numbers, the way they feel as they take up space in my brain. With each one, the urge to slide into the kitchen-door world ebbs. When I'm finally brave enough to look again, the forest is gone, all save a single flower: a purple, five-pointed star that sits atop a woody stem so long it almost reaches my thigh.

I swallow. It's a doraji—a perennial flower used in Korean

medicine, though the roots are also frequently eaten: with rice, as a seasoned vegetable, as liquor or candy or tea. In English, they're commonly referred to as "balloon flowers" for the puffy appearance of the buds before they open, though my mom always preferred their other name: bellflowers.

She brought the seeds with her when she first emigrated from Busan. She tended them until they took over half the backyard, a thicket of blue-purple flowers cheerfully impervious to the cold winters of Pleasance Village, Illinois.

Doraji weren't described in *Mi-Hee and the Mirror-Man*. That isn't to say they weren't there—it was a Korean children's book, after all—but what does it mean that after almost three years of seeing the book's imaginary forest in my kitchen, there's suddenly something new to find?

Though I know the flower isn't real, I can't help extending a finger toward it. Right before I brush the velvet of its petals, it shimmers into nothing.

When I said Mi-Hee's spyglass revealed the truth, I didn't mean *facts*, because people cannot be understood by their facts alone. I'll prove this later, but for now, here are mine:

Once upon a time, I was on scholarship in music school, after somehow nailing the audition on my clarinet—a life choice my high-school band director of a father had warned me against many times, because music isn't a career, not really, and no matter how much he actually loved his job, he didn't want me to end up like him, sublimating his artistic desires to teach a passel of horny asshole teenagers—though I, at least, would never feel the burden of white suburban parents bent on the Ivies pretending they didn't understand my accent.

And maybe my mental health was the best, and maybe it wasn't, but what I can tell you is that I was good—good enough that my sophomore year, I was selected for soloist on a performance of K. 622, Mozart's Clarinet Concerto in A Major. I'd aced the audition, in no small part because the K. 622 was one of my father's favorite pieces. The bouncy, mellifluous runs of notes that glide carelessly through the full range of the instrument, the way it'd been published posthumously without an autograph to explain how Mozart had wanted it to be performed. Musical historians can't even agree on the exact instrument it'd been made *for*: the basset horn, the A clarinet, or the basset clarinet, none of which are common members of modern classical ensembles.

By then, my parents had already started pulling away and weren't returning a lot of my calls. When they did, they always seemed distracted, as if there was something else they'd rather do. They'd assured me they would attend my performance, though—but when I sat there bathed in the bright lights, scanning the shadowy impressions of the audience for their silhouettes, I couldn't find them.

It was like my muscles just solidified—my fingers, my tongue, my guts. I couldn't move, and everything was going wavy. I managed to pull it together and blow into the mouthpiece, but it wasn't notes—just squawks. There I was, onstage in front of a packed auditorium, honking like a goose.

I ran offstage. Threw up. Skipped class—weeks, then months— and then nobody paid the measly tuition bill that was left over after my scholarships had been applied. When they evicted me from the dorms, I went to my parents' house, but my father wouldn't let me in. We stood there on the porch, a mist of sleet quietly falling around us, until he handed me his keys. "Go to a hotel or a friend's house," he said. "We can talk about this later."

Maybe things would have turned out differently if I'd confessed to failing out of college, to losing my scholarship. If I'd screamed at him about the bill. If I hadn't lied about having money, lied about having friends.

I took their car to the Pleasance Sunbeam Library. I knew from a thousand childhood visits that it wasn't open on Sundays, that it has a small employee lot around the back that's obscured from the main road. I slept there that night, in the back seat of my parents' car, my breath fogging the inside of the windshield as the evening cooled, eventually turning to frost. When I woke shivering at dawn and looked out, I didn't see anything through the ice but soft shapes—and then I closed my eyes, and there it was, a door hanging in the corner of my mind, one I hadn't seen since I was a child and obsessed with a book about a girl and a spyglass. I saw myself stepping through, and for a moment, everything smelled like smoke.

I turned the car on and let the engine warm. I scraped the ice—on the outside, on the inside, the legacy of my frozen breath—until there was a hole large enough to see. And then I pulled onto the highway and drove the two and a half hours to the big city, to Grand Station, Illinois, thinking I'd make a new life for myself, one where I was a hero, and successful, and loved.

And if I sometimes slipped into Mi-Hee's world and saw things that weren't really there, if I sometimes leaned into my fantasies just for the smell of smoke and beach sand, if I found myself drawing a special sigil on my apartment doors with my finger to ward off the deaths of my family in strange, gruesome ways—the same way Mi-Hee's counting warded off evils in the book—well, that was okay, because I had a dream, a story, a new life.

But I was wrong, because the life I live now isn't new. It's just a copy of the one I left behind, and I don't know the way back.

CHAPTER 2

A Box of Secrets

After I hang up on Leoni, after Mi-Hee's mushroom forest disappears, I take a seat on the plush gray-green couch—Leoni's couch, because I, of course, didn't bring any furniture with me when I moved in—and spend an hour trying to turn down the volume on the worries circling my brain, the feeling of *unrightness* that presses into my skin like insistent fingertips. I need to make sure I've got a handle on things, that for at least a little while, I'll be more firmly *in* this world than out of it.

There are rituals I can do, ones I started developing long before I'd first read Mi-Hee's book: counting, reciting, drawing my sigil, moving in symmetrical patterns with the right number of repetitions. Little actions that make me more certain nothing bad will happen, that I won't lose control of myself—but they're only partial measures. Not like going out to the Cayatoga Bridge, which tears out my bad feelings at the root.

But I can't go to the bridge right now. I always go right before midnight, because that's when I went the first time, when I discovered its power—and I'm terrified if I change any aspect of the ritual, the bridge won't work for me anymore, and I'll be stuck here, in this body, forced to trudge through this mess without it.

I decide to do the next best thing—draw my sigil, which is composed of four endekagrams: eleven-pointed, star-shaped forms made by connecting the points of an eleven-sided regular polygon. I draw it on the legs of my jeans, my pointer fingernail tugging gently on the bumps of the fabric. Eleven stacked sigils on one pant leg, eleven on the other, keeping careful count: the more elaborate the shape and the more powerful the number of repetitions, the better it will work, but only if I execute it perfectly, and keep it balanced on each side. Eleven is one of my favorite numbers to use: prime, hard to balance, and uncommon in nature, all of which give it strength—but it's still small enough and common enough that I feel I can control it.

By the time I'm done, another hour has passed, and I'm almost certain the mushroom forest isn't coming back. My anger at my roommate, though, is simmering to a boil.

I should be grateful to Leoni, who makes my entire life possible. This apartment may be a disaster—the spots of mold on the popcorn ceiling, the chipped stove with its single working burner, the unpredictable heat that sometimes roasts us in hellfire and sometimes leaves us chilled to the bone—but I also can't afford it on my own. I'm not even sure how Leoni affords it. I know she likes living in Grand Station for the location and transportation, that between the train, the highways, and the nearby regional airport, it's easy for her to get to her various travel therapy assignments. The hospital system is also pretty good, which is important—her sister is sick, some disease with a name I can never remember, though I know it's chronic and makes it hard to breathe, and it means she has to live in a residential care facility with round-the-clock monitoring.

I worry all the time that Leoni will move. If she decides she wants to relocate her main home hub and her sister to somewhere cheaper,

I'm not sure what I'll do. When my temp agency, Spectacular Staffing, called to say they'd found me a placement at a "hospital revenue cycle management" company called Advancex, I'd never heard of it, but they were offering me fifteen dollars an hour. I needed the money, because it was September, and I was sleeping in my car. The days were still warm, but that would change soon. The last remnants of summer in this part of Illinois always break like a wave, less than two weeks before the cold comes on, and the nights were already filling the windshield with frost. There was no way I'd survive dead winter, with its Lake Effect snow.

But I couldn't work at a place like Advancex without somewhere to stay. I'd just arrived from Pleasance Village and I didn't know anyone—and I'd been evicted when I failed out of school. Even if I somehow managed to talk a landlord into renting to me, the Advancex building was on Main Street, at the very throbbing heart of Grand Station. No way fifteen dollars an hour would be enough to rent anywhere close to there—and especially not fifteen dollars an hour at a *temp* job, which didn't count as real income for any rental agency I called unless I'd been working there full-time for at least a year.

I had no deposit, no acceptable proof of income. I couldn't get to the job without a nearby (enough) apartment; I couldn't get the apartment without a year at the job. The harder I tried to grab on to the situation, the more it slipped away.

I've done a lot of dangerous things in my life, but sometimes I think the worst was posting an ad on craigslist, detailing my situation, begging for help. If someone could take pity on me, if they had a room to rent—*I'll be a model tenant. I have a good job at Advancex and a car. Anywhere within an hour of downtown. Please.*

A lot of creeps replied, describing in great detail what they'd do to my hands, my face, my body. But then, like a unicorn parting the glade, Leoni arrived to save me, though I was no deserving virgin as per the medieval stories.

I have a place. It's not too far from there. You're ... not a serial killer, are you?

No, I'd replied, my heart beating as hard as it does when I hike across the bridge. *I'm a vegetarian.*

So was Hitler.

That was actually a myth created by his propaganda department.

As soon as I clicked SEND, the shock of what I'd done hit me. I'd corrected this person, the only earnest response to my ad. They were probably never going to reply again—

I hoped you'd say that. Do you want to meet up at Bin-Bash for some coffee and see how we get along?

Thinking now of how I'd held the phone to my chest and cried, my anger cools some—but only a little. The truth is that Leoni doesn't understand how I feel about Kurt, because she *can't.* She doesn't have a secret like Kurt and I do, access to a world larger than the one she sees.

But when that thought enters my brain, it drags in another—*Are you sure? Are you sure?*—and suddenly, all the calm I've bought myself drawing sigils on my jeans fades away into a sudden itch that can only be scratched by opening the box holding the proof of Kurt's secret— except that I can't. It's not safe time.

Safe time is the short window after I visit the Cayatoga Bridge when I can do things from my list of Nots: all the little indulgences I usually can't trust myself with, because I don't know how much is normal, when to stop, or when I'm close to losing control. During safe time, I can drink four iced coffees without feeling like I'm doing something wrong, or watch six hours of Discovery-Bang, a YouTube channel consisting entirely of voiced-over, shaky camera footage as two knuckleheads named Tyler and Josh crawl through Newfoundland forest and abandoned farmhouses to find evidence of fairies and Bigfoot. I can even listen to music, as long as I don't hum or sing or pay too much attention to it.

In my head, I think of "spending" safe time and "choosing" from the Nots, because safe time is like motivation: it's in limited supply, and each action brings me closer to the precarious state I spend most days in, when all the Nots start becoming dangerous again. Without the purge of the bridge, any indulgence that feels good—or that lets my guard down—could trap me in a loop, one where pleasure is secondary to stopping bad thoughts and emotions. If I go down that road, it's hard to come back, like the stomach-sinking feeling of getting home from work and seeing something in your apartment moved. No matter how much you try, you can't stop checking for more evidence that someone's tampered with your things.

Safe time is the only time I can look at Kurt's secret in the box without worrying I might slip into the kitchen-door world so deep that it's hard to come out—especially lately. But Leoni's criticism— *you don't even really know this guy*—has wormed under my skin like a splinter.

Why can't she understand that the holes in my knowledge aren't my fault? The harder I've tried to learn about the *real* man, about his life outside of work, the more elusive he's proved. But I know about the inside of his mind—that he, like me, contains a hidden depth he never shares. I know what's really important to him.

Don't I?

I know the answer, know I *know* the answer—and still, safe time or not, I get up and walk over to the shelf.

I keep my box with me, always. I even made sure to take it with me when I left the dorms, despite the fact that at the time, any reminder of my parents made me furious and despondent. It's made of dark brown wood, with turquoise-blue inlay on the lid. The inlay is shiny and ridged, like the rough edges I feel when I run the pad of my forefinger over my bottom teeth. The box has two fake brass hinges that hold the lid to the body, inset deep into rough-carved holes.

My parents got me this box during our only family vacation, when we all piled into the car during one high school summer and drove two days south into Mexico. I still can't understand why—neither of my parents seemed to like Mexico much, save the beach, and there are plenty of beaches closer to home—but it was the drive down and back that I most cherished: my parents bickering over which music to play, my dad favoring the classical masters, my mom demanding equal time on the tape deck for her favorite teuroteu singers. Each time she won, the car filled with a delicious sadness of floating vibratos and bouncy backbeats, though it was Shim Soo-Bong's "Geuttae geu saram" that made us all sway together, while Jang Yoon-Jeong's "Eomeona!" always had us clapping and dancing in our seats. Somewhere in Texas, they even let me play a song from my new teenage obsession, 14 Dogs, though my dad made a face the whole time.

Since then, I've kept my secrets in this box. Love notes from boys—and then girls, once I figured out who I really was. Report cards detailing failures in subjects as varied as chemistry, history, biology, and gym. A pornographic picture my once best friend Kim Scott printed from some website we never found again. Kim had run out of red ink, and the naked woman had been an alien blue shade, her body disrupted by static-like streaks.

The box is more dangerous than the other Nots, so I approach it carefully. I pick it up and replace it on the shelf eleven times—eleven is a good number, an endekagram number—and then I take it to Leoni's bed. Since it's farthest from the door, it feels like the safest place, the most protected. I can't risk having some part of the ritual go sour.

In this moment, it strikes me how illogical this is, how disrespectful I'm being of Leoni's space. I turn toward my bed, but the itching fills me again, and I don't go any farther. Instead, I push down that kernel of guilt—Leoni's bed, Leoni's place, Leoni's things, *oh*, but when I moved in here, I'd been so grateful, hadn't once considered how much *harder* sharing a bedroom would make everything, hadn't known about the kitchen-door world, how bad I would get—

There's a soft rattle emanating from inside the box. I almost drop it, but then I realize it's because my hands are shaking.

I sink down on her bed, careful, so as not to disturb the fluffy comforter. Bend my knees and drag my legs in close. Her bedding holds the soft scent of her, something clean and vaguely floral, something that makes me realize how stale the rest of this room smells.

I swallow and run my fingers along the box's edge. Its lid is so tightly fitted there's a soft grinding as I pull it open, wood against wood, a sound so pleasing my mouth almost waters. And even though I know what it holds, when I see its contents, the random pattern they've taken after the box's many trips onto and off the shelf, I quiver inside with excitement.

Pulling everything out is careful excavation. Somehow, in the shifting, the thing I need has worked its way to the top, the coincidence a proof that feels as strong as any tarot card. It's a postcard, face-down, just blank lines devoid of addresses, because it was never sent.

It's Kurt's.

I don't remove it. Not yet. Instead, I work my fingers under it, drag out something from beneath—a wooden key chain, the only thing in the box that is mine and mine alone, though I've never had it on my keys. The block lettering on the front reads: PLEASANCE TWELFTH ANNUAL BAND FESTIVAL, FIRST PLACE.

The white paint is starting to yellow, but its surface is as pristine as the day I was awarded it. I can still remember my father's face as he handed it over, the soft glow that could only be pride, though now I understand it stemmed from his role as band director, and not as my dad.

My chest throbs. I turn the key chain over and place it south of the box, wiggle my fingers back under the card.

I sneak out two cassette tapes with almost identical labels made of cheap printer paper, cut unevenly enough that they don't quite fit into their crystalline cases. They're both from 14 Dogs's debut album. I even went to a few of their shows, once they'd made it big enough to travel to Grand Station and then Chicago, although "show" is a bit of a grand word for an impromptu gathering of drunk teenagers and college kids in a park.

One of the tapes is mine—an ironic medium, since everybody had long moved past CDs to MP3s by then—but that was the kind of band 14 Dogs was.

The other tape in the box is Kurt's.

We were riding in the same elevator, and he bent over to tie his shoe, and the tape fell out of his bag and onto the floor. When it became clear he hadn't noticed, I opened my mouth to say something, but no words came out. I couldn't even look him in the eye. He got off the elevator, and the tape was still there, so I put it in my bag.

I put the tapes in their places on the bed, one east and one west. Now, the four objects—box, key chain, tapes—form a cross, with a large blank space in the middle. A good shape, a symmetrical shape, though it's still incomplete.

The last thing in the box is the postcard, which rests not quite flat against the wooden bottom. I pluck it out with both hands and set it in the center spot, still facedown, but I've spent so many hours staring at it that I can picture it clearly: a constructed thing, like a child's art class project. Most of the card's surface is covered with a roughly cut out swarm of black and white rabbits that I'm sure are from the office printer. There are gaps between the rabbits, though, places where the blue and white streaks of the card's background extrude out, like when you're riding in a car past a grove of tight trees and catch strobing flashes of a low-angle sun.

I peeled back one of the rabbits, once. It hurt as much as pulling off a scab, but from the revealed corner, I knew what was on the original postcard—Hokusai's famous painting, *Under the Wave off Kanagawa*.

A huge, swirling blue vortex, about to swallow the small mountain in the center.

I lightly drag my finger along the card's back, under the blank sender address lines. I can almost feel the shape of the letters on the other side. The blocky font looks like it'd feel at place in a seventeenth-century pamphlet were it not for the protective strip of clear packing tape pinning it to the ocean of rabbits:

SOMETIMES, I THINK THERE IS A SECRET WORLD ONLY I CAN SEE, AND ALL THE PEOPLE AROUND ME ARE JUST OBLIVIOUS ACTORS.

Can you understand, now, how it felt to read this? To be standing there in front of Kurt's open desk drawer, a stolen cassette tape I'd kept hidden for six months clutched in my hand, my heart beating wildly for fear that I'd be caught and have to explain why I'd waited so long to return it? And then to be accosted—no, *assaulted*—by a confession that mirrors my deepest secret?

Like a brilliant flash of light.

Of course I took it. *Of course* I'll never tell. I'd die to know exactly what he meant, how close his fantasy world is to my own—but then I'd have to talk to him. And he might ask for the card back, and I can't part with it, not yet.

After I first put the postcard in the box, I closed my eyes and tried to find Kurt's analogue in the kitchen-door world, but when I peered into it, there was nothing there, just a blank space where his kitchen-door form should've been. That usually means someone isn't important to me, but in this case, it confirmed what I'd suspected—that Kurt was a traveler between worlds like me, with no need for an analogue.

Except he's *not* like me. He doesn't have any trouble keeping it together. He's soaring through the ranks at Advancex, having somehow immediately identified everyone important and how to be their friend.

If I can divine how he does it, maybe I can do it, too.

I grab the corner of the postcard, ready to flip it over, but the urgency, the fire, is gone, replaced by a creeping fear. After all, this isn't safe time. I haven't gone to the bridge yet—I'm not supposed to be doing this. If I don't put this all back now, and shove it out of my mind, I'll upset the fragile balance I've reached with this world and Mi-Hee's. I could lose what control I have left.

I want to scream with frustration, but I don't make the rules. After a moment, I stick it all back in the box, get off Leoni's bed, and put everything back on the shelf.

I told you earlier about my life—the facts of my history, and that they wouldn't explain why I am the way I am, or how it feels to be the kind of twenty-four-year-old woman who hides stolen things in a box, who's unsure if a world from a children's book is real.

Here is a better version.

Let's say that when you were a child, you read about a girl named Mi-Hee. In your young imagination, she lived in a big, western-style ranch with gardens and a small pool filled with goldfish, because you didn't yet understand that most Korean houses in the 1960s when the book was first published didn't look like the homes in your tiny American village. They didn't have separate kitchens and dining rooms, and most of the doors in the house would've likely been sliding doors and not ones that swing out. You didn't know that the book that would come to define you was, in fact, translated, meaning you couldn't completely trust the accuracy of your mind's depiction of its contents.

But children are little egoists, and in your imagination, Mi-Hee's house was like your house. There was a kitchen just like yours, except this one had a skinny door that never opened. The knob didn't turn, and there was no keyhole or lock. In the book, once Mi-Hee was old enough, this door faded from her mind as if it had never existed—until one night, when she awoke to the smell of smoke. She sprinted out of her bedroom, feet thudding against the floor, only to discover that the entrance to her home was missing, the wall sealed over.

When she turned around, the kitchen door she'd forgotten was there again, only now it was open, and there was daylight spilling through it. On the other side was a white beach full of coconut palms and an ocean whose waves softly lapped at sparkling sand—and because Mi-Hee was young and curious and in danger, she stepped over the threshold.

Let's say you read this story, and loved it dearly, and then, like Mi-Hee's kitchen door, it faded from your mind—though not so easily. You were too attached to it, to this girl who was odd like you, who yearned like you, and it was a painful experience to forget it, one full of loss.

Then, one night, you, too, have an emergency. Maybe you are a new college dropout, shivering in the back seat of your parents' car, realizing that you have no idea what you're doing, that you've got no money and no place to stay. You pass the night in the employee parking lot of a small library, the one you practically lived in as a young child, because it's the only place that feels safe and quiet and familiar.

Just before dawn, after the stars have faded but before the sky starts to lighten, you think you see something through the glass of the side entrance—a short, bright flash, like the beacon of a lighthouse—and all the hair stands up on the back of your neck.

You crack open the car door and stare at the employee entrance. Something familiar-looking sits on top of the circulation desk, but the glass is translucent with frost, and you're too far away to be sure, so you creep out of the car, your feet crunching on frozen grass that was asphalt only a second ago. As you approach, the air around you fills with the smell of smoke. You know it's not real, but you keep moving, pulled forward as if on wires.

It's not until you're inches from the glass, until you've kicked the rock the staff use to prop open the door and sent it skittering sideways, that you can make out enough to be sure. A book, held up by a small wire frame. The cover faces the employee entrance and not the front door that patrons use, as if it was meant to be seen only by you.

You know this book, because you used to have one just like it. You lost it, somehow, right before you went to college. You tore through your parents' house on the verge of tears, unsure how you could lose something so important, so *needed*. Over and over, your mother asked you what you were looking for, but you were too embarrassed to tell her, and by then, she was used to seeing you cry for reasons you couldn't explain, reasons she would never understand.

But here is your lost book, in the glass. *Mi-Hee and the Mirror-Man*. You've read it so many times you can recite it from memory, trace the arc of the plot like an endekagram, but you've always wondered: If eleven-year-old Mi-Hee had known what would happen when she went through the kitchen door, if she'd known about the Wizard and the Mirror-Man and the empty-room ghosts and the unicorns and the *Forest That Shimmers as It Sings*—would she have still done it? Her house was burning, but there had to be other doors, other windows. The fire crew would have come. If she'd known, would she have stayed instead with her family, her sense of reality, her life? After all, no sane person just jettisons everything they know for a fantasyland.

You've read the book a thousand times and never managed to figure it out. But as you stand here, shivering outside the library, the sky just barely starting to pinken, you're seized with the belief that the answer is *in there*—in the library, in this book that is almost surely your copy, no doubt delivered to them by your mother as she disdainfully threw away your things. Your ears fill with a familiar piece of music—the one that recently humiliated you—as you grab the door and pull. You're almost surprised to find it locked.

And suddenly, you see it laid over the library door, as if the two somehow occupy the same space: Mi-Hee's kitchen door. In that moment, you realize—it doesn't matter what decision Mi-Hee made. It matters instead what decision *you* will make—you, who, unlike Mi-Hee, already knows the scope of what is being asked of you, that this decision is permanent—that some doors, once stepped through, seal up behind you, as if they never existed at all.

You, who doesn't like your life, who doesn't like your world. You, who'd rather go to never-never land, and never-never wake up.

As you bend down to pick up the rock, your nose fills with the smell of hot sand, and the music crescendos. You throw it, hard, and the door shatters into a crystalline rain, rendered silent by the calls of strings and flutes and horns. You bend down and step through the hole you've created, heedless of the jagged rim of glass.

When you straighten enough to get a good look at the circulation desk, the book is gone.

You're not sure it was ever there in the first place.

A horror overtakes you, but when you shut your eyes, you see around you a tall, enchanted forest, full of pines and spruce, and you realize what you've done. You've stepped through Mi-Hee's door, and now, it's *your* turn to enter a world full of fantastical, sentient creatures, friend and foe. It's your turn to go off exploring and have grueling adventures, sure the entire time that these challenges will turn out all right in the end—because, for once, you are the hero of this story, this story whose sole purpose is to mold you into a better version of yourself.

You get back in your car. You push the accelerator down as if the car itself has wings. Only then do you see the cuts on your legs, the red of your blood from the glass, and wonder at your own boldness.

You drive to your new life in Grand Station, because Grand Station is bigger and better, the perfect place to be a bigger, better you.

But shortly after you arrive, you realize how wrong you were. The challenges in Grand Station are no different from the ones you left behind in Pleasance: every problem you come up against here you've met before, but at an easier level of difficulty, when all you had to do was be a normal person in a normal place with normal rules.

In *Mi-Hee and the Mirror-Man*, when Mi-Hee breached the *Heart* of the mountain and uncovered all the mirrors in preparation for the spell that would bring the Mirror-Man into the world, her kitchen door once again appeared behind her—only now, it was painted black.

The sight of it, how closely it resembled something she yearned for, made her feel like she was being torn apart. She wanted so badly to step through it, but the Wizard had warned her in advance that this dark version of her kitchen door was not to be trusted, and so she left it alone.

And you? You leave *everything* alone, your whole life alone—at least, the best you can. You don't try too hard. You don't hope too hard. You tread water and go to work and go home and berate yourself for never being able to put pizza boxes away. Nothing ever changes.

Not until the night you realize that your coworker Kurt Smith is a better version of you, and you suddenly know how Mi-Hee must have felt when the shadow version of her kitchen door materialized behind her in the *Heart*.

As the teller of this story, I have to wonder: Where do you go from here?

If you were a smarter person, a better person, a more practical person, you wouldn't have stepped through the kitchen door at all—and even if you had, you would've marked where it was, and once you'd done all your growing, you would've returned with some new magic that your freshly enlightened self had discovered, and the door would've opened. You'd have gone back, back to your life with your many friends and your family that loves you and your good job. It's possible the door would've moved—such is the shifting nature of doors in fantasy worlds—but the point is, you would've figured it out. You'd be that main character, dutifully completing your arc of complex growth.

But you are neither smart nor bold. You are a broken person with nothing to go back to, so you decide to just stay in your new life without purpose—only now, you're damaged in new ways. Everything from your life in Pleasance feels like poison, too dangerous to touch, and over the last three years, in your shitty job, without the support of your family or friends, so many of the habits and behaviors that used to calm you have instead become your master. You're trapped inside of yourself.

Sometimes, when you sleep, you dream of climbing a mountain, but never reaching the top. In the moments before you awaken, you look down and discover your left ring finger has started to wither away, and you know that this process will slowly spread until it claims the rest of you.

CHAPTER 3

The Mirror-Man

The next morning, I wake up an hour earlier than normal, but I get stuck in the bathroom, because over the *shush-shush-shush* of brushing my teeth, I hear a sneeze.

I try to reason through my panic.

You live on the fourth floor. Logically, you have a downstairs neighbor. It's normal for them to be in their apartment. It's normal for them to sneeze. This is what you heard.

But I can't shake the feeling that the sneeze was too loud. Like it was coming from inside this room, from behind the toilet or the mildewed shower. And though it makes no sense, I'm too scared to check the mirror, too scared that looking at it the wrong way will give it power. Instead, I turn around by degrees, as if seeing someone in my bathroom out of the corner of my eye would make the experience less terrifying.

I think of Mi-Hee at the *Mountain of Cloudy Head and Underground Heart*, watching every one of the enchanted mirrors in the small room at the bottom of the well, trying to ensure the Mirror-Man couldn't emerge and catch her unawares, despite the Wizard's insistence that he could only be released by a spell.

There's nobody behind me, nobody in the cramped shower, but the feeling of being watched grows. If I don't ward it off now, it'll follow me all day. I draw my endekagram sigil on the bathroom door, but by the time I finish and throw my phone and keys into my purse, the green numbers on the coffeemaker say I'm running five minutes late.

Leoni texts before I make it out the door. *You forgot to pay the internet bill. I might be coming home in a few weeks. I'd rather not have to deal with all this then.*

All this. She means the bills, the mess, the way nothing is ever the way it should be. Given my money-management skills, she was smart not to put any of the bills in my name. Even though it's illogical for it to sting now, when I've just proved her right—it does. It also makes me feel guilty, like she knows I've been performing rituals in the bathroom.

Then again, judging by everything strewn around the apartment, there are much deeper shames to feel, at least where my faults as a roommate are concerned: plastic-windowed envelopes I was too lazy to throw away, like the Visa offers I don't qualify for, the stack of unopened petitions for donations to the local food bank. Five take-out containers from Hop Lo's on the corner, which have, at least, been scraped clean—I'm not the kind of woman who leaves leftovers. Pizza boxes; balled-up plastic grocery bags, the receipts still inside; a disconcerting number of paper towel and toilet paper rolls; and a constellation of discarded garments, as if a dirty-laundry bomb exploded on the coffee table, flinging unwashed socks and thrift-store sweaters this way and that. The other day, I spied a little pile on the closet floor that looked suspiciously like raisins, before shutting the door and fleeing.

I feel a twinge of pressure to retreat into the kitchen-door world, but I can't risk being sucked in. I reluctantly shove the urge away.

I'm almost at the door when I remember my work badge, which I thankfully locate in my purse. Right before the door shuts behind me, the overflowing kitchen trash catches my eye.

Today doesn't feel like *it*, as in, the day I start turning things around, especially given what just happened in the bathroom—but last night, I managed to push back against fixating on Kurt's postcard *and* kick the mushroom forest out of my kitchen. That's something. And if there's a chance Leoni will be home in the next few weeks, I'd better start cleaning this place up. I can't let her see the apartment like this.

I dart back in, tie the trash shut, and haul up on the bag. It's stuck, no doubt because of my stomping on the top to buy more time. I kick the plastic bin until the bag finally slides out, revealing an odd print of kittens chasing butterflies. Several of the cats bulge with white blotches: sharp trash corners trying to cut their way out.

The bag is a novelty print, a gift from Mrs. Marple and her horde of cats during the building's first—and, according to the super, who had to clean up afterward, *only*—secret Santa party. I actually hate the bags—hate shoving my trash into something cute and turning it grotesque—but they were free, and we've only got a few left.

I drag it over to the trash chute. It's harrowing, the way the bag strains, threatening to break under its own weight, thereby punishing me for my sins—but I make it. I heave it up and push it toward the chute opening—

Until I see the corner of my work badge sticking through my fingers.

I recoil, and the bag falls to the ground, the top splitting like a monster giving birth, its entrails streaming out. It's a huge mess, but I still have my badge. Relieved, I slump against the wall and take a deep breath.

If I'd thrown it down there, I'd never have gotten it back. The super, Mr. Sacks, slipped half-sheet flyers under our doors last week, warning us he was locking the trash room due to break-ins. I've tried *very* hard not to guess at the culprit—if someone around me is stealing from the trash of the people *in this crumbling-ass building*, I *seriously* do not want to know.

If I stay here and clean this mess up, I'll be late for work, and it's not like either Advancex or Spectacular Staffing have a real tolerance for tardiness.

Maybe I could leave a note? I bend over my purse and rummage through the contents for a pen and some paper. It feels awful to throw this on the super, but he'll understand, right? If I lose my job, I won't be able to make rent—

A shadow envelops me. Two sienna work boots slide forward, somehow occupying all the space that has ever existed in the world. I look up slowly, already knowing who I'm going to find. "Hello, Mr. Sacks."

"Hello, Katrina." He's got the gravelly voice you'd expect from a smoker, though I've never caught him smoking, and he never smells like cigarettes. He's a relatively short Black man, but given the way I'm hunched over, he looms above me.

I straighten up slowly. The added height doesn't make me feel better. I don't know what to make of Super Sacks—especially given that Leoni thinks he's not a super at all, but actually the building owner, affecting a role so we leave him alone. He rarely talks, and it's always stiff and humorless. Despite the boots and his emergent potbelly, he walks quietly enough to sneak up on you in a hallway, and he's always got a knife or some other tool visibly located on his person.

In short, he's either a mild-mannered, aging handyman, or a serial killer. I've only seen his kitchen-door analogue a few times, and that's proven no help: a black, anthropomorphic rabbit with an eye patch and a cigarette dangling from the corner of his clefted mouth.

I don't quite know what this means. While attempting to cross the

Beaches Strange and Wild, Mi-Hee was captured by a faction of rabbit-headed pirates, only to be rescued in the dead of night by the equally floppy-eared crew of the *Lepus*. But the sailors had a traitor on board, one Mi-Hee ferreted out with her spyglass, and as a reward, they let her sail with them all the way around the cape.

Mr. Sacks's furry analogue has a peg leg and sabers crisscrossed behind his back. He could be one of the *Lepus* sailors, although my gut says *pirate*—hardened, dangerous, and possibly criminal. Not the kind of person you want to be stuck in a hallway with alone.

I swallow. "I was just about to leave you a note—"

"Apologizing for the stain in my hallway?" He nudges the mess with his boot, unveiling a small pile of coffee grounds. "It's all right. I would've known it was you. Mrs. Marple wouldn't do something like this."

He's referring to the kitten print. "Right."

He frowns at me, the expression comically exaggerated. "Looks like you're going to need a bucket and sponge."

I see it, then, a time clock, and not like the computer program Advancex uses to log your punch. Instead, the space around me becomes a giant, rumbling factory, the air filled with steam, hundreds of industrious workers running up and down stairs and climbing machines like the masts of ships. A whistle pierces the air, and then the view zooms in on the old-fashioned time clock, men and women spinning a lever to stamp their cards with red ink.

I blink, and I'm in the hallway again. "I'm going to be late for work." It's the most my voice has ever sounded like a squeak—probably because I already know I've lost. Super Sacks *might* murder me, but according to Leoni, he likely has the power to evict us. With city rents being what they are, it's not really a risk I can take.

"I'll write you a note," he says. "Let me get you a bucket."

One thing only the chronically late can understand is that lateness is not linear. There are different *levels* of being late for work, and each inspires a different reaction.

At five minutes late, you put on a little burst of speed.

At twenty or thirty minutes late, you *really* hustle—pump the accelerator to the floor, drop things in haste, skip coffee, and try to breathe through the ensuing panic attack. It's almost impossible to catch up—but it *can* be done, even if there's no way to do it *gracefully.*

As someone who is twenty minutes late out the door, every single day, I know this feeling well.

Conversely, forty minutes late feels less pressing than twenty. Maybe it's because at forty minutes, you realize there's no catching up—that even if you push yourself to superhuman extremes, you'll still be late.

At Advancex, if you're more than ten minutes late, but under sixty, you get two action points. Sixty minutes late is four points. If you accumulate ten points (which never drop off, by the way), you come under review for firing.

Currently, I have two points. I am forty-two minutes late, which is twenty-two minutes later than normal, but I still hoof it when I hit the street, as the November wind is cold enough to freeze my freshly showered hair. I find my parents' car: an old, dark blue Buick sedan, the wheel wells disintegrating into chasms of rust. I noticed the first fleck last month. Since then, it's been growing almost daily, eating the car like a black hole, like the withering of my dream-fingers.

I get the passenger door open on the first try, which is lucky—the outside handle is failing, which means I have to leave the window cracked in case I have to resort to the coat hanger in my trunk. The driver-side door is superglued shut; after the latch broke, it kept flying open whenever I slowed down, which made for a harrowing highway experience. I bungee-corded it until I realized I'll never have the funds to get it fixed. I can't even afford insurance.

Truthfully, given Grand Station's stellar bus system, I don't need a car, though a vehicle was an Advancex requirement. I don't know that they'd still hold me to it, but as a fire-at-any-moment temp through Spectacular Staffing, I don't want to find out.

And I'd be lying if I said that part of my attachment wasn't the once yearly envelope I still receive, addressed to me, empty save for plate renewal stickers and proof of insurance. Each time, it feels like finding a message in a bottle on a beach.

I don't know why my parents keep paying for the insurance when they've made it clear they don't want anything to do with me. I sent letters when I first moved, long missives about what had happened, but they were returned unopened. After a month, I tried calling, leaving voice mails—until the number was disconnected.

Now, it's been three years with no other communication than the insurance envelope. I suspect it's because it's easier—if I have an accident in an uninsured car they technically own, they'd have to either report the car stolen or ask for it back. This way, they don't have to talk to me.

But in the kitchen-door world, it's because Pleasance Village sits on top of a mountain, around which a wild magic has grown an impassable dome of thorns. Only once a year does the barrier open enough to send out a single messenger pigeon.

It's stupid, thinking of it this way. But it hurts less, except when it doesn't.

I bore a hole in the ice on the windshield while the engine warms. Today, my car doesn't make *the noise*—a series of rattle-groan-shrieks like a dragon being sucked into a vacuum cleaner—but as I wait for a break in traffic, I can't help but feel anxious, as if I've forgotten something.

It's not until I'm in the flow of cars that I remember I didn't have a chance to draw my sigil over my front door when the trash exploded.

The flutter in my stomach grows teeth. Without the sigil, anything could happen.

Stop it. That's kitchen-door protection.

I still can't help glancing around the car. Thankfully, it's just a car, no hint of the large sailboat it becomes when I'm spiraling out.

Although there's a lot of traffic, I make decent enough time that when I pull into Advancex's boxy parking structure—a privilege I pay seventy-five dollars a month for—I'm still only forty-two minutes late.

I find a spot immediately, shaving off another two minutes. The time saved gives me a perverse impulse to turn on the car's tape deck, to lean back and listen to a little music.

Music is on the list of Nots, but I'm feeling weak. I turn 14 Dogs on for a minute, until my better judgment reasserts itself and I climb out. It's two blocks from the lot to the building. I'm not dressed warmly enough, so I throw on a little extra hustle rushing in.

Not too much hustle, though. I don't get much exercise these days.

When I turn the corner, the Advancex building swings into view—something that might've been called an Art Deco skyscraper if it hadn't been built twenty stories too short and forty years too late. Still, it has the almost wedding cake–like layers and curved lines, like a stretched-out morel mushroom.

At twenty-five stories, it's also the tallest building in downtown Grand Station, and it's impressive enough that I would've guessed it for the city's heart if I hadn't already felt the pulse throbbing at the center of the Cayatoga Bridge. As far as I know, it's always been office space, but in the kitchen-door world, it's the *Tower of Industry*: a self-contained steampunk city lorded over by an evil dictator. The bottom ten stories are a prison, with manual laborers forced to recapture waste and garbage. The next layer is made up of factory workers, then skilled artisans, and so on. The top layer, of course, is reserved for the elite, who look down upon the rest of us with impunity.

I realize that this *particular* depiction is colored by my own status within Advancex, but it's not like I've been able to see the building any other way.

When I push through the revolving door and into the lobby, I'm surprised at how empty it looks. Not a single body obscures my view of the marble floor—save Yuto, who smirks at me from his spot behind the reception desk. He makes a show of glancing at my badge before waving me toward the badge readers. My steps echo in the huge room like firecrackers.

I swipe through the turnstile and then again at the elevator, before hitting the button for the eleventh floor. My phone buzzes. I fumble for it as the doors close and the ground underneath me lurches.

I'm horrified by what I see. Three texts and two missed calls—all from my recruiter at Spectacular Staffing, who is none too pleased. The fact that she already knows about my absence means that Advancex has noticed, too. I stare at my phone, trying to compose a reply. I'm only vaguely aware of the elevator doors opening, the impression of legs and high-heeled black shoes—though the person I almost run into before I can make it off the elevator is not similarly distracted.

"Jesus, Katrina. Walk much?"

I flinch. This is the second time today someone unpleasant has snuck up on me. I go for the DOOR OPEN button, but it's too late—we're already descending. I punch in my floor again and plaster on a fake smile before looking up. "Hi, Yocelyn. How's your morning going?"

My heart sinks when she rolls her eyes. They're warm and brown, and when she used to sit next to me in the very back of eleven, I frequently found myself lost in them.

I'm not sure what I feel—*felt*—for Yocelyn. When we were seatmates, we were friends, and although I found her attractive, it wasn't like I wanted to date her. It was just nice to have something to liven up the workday. Navya, kindhearted and mom-tough, sits on my right. There was a time when I considered the three of us in the almost empty back row a bastion of plucky minority solidarity against Advancex's crushing weight—but then Yocelyn got promoted and moved to the very front of the floor, right next to Kurt, and became a real bitch to me overnight. Given that they're go-getters, I suspect it won't be long before they're both moved up a floor.

My stomach curdles. It's not like I can make up excuses to look for Kurt on twelve. My badge won't even let me on that floor.

"You're such a space cadet," she says coldly.

I realize she's been talking. "Sorry." I check my phone, but only two minutes have passed. "I'm, uh, running behind."

She looks me up and down, smirking. "Nice outfit."

We hit the lobby. The doors slide open.

She steps out, but before the doors close again, she pivots and grabs my arm, pulls me in so close I can smell the coconut in her conditioner. "Stay away from him," she growls.

I'm too shocked to react. The doors slide half closed around her before springing back open again. And again. The elevator makes a polite *ding*, which shakes me out of my trance.

I rip my arm out of her grip and take several halting steps backward, as if she's an angry dog that'll rush me if it senses weakness.

She, too, retreats. The doors slide closed, ending the conversation, the car lurching around me as I ascend.

She was talking about Kurt. She had to be.

I wonder if this coincidence is because of the unfinished sigil on my door—or if this is my punishment for briefly listening to music in the car. My skin itches already, but I can't exactly ride the elevator drawing endekagrams until I get fired.

When the doors open back up, I get off.

Sometimes, when I'm unsettled and can't do a ritual, I distract myself by focusing on minutiae. Like how Advancex positions higher status cubicles closer to the door, rewarding employees with easy access to the elevators. As spots go, Kurt's is pretty cherry—the first row of cubicles, all the way up against the wall, so he only has the one neighbor to the right side, which is Yocelyn.

I scan down the row as I pass. Her absence doesn't surprise me, of course—but when I see that Kurt's seat is also empty, my stomach suddenly feels like it's full of grease. The sensation sticks to me as I trudge to my seat in the back row.

Navya is on the phone, but she shoots me a look only the mom of four sons can successfully deliver—stern, worried, and curious all at once. She should be closer to the front by now, but she's had to take time away from work, some trouble with one of her kids—and Advancex *might* have let that slide, but time off is a cardinal sin in the Spectacular Staffing playbook.

Which doesn't bode well for me. The sinking feeling gets worse.

My chair groans as I slide in. I jiggle my mouse, and the monitor flickers to life. Navya must have turned it on when there was a chance I'd still make it on time.

I give her a nod, and she winks back before saying something about "the ease of the billing portal" into the phone.

I punch in and launch my email. Before it loads, the company messenger pops up, flashing to indicate a priority message. I swallow at the sender's name: Caressa, my immediate supervisor at Advancex.

Good morning, Katrina. Why don't you swing by my office.

No question mark. Not a question.

Caressa's desk is also on eleven, on a part of the floor for support personnel and management that everybody calls the Annex.

I should like the Annex. Something about its smaller confines and quieter population means that slipping into it makes all the noise of the kitchen-door factory melt away. But it's hard to enjoy when my visits to Caressa are always negative.

I gulp and stand up. Navya shoots me another look as I pass, though this one's easy to read. *Good luck.*

I check Kurt's desk on the way out of the room. He and Yocelyn are still gone. There's no reason this should make my skin prickle—after all, I don't have *romantic* feelings for Kurt—but it does. I'm sure part of it is just the *way* Yocelyn clutched my arm in the elevator.

But another part—and, if I'm being honest, a larger part—is that Yocelyn's analogue in the kitchen-door world is a creature known only as the Unfinder: a giant white rat with red eyes. Although the Unfinder's breed was never mentioned in the book, I can tell it's a lab rat.

I used to feel charitable toward Yocelyn's animal self—it was kind of cute, after all, and although the Unfinder's alchemically inclined character was chaotic and mysterious, she was never presented as outright evil—but given the way Yocelyn's moved up to sit by Kurt and her recent behavior, her beady eyes and scaly tail have taken on new implications: vicious and sneaky, hell-bent on getting ahead.

My back itches. Within seconds, the sensation grows until it covers my whole body.

There's something suspicious going on with her, and it likely involves Kurt.

Right before I reach the door, I slap my head as if I've forgotten something and pivot into Kurt's aisle. His coworkers shoot glances as I pass, but I pull a pen out from my pocket and wave it. "Thought I'd better return this," I say chipperly. "Just let me drop this off, and I'll be out of your hair."

An eyebrow or two rises, but everybody is tied to their phones, their screens. Being in the first row doesn't mean you can escape Advancex's productivity metric.

I make it to Kurt's desk and slide open *the* drawer—left side, second from the bottom. There's a book nestled in the back, something called *Illuminating the Secrets of the Monks*, but then my gaze falls onto a small card, just barely propped against the book's spine so that it rests at an angle, like one of the RESERVED SEATING placards you sometimes see on fancy restaurant tables.

It's another postcard. Kurt's sketched a drawing on the front in marker, flat washes of color that turn dark at each overlap. There are lines and lines of handwritten text, little blobs at the corners of the serifs that could only come from a ballpoint pen. It's a busy drawing, hard to parse, but when it finally comes together, my heart stops.

It's a hand, reaching into a drawer. And the text is just one line, repeated over and over:

THIEVES ALWAYS GET WHAT'S COMING TO THEM.
THIEVES ALWAYS GET WHAT'S COMING TO THEM.
THIEVES—

"Katrina?"

Caressa's voice, but echoing, as if from down a long hallway. There's a moment where the world wobbles on one corner, where I can see this room and the busy factory floor at once. My chest hurts, my head is spinning, I can't breathe—

"Katrina." Sharp, this time. I didn't imagine it. I lift my face—it's heavy, as if weighted—and look up at my supervisor, who is currently a red fire ant.

I focus hard, and after a moment, she's a woman again, dressed in a blouse and slacks, the white collar so crisp against her dark skin that I'm seized by a compulsion to feel the fabric. The pen's still in my hand. Kurt's drawer is open. Everything comes crashing down.

"Sorry." It takes a herculean effort not to snatch up the card. I drop the pen and slide the drawer shut. "Just had to return that."

Caressa's face contorts—angry, too angry for the crime—but then she straightens, her expression blank, and I suddenly can't tell if I imagined the crease in her brow, the curl of her lip. She looks like she always does, an archetypal middle manager, poised and vaguely annoyed. She waves her hand toward the door. "Do you mind?" Another not-question.

I nod once and turn, picking up the pace so she won't see my face. I don't know what she'd find there, but my heart is drumming, drumming, drumming. The first postcard might have been a mistake, but this one? It's clearly meant for me, and just like the repeating text on the surface of the card, a single line runs through my head, over and over. It doesn't stop as I perch in the tiny chair in Caressa's office, or when I sign the action plan she's put together, acknowledging how close I am to a point review. Not even when I'm back at my desk, clicking through the interminable slideshow on Advancex's lateness policy.

Kurt knows I've been going through his desk.

And the truth is that I've been so clumsy, so reckless—opening the drawer in plain sight, somehow certain that Advancex's grueling quest for productivity would shield me. There are a million ways he could've found out.

Part of me wanted this. How many times have I pictured him discovering my trespasses? But in my daydreams, he always flashes me a blue-eyed wink, a thinly veiled recognition of my place as his coconspirator, a person whose fantasy world is just like his—and now my refusal to look squarely at how being discovered might *actually* go has risen up and bitten me in the ass.

It's not until the fervor of being disciplined dies down that I realize I might be interpreting things the wrong way. I only glanced at the card. My perceptions were colored by the stress of knowing I was in trouble. And even if the card is exactly as I remember, it's possible that I missed the *intention*.

After all—if he's really angry with me, then why not just report me to management and be done with it?

Maybe he wants his original card back. Maybe he feels vulnerable that my observation of him has been so one-sided; maybe he's asking me to leave a card of my own.

You're not a thief if it's a fair exchange.

The thought's mine, but it feels traitorous. I know it's kitchen-door logic. The right thing to do is just leave this alone.

But it's like my entire being is pinned to the new postcard. When I close my eyes, it blinks in the back of my head like a radar dot. I walk past Kurt's desk on so many fake trips to the bathroom that Navya asks me if I have a bladder infection.

Every time, though, either Kurt or Yocelyn is there. No chance to open the drawer and make sure I haven't imagined anything. No way to push back against the subtle *clanks* of factory machinery slowly growing louder in the back of my mind, the kitchen-door world threatening to push its way in.

Until it's too much. Until it takes everything I have just to stay here, to stay *now*. I spend the rest of the afternoon on a steep incline, every part of me growing more and more exhausted by the constant attempts to keep from sliding down, but still, with every passing minute, the kitchen-door world becomes sharper, more real, my office slowly morphing into the factory as it fills with anthropomorphic workers: cats and rabbits, tigers and goats with animal heads and human hands and feet. Before long, the moans of prisoners drift up from below.

By the time I stagger to my car at the end of the day, I'm in two places at once. I question if I should be driving—but I'm fine, I think. Good enough to make it home. And although I spend more time maneuvering a sailing ship than my actual car, the groans and creaks, the calls of seabirds, and the *shush* of the waves are all strangely calming. It at least drowns out the times when my car makes *the noise*.

By the time I find a parking spot a street over from my apartment, I'm more centered. Even so, when I pull in, I don't take my hand off the shifter. This détente is only temporary; if I want to make sure I don't lose control—spiral into a panic, get stuck repeating a ritual, slip into the kitchen-door world and not be able to get myself out—I really, *really* should go to the bridge.

I'm afraid, though. I've always, *always* done it the same way. The same time of night, approaching from the same side. If I change something now, I could break its magic. Without the bridge and its power to ground me, to give me the chance to carve out small spaces of safe time to do the dangerous things that feel good, I'd go crazy.

My whole body starts to shake. For a moment, I'm trapped—but then I rip the keys out of the ignition, and everything's normal again.

Despite how tired I am, I race up the stairs. It's only when I'm inside, with the door locked, that I realize I'm crying.

CHAPTER 4

The Well in the Mountain

The forest of mushrooms is back in my kitchen. I can usually stand it—but right now, I can't force myself into its midst, no matter how badly my stomach growls. I feel like I've been caged outside of myself, like there's nowhere safe for me to be.

I should leave, maybe, but I'll be tempted to go to the bridge, and it's not even ten p.m.

I curl up in a ball on the couch and try not to think about things on the list of Nots, to ignore the music threatening on the peripheries of my hearing, but I can tell I'll lose it if I don't find some kind of distraction.

I turn in circles, like a cow in a pen. Go into the bathroom, take a shower. But then I get the feeling of being watched again, and I flee into the bedroom.

Thankfully, it's still just a plain, ordinary bedroom, but now that I'm seeing my surroundings with fresh eyes, I can't help but feel ashamed. I don't even know how a person accumulates this much trash. The garbage is like one of those spreading vines that's outlawed in half the country, runners that start in my corner of the room but swiftly consume the closet, the space under the bed, and the top of the squat dresser that Leoni uses as a makeup table and desk.

The odor assaults me. How did I not notice it before? Sickly sweet notes, the earthiness of mushroom gills, of moss, egg-sulfur, sour milk—and possibly mouse feces. I stumble over to the window and let in a burst of cold air replete with city noise, the mixture of car exhaust and stale fried food fresher than whatever rot pervades this room.

I can't get a trash bag to start tackling this, because they're in the mushroom kitchen, unsafe, *unsafe*—but I can at least sort things into piles. Maybe even venture into the basement of doom to do a load of laundry.

My thoughts creak to a stop when my gaze lands on Leoni's dresser. There are pens strewn all over the top, woven in between her massive collection of makeup—her pens, which I have borrowed from the bottom dresser drawer and not replaced. She gets bulk mistake-boxes from a website that makes custom pens: misspellings, misprinted phone numbers, ink that doesn't quite fit its embossed grooves.

It was one of her pens that I left in Kurt's desk, actually.

I sit down in front of the dresser and pull out some paper from the bottom drawer—I can't answer Kurt with a postcard, not without leaving the house—but I can write him a *note*.

Except I don't know what to say.

I need to talk to you, I start, then scratch it out. I decide to come up with a draft first, copy it onto a fresh sheet after.

There's something I need to tell you.

Scratch.

I saw your message for me. It's not what you think. We're more alike than you realize.

This last bit is not quite right, but I don't feel compelled to cross it out.

I—

My phone buzzes. I shake myself and pull it out of my purse. It's Leoni.

I don't want to talk to her. Not when I'm sitting in our bedroom, which I have destroyed with my disgusting trash. But I don't want to be alone, either, and she's waiting on the other end of the line.

I clear my throat and answer the phone. "Hi, roomie."

"Hey, Kat!" Her voice is too bright, like that sunlight flash through those trees. Something about the image threatens to tip me over the edge.

A long pause. "Um, Kat? Are you still there?"

"Yes. Sorry," I say, clearing my throat again. I hate it when she calls me Kat, although I've never managed to tell her that. "I was just…" I can't come up with an excuse. "How are you doing?"

"Oh, same old, same old. I want to talk to you, though."

Is the timing suspicious? She doesn't know what I'm doing, I don't think. "Okay."

"Well…my sister is getting worse."

Not for the first time, I'm hit by guilt—a sudden, irrevocable weight that pins me to the spot, and everything—the mushroom forest, Kurt, the factory—all just melts away, same as if I were on the bridge.

None of that is real. But Leoni, who has been so nice to me, Leoni and her sister are *real*, and I'm such a shitty roommate I can't even remember the name of her sister's disease. "I'm so sorry." My voice quavers.

"Oh," she says softly. I can't tell what she's feeling. "Kat, are you all right?"

Concern, then. She's concerned. But I don't know how to respond. "You were telling me about your sister."

"That's okay," she says. Her voice is comforting and warm, like beach sand. "That can wait. What's going on with you?"

Everything wells up inside me in a giant wave. "I don't…I don't know where to start. I don't know if I can get it out."

There's a long pause, one where I hear road noise, like she's driving—but it also sounds a bit like the ocean, and I suddenly can't tell which. "Maybe just start with something small," she says.

She's right. I can't tell her about everything, but there are small tribulations, relatable problems I *can* confide. I don't have to be so alone. "Okay. Um...I let the apartment get away from me again. It's a mess."

"Okay," she says. I can *hear* her donning her occupational therapist hat—she's a good listener, but solutions-oriented. Normally, this approach makes me recoil, but right now, I feel like I need the strength of her keel and rudder, or I'll drift out to sea. "Easily fixed. You clean it up. What else?"

"I was late today," I say, almost desperately—but this conversation feels *so* good already. It's like I've been wandering around in a dark, strange room, only to realize it's just my bathroom, that everything will fall into place if I just flip on the light. "I was late for work."

"Okay. Are you in trouble?"

I shake my head. "Well, no. Not yet. If I get another absence or late—"

"So you don't get another absence or late." A not-question. I've been receiving those a lot, lately.

"Right. Right."

"What else?"

"My car is making a noise. It's been doing it for a while, but it's getting worse."

"Can you take it to a mechanic?"

I close my eyes, consult my bank account. There's...forty, no, maybe forty-five dollars in there. I still haven't paid the internet bill, which is sixty. "Not until payday," I lie. I've *considered* taking the boat to a mechanic for damn near a year.

"Sounds like you have a plan! And you could always take the bus until then. Just in case."

I flinch at that. It feels wrong to change something in my routine when my world doesn't feel solid.

"What else?"

There isn't anything else—at least, there aren't any more *easy* things. But I sense an odd, tenuous thread of connection flowing between us, and when I look up, the mushroom forest is gone from the kitchen.

I'm amazed—and perhaps on the verge of an epiphany. There's some clue to my own mind in this conversation, some healing power that makes it good for me to continue.

I have to seize the moment.

"Um, well...something happened with a coworker."

"Which coworker?"

It strikes me that this is an odd question. Most roommates don't know all of someone's coworkers. I don't know any of Leoni's, though, since she's a traveling therapist, it's not like she'd have the same coworkers from one gig to the next.

But I'm a bad friend. Leoni's a good friend, and more than that, she's a unicorn—and once that image pops back into my mind, it looms large, threatening to overwhelm me. I need to stay here with this conversation. "Kurt." The word bubbles out. It feels good, like popping a blister.

There's an almost audible change, as if the vapor in the air has suddenly turned to frost. "Katrina," she says, very, *very* gently. "What did you do?"

I swallow. "It's not—well it's not something I *did*, exactly. At least, I didn't do it *today*."

"Okay." Still quiet. Still soft.

"I...a few months ago, I found something in his desk."

She doesn't try to hide her gasp. "You were going through his desk? Kat—that kind of shit can get you *fired*."

I almost start crying, but I hold on to the fact that even though I'm not on solid ground, I'm *better*, at least. Telling her is *helping*. "Yes. I think I'm in trouble. I can't stop…checking on him, you know? I follow him around the building. I know it's wrong, but I swear—sometimes it feels like he knows. Like he could be watching me, too."

There's a long pause, long enough to close my eyes and imagine the Cayatoga Bridge. I picture leaping off and tumbling down, the roar of the wind as it passes me by, and just that is enough to calm me.

"This is my fault," she says.

I snap back. "What? How could it possibly be—"

A groan. Something *ticks* in the background: four times, then it's gone. "You wouldn't have even noticed him if it wasn't for me."

I shake my head. "That's not…"

I can't finish the sentence, because it *is* true, in a way. I passed my first months at Advancex in a daze, and it wasn't until I was showing Leoni photos of an office Christmas party that she perked up and asked me about him and a few other guys, with lots of questions about my *type*. We'd killed a bottle of wine, and she'd teased me fast and furious. I was so flustered, it took me almost a week before I could admit to her that my *type* is *lesbian*.

But that's a technical truth. Technical truth isn't *real* truth. The kitchen-door world taught me that.

"No," I say, my voice suddenly firm. "It's not your fault. That's crazy talk. It's…Leoni, he had this *tape*."

"What kind of tape?"

I glance around the room, as if my gaze isn't being pulled to the brown and blue wooden box on the shelf by a force as sure as magnetism. "A cassette tape. Of one of my favorite bands."

"Oh." She sounds disappointed. "So?"

I shrug helplessly. "I don't know. Ever since then, I've felt like we were…*connected*, or something. It's not just the tape, either."

"What do you mean?" She sounds curious—but not judgmental. I can breathe again, at least a little bit.

"I don't know. Like...we're both super private around the office. I've never heard anybody talk about him having a partner or dating anybody—" Yocelyn flashes in my mind, her fingers closing around my arm, giving me pause. "Well, we have the same taste in music and movies. And we use the same little turns of phrase."

"I guess," she says, not won over by my arguments.

"Neither one of us has *any* social media presence. I've checked. It's like he's never been on the internet—although we're both interested in these weird pockets of things. *Different* things," I say, thinking of all the books I've seen in his drawer: *Medieval Battle Strategies* and *The True Ciphers of Da Vinci* and *The Lesser Key of Solomon*. It's not the same as my relationship with endekagrams and numbers and the kitchen-door world, but there's some key similarity behind it that I can't quite describe.

I let out a hard breath through my nose. "I just feel like...like our fates are connected." I cringe, my shoulders coming up until they almost touch the phone. "I know it sounds crazy."

"It doesn't matter if it's crazy," she says, and I'm glad I'm already sitting down, because I feel oddly dizzy. "Let's say it's true. Let's say your fates are deeply, irrevocably connected."

"Okay." I can barely eke the word out. The world is spinning. I feel like throwing up.

"So what? Does that mean he won't get you fired when he discovers you've been tailing him around—or that Advancex and Spectacular Staffing aren't going to throw you out on your ass once they find out? Not all connections are good, Kat. I'm sure the women who followed Charles Manson around also felt *connected*. I mean, they *murdered* people for him. That's a *connection*."

With the ringing in my ears, I hadn't realized how loud she'd gotten. "Please. Don't yell at me. I know. I'm *sorry*."

It's like a light switch, like that moment with Caressa when I was suddenly unsure if she'd ever been upset in the first place. "I'm sorry, Kat." A long sigh. "I'm just worried about you. I think you need to stay away from him. You don't know anything about this guy—where he's from, what he's like. People at work aren't their real selves."

It strikes me that this is one of the most medieval unicorn things she's ever said: it's wise and important, but also the kind of thing ingenue heroes in fables always ignore. I almost laugh.

"You need to get some professional help," she continues. "If it's about the money, I can help. At least a little bit."

It's not what you think, I want to say, but she wouldn't understand. Seeing a therapist won't make it go away. It'll probably just get me in worse trouble—or locked up in a mental hospital.

I'd die there—and for the moment, that thought is ghastly enough to cast long, cold fingers over our conversation, strong fingers that grab the wheel and steer us back to where we should've been in the first place.

"You're right," I say, and I hear her sigh with relief.

"I'm glad. I think that once you have a bit of space from this, you'll realize—"

"I don't feel like talking about this anymore." I take a beat to cool down. "I just mean, you're right, and talking about it more is just going to make me feel worse. I'm super embarrassed. And I'm suddenly really, really tired. Can we talk later? Maybe tomorrow?"

She doesn't answer right away. Then she says, "Okay." It sounds echoey, like she's a long way away—like she's at the bottom of a tunnel, but I know that's just in my head.

"Thank you," I say. "I'll get the internet bill paid and the place cleaned up."

I can tell she's not done, but she finally says, "I hope you feel better soon."

I close my eyes and count the hours until I can go out to the bridge. I notice that the rotting smell is back, stronger than before, though it bothers me less. "I will."

She hangs up. It's in that second—the sound cutting out, the phone becoming a dead thing in my hand—that I realize what that flutter in my chest was.

Hope.

It's a good thing I didn't tell her about the kitchen-door world. After all, you can love a unicorn, but it will never love you back. And you can't trust one to ever see things your way. They're too principled for that.

My belly's empty, but I don't think I can eat. I close my eyes and stumble toward the fridge, crushing mushrooms I dare not look at, until I find the bottle of wine in the door. It's half empty, and mostly vinegar, but I drink it anyway.

I only allow myself to venture out onto the Cayatoga at just before midnight, because that was when I first experienced its power to put control of my world back into my hands. I won't do anything to break that spell and run the risk of the bridge not being able to help me anymore.

But Leoni's insistence that I don't know anything about Kurt has burrowed under my skin. The kitchen-door world may not be *logical*, but the discoveries it gives me always turn out to be true, even if I don't recognize what they mean at the time.

I can't take how I opened myself up to her. I have to go. I put on two sweaters and two coats, even though I'll be hot until I leave the apartment. Once I start my rituals, I need to concentrate, or I risk breaking them. There won't be room for anything else.

There are three rituals, or keys, that have come to me over the years, three things that I instinctively know will help ensure my safe return from the Cayatoga. The first is storing my phone in the wooden box, because it feels wrong to bring a connection with the outside world onto the bridge. The second is my sigil of the four named endeka-grams, which I take my time carefully tracing with my finger on the outside of my front door. My hand is shaking—anticipation, fear, or just wine and an empty stomach, I can't tell—and when Mrs. Marple comes out to take her trash to the chute, with one of her millions of demon cats held under her arm like a handbag, I have to pretend I just got home and go inside and wait while she coos about how "Mommy will make things all better."

Any interruption or mistake is an imperfection, which means I have to start the drawing over. I do, again and again, until I've man-aged to trace the shape continuously and in one fluid movement, and then I move into the stairwell.

I take the stairs in an alternating triplet—one stair, then two stairs, then two stairs, then one stair—the complexity of the pattern, both balanced and unbalanced at the same time, being the third key. I don't always feel compelled to use the third key, but I'm leaving early, so I need to take extra precautions.

I pause on the way out the door, make sure I am safe to drive. Out-side, I even walk toe-to-heel on the line formed in the place where two pieces of sidewalk meet, just to be extra positive I haven't had too much to drink.

When I get into my car, I'm still an hour earlier than I should be, but I can't go back—if I open the door, I'll have to redo the sigil, and I might not be able to draw it as well a second time. And I can't sit here, not with this terrible feeling clawing in my chest. Leoni thinks she can make sweeping statements about my life and my relationship with Kurt. Not knowing his hometown, his dating history, or his philoso-phy on religion doesn't mean I can't tell that we're cut from the same cloth.

After all, I know Kurt's taste in music. Music tells you a lot about a person—can tell you *everything* about a person, if you know how to listen.

I swallow when I remember the source of that knowledge: my dad, the band teacher. He alone should invalidate this thought—his taste in music never told me he would be the kind of person to abandon me—but it doesn't.

I see no omens on my drive to the bridge, which both comforts and chills me. I'm approaching at the wrong time; I want some sign that I'm making the *right* choice. When it finally comes into view, I have to sigh at its balance, the way it's mirrored so perfectly in its middle. There are even four identical features at each exit, arranged as if they were the points of a compass rose: a car pool lot, a general parking lot, a bus station, and a tiny park. In the kitchen-door world, each of these manifests as a round pool with a jeweled floor of a different color: a verdant green, a brilliant gold, a fiery red, and an unending blue. The bridge itself is a set of stairs that rises straight up into the sky. At the top is a one-room cottage made entirely of stone and clouds, though you can't see it from the bottom.

I shove my purse under the passenger seat before getting out. I think it's best to carry as little of Grand Station as I can stomach onto the bridge, to avoid bringing something that could upset its balance of power. The dark presses in around me, heavy like the black water below, wind rising and dying like the voices of ghosts. I scan for cars. Nobody's supposed to be in the bridge-end parks this late, according to the signage. A ward put up to warn me off, but also my protection from being seen.

I creep forward, my pace measured despite the assault of the cold wind, because something is different: one lane of the bridge has been closed by a long red barrier. A number of orange barrels mark the lane like a spine, each one almost as tall as I am.

Construction. Coming soon. My stomach flutters—but that's a problem for Later Katrina. And besides, crews don't work all night. Maybe they'll put up a fence or something, but I'll scale it if I have to. Some rules are more important than others.

It's clear tonight, but the amber lamps above me drown out the stars and turn the lights of the city on the other side of the bridge into pinpricks. As I hike, the world around me starts to waver, the first sign that I'll soon be in the kitchen-door world, on the *Mountain of Cloudy Head and Underground Heart*—but this time, I'm not worried about the transition. Sometimes the poison is part of the cure, and once I'm finished here, safe time will start. I'll be anchored in the real world again, and not just for a moment. I'll once again be in control.

I've kept a brisk pace, but after what feels like twenty minutes, I can't tell how far I am from the midpoint of the bridge. Sweat is beading across my forehead and turning my back damp. My breath comes hard and sharp and cold needles stab my ribs, but I welcome it, because pain's real, no matter the source—a broken heart, a broken bone, a broken soul, the imagination. I should've left one of my coats behind, but I'd forgotten how much work this is. I haven't had to come since September, when the air was only starting to turn crisp. *Almost two months ago,* I think, amazed by the duration of my absence. Maybe the kitchen-door world hasn't been pulling me in as much as I thought.

It takes forever, but I can finally feel that I'm approaching the midpoint of the bridge. By now, I'm not sure if I'm in the kitchen-door world or in Grand Station. I can still see the bridge, but Mi-Hee's mountain stretches high in front of me. With each step down the Cayatoga's length, I watch myself climb the stone stairs that cut up the mountain's rocky face. Before long, the view and my body are in separate worlds, the sensation of the flat bridge competing with an incline my eyes refuse to let go of.

I have to hold on to the rail and feel my way forward, and still the wind drives at me, forbidding me to pass. There's wind in the kitchen-door world, too, though this wind has a voice, a human moan that grows as I climb, climb, climb.

And then I'm there. The midway point of the bridge, the apex of the stairs, the nexus of everything. I can see a small cottage—the one that leads to the room Mi-Hee called the *Heart*. I enter its stone and cloud walls, not with my body, but with my mind.

It's cramped inside—nothing to see, save the rough lip of a well in the middle of the floor. I approach its sides until my fingers touch its dream-rim.

I brace myself and peer inside. The entrance is round, the interior dark. My gaze falls down a long, long tunnel, one that leads straight into the heart of the mountain. A dangerous drop, a dangerous drop—

A drop my body knows is too far to be real.

Just like the first time—and just like every time since—something snaps in my mind, and then my stomach churns as the vertical distance between me and the bottom of the stairs folds in on itself, fantasy morphing back into reality.

In my mind, I go plummeting down, so fast I have to close my eyes, so fast it feels like I will throw up if I open them—

And then everything is calm. I am on the bridge. No kitchen-door world—just me, Katrina Kim, on the Cayatoga. I grip the side rail on the bridge, because it's suddenly hard to stand, because the last part of the ritual is the most difficult. I gather myself and take a few shuddering breaths, and then I open my eyes.

The water is two hundred feet down and dark as molasses. My heart thumps like a rabbit, but I force myself to look.

I imagine tossing myself over the railing: the wind screaming in my ears, the shock of my body slamming into the water's surface, the thunderous pain of my organs tearing loose from their anchors as inertia propels them forward.

I've read articles on this. Jumpers break bones, lacerate hearts and spleens, knock their brains against their skulls. Death comes for you fast—hopefully instantly, although it can take a few minutes if you're one of the unlucky ones who survives the impact and has to either bleed out or drown.

Many people they just don't find. They're swallowed up, as if they'd never existed at all.

I stand on the bridge and stare at the water until I'm sure it's enough. Until I'm sure I got what I came for, until I understand the dangers of letting go.

Of losing control.

I don't know why the bridge works for me when all my other rituals fail. I think it's because not wanting to live in this world is not the same as wanting to die—and when I'm on the bridge and looking down, it forces me to choose.

I collapse against a support pillar, the fierce cold seeping into my coat despite my buzz. The concrete is a slab of ice against my tights, but I wait until my legs feel solid before standing. The world is calm and bright again, even if this visit sapped more energy out of me than it normally does.

I pivot back, toward the parking lot. As if on cue, a car turns onto the bridge, and then another. Although I have nothing to be ashamed of, not now, my stomach flutters, and I shrink behind the pillar to watch as they approach.

The first car is small and white. It slows some, as if the driver has spotted me, some Good Samaritan maybe—but then the dark SUV behind it flicks their headlights on and off, obviously intent on overtaking, though they can't, not with the lane closed.

Both cars speed up and pass me, their taillights glowing like embers.

I need to get going, so I do, but now that I'm calmer, I feel like I'm drifting. I can't help glancing up at the moon as I walk. The trek back from the center of the bridge is always hard, my body always weak. I feel dizzy and clearheaded at the same time, like an acolyte who's fasted for days in search of enlightenment.

But without the threat of the kitchen-door world pressing in on me, my universe changes. I feel like I'm floating, safe and cocooned, and all my habits, my faults—the way I avoid people, the way I keep fucking up, over and over again—are no longer so sharp.

It's so cold that my fingers have gone numb, so cold my face burns and my eardrums throb with a dull ache, but I'm grateful as I walk back to my car.

I realize I am humming to myself and stop. I am better, but not invulnerable, and some stones are better left unturned. I can't go mucking around in my past, dwelling on my father and that disastrous performance and the library—

A thunderous crash echoes through the night, one so long and loud that the sound fragments in my mind.

I spin, and just like when I was staring at Kurt's postcard earlier today, I can't understand the jumble in front of me. There's a huge mess at the end of the bridge, signs and barrels going every which way, the dark SUV at an angle, blocking the only open lane.

I'm paralyzed. I watch as someone gets out—they're all the way at the end of the bridge, in the shadows, but I can *just* make out the shape of their head above the top of the car, so tall I'm pretty sure it's a man. He sprints forward, so fast that I can't pick him out—until he stops near the front of his car and is caught in one of his headlights. The sight of him is ice water down my spine.

I yell his name into the wind. "Kurt!"

His head snaps in my direction, then away—he must not know where I am, must be blinded by the brightness.

I dash to the right, trying to get under one of the bridge lights, to where the car won't block so much of his view. I wave my arms at him to get his attention. "Kurt!"

He turns and finds me—and despite the distance, despite how far we are, I stop and take a step back at the rage on his face. I can only see a small sliver of him between the car and the construction barrels, a tiny window that reminds me of Mi-Hee, staring into the small, gilded pane as the Mirror-Man emerged into her world.

For a moment, I can't breathe.

"You," he screams, pointing a finger at me. "I knew it was you!"

I don't understand. He's angry, too angry for stealing a postcard, for any other crime I've committed. "I'm sorry!" I cry out, but he's not looking at me anymore. Instead, he takes off running, then ducks as he hooks back behind his car. I lose him in the dark.

Where is he going?

"Kurt!" I run after him, calling his name, but the wind roars, sucking away my voice. "Kurt!" I'm so fixed on trying to pick him out that I almost run into one of the orange barrels. I slide to the right, the air suddenly pungent with the scent of burning rubber—

And then I see him again, cresting over his car like the moon, his clothes flapping as he ascends. For a moment, I think it's a mountain, that he's climbing the mountain I already banished, but then I realize that it's the side rail.

He's going to jump off the bridge.

"Kurt, no!"

Everything unfolds in slow motion. My vision narrows to a tunnel as I sprint toward him, but he's far, too far—and before I'm even halfway there, he's on the second to last rail. One rung before the top.

Suspended above the railing, he seems to glisten like the dark water below. He sweeps the bridge with his gaze, and I have just a flash of his face in the bridge lights, his expression strangely triumphant. "You just had to fuck everything up, didn't you?"

Then he laughs, and he's up and over.

I hear the splash before I make it to the spot where he was standing. When I look down into the water, there's nothing but the dark.

SECOND
STELLATION

Fig 2. The Medial Hendecagram, created by taking the second stellation of a hendecagon. It can be described by the notation {11/3}. If the words "endekagram" or "hendecagram" are used without a prefixing word (such as "small," "great," or "grand") to describe a regular eleven-sided star-shaped polygon, it is usually assumed to refer to the medial hendecagram.

—The Magical World of Geometry

Mi-Hee braced herself for the first question as the unicorn dipped her horn—a horn so sharp it cleaved the air itself in two, so that Mi-Hee had to take shallow half-breaths, just like the Wizard had warned.

She'd made it past the beaches and the strange rabbit sailors, the terrible howling snowstorm that had attacked the abandoned hut as she'd huddled with the empty-room ghosts. She'd covered her ears and sang at the top of her lungs as she maneuvered through the forest—but she'd never been as afraid as she was right now, in this moment, not even when her house was burning, not even when the door back to her kitchen had shut behind her.

If she couldn't solve the creature's riddles, it would spear her body and tear her apart with its hooves and teeth, and she'd never learn how to get to the Mountain or its Heart. She'd never find her way home. "Why are you here?"

Mi-Hee blinked. For a moment, her hands stopped moving, her fingers interrupted from their careful count. Should she mention the Mirror-Man? Surely, the unicorn already knew about his banishment to the Mirror-World, the terrible magic he'd left behind—but the creature might not like her letting him back into this world, where he might be able to pick up his dark work again—even if letting him in was the only way he could be defeated for good.

The Wizard had warned her not to lie to the unicorn. What if she just said she wanted to go home? Was that enough truth?

She didn't know. She needed more time. "Excuse me for asking, unicorn. Is this the first riddle?"

The unicorn laughed, and it sounded like waves on rocks, like ringing a great gong of brass. "There are no riddles." She tossed her head, making her mane dance in the moonlight. A thousand fireflies suddenly blinked in the air as one. "There is only truth."

CHAPTER 5

The Truth, Whole and Nothing But

I drive to the police station. I know this is true, because I remember doing it—jamming the accelerator to the floor, running red light after red light, the city shifting around me in flashes of reflections—but it still doesn't feel real.

The police officer in front of me, Officer Hanson, looks tired. There's a rumpled quality to her uniform and hair, like something pulled out of the dryer and left too long in the basket. She speaks in a slow monotone that doesn't give anything away, but I can tell she doesn't believe me.

"It's the truth," I say, for what feels like the thirtieth time—and all thirty times, it's been a mistake. Wouldn't a liar say the exact same thing?

Despite her neutral face, I can guess her thoughts. After all—why was I on the bridge in the first place, alone, at almost midnight? Why would I leave my car in a parking lot and walk all that way?

If I close my eyes, I might be able to find her kitchen-door analogue and learn something from that, but I don't want to break my new seal. Not yet.

"Listen, miss." She rubs her face with her hand, the first emotion she's betrayed since she brought me into this little room. "I'm going to need you to take a Breathalyzer."

"I can't believe this!" I don't mean to sound angry, but I do. "I *saw* what I saw. And I came straight here to report it. *I* came to *you*."

She nods. "Yes, you did. In a car. A car we're going to need to look at, by the way."

I bite my lip. I feel like a child caught trying to sneak out of the house—yes, I had some wine, but that was *hours* ago. "It was an *emergency*. What was I supposed to do?"

"You could've called 911—"

"I don't have my phone on me." I don't explain, of course, about putting it in the box, one of my keys for safe return. I even did the third key to make up for the fact that I left my apartment an hour early. Stupid, stupid. I should have known better, and now this is what I get.

She raises an eyebrow, and I have to look away. I'm tearing up—I hate that, hate that it always happens when I'm upset, that I can't control it. I scan the room. It's not like in the movies. The table isn't made of metal or bolted to the floor. It's just a normal table, some cheap, prefabricated thing that looks like they put it together with an instruction pamphlet and an Allen wrench.

"Miss?"

I snap out of it. "No. I'm not going to take a Breathalyzer."

She purses her lips. "I can't compel you—"

I breathe a sigh of relief.

"But if you refuse, I have the right to hold you in jail—and frankly, maybe the obligation. *What* were you doing on that bridge?"

Under the table, I squeeze my thigh with my right hand, hard enough to hurt. I concentrate on the scratchy feel of my tights under my fingers. *"Listen."* It's quieter, but forceful. I do my best to look her in the eyes. "You have to listen to me. This isn't…it doesn't matter what I was doing there. This isn't some cry-for-help situation. I'm not a danger to myself or anybody else—"

The expression on her face—just a flicker, but I caught it. It was a mistake, that phrasing. Normal people don't talk that way.

I swallow and soldier on. "I *know* it was far away. I *know* I've been drinking, and now I'm crying like some stupid little baby—but you have to believe me. It was Kurt, from my job. The car—"

"There was no car."

My whole body goes numb. "What? What do you…"

"I sent an officer out to the bridge before you even sat down. There was no car there." She holds her hands palm up, gesturing out in front of her, as if saying, *See? See for yourself.*

"But…the accident. The barrels and the signs. There must be glass—"

"There *is* some glass, actually. Which is one reason we need to look at your car and inspect it for damage. You said it's in the lot across the street? What's the make, model, and license plate?"

I swallow. "My bumpers are cracked, but that's old."

"We should be able to tell. Make, model, and plate?"

I tell her it's a 1999 Buick LeSabre. I don't remember the plate.

"Okay. Is it registered to you?"

My heart beats so hard I can hear it. "My parents."

There's no way Kurt could've driven away from the accident. Not when he went over the railing.

I close my eyes and picture it, the two cars, the dark SUV in the back—Kurt's car, now, I'm sure of it. He'd been tailgating someone. What did he hit? There'd been so much blocking my view, both before and while he jumped. "Listen. There was another driver. They must've come back and gotten his car—"

"Maybe," says Officer Hanson, though it's clear from her tone she doesn't agree. "And I wrote down what you told me, and we'll check on this Kurt. If he's missing, I'm sure you'll be hearing from us soon." She tilts her head to one side—not cocking it, but slowly, like she's pondering a painting at the Guggenheim. "Listen, Katerina—"

"Katrina." Even now, I can't help but correct her.

"Right. Katrina." She nods. "The way I see it, you have two options here. You can submit to this Breathalyzer—and given that you've already admitted to me that you've been drinking and driving, you've kind of tied my hands here—or you can refuse. If you refuse, I'll get a warrant for a blood test. Your license will be suspended until your court date—"

It hits me like a battering ram. *"What—"*

"—and there are a number of penalties that we can impose, should the DA so choose." Her chair squeaks as she leans back. I haven't heard it do that yet, and the noise startles me. "There is another option, though."

I swallow. "What's that?"

She folds her hands in front of her. "I have a daughter about your age. Let me drop you off and talk to your folks or your friends or who-ever you stay with, recommend you get some help. As long as you haven't damaged anything and agree to cooperate—"

"I'll take the Breathalyzer." It's out of my mouth before I've really put the thought together. I know I don't want her to come to the place I live. I definitely don't want her to talk to my parents back in Pleasance.

After today, I *never* want to see her again.

She furrows her brow. Consternation or worry, I don't know and don't care. I'd peel off my own skin if it would get me out of this tiny fucking room. "Listen, we all need help sometimes—"

"Give me the Breathalyzer. *Please.*"

She pauses, but she stands and leaves the room. As soon as she's gone, I slump back in the chair—mine does not squeak—and wipe my face on the sleeve of my outer sweater. I need to blow my nose, but at least I've stopped crying.

I close my eyes, just for a moment, and I see Kurt's face, that mask of rage. His posture as he went over the edge. It was...*resolute.* Defiant. I tried to describe it when I was talking to Officer Hanson, but I was panicked and hyperventilating, and it all came out wrong.

The door opens—no knock, because cops don't have to be polite—and Officer Hanson holds the device up and points to the mouthpiece. "Blow right here."

I blow. She takes it away and looks at the screen. Sucks on her cheek. "Your car looks clear, and you're under the legal limit. I don't have a reason to hold you right now, but I think—"

"Goodbye." I get up, my legs trembling, and make my way out to the parking lot.

The drive to my apartment doesn't feel real, either. So much so that when I'm in front of my door, key in hand, an odd fear strikes me—even if I don't know exactly *what* I'm afraid of.

It's so intense that even though I'm not ready to go into the kitchen-door world, I close my eyes and lean toward that place, just a bit. Almost immediately, the sigil I drew on the door before I left flares to life in my mind, brightly colored against the darkness behind my eyelids. Four endekagrams—star shapes, each laid on top of the other, like the designs I used to make with my spirograph when I was a kid, hours and hours of sticking a pencil in one of the center holes and circling around the frame until a perfect shape was drawn.

When I was younger, my imaginary sigils started as simple shapes: runny circles that became triangles, squares, and octagons, but the protection of a sigil correlates to its balance and how hard it is to draw.

When I was a teenager, I discovered the hendecagon, a polygon with eleven sides, so many that it's almost, but not quite, a circle—like looking at the underside of an opened umbrella, the straight lines between each point formed by the tension of the panels.

Because 11 isn't a special kind of prime number called a Fermat prime, you can't construct a regular hendecagon with a compass and a straightedge—each point inside forms an angle of 147 and 3/11 degrees, and 3/11 is one of those fractions that just stretches off after the decimal forever. But with enough practice, you can *learn* to draw one, and I spent hours when I should've been studying tracing my finger over the thick lines of a design I'd printed off, burning the feel of the correct spacing and angles into my muscle memory.

Until even that wasn't enough.

When I was sixteen, I opened *The Magical World of Geometry* and discovered *stellations*—the stars formed when you skip adjacent points on a polygon. Some stellations are so important they have names. For the hendecagon, there are four named stellations, or endekagrams. It's these four shapes, laid on top of one another—each the color of one of the kitchen-door pools on the sides of the Cayatoga Bridge—that form the basis of my sigil.

In my mind, though each endekagram is a different color, there are so many overlapping lines that the shapes merge together. I concentrate intensely, pulling each one to the fore in turn.

I start with the red one, the first stellation, the figure known as the *small hendecagram*, which looks like a sawtooth image of the sun. *Intact.*

The second stellation, the *medial hendecagram*, is gold. The medial hendecagram's center is slightly smaller, the insides busier; each new set of points skipped forms an extra layer of nested triangles on the inside of the shape. Also intact.

The third stellation, the *great hendecagram*, is green. Each segment of this star-shaped figure skips three points from the base hendecagon before connecting to the next. It looks almost like the Star of David, as long as you don't count the points. *Intact.*

But when I pull forward the fourth stellation in my mind, the *grand hendecagram*—a blue, flowerlike structure, the center a tiny circle, each point a long, straight fang—I spot the flaw. Three arms are broken by scratches, as if someone has taken a thick roofing nail and gouged right through the middle.

I don't know what this means. Despite how carefully I was drawing it, I could've made a mistake, although I feel like I would have noticed. Or maybe it's an effect, and not a cause—damage rendered as it tried to protect me from what happened on the bridge.

Most likely, though, I'm imagining the scratches, just like I'm imagining the sigil in the first place.

I open my eyes. The back of my neck prickles as I try the knob. Still locked. This, at least, is a relief; it held up where my sigil failed.

Heart thumping, I unlock the door. My nose fills with the smell of peppermint as light spills into the hallway.

I'm stunned. Leoni's sitting on the little couch, bent over with her face in her hands, her short, blond hair floating above. She hasn't seen me yet, and I don't want to startle her, so I clear my throat and rattle my keys. When she looks up, her eyes are red and wet, and the mask of makeup she always wears is smeared into odd shapes. She looks like a panda bear.

But when she sees my face, she asks before I can. "What's wrong?"

I shake my head. "No, you first. I thought you were in North Carolina for a few more weeks. Did the job end early? Did you just get in?"

She nods—not really to me—and picks up the cup of tea in front of her. She's dug a hole for the cup out of the crap on the coffee table and added one of her little matching tea saucers, an affectation I've never seen anybody else use, although I like it, like Leoni's sense of ritual. "Yes, sorry. I got a call yesterday that my sister wasn't doing well, and I should come right away. I hopped straight in the car. I didn't even think to call until I was four hours out, but..."

She trails off, polite, even now.

"But you couldn't tell me, because I was acting crazy."

She laughs—brittle—and then starts crying again. "Oh god. I'm... sorry. It didn't seem like the right time."

The right time. Less than an hour ago, I was sitting in front of a police officer, blowing into a little machine and waiting to find out if I was going to be held for a DUI.

And before that, I was watching Kurt go over the bridge.

"Kat?"

I blink, refocusing. "I'm sorry."

She squints at me. "Kat, what is it?"

I tread carefully. I can't tell her—not after her comments on the phone about my mental stability and obsession with Kurt, not after finding out what's happening with her sister—but I don't know what else to do. I open my mouth, desperately searching for a lie, and then it's like someone else takes over my body. I start crying—heaving, crazy sobs.

Leoni leaps up, jostling the table, spilling mint tea over the debris on its glass top. "Oh... oh fuck, look, it's okay. Whatever it is, it's going to be *okay*..."

And then I can't really hear her anymore. I'm vaguely aware of her coming close, making *shhh-shhh* noises, but my head is filled with images of Kurt climbing those railings, and that angry, proud expression on his face. I went to the bridge with almost the same intention—to look down into that water, to think about jumping, but Kurt? Kurt actually *did* it, and I don't even know why.

I'm getting less and less sure it even happened.

"Hey." She wraps her arms around me and pats my back. It's the first time we've ever hugged this close. We're almost the same height, and I'm surprised to find my chin fits over her shoulder perfectly.

She guides me to the couch, somehow devoid of my errant laundry, and pats the cushions. I collapse into them, and she brings me a big fluffy blanket and wraps it around me. It smells clean. "I need a fresh cup. I'll make you some too," she says, before spinning away.

I hear her turning the knob on the stove, the *click-click-whoompf* of the burner catching flame. In some of the old stories about unicorns, they died out because they couldn't put their own needs and tragedies first. I feel guilty, but I think there's something to her bustling, this doing for others so they cannot do for you, and I'm content to play my part as her patient.

In the interim, though, I'm forced to look around the room, at the trash I failed to dispose of. This isn't the first time Leoni's come home to a dirty apartment, but it's certainly the worst it's ever been. Did she walk inside and start screaming? Kick things out of the way while cursing my name?

I feel nauseated.

It takes almost ten minutes for the water to heat, ten minutes for me to compose myself before she takes a seat next to me, sets the steaming mugs on the table, and pats me on the hand. "You look calmer."

"Yes. Sorry. I got spooked. I didn't expect—I mean, I didn't think you'd be back so soon. I'm *glad* to see you, even if I wish it was under better circumstances."

Leoni smiles, although it's bitter and thin. "She's got pneumonia—happens sometimes, when people are on ventilators. She's drowning. They're not going to be able to save her." She says it with distance; I can tell this is the therapist in her, making a wall of space between *provider* and *patient*.

But at the mention of drowning, I think of Kurt being swallowed up by the river.

She takes a sip from her cup and makes a face. "Ugh, this one's yours. I don't know how you stand it like this."

I take it gratefully. I don't want the tea, not really, but it feels like I'm holding something magical in my palms, a small oasis that radiates warmth and coziness. I take an experimental sip, and four tablespoons of sugar explode over my tongue. "I don't know. It's just good like this."

Leoni snickers. "Tea is supposed to be healthy, you know. Not a candy bar." She gives me a wink that makes my stomach clench—she's working so hard to keep a stiff upper lip, when I know her life's falling apart. "Now, what's got you all in a twist?"

"Uh—I just…there was an accident in front of me on my drive home."

"Oh?" She raises an eyebrow, but it's not like the cop: fascination, not doubt. I hope. "Was anybody hurt?"

I don't know how to answer that, so I just shake my head.

We sit quietly, her in her thoughts, me in mine. After a moment, she sighs and stretches, hands overhead, and walks away.

At first, I think she's going to bed, but then she comes back with her laptop and queues up a playlist on YouTube.

I read the title. "'Cats Knocking Things off Shelves'?"

She snorts. "Yeah. These little fuckers get me every time. Maybe later, you can show me that thing you were talking about, the one with the Canadians who hunt those imaginary creatures—Discovery Fuck?"

"Discovery-Bang!" I say, my eyes wide, but already, I'm laughing, if only a bit.

I don't remember falling asleep on the couch, but that's where I wake up. It's bright as I rub crud out of my eyes and take stock of my surroundings. Before Leoni went to bed, she wrapped me up in the blanket, even tucking it down beneath my feet so they would stay warm.

I swallow when I see that. I can't remember the last time someone did something so tender for me. The mugs are both gone, whisked away to the kitchen, along with all the other clutter that had once crowded the table—save a yellow sticky note in the middle. It's oriented so perfectly, I imagine that if I measured, I'd find it was dead center: parallel lines inside of parallel lines.

Kat—

The hospital called. It was a bit odd—last night, I said my goodbyes, but this morning, they're reporting she's doing slightly better. I'm going to go spend some time with her, but if anything happens, or you're not feeling well, please call.

—Leoni

I blush from my ears to my knees. It's a kind offer—and she didn't mention the state of the apartment, for which I am grateful. I don't deserve her diplomacy, but combined with this new, vulnerable side of her, it makes me feel warm.

With a night of sleep under my belt and the sun shining, last night feels like a movie, not like something that really happened. I know I saw a man on the bridge, but when I close my eyes and picture it, the edges turn fuzzy, distorting like a twisting piece of sheet metal. Kurt drives (*drove?*) a dark SUV, but so does half of Grand Station. I'm *sure* it was Kurt's face—he recognized me, even, called out to me—but not by name.

But Kurt's all I think about these days. It stands to reason that I'd see him.

The more I wrestle with it, the more it feels like I might grasp what threads tie together all these clues—like the car. It was missing when the police got there, but if some man had really crashed his car on the bridge, it makes sense that he'd flee the scene, especially if he was drunk. And I saw someone jump, but it'd been dark, and from a distance. He could've easily jumped *forward* onto the bridge, instead of backward into the water. His car and the rest of the bridge would block my view either way, and then he could've run away before I got there.

Which means that even if it *was* Kurt I saw, he isn't necessarily dead.

I can't trust any part of last night. It's like that time in college when I forgot to buy tampons, only to get my period in the middle of a late-night study session. I'd been so tired driving to the store, I almost fell asleep behind the wheel. Then, I saw a deer with massive antlers, clear as day, but it wasn't until I swerved and slammed on the brakes that it morphed back into the cast-off shadow of a waving branch.

The dark plays tricks, even when you're not drinking. And I'm the kind of girl that sees illusions in the daylight. The kind of girl that gets half loaded, drives out to a bridge, and walks to the middle for the express purpose of imagining her own death.

I compose a text on my phone.

Hey Leoni! Got your message. Sorry about last night—I was spooked, but I'm fine now! Please take care of yourself.

I add the requisite number of emojis for *Sorry I acted like a total weirdo*—five, including two smiley faces, a laugh-cry, and two of the ones with a little star of shame exploding on their forehead. I set the phone back down on the coffee table, but I still feel uneasy. Now that I've opened that door—*what if Kurt's still alive?*—other questions slide into the light.

Like: If it *was* Kurt on the bridge, then why was he there?

The fact that I have no idea dredges up a list of all the things I've wondered about him—the things I don't know despite my constant surveillance. Questions that have settled at the bottom of my consciousness, waiting to be stirred up like lake muck.

Is Kurt originally from Grand Station? If not, where did he come from, and what was he doing before this? I know he started at Advancex sometime before me, a Spectacular Staffing referral who was hired in almost right away, which always made me suspect nepotism of some kind—although Advancex has been growing rapidly, given how quickly hospitals have warmed to the idea of an outside company handling most of their day-to-day insurance verification, billing, and collections. Still, Advancex isn't quite big enough for one of those highly regimented hiring processes with all the checks and balances to make sure you don't stick your son in a cushy position.

That said, I can't blame nepotism for my lack of progress. In the entire time we've both been there, I've moved up only one floor, from the grind of ten to the slightly-less-grind of eleven, although who knows how long that will last. I just barely made it into the back row, and that was only because they ran out of seats on ten a week after they hired me.

But Kurt? Kurt started somewhere below, I think, although I don't know what infraction would have led him to be initially classed as less-than-ten material. And in the space of months, he'd skipped from collections, to preauthorization, to back-end rebilling, before being moved up front as an assistant team-lead, with Yocelyn trailing right behind him. And now, there's talk of him getting some kind of manager slot.

I'd chalked this up to lots of factors. His age—older than me, maybe midthirties—the fact that he was male and white. Having more experience, being more self-assured. I'd gotten the feeling there was family money somewhere in there, from his fancy phones and watch—there's no way he paid for any of that making close to what I make. And it isn't like I've really been *trying* to move up; if anything, I carefully cultivate the amount of work I put in so I don't stick out in any way.

He's always been quiet, friendly. Assertive without being too aggressive. Well-liked by mostly everyone—though lately, I've noticed a weird pattern to the people in his orbit, managers hovering around him like bees before disappearing again, as if avoiding him. I'd assumed they were just checking in on their rising star and trying not to be too obvious about it, but now, I'm not so sure.

What else? There's his hair, which is always shiny and looks like it would be hard to the touch, and he's got one of those perfect smiles that's been whitened within an inch of its life. He talks like someone highly educated, and I've always assumed he'd once been on "the fast track" and messed it up in some way and had to start over, like a drinking problem, or maybe coke.

Looking at it now, I wonder how many of those assumptions came from solid evidence—and how many were just me trying to retroactively explain my fascination with him. But in the years that I've been following him around, nothing matches the rage I saw on his face last night.

I'd never have guessed he was capable of that.

My phone vibrates—Leoni likely responding—but I don't pick it up.

I have to get off this hamster wheel or I'll go crazy. Right now, Kurt is Schrödinger's corpse. If it *wasn't* him on the bridge, then I'll see him at work on Monday.

And if he's not there? I can look into it. I can ask around and find out if he was okay Friday before we closed up, try to figure out why he'd jump. Maybe even approach Yocelyn, if she seems receptive—though at the thought of her grip on my arm, I change my mind. I'll do my own research.

After a moment, I stand up, dislodging a hard lump lost somewhere in the cushions. I reach under the blanket and drag it out.

My wine bottle. I'd been sleeping on it and *didn't even notice*, like the world's dumbest princess on top of the world's biggest pea.

I take it over to the kitchen trash. The bin is empty, the bag replaced with a fresh one. Kittens dance over the folded bit above the can rim. Leoni must have put in a new bag the second she got home.

I throw the bottle in—*clunk*—before remembering that glass is recyclable. I fish it back out and find that the bin isn't empty, after all. Instead, there are five used tea bags in its depths, scattered like the points on a star.

CHAPTER 6

When You Smell a Rat

When night finally falls, I find I can't sleep.

I don't sleep for two whole days.

I feel my systems breaking down. I keep drifting off and restarting like a hanging computer, only to find something has gone cold: my coffee, the car, the shower. I know this is dangerous, that without sleep, neuroses—kitchen-door or otherwise—all grow teeth. Insomnia distorts perspective, turns ordinary air into toxic gas.

But there's no escape. At this point, I'd almost welcome a permanent embrace by the kitchen-door world. I'd welcome anything other than staring at the ceiling, circling back to the moments after I threw away the wine bottle, when I turned and glimpsed myself reflected in the microwave glass. My lips were purple, as if stained with sin. No wonder Officer Hanson had insisted on a Breathalyzer.

Leoni has become my ghost—spending her days and most of the night with the sister who somehow clings to life, coming home only to shower and change. Even so, I can tell she's trying to take care of me: teacups with four tablespoons of sugar staged on saucers. Yellow sticky notes with encouraging messages: *Are you okay? Try to relax a bit this evening.*

As if it were *my* sister who was dying.

Finally, it's Sunday night. At three a.m., I hear the click of the lock, the swing of the front door. Leoni pops into the shower, followed by the *schink* of curtain rings being dragged across the bar. Later, I close my eyes when she steals into the bedroom, soften my breathing. It feels like I'm spying on her, feels worse than it ever did spying on Kurt.

She grabs clothes out of her dresser. I flinch when she kicks a piece of crinkly trash and sighs. When she leaves, she's like all good ghosts, like the ghosts Mi-Hee found in her abandoned hut: there's almost no sign of her passage.

When my alarm goes off at six on Monday morning, something changes despite my exhaustion. It's like those cartoons of steam trains: swing open the furnace and shovel in coal, and the engine instantly roars to life.

I almost leap out of bed. I'm too anxious to eat, so I just shower and throw on clothes.

My body feels weak. When I shut my eyes and open them again, I've teleported from the bedroom to the front door, facing it as if I'd been locking it. I've still got the keys in my hand.

I don't like this. Don't like "coming to" on a threshold, where everything always feels precarious, unsafe. If I *am* going into work, I need safety.

I close my eyes. In my mind, I pull out the pieces of my sigil, the endekagrams. The grand hendecagram is still scratched—in four places, though, not three, which is strange—but the final scratch is so tiny, like the impression of a fingernail in wax, that I could've easily missed it. I could be imagining it right now, trying to avoid leaving this moment for what comes next: either facing Kurt's death, or seeing him at work and wondering if it really *was* him on the bridge.

Still, I need to redraw the sigil. It can't protect me otherwise.

Tracing it takes me long enough that I've gone from early to right on time when I get into my car. I try not to speed on my way in, because I don't want this to be the one day a year I get pulled over. My recent encounter with Officer Hanson is probably recorded somewhere.

I glance in my rearview a thousand times. I don't even know why until I catch the first dark SUV and find myself checking the front bumper for telltale cracks. Every time I see a car that *could've* been the one on the bridge, it gives me an electric jolt—but in the end, none of them look like they recently had an accident. None of them are Kurt's. Nobody's following me.

When I get to Advancex, I fumble through my purse for my badge. It's not there.

I close my eyes and try to remember Friday night—if I had it on the bridge, in the police station, in the apartment afterward—but there's just a hole where my memory of it should be, as if the shock and fear of that night have eaten it away.

Behind me, someone honks. The gate attendant—a new one I don't recognize—shoots me a quizzical look.

Fuck. If I go home to get my badge, I'll be late. *Really* late. I don't have the points for that—and if I get fired now, or even just sent home while they review my case, I might never find out what happened to Kurt.

I need to find street parking, though I still only have forty-five dollars in my bank account. Not enough to cover an entire day on a meter, so I'll have to run home at lunch to get my badge. At thirty-five minutes each way in midday gridlock traffic, I'd have to bend the laws of physics to make it back in time.

My stomach churns.

I circle a four-block radius like a frantic shark for ten minutes before I find a meter. There's a kiosk right in front of it, so I buy five hours and print off a ticket—thirty dollars, please, God, let me not have bought some gas and forgotten about it—and sprint into work.

When I make it into the lobby, I'm panting and covered in a fine sheen of sweat. It's surprisingly empty; I'm the last straggler. "I—*huff*—forgot—*huff*—my badge."

From behind his giant desk, Yuto rolls his eyes. "Fine. Employee ID number?"

"It's, uh, four-two-three…" I make a face. *Nobody* remembers those. That's half the reason to wear the badge in the first place, so you can flip it over and check the number for the computer. "Can't you just look it up?"

He lifts an eyebrow. I graciously refrain from snapping as he wiggles the mouse on his computer. "I'll need to see some ID."

"Sure, I—" I reach down for my purse before remembering I left it in the car—and now, I've got less than five minutes before I'm late.

It feels like I'm the commander of an army, my advance stymied by a sudden blizzard. "I forgot my purse."

Yuto shrugs. "Sorry, honey. It's policy. No ID, no ID number lookup, no visitor's badge—"

"Oh, *come on*, Yuto! You know who I am!"

Yuto tilts his head, appraising. "No, can't say I do for certain—"

"We *just* had your birthday party in the break room, like, a month ago. I brought the chips."

He looks down at his nails. "What kind of chips?"

My mouth falls open. "I don't know…potato?" I look at the clock again—four minutes. I have to get past Yuto, make it up to the eleventh floor, turn on my computer, and clock in. All in four minutes.

Time for drastic action.

I lean over his desk and lower my voice until I'm basically wheedling. "Listen, Yuto. You and I, we're two out of the, what, six Asian people who work here? And we're the only two East Asians."

An alliance between Japan and Korea? My mother would die, just to roll over in her grave—but from Yuto's sniff, I can tell he's listening.

"So I *know* you've seen me around, because there's *no* way you don't notice something like that, even if we all pretend we don't." I consider batting my eyes at him—I'm a pretty good flirt, when I want to be; the key is to hate yourself and have no sense of shame—but I've always assumed Yuto is gay, although that could just be wishful thinking. It's nice to imagine you have allies in the office.

"You know," says Yuto. "You're really boring me right now."

I give him my fiercest squint. "Yuto, if you don't write my ID number down on a sticky note and let me into this building *right now*, I'm going to make it my personal mission to make your life miserable."

He scoffs. "Yeah? What exactly are you going to do, *temp*—"

"I'll go around telling everyone about dumb Japanese customs that aren't real. Like how you're all in love with country music, and how the nicest thing you can do for someone in Japanese culture is set them up on a blind date with a good, church-fearing woman, and how your people—"

Yuto's mouth falls open. "*My* people? Katrina, I'm from *Skokie*. You know, *Chicago*? You can't seriously think they'd fall for that—I mean, they have *Google*—"

I shrug. "Maybe. But remember last year, when they all got fooled by that *Onion* article and started that argument about bombing Agrabah? It's from *Aladdin*, Yuto. The article was over five years old. Is this a chance you really want to take?"

He purses his lips like he's sucking on a lemon. "You have no shame, do you?"

I glance at the clock. Three minutes. "No, right now, I can't say I do."

When I look back down, he's holding out a visitor's badge with a sticky note on it. "Fine, you win. It's already programmed for eleven."

I snatch it and take off running.

"And Katrina?"

I smash the UP button before I turn around. "What?"

"Oh, *nothing*." Yuto smiles—smug, satisfied—and my stomach drops, but the elevator dings behind me.

I leap on, hammer DOOR CLOSE, and check the clock. Two minutes. If Navya's already turned on my computer, I just might make it.

Victory tastes good, until I remember Kurt, and all the joy dribbles out. By the time the door opens on eleven, the miasma of my anxiety has seeped through the elevator car.

When I get to Kurt's row, there's a small crowd of people around a computer, blocking my view. I don't have time to wait for them to clear out—and if Kurt's missing, he'll still be missing after I clock in.

And if Kurt's still alive?

Could we pretend the incident on the bridge never happened, find some way to sweep it under the rug?

When I make it to the back row, my computer has already been on long enough that it's flipped to a black screen, a small "Advancex" bouncing around in a ball on the desktop. "God, thank you, Navya, you lifesaver."

She gives me a long-lashed wink.

Thirty seconds to spare. I hunch over my keyboard, shake the mouse, type in the number from Yuto's sticky note, and hit ENTER.

Incorrect login credentials. Two attempts remaining.

"Fuck." I type it again, this time slower, taking the time to concentrate. ENTER.

Incorrect login credentials. One attempt remaining.

My stomach sinks as I remember Yuto's smirk. No, he wouldn't do that, would he? Screw a girl over when she's down?

I carefully punch each number in, one at a time. ENTER.

This computer has been locked.

And now, I'm officially late. I thunk my head into the desk and imagine hitting Yuto with my car.

Navya slips a hand behind her headset microphone. *What is it?*, she mouths.

I point at the screen. She nods and opens the interoffice messenger, before typing: *Wanted to let you know that Katrina's been trying to punch in for five minutes, but she's locked out.*

The reply is swift, so swift that I can't help picturing Caressa as her kitchen-door analogue: a red ant, her segmented body curved like a bow as she hunches over the computer, her mandibles clacking in disappointment when she gets Navya's message and realizes she cannot fire me yet. *Then why isn't she at IT?*

She just left, responds Navya, before giving me a meaningful look.

A lifesaver, I mouth, but Navya just points behind her: haughty, imperial, every inch the mother of all those sons.

The giant mess of people is still in Kurt's row.

In order to get to Enrique, our technical support king, I have to venture into the Annex *and* make it past Caressa. I hold my breath as I exit to the hallway and hook left at the elevator. When I'm this tense, every movement I make is punctuated by the factory's hum.

Caressa's standing at the door of her office—it's clear she's been waiting for me—but then her phone rings. She frowns, but turns away, and I breathe a sigh of relief as I dash into Enrique's row and plop down in a seat. "I'm locked out of my computer."

It only takes him a second to realize that two of the digits are transposed—*Damn you, Yuto!*—and then I'm dashing back past Caressa's office. I can't help peeking when I hear, "I don't understand! We went through all the reports. There's *no reason* for that money to have moved. Who accessed those files?"

She looks *pissed*—like all ants, Caressa's all about order and hierarchy. I envision her antennae twitching furiously as I fly back into the safety of the main hall.

I stop at the restroom to splash cold water on my face and dry off with paper towel so rough it feels homemade. When my loins are sufficiently girded, I hold my breath and make my way back to the floor.

Even from the doorway, I can see that the group blocking Kurt's desk has dispersed, like dancers after a flash mob.

I turn into his aisle, leaning side to side to see past everyone. It takes a moment for me to find the right angle.

Kurt's not at his desk. Yocelyn, however, is at hers. And although she's mostly obscured by the cubicle and the people around her, just from the tension of her leaning body and the tilt of her head, I know she's looking in Kurt's desk drawer. *The* desk drawer.

The world around me slows. I advance down the aisle as if pushing my way through a stadium crowd, squeezing past pulled-out chairs without an "excuse me" or a gentle throat clearing.

It's not until I'm almost on top of her that I can *see* the evidence that I'm right. His drawer, *the* drawer, is open. I press closer, so close I could reach out and touch her, could grab her arm like she grabbed mine.

There's a book in the back of the drawer, like there always is. The postcard about thieves from Friday is missing. Instead, nestled next to the spine of *Military Ciphers* is a cheap flip phone with EPOCH PRE-PAYED stamped on the front.

I don't understand. I've seen his phone a million times, always the newest iPhone, and while Advancex occasionally gives out company phones to managers, they're always smartphones, and Kurt's not a manager.

Yocelyn shifts the phone aside, making something below glint. I lean closer.

It's a key ring with four keys on it. One of them looks like a car key.

Some part of my brain, buried deep, hears my own gasp. Yocelyn's head snaps up, the expression on her face contorting as she recognizes me—but it's like trying to cover the third stellation of a shape with its second: no matter how hard, how deep, how completely you draw those lines, there'll always be something poking through. Her blank face can't disguise her rage or her wet, red eyes. There's a ruddy patch that stretches over her cheeks and nose, a slump to her shoulders not canceled out by the stiffness that now infuses them.

She's been crying. Crying for Kurt, who has only been missing—as far as she knows—for a few hours. Crying as she went through his desk.

If that key *is* Kurt's car key, and it was Kurt's car on the bridge—then how did it get into that drawer?

Yocelyn slams the drawer shut, but it's too late. The *thump* just punctuates my suspicions.

"Is there something you want?" she snarls, but I see all the way to the rat: worrying its forepaws, licking its scaly tail. Yocelyn is scared. Scared of *me*.

I realize I should be scared, too, but I'm not. Instead, my core feels cold and dead, my outside stiff and plastic. "I had something I needed to tell Kurt," I say slowly, waiting to see how she'll react.

She grimaces, as if I'd pinched her. "He's not here, *as you can see.*"

I nod and turn away. There are more things I should say, should ask, but I suddenly feel like I'm floating—no, like I'm *falling*, the stone sides of the well whistling by my ears as I plunge into the *Heart*, and there's nothing to do but let gravity carry me back to my desk.

CHAPTER 7

The Flimsy Fetter Flies
in Sunder

I walk back to my desk in a daze. For a moment, I can't hear the factory anymore, but then something soft and haunting weaves itself under the rasp of my breath, plucking sounds that ring like bells.

It's a harp. I can even place the piece. The oboe hasn't started yet, the plaintive, repeating call instantly recognizable to half of America, despite being written almost 150 years ago. I crush the memory down with the force of the blue wave on the postcard. There are things I cannot afford right now. Getting lost in the main theme to Tchaikovsky's *Swan Lake* is one of them.

A sudden pressure encircles my arm. I tear myself away, ready to come to blows with Yocelyn if that's what it takes, ready to—

Navya's mouth falls open, her brown eyes wide. She's so stunned, she doesn't even put her hand down, and it hangs in the air between us, as if she's a petitioner about to make an offering.

"I'm…I'm sorry." Even though it's not Yocelyn, my arm burns with the pressure of the remembered touch.

Navya recovers. She guides me to my seat before wheeling her chair up. When she speaks, her voice is low, but I can hear her, because the music *and* the factory noise have stopped; even with the hums and mutters and ringing phones of an entire working floor in front of us, it's suddenly eerily quiet. "Katrina, what's going on with you?"

She looks toward the front of the room, toward all those people.

It's the wrong thing to do. I'm primed and prompted, and I can't stop my mind from rolling down the track: any one of them could be a spy, for Advancex or someone else—

I grab my thigh. Squeeze so hard the tips of my fingers feel like little knives, until the whispers of *conspiracy* fade away. "I'm sorry." It's clear from the lines on Navya's forehead that she needs an explanation. "I just—Caressa was really mad. I don't want to lose my job."

She nods slowly. Listening, but not placated. "I'm worried about you, Katrina. This"—she waves her hand around her, as if the sweep of her arm could summarize my behavior—"isn't *like* you."

It's my turn to nod. "Would you mind grabbing me a coffee?"

Her face twists. At first, I think it's disappointment—but then she glances down at the little clock in the corner of her screen. I can trace the shape of her thoughts: How many minutes has it been since she marked herself *unavailable* for the next call? How long before she gets flagged for a lack of productivity?

"I'm sorry," I say, clearing my throat. "I just—"

And then I picture Navya as her analogue: Mama Dak-Dak, a gigantic, red French hen, sitting on a brood of eggs. It fills me with guilt—despite how accurately it summarizes her warmth, her caring, her sense of purpose, something about seeing Navya as a chicken doesn't seem complimentary to her, to what an amazing person she is. I try hard to avoid imagining her that way, but now there's something else underneath the image, an idea not quite fully formed. I trace down its length, hand over hand, despite my suspicion it's something to be ashamed of.

Family. If Navya has a weakness, it's family. "I…it's my cousin. He's gone missing."

A *flash-flash-flash* of light through the trees.

Navya's face suddenly looks haggard. "Oh, Katrina. No wonder you've been so strange. I'm so sorry—" Another reflexive glance at the clock, and I suddenly hate Advancex for reducing us to this, for making us the kind of people for whom the time clock is as pressing and omnipresent as our own heartbeats. "Did you go to the police?"

My intuition was good. She's completely forgotten about my strange behavior—and all it took was me tapping into her worst fear.

"The police," I say, remembering Officer Hanson. What kind of person am I? I thought I knew. "The police. Yes. They won't help. Say there's nothing wrong, but I'm not sure. It's not like him to just disappear like this."

She bites her lip. "Is he on drugs? Has he been stealing things?"

My gut spasms. Her question reveals more than she probably meant. I feel like a serpent, slithering forward to suck the yolks from her brood.

It's too much. I need to back off.

"I don't think so. And maybe it's nothing. Actually, I *think* he mentioned something about going on a trip to visit a friend. I can't believe I forgot that."

She covers her stomach with her hand, bends forward until her head almost touches her knees. "Oh god. You poor thing," she says, although it's not really to me. "His poor mother. You have to check his social media accounts, his phone. How old—"

And then she stops and looks down, still as stone. She's tapped into some bad memory. I never said anything about my hypothetical cousin's age, but Navya assumed he was a child. Whatever trouble her sons have gotten into, it must be terrible. I can't help but picture a young man, one that looks like Navya, collapsed on the ground, a needle in his arm, his lips turning dusky—

I can't breathe. "It's okay," I say, backpedaling, though it feels like trying to back a raft up rapids. "It's probably nothing—"

"You need to hire a private investigator." She says it so fast, so assertively.

"Really, I think—"

"Here." She scribbles out a number on a sticky note and pushes it my way. "You can go now and call. I'll figure out a way to cover for you—"

I can't even see the note, not with the way my vision is blurring, the heat in my eyes. "No." My voice is hoarse. "I don't want to get in trouble with Caressa—"

"Then go at lunch." She glances down at the clock, and from the way her eyes widen, it's like she actually *sees* it for the first time. But her face hardens as she refocuses on me.

Navya treats our job like the law itself, but she's willing to get into trouble for me.

I've made a terrible mistake. And I can tell it's one I'll pay for—day after day, month after month, she'll check on me and my cousin, will ask us how we're doing. I'll have to spend the rest of my time at Advancex rehearsing new lies, making sure they fit more perfectly than the dovetailed joint of a drawer corner, because Navya will never forget. We're two of her eggs, now, and one of us doesn't even exist.

What will she do, when I finally slip up, and she finds out I've lied to her?

And just as the implication of that hits me, a window opens, a patch of light: maybe a private investigator *is* the right way to go. Because despite all the hours I've spent studying Kurt, his tape, his postcards, his books—the truth is that Leoni is right. I don't know that much about him.

And if Yocelyn really did have something to do with his death, if *she's* the reason his keys are in his desk? I'm going to need evidence. "Okay," I say. "I'll call at lunch." I'll do it from my car, because somehow, despite all of this, I still have to face the cold reality of having too little money in my bank account to stay at the meter.

Her relief is written on her face in disappearing lines and slackening muscles. "Good. You're doing the right thing."

I nod and pretend to go back to my work, but I watch her out of the corner of my eye. I see her, *really* see her, the way I first noticed Kurt after that conversation with Leoni, poring over the Christmas party photos. I'd pictured before the scrapes that Navya's sons had gotten into, the reasons for her absences from work—but how many times do you call a private investigator's number before you have it memorized like that?

Does everyone in my orbit have a secret tragedy, just crawling underneath the surface?

The next two hours are not a blur, exactly, because I sense the time pass like the dangerous, pendulous feeling of a low-hanging power line, but my ruminations have no clear shape or direction.

Despite Yocelyn's ire, I'm no longer sure of her guilt. I sat next to her for so long, observing as her lunches of enchiladas and tamales turned to "healthy" grilled fish and broccoli, the rapid improvement in her labored typing. Listening to her phone calls with her mother and her sisters and her carousel of boyfriends—though that all stopped shortly before she moved up next to Kurt. I can't decide what that means.

And even if she was on the bridge, even if she did put the keys in the desk—it doesn't make her a murderer.

I fight the urge to walk over to her seat and just ask. Maybe Navya's investigator can give me something that will determine if Yocelyn is enemy or comrade.

At lunchtime, I stand up to get my badge. I'm going to be late coming back. *Unless?*

I've done a terrible thing, manipulating Navya like this. It's unforgivable. And still, I write my password down on the sticky note below the corrected ID number.

"I'm going to make this call now. I think I should do it in my car," I say to her, before glancing at the people in front of us.

"Okay." She actually manages to smile.

I drop my voice. "It might go a little long. I'm worried about clocking in late." I suddenly lose my nerve and look down at the note, my shaky penmanship.

She stiffens, but just like before, her face becomes resolute. "Okay. I'll clock you in if I have to, but try not to be late. *Please.*"

There's no way to drive home and back before the end of my lunch. I know this, just like I know that if Advancex ever finds out that Navya punched me in, our time temping here is over. "Sure. It's just in case."

I wonder what penalty I'll pay for this, if there's a special place in hell being reserved for me right now.

We ride down in the elevator together. For the most part, she's in her own little world—head down, her black hair falling forward to frame her face. She sees me, though, as we step off, and I can't get over how big and sad her eyes are, how full of hurt.

Although I'm not the praying kind, I say a little prayer for her family as I head out to my car.

Once I'm sitting behind the wheel, I take out the sticky note and read the number. It's local, with what looks like the word "Sunder" written underneath, though it's hastily scrawled and could easily be "Sumdar" or "Sunoen" or a thousand other things that don't make sense—but my mind keeps coming back to "Sunder."

Sunder. As in, "to tear apart." I wonder if Navya was trying to tell me something. I enter the number but don't place the call; instead, I work on pulling out of the parking space. It's congested, now, a thousand people going to lunch at the same time. Each passing second is another Navya will have to cover for.

I give up on waiting for someone to let me out. I stomp on the gas and shoot in front of a car. My Buick groans and sputters, but the noises are absorbed by angry honking, long train horns of sound that make me picture the driver leaning their entire body onto the steering column. Any other time, this kind of confrontation would almost give me a heart attack, but I've already reached the peak of what I can feel, and there's nothing but the soft jolt of an ascending elevator where the fear should be.

Once I'm secure in the flow of traffic, I place the call. It rings four times, then a *click*. "Sunder Investigations." A woman's voice. Low, and kind of gravelly. She says it like *Soon-der.*

I should've rehearsed, but I was too wound up in guilty thoughts of Kurt and Yocelyn and Navya. "I...someone recommended you to me and, uh..."

What can I tell this woman? Obviously not the truth—but in movies, good PIs have what my mom calls "nunchi": they can tell when you're lying. And this person is better than good, because Navya no doubt filtered through every single PI in a four-hour radius before choosing one.

I realize I've been sitting quietly on the phone for what feels like a *very* long time.

"Listen, kid," says the woman, and for a moment, I'm peeved, even if she does sound old enough to be my mother, "someone your age calling me, it can only mean one of a few scenarios, so how about we whittle this menu down so we can both get on with our day?"

Her voice is kind, some smooth warmth under the gravel, and the efficiency of her statement makes me feel like I'm in capable hands. I find myself suddenly able to concentrate again on the flow of cars around me. "Okay," I say, as I pull up to a light, and it's only then that I realize how stoppered my voice sounds, as if I've been crying, though that's just from the cold on the walk over.

"Right, so someone like you calling me, they've either: *one*, lost something. *Two*, lost some*one*. *Three*, been deprived of an inheritance they feel they should have rightfully received or in some other way been taken advantage of financially, or *four*, suspect their spouse-*slash*-girlfriend-*slash*-boyfriend-*slash*-partner has been jumping into the wrong bed." She pauses. "Although, I should add that looking for birth parents falls under the header of *lost someone*. So, which is it? If it's none of these, I automatically accept your case, because at this point, I've been doing this long enough to have investigated every-thing under the sun, and I absolutely hate being bored."

There's another long pause, followed by a noisy exhalation. She's smoking. Inside. Which is so horrifying I almost hang up the phone. "Lost someone," I manage to eke out. "Well…not exactly."

Another pause, and then she actually says, "Go on," like we're in a movie and not just on the phone, me awkwardly guiding the sometimes-sailboat through traffic as my breath draws an ever-widening circle of fog on the windshield. In fact, I realize a movie is *exactly* how this feels—I can almost picture this woman in a *Dick Tracy*-ish raincoat and hat, the room around her in stylized shadows. It's uncanny, like something that doesn't belong in either this or the kitchen-door world.

The windshield fog-circle is too big for comfort, and I'm freezing. I flip on the heater, but the air that comes out is still cold. "Right. It's a man. I know where he is, though. He killed himself. At least, I *think* he killed himself. I just don't know why."

Another long inhale. "No note?" She's holding her breath. She lets it out.

"No." I slow for another red light. "I mean, I don't think so. I don't have access to his apartment. I don't know where he lives." *Not for lack of trying.*

"Then how are you so sure there's a *reason*?"

"There's always a reason," I snap, but that's not what I meant to say. "I just—I don't think he did it for the *normal* reasons. He...didn't seem the type."

A snort. "There's no *type* for suicide—"

"I know that!" It comes out so loud it's almost a shout. I have to take a breath. There's something about this woman, her directness—I want to close my eyes and seek her out, see if I can find her analogue, but I'm still driving. "Can you just...how much would it be, to find something like that out?"

She hums to herself. "To be honest, this is sort of boring, but also sort of interesting—mostly because of *your* interest. Tell me, were you sleeping with him?"

"*No.*"

Behind me, someone lays on their horn. The light is green. I'm not sure when that happened.

"What information do you have?"

A glance in my rearview tells me the asshole behind me is in a silver pickup truck, and that he also feels it's necessary to tailgate me. "What?"

The woman becomes an auctioneer: "Date of birth, social media, vehicle make and model, license plate, place of employment—"

"No," I say, overwhelmed by the barrage of options she just rammed in my direction, by how little I actually know. "His name is Kurt Smith. I think he's around thirty-five, although I don't know his birth date for sure. He doesn't—didn't have any social media, and—"

"No social media?" she scoffs. "Everybody's got social media. Maybe not an account on every site, but everybody has *something* they use to track the activities of their past and peers. It's monkey psychology."

"He didn't." I glance up at the roof of my car, half expecting to see a view of the sky, but there's just a corner of falling felt, sagging down from the ceiling like peeling wallpaper. "I'm sure."

"How can you—"

Because I'm a fucking stalker. Because I've literally spent a hundred hours trying to find it. "I'm just sure."

"Okay," the woman says, clearly not believing me.

"And he works—worked at Advancex, on Main Street. He drives a big black SUV. It has…" I shut my eyes, trying to concentrate, wishing I knew just a bit more about cars. "The plate starts with 'VO,' I think."

I open my eyes and slam on the brakes. Traffic has bricked up in front of me. The silver pickup squeals to a stop just inches shy of my rear bumper before laying *hard* on the horn.

"Are you okay?"

I'm panting. "Yes, sorry."

"This isn't a lot to go on." Another drag of a cigarette. "Did you try the police?"

"Yes. They don't believe he's dead. Or missing, or whatever."

"Interesting. And you do, because?"

I don't need to close my eyes this time. I'll see Kurt's angry face until I die. "Because he jumped off a bridge right in front of me."

Another long pause. "*Well* now," she says. "That *is* interesting. I'll take your case, and I'll do it at a discount."

All the weight that's ever sat on my shoulders falls away in a single, swift movement, like shedding a waterlogged coat. "Oh. Thank you. Thank you."

"Sure. I have flat rates for single services, but I don't think that applies here. And I usually charge a hundred dollars an hour—"

I can't help gasping.

"—but since there's so little to go on, this could be a lengthy job. Could take days. But it sounds interesting. I'll do it for half," she says. "Fifty dollars an hour, with a three-hundred-dollar retainer."

She should've asked me for one of my kidneys. It would've been easier to come by. "I...I'll have to think about it." My whole body's numb.

"Yeah, no problem," she says. "Anything else I can help you with?"

"No—"

"You should be more careful while driving." And then she hangs up the phone.

I realize I don't even know her name.

CHAPTER 8

Recapitulation

I tear through the apartment—an easier task than normal, since Leoni's been slowly asserting her organizing influence on the place, like a magnet pulling iron filings into shapes. Things have been sorted into piles, staged in their proper corners to be reshelved, hung, and put away. Several bags' worth of trash are missing, and even the smell is different: aired out some, the worst of the rot gone, the rooms touched with notes of Leoni's soft floral scent.

The changes are both welcome and guilt-inducing.

The apartment's now foreign topography presents a new obstacle: I can't find my badge. I excavate the closet, my drawers, check under my bed. I scour the counters, the little organizer near the kitchen sink, the medicine cabinet, the spaces between Leoni's makeup containers on the dresser.

I realize it's most likely still attached to the shirt I was wearing Friday. If Leoni's moved it, there's only one place it could be.

The laundry hamper is a big, freestanding cylinder of wire and mesh inside the bathroom closet. I dump it out onto the tile, clothes spreading across the narrow stretch like an avalanche. Each second ticks away, reminding me of my sins against Navya—

But there it is, still paper-clipped to the right side of the collar. I pull it off and awkwardly twist my arm to attach it to my shirt. It's a movement I've practiced a thousand times, but something feels wrong, and I can't quite put my finger on it.

I step out and glance up at the coffeemaker—running on forty-five minutes, now. I'm going to be so much later than I thought. I leave the hamper on its side and sprint for my car.

I'm more than a half hour late when I finally make it onto the floor. I glance at Kurt's aisle as I pass and cringe when I notice that Yocelyn is gone. A perfect opportunity to grab the phone and whatever other clues might be in that drawer, but I can't slow down, not when Navya is waiting.

She spots me long before I slide into the seat next to hers. As soon as I wiggle the mouse, the interoffice messenger pops into view.

Where were you?

I'm so sorry, I type back. *She had a lot of questions.*

You don't understand. Caressa was here.

I feel like I've been dunked in cold water, but Navya is typing something rapidly—not to me—and then she turns and raises her eyebrows, trying to signal me. "Thank you, ma'am. Is there anything else I can do for you today? Thank you." She hangs up and turns toward me. Her eyes are huge.

"What is it?" I can barely speak.

"She came by three times, looking for you," Navya hisses. "I said you were in the bathroom, that you might have food poisoning or something."

At this moment, throwing up might not be such a stretch.

"You'd better message her. She said something about your email." She hops back on another call, but I can tell from how pale she is that she's worried.

I swallow and check my email. There are over *twenty* messages, time-stamped back to last night. *Fuck.* Is it possible I haven't opened it since yesterday?

I scan through subjects and senders, and there it is, from nine fifteen in the morning, an email from Caressa with the subject line *Lunch Meeting.*

Before I can click on it, the office messenger pops up on the corner of my screen.

So, Navya says you haven't been feeling well.

This is an understatement. *Yes. Maybe it's something I ate?*

Could be viral. I think you should go home.

For a second, I'm elated—how many times have I dreamed of throwing up at work, just to be freed from an afternoon of drudgery? The fact that I need the cash—especially now, when I've burned through everything but my last fifteen dollars—doesn't change the *relief.*

But then I remember Yocelyn. Kurt's desk. I *can't* go home.

I don't want to let you down, I type, cringing, but I don't hit ENTER. Caressa's not going to believe that coming from me. *I can't afford any more points.*

The reply is almost instant. *Sorry, but we already had to send someone home today. I don't want whatever it is to spread through the office. You'd better go.*

There's no use arguing. I say thank you and fill Navya in when she wraps up her call.

"She didn't seem suspicious or angry?" she whispers, her gaze trailing down to the sticky note.

My stomach turns. It must have been hellish: clocking me in, then sweating every minute I was late, Caressa swinging by three times. Navya must have felt the walls closing in on her.

"No." I have to clear my throat. "She just doesn't want me to get anybody else sick. You could probably even go home early, if you say you're feeling flu-y."

"Maybe." She turns back to her screen.

After a moment, I stand and grab my things. Something tells me I'm not going to come in tomorrow and find she's turned my computer on for me.

On my way out, I check Kurt's aisle, though my stomach is churning. Yocelyn's desk is empty, the chair tucked in—

Caressa said somebody had already been sent home.

Yocelyn could've faked it. If she wasn't the one who put Kurt's keys and phone in the drawer, she could've used the opportunity to take them somewhere—

I freeze at a light tap on my shoulder. "Aren't you supposed to be leaving?" Caressa's voice.

I turn around stiffly, as if my spine no longer works. "Sorry. I had plans with Yocelyn this evening. I just wanted to let her know that I was sick."

Caressa crosses her arms, looks me up and down.

I haven't really slept in two days. I probably look like death.

She rolls her lips in, presses them together, and shakes her head. "She's not here, Katrina."

"Okay." I turn around. I can feel her following me, like those old movies where the feds are tailing some mafioso, except I'm making no attempts to hide.

She stalks me all the way to the elevator. My last view as the door closes is her face, a single brow raised. I can't tell what she's thinking.

In an elevator, eleven floors don't take a long time. Less time than it takes to check your makeup, to listen to a voice mail, to walk from the Advancex lobby to your car.

And yet, with the way the world is swirling around me, as if the rules of gravity have suddenly changed, I have time to contemplate each of my sins, one per floor, like I'm descending the layers of hell.

Floor ten is for what I did to Navya. Nine for trashing the apartment and leaving it for Leoni to clean up. Eight is for not realizing sooner that something was wrong with Kurt, despite watching him so carefully.

Floor after floor after floor. It's not until passing three that I realize that even if Yocelyn took Kurt's phone and keys, there might be other clues in his desk. Clues Yocelyn forgot. Clues she might come back for tomorrow.

And I can't let her do that.

I smash the button for eleven right before the elevator hits the ground, and then I shrink against the back wall of the car, away from the door and Yuto's spying gaze. I count my breaths—five, ten—and then finally, *finally* the doors close again, and I'm on my way back up.

This time, the ride feels faster, breath after breath, floor after floor. I exit the car, but I don't turn toward the Annex or my desk. Instead, I slide into the bathroom—where I'm sure there aren't any cameras— and pick one of the stalls, right in the middle of the row.

I shut the lid, have a seat, and hide my shoes by pulling my feet up onto the rim. Immediately, my vision swims, exhaustion catching up. Despite how anxious I feel, there's a very real danger I might fall asleep—four hours is a *long* time—and if I'm in the building *too* late, I run the risk of attracting the attention of a security guard or setting off some kind of alarm. I've got to time this right.

I set my phone for five twenty, late enough that the push of people leaving the office will be over, but not so late I won't be able to make up some excuse for the guard—that is, as long as Caressa doesn't catch wind of it. I check three times that the alarm is on vibrate only, and then I tuck my phone into my bra.

And yet, now that I can safely fall asleep, I'm suddenly awake. I stare at the stall door and imagine the back covered in overlapping endekagrams. I think about the stars in Mi-Hee's kitchen-door world, foreign constellations swinging across the heavens.

Somewhere in Kurt's desk, there has to be a clue, something that will tell me what happened on the bridge.

When the alarm goes off, I spasm and almost drop to the floor. For a second, I have no idea what's happening, but then I remember Yocelyn's tear-streaked face as she went through Kurt's desk, and I uncoil myself from my purse and ease off the toilet. I have to stand in stages, vertebra after vertebra, my knees and spine aching from being curled up in a ball for hours. Only then do I reach down and pull the phone out to silence the alarm.

I have a number of texts, all from Leoni. I scroll through them with my thumb.

Can you call me when you get this? I need to talk to you. Received at 2:07 p.m. I can almost picture her gnawing on the corner of her bottom lip, her expertly applied lipstick somehow not bleeding onto her teeth.

An hour later: *Seriously, I know you're working, but it's important.*

And then another, from less than ten minutes ago. *Please call me as soon as you get off work.*

My stomach tightens. I want to call her—but every extra minute is going to look more suspicious, another chance to be caught.

I make a mental note to call her afterward and put the phone away.

I venture out into the bathroom, the tap of my shoes softly echoing off the tile. I walk to the sink before I realize I shouldn't create extra noise by washing my hands, so I creep out into the hallway, my skin crawling with invisible germs, and peek around the corner.

It's completely silent. I don't even hear the factory—as if my subconscious has decided my survival is more important than whatever would normally be kicking around in my brain.

I take a few sneaky steps before I realize how suspicious I'd look to anybody watching on a monitor, so I swallow hard, straighten the front of my dress, and throw my shoulders back. I waltz onto the main floor like I'm a rich lady at Bloomingdale's. When I get to Kurt's aisle, I even pull out my phone and scroll through the apps a few times, as if I'm bored and checking messages.

Still, by the time I sit down in his seat—*my seat, act like it's my seat*—my pits and back are prickling with fear-sweat, and I feel like a kid about to tear the wrapping paper off a package that has an equal chance of holding a game console or an eldritch horror.

I open the drawer. The phone and keys are still there. Stunned, I pull them out, one in each hand, and then Kurt's book, and set them all on the desk. I try the phone—it's still on, still has juice despite sitting in this desk for at least three days—but when I flip it open, I'm immediately asked for a PIN.

It's a burner phone. It has to be—which means what? He's got a mistress? He's dealing drugs?

I examine the keys. Four keys, including a car key, two house or apartment keys, and then a final, small copper key that could be for a padlock—or an apartment mailbox, now that I think about it, because it looks *just* like the one to *my* mailbox.

In fact—

I pull my keys out to compare. One of his apartment keys looks just like mine. It even has the same stamp on the back, an sc4 in tiny, laser-etched letters, but when I put the key up to mine, the teeth look completely different—

"Miss?"

A deep voice startles me so badly I almost fall out of the chair. I spin to face a security guard I don't know—a white man with a soft jaw and graying temples. "Sorry, miss. I called out, but you were somewhere else."

"Yes, I—" I have to swallow. My heart's turned into a hummingbird. "I was, um, thinking about something."

He gives me a dubious nod. "Right. Can I ask what you're doing here?"

I almost forget to lie. "I, uh, one of my friends is picking me up, and I didn't want to wait outside. It's cold and dark…" I look down at my feet. "I guess they're running a little late."

"I see." He shakes his head, fumbles around with something at his hip—I panic, but it's a flashlight. "Technically, if you're not working, you're supposed to be off the property. I understand why you wouldn't want to be outside alone in the cold—city can be dangerous—but you can't wait up here." He rubs his chin with his fingertips. "If you like, you can wait in the lobby. I'll walk you down now, if you don't mind."

I stand. "Yes, of course, thank you."

I try to convince myself that I hadn't planned on taking anything. That it's because the guard's staring at me, that it'll look even more suspicious if I leave everything here.

I open my purse and push it all in—the phone, the keys, Kurt's book. In the move, something flat and square slides out from beneath the front cover, a corner like a business card. I catch the edge of some design: curved, parallel lines, like a spiderweb.

Postcard. A shiver goes down my spine.

"All right, miss." The guard actually beams at me. "Let's get you downstairs—are you okay with taking the elevator?"

And even though I don't relish the idea of being in that enclosed space with him, I've already drawn enough attention to myself, so I nod meekly, and he leads me out of the room.

He waits in the lobby with me, which makes me feel trapped. I count to a hundred and twenty-one and pretend to get a text. "That's them! I guess I should've just waited outside." I give him my best smile and wrestle down the urge to run. On the way out the front door, I hear the *doot-doot* of a two-way radio.

"Yeah. She's on her way out," he says, and then the door closes behind me.

Who was he talking to? Who else saw me?

I make it to my car in a semi-daze. I can't get the door open on the first try, or the third, or the fifth. Just as I'm about to dive into my trunk for the coat hanger, the latch on the passenger door finally disengages.

I crawl over the center console, into the driver's seat. It's not until the car's in motion that everything hits me—how crazy I'm being, how close I am to losing my job. Caressa almost caught me *and* Navya. She also sent me *home*. If the guard had recognized me, if he'd known that was Kurt's desk, *if, if, if*—

She's on her way out.

I start crying. I have to take deep, slow breaths, but everything is spiraling out of control. I need to re-center myself, and if what I've done has broken the bridge's magic, it might not be able to save me anymore.

Is this my life, then? An unending series of hallucinations and delusions, an endless cycle of fear and failures? My vision flashes with stage lights. I'm gasping, taking huge breaths. I look for an exit from the busy street, a place to pull over. There's nowhere, but it's not safe to go on.

I slow to a stop in the middle of the road as sweat breaks out across my whole body. The driver behind me lays on his horn. I smash the button for the hazard lights and try not to vomit, try to focus on their indicators on the dash, the rhythmic *click-click* of them blinking off-on, off-on, because they're real, they're real—

The driver lays on the horn again. "Shut up!" I scream back—

And then everything goes quiet, like the shush when the house dims the lights, nothing left but a white baton hanging in the air, nothing but

Click-click
Click-click

As if beckoned, my ears fill with the first notes: a ritornello of bouncy strings and regal horns as they introduce and reinstate the themes. K. 622, Mozart's Clarinet Concerto in A Major. I haven't heard it, in my head or otherwise, since the night I broke into the library.

I'm not allowed to listen to this anymore—

But I lean into it anyway, push to the first clarinet solo, the one I know—not as Mozart originally intended, *because he didn't leave an autograph explaining his wishes—*

(My father's voice)

The man leans on the horn again, but it's like when you're onstage, and you're so afraid, and the lights are so bright you can't see a single face in the audience.

Are you there Mom and Dad are you there?

The baton waves, your heart is hammering like timpani—and then you start your solo, and the entire world fades away. Just you and the music.

I'd forgotten. How could I have forgotten?

I ease onto the gas. I maintain speed. I find my way through my favorite part—right after the leaping triplets, blazing fast, so horrendously waltz-like and playful in the middle of all those flurries of notes, as if you've suddenly fallen out of time.

The car transitions into the ship around me, metal and the terrible engine noises changing to the creaks of wood, the roar of waves, but I'm no longer panicking, no longer afraid. I am myself, more than I have ever been, my tongue dancing on the back of my front teeth as my fingers flutter over the keys. I am Katrina Kim, doing the only thing Katrina Kim ever did right.

And then I'm in front of my apartment.

I circle around for a space. Get out. Lock the doors. Stumble a bit as the song in my head moves toward the recapitulation, where the soloist and the orchestra are again reunited, the feeling of a rough reed on my tongue. I can even taste its woodiness, feel the soreness along the edge of my fingernail from holding up the weight of my clarinet, the groove in my bottom lip from years of being curled over my teeth.

I climb stairs in time, always in time. I wait in front of the door until the piece ends, until I hear applause, and only then do I pull out my keys—except they're not my keys, they're Kurt's keys. I try them in the door anyway, but they don't fit.

A moment later, the door swings open. I think I've got the right key after all, but then my world fills with Leoni's concerned face. "Katrina?" She sounds like I'm underwater. "Katrina, what is it? Are you okay?"

"Sorry," I mumble. "Exhausted."

She steps aside as I make my way in and tries to guide me onto the couch. "Here, sit down—"

"Going to bed," I grunt, evading the couch. I make it halfway to the bedroom before I feel the pressure on my arm, and even though I know it's Leoni and not Yocelyn, I pull away, hard.

"Do you know what time it is? Katrina, stop. Katrina, we really need to talk. Katrina, don't go in there yet—"

But I'm on rails. I'm through the bedroom door before I hear her say anything else. I run into something—*chair, her chair's pulled out*—and trip. I grab for the edge of the dresser, but I'm still holding my purse, and it smashes into the top, into a folder and a cup of mint tea and a hoard of makeup containers. Everything scatters, glass and liquid and papers and all her careful notes, and with it comes an avalanche from inside my purse, pens and ChapStick and tampons and keys and Kurt's phone and Kurt's book—

Leoni grabs me then. I don't know when she came in. "Katrina, stop. Are you drunk?"

My eyes are filling with tears, and my body is so heavy, and if I think about any of this, I'll lose the ability to breathe. "I just have to go to bed," I say, stooping down to grab Kurt's things.

Leoni squats in front of me. "Okay. Let me help you." She says something else, but I'm back to being underwater.

She scoops Kurt's keys and phone and the rest of my things back into my purse. She hands it to me and guides me toward the bed.

I don't take off my clothes, my shoes. I drop the purse on the bed and curl around it, and then I'm falling asleep to the sounds of her putting the room back in order, the way only Leoni can.

CHAPTER 9

A Message from Beyond

I wake up an hour before my alarm.

I lie there in the silence, feeling strangely, impossibly calm, like I've just gone out to the bridge, but then it catches up with me: I don't really know what happened on my way home from work, what it meant. I've spent the last three years staying away from my past life, from the parts I'd assumed were over: Pleasance, my parents, music.

I thought I'd moved on from everything, but instead, I've just been treading water.

Then again, things are changing. Talking to Leoni, listening to music—I've managed to push back against the kitchen-door world, at least partially. Even though I'm desperately flailing around, things aren't as written in stone as I'd thought.

I roll into a seated position. Everything feels heavy, like I'm hungover. I have to peel myself off the mattress.

Leoni's gone, her fluffy comforter folded up at the foot of her bed, the pillow on top, her sheets stripped. She must have taken them to a laundromat.

I take Kurt's apartment key out and confirm again that it's *not* a match for mine. I open his phone and play with it, even trying a few combinations for the PIN, but no luck. And then I remember his book, the postcard inside. I pull it out.

I have to hold my breath, because *this*, this is not possible.

It's black and white, hastily sketched, a set of symbols I'd know anywhere: music staves, though they're oddly shaped, peaking up in the middle like a mountain. Black notes are buried between the lines: a repeating sequence, iterated over and over again.

I didn't know—and yet, I must have, must have gotten a fuller glimpse of the card than I realized in my hurry to rush out of the office. Music's been turning there, in the back of my mind, daring me to reach out to it.

But this isn't my K. 622, or even really music at all. They're all quarter notes, too simple and repetitive to mean anything. And the shape of the staves, like the top of a circus tent—

My stomach churns as the names of the notes pop into my head.

D-E-A-D-D-E-A-D-D-E-A-D

Dead. Dead. Dead.

The arching staves suddenly make sense. They've been sketched to look like the lines of a suspension bridge. Which means this card must be Kurt's suicide note.

I'm there again, chilled to the bone, listening to the crash of metal and glass, watching him disappear into the shadows, into the black water—

Why are you always disappearing, Kurt?

I spend another ten minutes trying to rustle some other clue out of the card, but there's nothing. I even take the first card out of my box, the bunny-clad reference to a fantasy world, but it doesn't tell me anything.

First the fantasy card, then the thief card, then this: Kurt must've known I was watching him.

What else did he know about me?

My head's spinning, but I can't be late for work. I shove this inquiry aside, get washed and dressed extra quick, grateful that Leoni isn't here to see me run around wet and half naked, and spend a few minutes researching keys. I learn that the "SC4" stamp identifies a specific *blank*: a key-shaped piece of metal with no teeth. To *cut* a key, you put an original and a blank into a grinding machine, which then carves the teeth from the original onto the duplicate.

The Schlage SC4 blank is one of the most common blanks *in the world* for commercial six-pin locks—which apparently includes a lot of apartment buildings. In other words, the fact that Kurt and I have the same stamp on our keys probably doesn't mean anything.

Still, I have to fight the urge to try his key in all the doors in the hall. Instead, I go into the mail room and try the little copper key in the mailboxes. None of them open, which lends more evidence to the SC4 being a coincidence.

I'm relieved, but also strangely disappointed.

On my walk to the Buick, I focus instead on the clues I *do* have—like the car keys. The dark SUV I saw on the bridge *looked* like Kurt's car, but it's possible I was wrong, or that he has more than one car. It's not a very good clue, but if I have to, I'll search the entire city for a car that lights up when I hit the button.

I also have the advice from the Sunder Investigations woman. I *know* Kurt doesn't have a social media presence, but there are other kinds of sites, right? He could be part of a forum for 14 Dogs, or on a college alumni mailing list. I've limited my search for him to the Kurt I thought I knew—but there were parts of him I never even glimpsed.

As I drive to Advancex, I list more things to research. I need to figure out that phone PIN: there are only so many possible four-digit combinations. And I have the titles of most of Kurt's books written down in various places. They're all history books—medieval history, mostly, with a lot of books about demons and secret societies and codes. There could be a clue in one of those.

In fact, the more I think about it, the more it makes sense. I have his postcards, his books, his phone and keys. With a little time, I'm sure I can figure this out.

I park at the very top of the parking structure. I press the key fob several times on every floor, waiting for a telltale *beep-beep*, but I make it down without incident. Kurt's car is definitely not here.

Yuto gives me the stink-eye on my way in, but I've got my badge, and I'm early enough that there are other people in the lobby, so he can suck it. I spy on Kurt's aisle when I pass. He's not at his desk, of course—but neither is Yocelyn. Maybe she really was sick.

When I make it back to my desk, my computer is off. Navya nods a hello and ignores me. She hasn't forgiven me for what happened yesterday, and I'm not really sure she should. I put her in a tight spot.

I clock in and check my messages. Nothing from Caressa, thank god, although there's an email from my Spectacular Staffing recruiter, who needs me to fill out a number of forms pertaining to the hours I've missed.

I work for a bit, taking calls from people who are sure their insurance has been billed incorrectly. They're usually right; most of my and Navya's job involves figuring out ways to rebill things so that insurances will reverse rejections, recapturing revenue the hospital assumed was lost, which also shifts the burden of payment away from the patient. It's a job that requires concentration—juggling regulations and billing and procedure codes, shuffling times and dates—but I can't stop obsessing over the burner phone.

I slide it out of my purse and under the desk, trying to think of likely combinations. I don't know Kurt's *entire* birth date, but I know he was born in June, because he's always on the list of June birthdays in that month's Advancex newsletter.

0-6-0-1, enter. 0-6-0-2, enter.

After *0-6-0-5*, the phone says I've been temporarily locked out. I make a note of this. Depending on how long it lasts, I can alternate working and trying codes without disrupting my productivity so much that I attract Caressa's notice.

I take another call, one that lasts two minutes and twenty seconds. At the end, the phone is still locked, so I take another call, and then another, checking the phone each time.

Still locked. Maybe for good.

I start panicking. I turn it off and back on. I pull the battery. I reset it four, five times, but it's still locked.

When I look up, Navya is staring at me, but her phone rings, and she turns away.

I glance at the clock. Twenty minutes and seven seconds, now. I've been unavailable for four minutes, ostensibly typing notes. Too long.

I try the phone again. This time, it opens. I'm so relieved that I feel a rush of cold air around me, like plunging into a pool.

Okay. Five more codes.

I try *0-6-0-6* through *0-6-1-0*, and then I set a timer for twenty minutes on my computer.

By the end of the day, I'm feeling less hopeful.

I get through the entire month of June before surreptitiously taking the phone apart. There's no way to see what number it's been assigned, and without the number, I can't log into the Epoch Prepayed portal. And the specs for Kurt's burner phone state it supports PIN combinations of up to *six* digits.

Kurt looks like he could easily be anywhere from thirty to thirty-five—so even if he *did* use his birthday, that's at least 150 possible six-digit combinations. With twenty minutes in between every set of five, just trying the different variants of a June birth date in a five-year window could take ten hours.

I try searching for college alumni, medieval forums, 14 Dogs fan sites. I even try just typing "Kurt Smith" into Google images and looking through them all one by one, trying to find a man who matches the Kurt I know, but there's nothing.

The only new helpful development comes from a search for "Kurt Smith historian," which leads me to a professor of medieval studies in England with the same name. I send one of his colleagues an email, making up an excuse about a research paper.

I check the parking garage again after work, though I don't expect to find anything. I set out for home—but then an odd itch comes over my limbs, like a scratchy sweater.

If these keys *are* from the car I saw on the bridge that night, then given the way the front of that car was crushed, I'm not entirely certain how far it could drive—so the best place to start looking is probably somewhere near the bridge.

It's a thin lead, but I turn around. After a moment's contemplation, I shove a tape into the tape deck, an artifact of another time, and the growling strains of 14 Dogs come shooting out of the speakers.

My phone lights up and vibrates on the dash. Leoni again. I feel guilty—I mean, her sister is dying, and she tried to call me yesterday and I didn't pick up then, either—but part of me worries that if she hears my voice, she'll know what I'm up to, how crazy I'm being, and I just don't want anybody to know.

Traffic picks up about five minutes out from the bridge. It's always congested, but this rapid devolution into total gridlock doesn't make sense until I get close enough to remember the orange barrels, the closed lane. Now, giant cranes swing their heads back and forth like dragons.

I park and get out. Try the key fob, but there's nothing—and worse, I don't feel any trace of the bridge's power. Its magic is broken for me. Possibly forever.

I force my thoughts back to Kurt. There are lots on the other side. I could drive over—but I don't want to get snarled in the construction, and my muscles are jumpy.

I decide to walk the bridge instead, hoping to feel some hint of the kitchen-door world, some comforting thrum, but it's quiet all the way across.

The evening stretches into night. I pass the time going from location to location, creeping through rows, trying to find the car: parking structures, used car lots, grocery stores, schools. I stop for gas and put ten of my last fifteen dollars into the tank. I take advantage of the opportunity to stretch my back and pull out my phone to check the time.

Leoni's called twice more, though I didn't notice it over the music. By now, the tape's been played, both sides, several times. My gut twists, but it's going on midnight, and I'll see her soon.

I shut off the music and drive home in silence. Half of the signs around me are lit, and the effect of these alternating patches of light and dark is like a mouth missing teeth. I name the dark signs from memory as I drive past—*Walgreens, Supercuts, that clothing store with the word "bird" mixed in somewhere.* The car makes *the noise* four times on the way, which *seems* like more than normal.

When I get home, I test the doorknob before I open it—locked— and then I unlock the door and push it in.

The lights are all on in the apartment. My heart stops. Nothing is where I left it. My first thought is *we've been robbed*—but then I realize how silly that is, because what robber puts books back up on bookshelves, clears the clutter off the floor, and takes out the garbage? There are *vacuum tracks* in the carpet, perfect diagonal lines like a mowed lawn, and the air smells faintly of citrus.

I wander in, mouth open, like Mi-Hee stepping into the kitchen-door world for the first time; this version of my apartment is 50 percent larger than the one I left. I circle through the space slowly, finding objects that were long forgotten, like the orange pillar candle in the middle of the coffee table, which flickers invitingly, though it's burned through half the jar in my absence. Three pairs of shoes, neatly placed in a row by the door. A padded oven glove with a print of cats playing with a ball of yarn I dropped behind the stove. When I pick it up, the fabric is soft and clean, the insides fluffy. Just washed, then.

There's a card on the kitchen counter, sealed in an envelope. Even upside down, I can read my name in Leoni's curling script. I pick it up, tear open the side, and pull out the card. It's facedown, and when I flip it over, it sparkles in the light.

Glitter. It's already all over my fingers—will certainly be all over the counter before I finish reading it. The image on the front is brightly colored, a Lisa Frank–style horse running on what appears to be a rainbow made of different colors of fruit. There's nothing printed on the inside—just Leoni's tight writing, sloping down slightly as it crawls across the page.

> Kat—
>
> *I was hoping to catch you, to say something in person, but I couldn't get you on the phone. My sister died*

I have to swallow, to blink back tears. My hands are shaking. She'd been calling me, and calling me, and I never once answered.

and I need to go take care of my mom. I don't know when I'll
be back, but there's three months left on the lease, and I've left
Mr. Sacks a check to cover that much. You'll have to find a new
place after that, though.

I start crying, hard enough to make her writing swim. She'd been
trying to say goodbye.

I've been thinking for a while about what to get you as a
going-away present, because although we were sometimes
like two ships passing in the night, I definitely enjoyed our
conversations. But yesterday, when I got home, I opened the
closet and saw a MOUSE—and I realized EXACTLY what I'd
be leaving you with. Hopefully, a clean apartment will help
you find a new roommate. I left a note explaining the situation
with Mr. Sacks, too, so I think everything will be fine.

Also, there's one last thing: I've been thinking about you and
your fixation on this guy Kurt. I know I haven't always been the
most supportive—but Katrina, I really don't think it's healthy.
You need to let it go. If you can't, get some professional help. He's
all you think and talk about, and I'm worried about how it's
going to affect your job and your well-being.

Also, I didn't have room in my car for the furniture. I
thought about coming back for it later, but then I realized you
could probably use it. Feel free to sell it for the therapy, because
you deserve better than this. Everyone deserves to be happy.
Even you.

Love, Leoni.

One moment, my legs are doing their job, holding my body straight
and erect like they have every day since I learned to walk—and then

I'm sinking toward the ground, the handle of the silverware drawer jabbing me in the back as I slide down.

Leoni's gone. And because of my stupid obsession with Kurt, I didn't even have the chance to say goodbye.

Numbness seeps through my skin, and out of nowhere, the Tea Closet Incident pops into my mind.

It was shortly after I moved in with her. One morning, I got a call from my recruiter that Advancex was likely going to cut me as a temp, but they needed to finish the quarterly budget to make sure. I waited two weeks, the guillotine hanging over my head, frantically putting out applications for jobs that paid half as much because they'd likely hire fast, because I couldn't afford to miss even a single check.

And then one day, I completely lost it. I squeezed into our tiny closet and shut the door and started crying hysterically. A few minutes later, I heard a soft, rattling knock. "Kat? Are you okay?"

"Yes," I lied.

I heard her walk away—heard her step all over the apartment, heard things clink and the kettle go, and then she came back and slid the door open a tiny bit, just enough to push in a small tray with a lit candle, a cup of peppermint tea, and a romance novel.

It was a silly thing to do.

It was just the right thing to do.

Leoni had been the best fucking roommate, and I hadn't appreciated her. Worse, I'd completely failed to hold up my end of the bargain—sometimes, it was all I could do to just get dressed and make it into work, but not *all* times. There were days when I could have cleaned up a bit, could've done something to make her life easier. Instead, I'd let things get so bad we had a literal infestation of vermin.

And Leoni was good for me, grounding. I could feel it. And if the only person I've gotten close to in the last three years tells me to get help—well, shouldn't I listen to that?

I lean my head back against the cabinets. I desperately want to go crawl into bed—but I also don't want to leave this spot, don't want to figure out somewhere to put this card that won't destroy all of Leoni's hard work. If I get up now, if I go to bed now, then all of this will have really happened, and I can't do that, not yet.

So instead, I hold her card in my hands, curl my legs into my body, and wait.

CHAPTER 10

Ad Libitum to A Tempo

I wake up before dawn, the soft piano of Debussy's "Rêverie" uncoiling through my head. I wonder if the music is here to stay.

The clock says it's 6:05 a.m. Wednesday, I think.

Despite spending the night on the kitchen floor, I don't feel tired—but my body is stiff in a thousand places, and it cracks audibly as I attempt to stand. Worse, though, is the sore spot in my chest, the mocking shine of the clean surfaces.

Leoni's check will cover three months' rent. After that, I'm on my own.

When I first came to Grand Station, I had daydreams about striking it rich and moving into a swanky place by myself. About shopping for curtains and tiling backsplashes and uncovering virgin brick fireplaces behind crumbling walls, their hidden contents somehow untouched by the ravages of time—but now I understand how ridiculous that was. I haven't even been doing my fair share in a joint-living arrangement.

I ease myself onto the couch. There's still a little time before I have to start getting ready—not so much that I can actually *do* something, but enough that I don't feel like pushing into work quite yet. And there's something about the quality of the not-light outside, the softening of an impending dawn, that makes my mind feel clearer and stronger than it has in a long time.

I could stop doing all of this, I think. I did it once before—drove away from Pleasance Village and found myself a whole new life. I could make a new life again. I wouldn't even have to leave—just no more distractions. No more phone, no more keys. No more wasting precious time and energy driving around at night looking for Kurt's car, trying to find him online. Instead, I could start buckling down like a real professional, actually *work* at getting hired in and promoted—that's what Kurt did, right? Just played the game? Showed up on time, looked industrious? Maybe it took making a few friends in high places, but I could do that, couldn't I?

And though the outside hasn't changed, I feel like I can see the sunrise, gold and orange and pink. Maybe it's the fact that my ass is numb and half the floor is covered in glitter. Maybe it's the fact that for the first time, I'm realizing I *can't* do it alone—but something is shifting inside of me. I can feel the trajectory of my life, the fact that I am my own worst enemy—my own worst danger—and I'm afraid.

I need help. The thought is quiet and thin, like the see-through lace curtains on magazine kitchen windows. It feels like it tears me in half, like a river comes pouring in through the gap. *I need help. I need to get help. I've got to do something, before—*

Before I die.

I can almost see it below me: dark water, light flickering across the surface. A portal to another world. If I don't do something, one day, I won't be able to walk away from it. Kurt couldn't, after all. And he blamed me for that.

I don't want to die.

Wind whistling through my hair off a bridge.

I *don't* want to *die*.

I rub tears off my face and stumble to my feet, sending shocks of pins and needles through my leg. I grind my foot into the floor and feel it—really *feel* it—the numbness, the pain. I am alive, and I *will* feel this, and when I can move my legs again, I'm putting Kurt's things in the trash. I'm going to shower and go to work, and I'm *not* going to forget my ID, and I'm going to do the best damn job I've ever done.

And when I get home, I'll call therapists. A lot of them, until I can find one that takes Spectacular Staffing's godforsakenly terrible insurance. I'm going to go back to therapy and tell the truth this time, and maybe get back on some medication. Figure out my living situation. Come up with a plan for my career.

I stand up, say a silent thanks to Leoni, and throw Kurt's stuff in the trash bin. I tie a knot in the top of the bag, pull it out, and leave it next to the door so I don't forget to chuck it in the chute.

And then I get into the shower.

It feels like my skin is peeling off, but I don't make my endekagram sigil on any of the doors. Instead, I toss the phone and keys into the building trash chute. They hit the bottom with a metallic *clang*, and I feel a hundred pounds lighter.

When I get to my car, I can't get it open—and given what happened last night, I didn't have the presence of mind to leave the window cracked. But I am calm enough to think, and I need to solve this problem, and not just for now.

I sort through the trash in the trunk until I find the car's crumpled manual and cringe—my parents always took such good care of it.

I smooth the pages out and flip to the section on removing the back seat. Between the bolt and the clips, it's not the easiest-looking procedure, but when I check my phone, I have plenty of time, and I'm suddenly hopeful—how much more time will I have, if I'm not always beholden to my rituals?

I manage to get the passenger door open *and* remove the seat. There's a hole behind it, rimmed in rusted, sharp-looking metal. I break off the clip that fastens the seat before sliding it back in.

It looks almost normal—and now, there's direct access to the back seat from the trunk. I'll be able to climb through in an emergency, though I should put some tape or a pool noodle around the edges of the hole, because it's not exactly *safe*.

I am early enough that Yuto raises an eyebrow, early enough that I beat Navya to her desk. I lean over and turn on *her* computer, though she'll doubtless get here in plenty of time. It's going to take me a while to win back her trust, but I will.

I fire off a message to Caressa, apologizing for my *recent struggles with tardiness*. I fill it with exuberant buzzwords and a final *thank you for this opportunity, I'm so excited to recommit myself to the work*.

The check mark in the corner of the screen tells me that it was seen, but Caressa doesn't answer. Busy, or maybe not at her desk. I don't let it faze me. Today, I am invincible.

I open up the hospital insurance portals, my Excel spreadsheets, the phone dialer screens, and start doing the best damn job I've ever done, for Advancex or anyone else.

By midday, my resolve is bent, but not broken.

It starts with my computer, which has decided to be ornery: slow and prone to freezing. I have to reboot it twice. Every so often, I glance to my side, looking for Navya. By nine thirty, I have to admit she's actually late, and by eleven, that she's not coming in at all.

Right before lunch, I get stuck on a particularly bad call—a man incensed about his hospital bill after an ER visit for chest pain. I—and, from the notes, Navya and three other representatives—have already looked at this account several times and explained to him the problem: there is a difference between the facility fee, which includes the emergency room, and the *provider* fee, which is billed by the individual doctor. And in this case, the doctor was part of a traveling group of emergency room physicians—a staffing company, not unlike the one that employs me, which makes them out of network. It's frustrating, but legal, and yes, he's on the hook for the whole bill.

But he refuses to understand me. He just keeps repeating, over and over, "But I have insurance. Don't you understand that? I have insurance. *Good* insurance."

And maybe it's because I *don't* have good insurance, but I cringe every time he says it. Eventually, I pretend to transfer him and hang up. He'll call back, and hopefully, he'll be rerouted to someone who can actually make him happy. It seems cruel, but it's the best thing— because I can already hear rumbles of the factory around me, and I don't want either of us to see where that leads.

It takes me a while to finish my notes, to craft the flow of this narrative into a customer service document that would stand up under scrutiny in court, that wouldn't cast blame on anybody at Advancex. When I reach for the mouse to click the button that will stamp this onto the record, my cursor goes traveling across the screen.

I watch it float. It's a curling, lazy movement, but one that feels like it has some intention—like the path of a nervous, well, *mouse*, finally venturing out into the middle of the kitchen floor.

When I blink, the cursor is back in the corner of the screen.

I wiggle it tentatively, and it responds like normal.

A few hours later, I'm starting to feel better when the computer freezes again. I hit CTRL + ALT + DEL to restart it—but then I remember the mouse and check the running programs. Maybe there's some process I can close that will at least get me through this day.

There's a program I've never seen before listed in the task manager: SNTLKL.exe.

I don't know what that is. I search for it using DuckDuckGo, but the random configuration of letters is so generic that tons of different matches come up. Some are blocked by the company browser—which usually means the software thinks it's porn. Either that, or a union website.

It's probably nothing, but I still feel uncomfortable. I write the letters on the last sticky note on my pad before throwing the empty cardboard into the trash.

I message Caressa again. *My computer keeps freezing. Do you want me to go down to IT?*

The reply is almost instant. *They're doing something on the server for the next hour or so. Let's wait, and if the problem keeps happening, we can reassess tomorrow.*

Okay, I say. *Sounds good. I'll make a note.*

I open my drawer to get out a new package of sticky notes, but something's wrong. I stare at it, the paperclips and highlighters and capless pens, the cellophaned packages of sticky notes, the roll of tape—

The tape is upside down. I *never* put the tape upside down. It feels mean, shoving the poor tape's face into the darkness of the drawer.

Which means someone has been in my desk.

My stomach churns, but Advancex has cleaners who come at night. They're not supposed to move your things around, but one of them might have found the tape dispenser on the ground and popped it into my drawer.

Or it could've been Yocelyn, jealous over Kurt—but no, it had to be someone between yesterday evening and today, and she wasn't here. Unless she snuck in later.

Navya, maybe? Would she have reason to go through my desk?

My computer dings. It's the office messenger.

Just got memo. Server problem is fixed. Why don't you try restarting, and see how your computer is doing?

I swallow, but I reboot and check my running processes again. The new one, SNTLKL.exe, is missing.

Was it some IT server tool? My stomach crawls.

I glance over my shoulder, but nobody appears to be watching me, so I get back to work.

By the end of the day, I'm back to wondering if maybe I'd imagined the whole thing—although I still have the SNTLKL.exe note in my purse. I know because I checked it twice.

And even if this program is some new nefarious Advancex spyware—well, so what?

Maybe the best way to deal with this is to be so squeaky clean there's nothing to find. A hard thing to do, when you've already stolen a bunch of items from a coworker's desk—but that evidence is at the bottom of my apartment building's trash chute, and the only person who would point a finger at me has jumped off a bridge.

And none of it changes anything. Leoni's still gone. I still need my job. I still need to drive home and somehow find a new therapist and a roommate. If I get lucky, maybe I won't have to move—though it's going to be hard to find someone else willing to share a bedroom, even at this price, so we'll have to figure out a new arrangement for the space.

Life is scary enough. I don't have to go poking around in a fantasy world.

I'm almost home when my phone startles me from somewhere deep in my purse. I jerk the steering wheel, but then I crouch down, keeping my eyes trained on the road, and fish it out.

It stops ringing by the time I get it in my hand. I glance at the vaguely familiar number. Seeing the arrangement of the digits makes a strange beat bloom in my body, like the "Closing Rejoicing" section of Stravinsky's *Firebird*—the distinctive press of 7/4 time, the same meter used for the stomp in Pink Floyd's "Money."

One-two-three-four, one-two-three. One-two-three-four, one-two-three.

As if summoned, the two pieces overlay themselves in my head, a discordant clash that shouldn't work but does—and then something else breaks through, something wrong, something more annoying than disconcerting—

It's my phone. It's ringing again.

I'm still driving. I put it on speaker. "Hello?"

"This the young woman that called me earlier?"

The investigator's gravelly voice zaps me straight in the spine. Déjà vu.

"Hello?"

I clear my throat. "Yes, that's me."

"I have something to tell you."

I don't know how to respond. "Okay."

"Keep in mind that if you lie to me, I'll know. I do this for a living."

The music is back. I hope she can't hear it. "Okay," I say, because she appears to be waiting for an answer.

"Why are you so interested in this guy?"

My mouth is dry. "I told you. I saw him die—"

"Right. Jumped off a bridge—but *before* that, did you have an existing relationship with him?"

She asked this before. I can't remember how I answered. "Not in any way that matters." It's true enough to hurt.

"And why are you pursuing this when the police have decided it's not worth pursuing?"

This gives me a jolt. I can't remember if I told her that—if not, she's got good sources. "I don't know. Honestly—I just can't let it go. He looked at me before he jumped, and there was something in his expression…" *Anger, hatred.*

"Something that didn't make sense?"

I nod, grateful. "Yes. And it's eating at me."

"Interesting." There's a long pause. I wonder if I've missed some cue. "So, here's the deal. This conversation never happened. I have no idea what you're getting involved in and, frankly, don't care, but if this goes bad, I do *not* want to be dragged into it—not for free. I don't care if you're on the witness stand in front of the president, one hand on the Bible—if you're asked why I called you at this time, on this date, you tell them it's because I wanted to offer you a discount of ten percent to start this investigation."

"Yes," I say. I'm not *hopeful*, exactly, but there's a curious tingling filling my body, like it's fallen asleep and is on the verge of waking up.

"Repeat it back to me."

"What?"

"What I just said. You're being interviewed by the president. Repeat it back to me."

I rub the back of my neck. "You called me at this time to offer me a discount of ten percent off this investigation—"

"—to *start* the investigation." Her correction is sharp. She's not playing around.

"Ten percent to *start* the investigation," I say, hoping my tone sounds dutiful.

Another long pause. I hear a crinkling, a soft *snick*—but it's not until she takes a long breath that I realize she's lit a cigarette. "Okay. I was following up on something for another client and a vehicle caught my eye. I realized it matched the description of the car you're looking for, especially given the location."

My head swims. "Okay," I say, too afraid to say anything else.

Another drag. "If this is your guy, something tells me you should be careful. Like the plate—it's seven alphanumeric characters, same as a standard plate, but given the pattern, it's a vanity plate. You can't just randomly alternate numbers and letters. Know what I mean?"

"No," I say, because I don't. My body is still doing the numbly-tingly thing, although a bunch of questions are now darting through my head, anxieties fleeing like deer across a road. What if it's not his car? What if it is, but by the time I get there, it's moved again, like some infernal ghost car? What if it's his car, but the key I have isn't his car key?

Shit. The key. Which I have thrown away. And for good reason.

This is the universe, trying to tempt me down a rabbit hole. I can't do this. I need to find a graceful way to exit the conversation and stay strong.

"I mean," she says, clearly unaware of the tracks my mind has just taken, "a plate like this? This guy thinks he's really clever. It's obnoxious. You gotta wonder what kind of person he is."

I want to tell her that I *do* wonder, but I don't.

"Anyways, here's the deal. You on a cell phone?"

"I—yes."

"I'll text you the location. *But* I don't work for free, remember?"

My mouth goes dry. I can feel Kurt's car slipping through my grasp. Which, on second thought, is where it needs to be—out of my grasp, out of my mind, and out of my life. "I don't have any money," I say, hoping it will make her leave this alone. I'm too weak to hang up on her myself, but if she doesn't feel like she'll be compensated—

"That's okay. You can owe me a favor. Always good to have favors in my line of work. Sound good?"

I shudder at the thought of owing her anything. "I'm not sure—"

"By the way. The front of the car is all smashed up."

There's nothing else she could've said that would've had this effect. It's like falling through lake ice. "Oh," I say, as if that means something.

"All right. I'm going to go."

"Just—" It hits me then, that I *still* don't know who I'm talking to. "What's your name?"

"Sunder," she says, as if it's obvious. She hangs up before I can reply.

CHAPTER 11

Another Man's Treasure

Once upon a time, there was a girl who wanted to be a better, healthier person than she was. But change is exhausting, and sometimes requires therapy, and it's hard to find a good, affordable therapist when you have shit insurance.

Maybe I should've phoned the police when Sunder called about Kurt's car—it would've been the healthy thing to do—but they didn't believe me the last time I spoke up. They acted like I was a perpetrator, so really, the smart thing to do is locate the car (and the keys) and see if there's *really* anything nefarious going on.

This is the story I tell myself as I descend into the basement of my apartment building. I try not to think about spiders, about the way the narrow stairs feel like they're slanting under me, *Haunting of Hill House*–style.

The cramped hallway at the bottom is dim, even with the lights on. I let my eyes adjust before creeping farther, to the laundry room and then past. I know the trash room's down here, somewhere, though I've never ventured this deep into the bowels of the beast. With every step I take, it gets darker—and when I look up, I can just make out a naked, burned-out bulb in the shadows on the ceiling behind me.

I proceed down the hallway, looking for a bend, a branching path, another door, but there's nothing. The hallway just terminates abruptly in a wall. I must've missed something. I double back—and catch the unmistakable odor of garbage.

I return to the wall. The movement makes light glint dully on something almost too high to reach. A hasp, secured with a rusty padlock, tucked so far in the shadows it's no wonder I missed it.

Staring at it now, I can easily make out the edges of a door. The trash room must be behind it. I've got to get into that room, but I don't have the key.

I inspect the hasp, reaching to prod its edges with my fingertips. It's anchored with four slotted screws. I could probably rip the padlock off if I jerked hard enough, but that would damage the door.

I decide to try taking out the screws and search my pockets for something I can use as a screwdriver. There's nothing, until I pull out my own keys. It looks like the mailbox key might fit.

I have to stand on my tippy toes to reach, pushing the key hard. I try four times, five, but the screw refuses to turn. I give up and yank the padlock, but the metal loop is affixed to the door more solidly than I'd guessed.

Well, fuck. I need a better grip and some leverage.

I steal into the laundry room and look around. It's empty save a basket in one corner, a square plastic number that looks like it *might* support my weight, if I'm both careful and lucky. I grab it and turn it upside down in front of the door. I pull hard on the lock and haul myself up onto the basket, taking care to keep my feet directly over the sides where it's strongest. It creaks under me, hairline cracks appearing in the plastic, but it holds.

With my other hand, I drive the mailbox key into one of the hasp screws. This time, it turns, just a bit. I work as fast as I dare, skinning my knuckles over and over, trying not to think about the sounds the basket makes under me every time I shift.

I'm halfway done with the last screw when the basket collapses. My fist clenches around the padlock for a moment before I lose my grip and crash to the ground, my whole side lighting up with pain.

When I finally crawl to my feet, I discover a trickle of blood stretching across my forearm. A glance down reveals the cause: a sharp piece of plastic, sticking up at an angle—no, wait. I've also cut my hand.

I look up. The padlock is still in place, but the hasp is free. Nothing to stop me, then.

I swallow and pull open the door, revealing a giant blue dumpster. Its ripe smell spills into the hallway. I drag in what's left of the laundry basket, away from prying eyes, and shove it into a corner.

I'm in a storage room. It's about as large as my apartment, full of shelves of cleaning supplies and tools and random parts: the front of a dishwasher, the insides of a window air-conditioning unit. I wonder if all this stuff was here before, or if the super dragged it in after he started locking the garbage room. I imagine it's the latter, because if not, I can understand why people keep breaking into the place. The tools alone look valuable.

I step closer and gag as the smell assaults me. The bin is completely full—bags of ramen noodles and Styrofoam meat trays and banana peels. Several have burst open from the impact of landing, like overripe tomatoes. A huge, heaving mass of black and white plastic, and somewhere, at the very bottom, is a tiny, cat-print bag of Kurt's things.

I take stock, trying to strategize. I'm too short to reach anything but the top bags. I need a ladder and some gloves, a tarp or something to put down on the floor—somewhere to deposit the bags without making a mess. I'll put it all back before I leave, and the super won't know the difference.

Something catches my eye in the back of the dumpster: a little tuft of plastic, sticking up like one of those flags they use to mark gas lines. I can't be sure—but I *think* I spy a kitten on it.

I could've sworn I'd heard the bag hit the bottom of the dumpster this morning, but it could've hammered into the side or landed on top of some other hard piece of trash. It's right on top. If I can find something to stand on, I *might* be able to reach it.

I search the utility room. I find a small Ikea-style shelving unit that deforms when I push the sides in with my hands. I only need it to hold me up for a few seconds, but given what just happened with the laundry basket, the idea makes my stomach queasy. Right as I'm trying to remember the exact amount of the deductible on my crappy health insurance, I discover a metal folding chair, hidden in the shadows and covered with dust. Perfect.

I unfold it and clamber up. The little tuft of kitty plastic is all the way in the back. Even leaning over as far as I can, I can't quite reach it, but it's close.

The rim of the dumpster is flat, though, and a good three inches wide. I plant my foot and bounce, trying to see if the dumpster will roll. It doesn't move, though I can feel it *wanting* to.

In other words, this is a dumb idea. But the bag is *right there*—and it's not like I have a ladder in my apartment. And if I leave, I might not be able to find it again, or I could come back to an empty dumpster.

I take a deep breath, and then I push off my rear foot, swinging my weight forward—and overbalance. I desperately grab for the only hard thing in front of me—the rim of the dumpster—which brings my face inches from garbage. The smell is...not pleasant. I reach for the bag, but it's still too far.

I walk my hands around the rim, the cut on my palm burning. My abs protest, indignant that I would demand *planking* when I normally need a break walking up the stairs to my apartment. As I stretch farther, the burn gets worse, giving me plenty of time to regret this and all my other life choices.

Finally, though, the little tuft of plastic is in reach. I brush it with my fingertips—just a bit closer—and then I finagle it between my index and middle finger.

A loud bang echoes behind me. I scream and face-plant into the dumpster, straight into an open Styrofoam container of half-eaten chicken Parmesan. One of my hands lands in something slimy, but it's not until I'm rolling over onto my side that the stink hits me, and even then, it's not until I see it—

Baby diaper. I've just stuck my hand *inside* a strange baby's diaper. My hand with an *open wound*.

Inside.

a.

baby's.

diaper.

I look up. It's the super. I scrabble for an explanation, but my mind is hijacked by disgust. Before I can come up with a single word, I vomit all over the inside of the container.

Mr. Sacks takes me in—shit-handed, vomit-faced—and takes off running.

For some reason, that makes it worse. Before the door even bangs behind him, I throw up again and start crying. Half blind, I grab the little tuft and pull—and it sticks, wedged too deep, and that fills me with worse horror, because *it's just a little bag, it should come out easily*—and then it finally, *finally* pulls free, a hundred frolicking kittens dancing across the surface—

It's stuffed a quarter-full, easily ten times the size of what I threw down the trash chute this morning. I've defiled my body in ways I'll need drugs to wipe from my mind, and it's not even the right fucking bag. I was crying before, but now I'm *wailing*—a crazy, hyperventilating ululation that erupts up the trash chute like a banshee's scream.

I try to clamber out, but the trash is like quicksand. Plastic bags rustle and shift around me, some of them tearing as I go, releasing new smells into the mélange. I gag and gag, and everything is terrible—

The door creaks open just as I get my hands on the side. I pull hard, but I'm not strong enough to drag myself out. The super's steps echo, bouncing around the small concrete room as he runs toward me, and for a moment, a horrible image fills my mind—him shutting the lid, forever confining me to trash-jail, me asphyxiating in my own vomit, the truck later coming to dump my body in a landfill.

This is how I die. I never would've guessed—though I should've known. I should've known it from the first time I saw his kitchen-door analogue, that menacing pirate bunny with its peg leg—

"Stop moving," he says, and out of options, I obey.

He dabs something under my nose with a gloved hand. I'm assaulted by the smell of menthol, so loud it drowns out everything else. The air is acerbic but fresh, and I start weeping again, this time from gratitude.

"Thank you," I manage.

He nods, but from the way his top lip gently tugs upward, as if caught with a fishing hook—he's disgusted, and I don't blame him.

He sets down the little tub of mentholated rub. Under one arm, he's got a small container of disinfectant wipes. He pulls a wad out of the top, the wipes making soft grinding noises as they exit the hole, and hands it to me. "You can clean up your..." From the way his eyes dart around as he takes me in, he can't settle on a part. "Body."

None of this is what I expected. I take the wipes and clean off my hand. They're the heavy-duty, industrial kind you're not supposed to let touch your skin, but after what I've just been through,

I'd crawl inside the wipes container if I could. My hand stings so sharply I almost cry out, but I don't stop, because I will never be clean again.

When I'm done, I look around for a place to throw them away, before realizing that I'm standing inside of a literal dumpster—but before I drop them, he holds up an empty trash bag, fresh off the roll. "Don't want to just leave human shit lying around in the open like that." And then he sighs. "God, some people are nasty."

I think about the mouse that compelled Leoni's cleaning spree and wince. I drop the wipes into the bag.

He pulls out some more and hands them to me. "For your face."

I shiver and clean my face. The wipe turns red with old spaghetti sauce. And then I look down and see my shirt, and I do the best I can to remove the worst of the vomit.

"Okay," says Mr. Sacks, once I throw the wipes in the bag. "Why don't you tell me what the *hell* compelled you to break into the trash room and go rooting around inside my dumpster?" His face morphs, turning stony. "Are you the one that's been stealing my—"

"No, no," I interject, afraid of the end of that sentence. "I, uh, accidentally threw away some keys."

He sighs and shakes his head—but when he looks up, I'm surprised to see what looks an awful lot like *guilt* cross his face. "Look...I mean, yeah, you need to get better about keeping track of your things and all—but if you really can't pay the seventy-five dollars to have a new key cut, why didn't you come to me and talk it out? Was all this really necessary?"

I bite my lip. "The thing is...they weren't my keys."

His mouth falls open. The muscles on his face flicker and twitch, like the first shivers of life in some gelatinous horror-movie blob. "You...you threw away *someone else's* keys?"

I nod. "Yes. And a phone. I—"

Before I can finish, he whoops and doubles over, just exploding into a laughter that takes forever to die down into small, periodic rumbles.

"Well," he says, wiping tears out of his eyes with his forearm, "how about this. Let's get you out of the dumpster. Go upstairs, take a shower, and change your clothes. I'll meet you back down here in an hour, and we'll see if we can't find those keys."

He chuckles again, but then he climbs onto the chair and holds out a gloved hand, still shining with mentholated rub. I manage to get into a semi-squat, enough to reach for it, only to fall forward—but he catches me and jerks me upright, before hauling me out like a little kid.

"Go on, now," he says. "And don't be late—or too early. I don't exactly feel like hanging around down here a minute longer than I have to. Seven-oh-six p.m., on the dot, got it?"

"Got it."

"Oh. And I'm billing you for the repair to the hasp."

I'm too ashamed to answer, so I just run upstairs—fast at first, and then slowing down. *Way* down. When I finally make it past my door, I drop my keys into the sink to be washed, and then I strip and jump into the shower.

By the time I head back downstairs, hair wet but body clean, I'm not in a *good* mood—but I'm certainly in a better one.

Mr. Sacks is waiting right outside the trash room. "I sprayed some air freshener in there. I don't know how much it'll help."

He hands me the jar of mentholated rub and a fresh pair of gloves.

I put them on and dab some of the rub under my nose. "Now what?" My stomach churns. No amount of gloves or menthol changes the fact that, at some point, we're going to be digging through the trash. And by *we*, I mean *I*, because I doubt Super Sacks likes me *that* much.

"Well, it depends. What time did you throw everything in the chute?"

I swallow. "Like, seven a.m.? It was right before I left for work, and I was early today."

He nods thoughtfully. "That was right around the time I swapped out the bins, I think. So depending on if it was before or after—"

"After."

He raises an eyebrow, and I shake my head. "I heard it thunk against something when it fell in. Sounded like the bottom of an empty bin."

He nods. "Okay. Was it just—was it just the one key, or was it a whole key ring?"

"The whole ring. And a small phone. But—if we move the trash around a bit, I can maybe find it. I have pretty distinctive trash bags—"

"Yes." He glances over his shoulder at the trash room door. "Little kittens." He makes a face, then, the kind where your lips pull back to show all your teeth. I get the feeling I'm not going to like what he's about to say. "Unless you threw away a dead cat earlier, I'm pretty sure that wasn't your bag."

"A dead cat?" I blink as the words sink in. And then, in a moment of utter horror, my still unsettled stomach roils, and I shove the image out of my head, before I can throw up all over again.

"Yeah," he says, oblivious to my pain. "I've talked to Mrs. Mar—to the *tenant* about it before, but I guess we'll be having that discussion again. Stuff like that is how you get rats."

Oh god. It's Mrs. Marple. Mrs. Marple, who gifted us the trash bags—she's been throwing dead cats away in the dumpster.

How many cats does she have now? Ten? I don't know them well enough to notice if one's been recently replaced.

I gesture grimly toward the door of the trash room, eager as fuck for this to be over. "So, I've been trying to come up with a plan..."

"Right." He rubs his face with his forearm. "Is there any reason you didn't call the phone?"

Because I don't know the number. "It's off. Can we maybe try to get the keys with a magnet?"

"Keys generally aren't magnetic." There's a sudden harrowed look on his face that makes me think this is a road he's been down and would not like to revisit. "But the dumpster walls are. A magnet won't do us any good."

"So what do we—"

He pushes open the door without answering. There are a bunch of flattened cardboard boxes laid on the ground around the dumpster, a tarp spread out on top. Next to the tarp is an organized line of objects: two of the long-handled reachers with grabby pinchers that are advertised on TV for seniors, a shovel, an open utility knife, and what appears to be a long-handled pool skimmer. There's a tall stepladder next to the bin.

I realize it's just a bunch of maintenance supplies, but it's also kind of beautiful.

"You're sure," he says. "About the kitten trash bag. And the empty bin."

For a moment, even though I watched that bag disappear down the trash chute just this morning, even though I heard the *clang*, I'm not sure. I picture four different trash bags, hear four different sounds.

It's not the first time I've wondered if I'm completely losing it, but the banality of the trigger—a trash bag, a fucking trash bag—makes this one cut deep. "Yes," I say finally. "White trash bags, little prancing kitties. Same as Mrs. Marple's."

"Right," he says, and he hands me a reacher.

After a few minutes, we hit a good rhythm. He won't let me stand on the ladder, not after what he just witnessed, so he climbs up and grabs bags with two reachers in concert, because one isn't enough to support a bag's weight, and a single little rubber pinchy-part is too likely to puncture the bag. I wonder how many times the man's had to dig through trash to know this.

I stand below with the pool skimmer. Most of the bags are too large to really be *caught* by it, but I can break their fall and steer them onto the "landing area" without rupturing them. Most of the time. Getting the bags back into the trash is going to be a real pain in the ass.

As the minutes tick by, he disappears farther and farther into the dumpster. Just as the pile is getting too big for the landing pad, leading me to nervously run circles around it as bags slide down its sides, he lets out a triumphant shout, as if he's sighted the white whale itself—and then he straightens. Dangling on the edge of his reacher is a white kitten-print bag, just the right size.

He grins and carefully swings it over toward me. I catch it in the pool skimmer. It's everything I can do not to tear into it with my bare hands, but it *was* in the garbage, so I wait as he grabs the utility knife, cuts the bag open, and spills its contents onto a clean piece of newspaper below.

"Wow," he says, clearly impressed. "You managed to throw the phone and the keys into an empty trash bag, tie it off, and send it down the chute. I don't know how a person does that."

I blush so fiercely it hurts. "Yeah, I—I didn't have a good morning."

I go to grab them, but Mr. Sacks blocks me with an arm. "Not so fast, Ms. Kim. We need to clean up first."

This part, at least, goes faster. We have to be careful, because some of the bags are broken—either from the fall, or being moved onto the landing area, or from my flailing around inside the dumpster like I was about to have a prophetic vision. The bags that can be tossed back in are heavy enough that after a few minutes, I'm breathing hard. My arms already ache from holding up the pool skimmer and catching things; by the time we get all the bags and the tarp and the cardboard and our gloves into the dumpster, they're half-dead, and I'm covered with sweat.

When we're done, I look up at Mr. Sacks, afraid of what he's going to say next, but he just motions at Kurt's things. I step forward and scoop them up, glad the kitty bag turned out to be as durable as its box proclaimed.

"Thank you." I misjudged him so badly, and he's been so kind despite what an asshole I've been. I'm so mortified I could crawl back into the dumpster and shut the lid. "I'm sorry about the door. I didn't mean to break it."

His eyes widen, but he recovers quickly. "Like I said, I'll put it on your next rent statement. I have a bunch of repairs to get to, so I'll see you. But if you could do me *one* favor?"

"Name it."

He nods, a bobbing motion, mostly to himself. "The last time I went up to your apartment for the quarterly fire inspection, it was so dirty that I was honestly afraid you were going to get an infestation. I know you've been going through a lot, but you really, *really* need to clean that apartment. I don't want to have to take action—"

"Consider it done," I say.

He nods again, this time suspicious—but perhaps a bit hopeful, if I'm being fair—and then he leaves me alone with my treasure.

CHAPTER 12

X Marks the Spot

It's almost ten p.m. when I manage to get into the car, exhausted but wired at the same time.

The GPS says the address Sunder gave me is only about ten minutes from the bridge, though on the opposite side. I've never been in this neighborhood before, and as I approach, it becomes clearer *why*. Minute by minute, the streetlights get dimmer and farther apart, the encroaching shadows made worse by the widening gaps between buildings. Places are missing—torn down, burned down, or just plain collapsed. Nobody has seized the opportunity to redevelop these lots, despite the city's crowding, though gentrification will surely come for them one day.

The road turns gnarly, the borders rough and cracking away in places like scabs.

The GPS lets me know I'm close, though I don't see anything. I turn at a building—

A lot pops into view. It's got cars in it, at least twenty, surrounded by a tall chain-link fence that hangs off bent metal poles. The gate's closed. I think it's a used car lot until I spy the sign over the office door—BERTOLINI'S AUTO REPAIR.

The lot's dark, and I don't see anyone nearby. It'd be trespassing to enter. I don't even know if the car is in there.

But I have Kurt's fob. If the signal reaches, I can check without getting out of my car.

It takes some maneuvering, but I back into the driveway, all the way to the gate, to make it easier to flee if someone jumps out at me. I fish Kurt's fob from my purse and press the lock button. Somewhere behind me, a light flashes, *beep-beep*.

I open my window and lean out, before pressing the button again. I catch the flash's origin out of the corner of my eye, down at the end of the row. I can't see the car, but it's here.

My skin feels tight. My motor clunks and groans. In my rearview, the glow from my taillights just barely catches the cloud of steam rising behind me, red glints on whispers of smoke.

I absolutely should *not* get out of this car. No way, no how.

But—*but*—Kurt's car is here, in this mechanic's lot. And I'm *certain* he didn't drop it off.

I imagine returning to my apartment. Coming back in the morning, sun hitting broken sidewalk and weeds, dully lighting the ancient chain-link—and finding the car no longer here. I imagine never knowing what really happened to it—and in that moment, something plays inside my head, just a few bars of horns and a timpani roll, and I know I can't let this slip through my fingers. That's why I'm here, isn't it? To *know*.

I grab Kurt's keys and my phone before dropping my purse in the footwell and climbing over the center console. When I crack the passenger door, the dome light glows, bright in this place, but the beam doesn't penetrate the shadows behind me.

I close the door just enough to kill the light and walk toward the fence. Cold drives into my neck, my hairline, my fingers and ears. The world reacts to my movements, light shifting and bouncing off surfaces, my reflection refracting onto side mirrors and auto glass and flat planes of shiny paint.

I slow down as I get closer. I don't try the button again, don't want to break this odd silence or give myself away. It's almost like a spell: if I can pick out the car by sight, then maybe it'll be real, maybe I'll be rewarded for my cleverness—

There, in the very last spot, is a boxy, black SUV. Part of the front end is crushed in, the headlight smashed and the bumper dragging on the ground, like a sneer.

It's Kurt's car. I know it is—but even so, I hit the fob again. The lights flash, the locks engage, and I feel the itch. How stupid, to think I could outrun this need, could keep it away with the force of my will. I have to see. I have to *know*.

I check the top of the fence for barbed wire. *Safe.* I take a long breath, and then I grab the chain-link with my fingers, testing its strength. My hand aches where I cut it, but I pull and ascend, as if I'm climbing the kitchen-door mountain on the Cayatoga Bridge. Music fills my mind—quiet at first, and then louder, the bouncy bassoon of Grieg's *Peer Gynt* Suite no. 1, "In the Hall of the Mountain King."

The whole way up, I tell myself I'm not doing this. I struggle at the top, balancing precariously as I get one leg across and then the other, before starting my descent. By now, my arms and fingers are screaming. The toe of my left shoe gets caught in the fence, wrenching my ankle.

About four feet from the bottom, I fall flat on my back, so hard my head smashes into the ground and my teeth smack together. It fucking hurts, hurts enough I'm afraid to move at first, too scared I've broken something, that I'll find out I'm paralyzed.

But then I see the car, leering at me. Making me itch. The music starts again, strings entering as if on cue.

I roll over like a turtle and find my feet, but now, I'm too scared to approach the car head-on—like it's the Mirror-Man, waiting to crawl out from above my bathroom sink if I look at him wrong.

I circle behind it, envisioning invisible monsters hiding between the gaps of the cars, hands darting out to grab me by the ankles. I shift farther away, hopefully out of reach, until I'm close enough to read the license plate:

V01N1CH

I freeze. A small light goes off in the back of my mind, as fuzzy as my car's dome light. I've seen this word before, I think. What did Sunder say? Something about the vanity plate being clever—no, *obnoxious.*

I open up the notes app and copy it down, being careful to make sure I get the zeros and ones correct, and then I circle around to the passenger window and peer in. The car looks bare and, as I suspected, immaculate. Something tells me I could run a finger into any crevice on the dash and come away clean, that there are no crumbs hidden deep within the seats.

But I'm still afraid to open it, afraid of how much it feels like a tomb. Instead, I pop the trunk. Like the rest of the car, it's empty—I can clearly see the carpeted flap that covers the emergency tire storage.

I pull back the flap. It's showroom perfect: a spare tire, a jack, and a tire iron, a flat piece of cardboard from what used to be a shipping box underneath. The cardboard's clean, but I know instinctively it's for a blown tire—something to keep Kurt's skin and clothes off the road as he replaces it.

After a moment, I lift up on the corner of the tire. I'm treading water, I know I am, but I'm still too afraid to break the seal of the car doors, to set the next thing in motion.

Underneath, *306* is scrawled in black on the cardboard, some fat pen that looks like a marker, or maybe grease pencil—but there's nothing else of note.

It's time. I unlock the doors and reach for the handle, before I remember: if this is a vehicle dump, or whatever, I shouldn't touch anything with my bare hands. I pull my sleeve over my fingers and grab the handle.

Kurt's interior light comes on, startlingly bright compared to mine. I don't want to get in all the way, in case I disturb some hair or DNA or something else the police might need—but both the front and the back are completely empty. Even the cupholders are clear.

And then I remember the glove compartment. I circle around to the passenger side and push together the buttons that pop the compartment open. The door falls hard, bouncing at the bottom of its arc.

There's an owner's manual, still shrink-wrapped in plastic. I pick it up, hoping to find something underneath, but there's no registration, no proof of insurance.

It makes no sense. It's not like the car's been dumped in such a way that it's unidentifiable—the plate's still on it, and probably the VIN number. Removing his documents wouldn't hold the police up any.

I inspect the manual, hoping the documents are in the plastic somewhere, or stuck to the outside. I don't see them, but I catch a whiff of a distinctive floral scent, some air freshener or—

"What are you doing?"

At the voice behind me, I jump and drop the keys, and they sing to the ground, alarming as bells.

I whirl to face my attacker. An East Asian man, wearing one of those ridiculous train conductor hats. He holds his hands up in front of his face. I realize for an incredulous moment that *he's* afraid of *me*.

"I've already called the police." His face is streaked with something dark, and there's a nasality to his vowels that you only get if you grew up in the city proper and not hours past the outlying suburbs like me.

Wait—the *police*?

Oh, fuck. I *don't* want to be here when they arrive. "Pardon me," I say, doing my best impression of a fainting Victorian housewife. "I just—I needed some stuff from the car, and I didn't want to bother you."

He looks me up and down. I can see him doing the math, that I'm pretty well dressed for a car thief. I'm lucky that I put on something nice before leaving the house and not a pair of sweats.

"How did you get in here?" Before I can answer, he adds, "What did you leave?"

"My medication. My...uh...my birth control."

A smile slowly spreads across his face. It's a beautiful smile, the kind that just completely changes a person. "Seems like a problem."

"Yes," I say, the edges of my world turning wavy. I close my eyes for a second, force myself back to the present.

"You dropped your keys."

"Right." I keep my eyes trained on him as I squat. Perhaps sensing my reluctance, he takes a step back. I fish around until I finally feel metal under my fingers. I'm sticking them in my pocket when he holds his hand out. "We didn't get any work done—she said you were going to drop off the deposit, but we never got it."

"I'm sorry," I say, which is ridiculous—but then his words catch up with me. "Who said that?"

He shrugs. "The other girl. The one who dropped it off."

A lump forms in my throat. *Yocelyn.* That explains what she was doing in Kurt's drawer. "What time was that, do you remember?"

He nods. "First thing Saturday morning. In fact, I was about to have your car towed—we don't usually hold them this long. Don't like people to get into the habit of storing them on the lot, and we don't really have the space."

"Can you describe her?"

He purses his lips, clearly thinking it an odd question.

"Sorry," I say. "My sister was supposed to do it, but she's so lazy. I just want to know if she let somebody else drive my car when she wasn't supposed to."

When did I become such an excellent liar?

He reaches behind his ear. A cigarette materializes in his hands, which makes me think of Sunder. "She wasn't your sister, unless your sister's a white girl with short hair. The way she's got it bleached and styled, it reminded me of a boy-band singer from, like, 2005—or like, K-pop, ya know?"

He gives me a conspiratorial wink, acknowledging our Asian connection, perhaps, but I can barely breathe. There's only one person I know who matches that description—both in the hair and that half-shiny, half-sticky impression of not-quite-glamour. *That sounds... like it could be Leoni?*

Which doesn't make sense. It should be Yocelyn. And there's no way Leoni was here, because she was out of town, because she's always out of town—

He cups his hand around his cigarette and lights it. "But, yeah, we're going to need that deposit."

"Sure." My mind feels like a computer mining crypto, just computation after computation: I found the keys in Kurt's desk. Yocelyn likely put them there. But the mechanic's describing Leoni, which would mean Leoni drove the car here on Saturday morning. It seems impossible—but then again, she was there in the apartment when I got home from the bridge on Friday night. So, not so impossible. Just crazy. And she'd been crying, and I'd been so sure it was because of her sister—

A sister I've heard of but never seen. A sister I don't even have proof is real.

The air goes out of me. "Just...let me run home and grab the money."

"You know, it's cold out here, and I've had a long day." He squints at me. I've seen this expression often enough—particularly lately—to know he's doubting my sanity. He squints even more as he takes another drag. "So tell you what—how about you give me the keys, along with a good phone number, and—"

"No!" I wince. "I, *uh*, can't give you the key."

His brow furrows. "Why not?"

I'm not as accomplished of a liar as I thought, because I can't think of a good reason. "I mean...I *can* give you the key, I just have to get it off the key ring."

He blinks. "You...can't get it off the ring?"

I can follow his struggle to process what I just said. He spends most of his day solving complicated mechanical and electrical issues, in a city where there are few enough people of Asian descent that every single one of us feels like an ambassador, where we have to work harder and be smarter and more literate and just plain *better* so that our white peers don't attribute our personal failures to our race—and now he's confronted with a woman who looks like she could be related to him, and she *doesn't know how to get a key off a key ring.*

It takes him a full ten seconds before he manages to make words. "Um, can I see them?"

I hand him the keys. It makes me nervous, giving away my best link to Kurt, to his past.

He pulls off the key and hands me back the ring. Somehow, he manages to keep his expression calm, as if this is a perfectly normal thing he has just done, and not evidence of my complete lack of intelligence.

"Thank you." I can barely make the words.

"You're welcome." He clears his throat. "The deposit for the bodywork will be four hundred."

"Right," I say, turning anxious again. If he did contact the police, they'll be here any minute. "Let me go get that."

"Sure. But bring it back tomorrow, when we're open. Follow me, I'll let you out of the gate."

He, at least, seems to have forgotten about the police—or maybe I got lucky, and he didn't call them in the first place.

He guides me out. My car door is still open. I'm sliding into the passenger side when I hear him call out.

"Oh, and miss?"

I freeze. It's hard to breathe again.

"Is that your Buick?"

I clear my throat. "No. Just borrowing it."

"All right. Well, let the owner know that noise is a bad one. If they don't get it fixed soon, they'd better sign up for Triple-A—like, yesterday—and baby the gas while you're driving it, or you'll flood it."

He walks away before I can answer.

I pull away. As soon as I ascertain there aren't any police following me, I call Leoni.

Three ascending tones, and then: "This number is out of service."

It doesn't make sense. I try again. And again. And again.

"This number is out of service."

There's an odd, hot feeling in my chest, as if my internal machinery has jammed, but it's not until I'm a few blocks from the apartment that it breaks into something I can understand. By the time I make it into a parking space, my eyes are filling with tears.

It was Leoni. Tea-Closet Leoni. Clean-the-apartment Leoni. Talk-me-off-a-ledge-on-the-phone Leoni. Somehow, she was involved with Kurt's jump, his car's disappearance.

No wonder she kept telling me to stay away from him.

I dial again, listening to the automated message, crying too hard to breathe.

⬥⬥⬥

I drag myself up to the apartment. I don't try to block out the mushroom forest. I text Leoni hundreds of times, despite her disconnected number.

I found the car. Now I know it was real—the accident, the jump—and I still don't know anything new.

Except for the license plate. It floats in the back of my mind, tugging just hard enough to make me stop blubbering. I pull out my phone to check the plate number: V01N1CH. I know, *know* I've seen this somewhere before.

After a moment, I copy the entire word and paste it into Google. Nothing relevant comes up.

I close my eyes and take a deep breath. I can feel it there, like a crooked picture frame, so close that if I just reached out, I could knock it off the wall.

I try changing the numbers to letters: *Voinich.*

Did you mean, "Voynich"?

I don't fucking know if I did or didn't, so I click on the word, and the search results repopulate. I pick the first link, Wikipedia.

The Voynich manuscript is a document named after its discoverer, Wilfrid Voynich, who purchased the codex in 1912. The text is hand-scribed in a writing system that as of yet has not been translated—and may in fact be meaningless, as it has been studied by numerous professional codebreakers without clear results.

The vellum of its manufacture has been dated to the early 1400s, although that does not necessarily indicate that the text itself is that old. The total number of original pages is unknown. Approximately 240 remain.

The majority of the pages are illustrated, with diagrams that may reflect flowers or other natural phenomena.

There's a picture on the side. It says "floral illustration," but to me, they look more like stars than petals.

Like endekagram stellations.

I think about all the times I saw Kurt in the break room, reading books about Masons and medieval history and ancient magic and military strategy. No wonder Sunder implied he thought he was smarter than everybody else; his license plate's literally a reference to undecipherable codes, to a book full of stellations—

The skin on the back of my neck crawls. I'm still missing something. I close my eyes and try to picture the car again, walk myself through the night. The license plate, the spare tire in the trunk, the number scrawled in black on the cardboard under the tire:

306.

I didn't think about it, at the time—but when I first moved into the building, before we got a special bin of lockers last year to hold packages in the mail room, they used to be held for us in the office. And if I'm remembering correctly, our apartment number was scrawled on the side by management to make them easy to locate on their holding shelves.

306. And right now, I'm in apartment 406.

That can't be right.

The world goes wavery around the edges. I let it happen, because I don't have enough willpower to fight back and try to think, to figure out if this makes sense.

306.

406.

Three plus zero plus six makes nine.

Four plus zero plus six makes ten.

306, 406. Nine, ten.

A nine-pointed figure is called an enneagram. Ten-pointed, decagram.

And next comes the hendecagram, or endekagram. An eleven-pointed polygon, part of the sigil that keeps me safe.

Secrets and codes.

The world around me morphs and distorts, no clear shape or color or form—then returns. Distorts and returns. Not so different from a beating heart.

It feels like I'm in a dream. Like I'm in the kitchen-door world. Like I'm hurtling away from Pleasance Village again, my breath wispy inside the warming car, hunched over the steering wheel, glued to that little patch of clear window, blind to everything else.

I stare down at Kurt's key and rub the SC4 stamp on the back, same as mine, and then exit my apartment to descend the stairs.

When I get to 306, it occurs to me that I should knock on the door, but I don't. Don't want to break the spell.

His key glides into the lock, smooth as if it was made for it—because it was. That's the whole point, isn't it?

I turn it, and the door opens.

THIRD
STELLATION

Fig 3. The Great Hendecagram, created by taking the third stellation of a hendecagon. Like the medial hendecagram, a prism
over the Great Hendecagram can be used to approximate the
shape of a DNA molecule. It can be described by the notation
{11/4}.

−The Magical World of Geometry

It was dark and quiet in the Heart.

After she cast the spell the Wizard had given her, Mi-Hee sat for many hours, counting her fingers, watching the darkness turn into shapes and colors and back again, and all the time, she tried to muster up the strength to uncover one of the mirrors, to bring the spyglass to her eye and bring the Mirror-Man into this world.

And though she was afraid, so afraid, she thought back on all the things she'd conquered to get to this point—the sleeping trees, the vicious unicorns, the dense thicket of roses that grew teeth instead of thorns. Mi-Hee was tired, and cold, and lonely.

The door the Mirror-Man could open was the only way home.

She gripped the cloth.

She pulled.

CHAPTER 13

When Worlds Collide

Once upon a time, there was a girl with a vivid imagination, one who was not entirely sane. She was afraid of many things that weren't real, but she didn't tell anyone. They would've sent her far, far away, and she wasn't ready to go.

Most of all, though, she was afraid of the mirror in her bathroom, the man she saw out of the corner of her eye when she looked at it the wrong way. She liked to think it was because of a silly book she'd read as a child, but we all know that's a lie.

When the door swings open, my eyes struggle to understand the room. It is achingly, shockingly empty, as if the room is the tunnel in the middle of the mountain, as if the room is the air between the bridge and the water—

As if the room is me.

I can't stop thinking about the Mirror-Man. About the danger of looking at something in the wrong way and imbuing it with too much power, and it makes me afraid to turn on the light. Instead, I step in and shut the door behind me, wait as my vision swims. It's hard to breathe, but the dark softly falls away like snow, leaving the details to materialize.

It's a room of Nots, no, of *things* that are not. There is no television, no sofa, no kitchen table—but hunched in the very corner is a small writing desk, hiding in the shadows like a wounded animal.

I steel myself. I approach as softly as I can, toes touching down on the carpet so gently I wonder if the fibers underneath are really bending— or if they hold their shape and suspend me, cloudlike, above the floor. The room opens to me: the bathroom door, the door to the bedroom— both closed, but I know them intimately, the number of steps to each, can mark the distance in elevens or even-odds or prime numbers with my eyes closed because my apartment, of course, is the same.

Same, were it not for the shut doors. I never shut doors, not unless Leoni is home. Never want to run the risk that something is happening in another room I can't see—like right now, in the bathroom. The Mirror-Man could be there, pulling himself out of the glass. I can't let that happen—I know, I *know* it's crazy, that I'm spiraling into new, confusing places. Everything is colliding together, and I can't keep straight which rituals belong where.

It doesn't matter, because the Mirror-Man is dangerous.

My heart hammers, hammers, hammers. I change directions and tiptoe over to the bathroom. Silently, so the Mirror-Man can't know—except that when I reach for the knob, I see through the door to something different: Kurt, his skin bloated and white from the water, seaweed in his hair. His teeth gnashing and fingers clenching as he waits for me to open it.

I turn the knob, and it's like inviting in my own death.

I push the door open.

It's empty.

I'm so relieved, I could collapse. It's just a room, a normal place, no magic, no fear. There is nobody in the mirror but me—

And then I see the writing above me, reflected backward by the mirror, swallowed by the shadows that descend from the ceiling. I turn away before I can read it, before seeing it fully can make it real— but the movement just brings another strange thing into view: a long, dark vine climbing up the white wall, so straight it feels rigid to my eyes.

My blood turns cold. I close my eyes to protect myself from the mirror and turn to flip the light switch. Only then do I allow myself to look.

A long, black wire stretches up from the floor, covered in glinting packing tape. I follow its ascent, right up through the ceiling, and my head swims.

I can't look at that, not yet, so I trace its other end—because that's where the answer is, isn't it? Not at the top of the mountain, but at the bottom, deep in the *Heart*?

The wire dips behind the toilet. It's only now, with the light pinning this world down to one place, to *this* place, that I see that the wire actually reemerges on the other side, snaking around behind me.

I hold my breath and turn to the back wall. Before I can locate the other end of the wire, I find the message in two-inch-tall capital red letters, in a square handwriting I recognize from years of peering over Kurt's shoulder:

DEAR KATRINA, THIS IS FOR YOU. I PUNISHED HARRY, AND I'LL GET YOU, TOO.

I can't move. My stomach churns, questions barraging me like hail. Who the *fuck* is Harry? And why would Kurt leave me a message on his own wall—how could he have known that I'd see it, that I'd invade the place he stays, the place he sleeps—

And then I remember the wire. My gaze drops down, as if I am on a roller coaster, slowly rattling my way to the top.

The wire curves around the bottom of the wall, hugging it above the baseboard. It exits three feet below the message through a hole that leads back into the living room.

I don't want to see. I have to see.

I leave the bathroom, counting steps—*one, two, three, four.* I keep walking until I get to *eleven,* and then I stop and turn.

The bathroom light is on. The living room is dark. It's easy to spot the hole, a bright ring of light spilling out around the dark body of the cable, like a solar eclipse in miniature. There's just enough light, now, to trace the cable's path straight to the desk, to a rectangular shape that's dark and slightly raised. A laptop.

The wire *plugs into* the laptop.

It's like the *snap* of the world collapsing on the bridge, all my realms folding into one.

I sprint for the bathroom, my steps thudding across the floor. I grab the tape and tear it off. I'm crying hysterically, *when did I start crying, when did I start crying, I can barely see—*

I grab the edge of the wire and yank hard. There's the briefest pause, a moment of resistance, and then the wire falls straight down, pooling like the coil of a serpent, revealing its head at the end, its gleaming eye, a mouth made of mesh. It's a camera and microphone with a small circle of bathroom-floor vinyl glued to the top, like a tiny fascinator hat.

He was spying on us. On our apartment. All the times I'd frozen up in the bathroom—someone really had been watching me.

I bend over and vomit into the toilet.

When it's safe to stand, I wash my mouth out in the sink. It, like everything else in this room save the wall with the writing, is bare: no cup, no toothbrush or paste, no bottles in the naked shower. Even the toilet paper holder is empty—so if he was living here, he's definitely moved out.

I don't think he was, though. When I close my eyes, I see Mi-Hee's empty-room ghosts: soft, spectral forms that float through the room like dust motes, the occupants of the hut that Mi-Hee took refuge in the first night she crossed the beaches. They like vacant spaces, because they dissipate when disturbed.

I've never seen them in my apartment, even though my apartment is supposed to be the hut. Once again, it never occurred to me to wonder why.

Somehow, it makes this place even more malevolent. If he didn't live here, then it was just a place to spy on us, a place to leave threats on the wall.

I knew it was you. That's what he'd said on the bridge. *You just had to fuck everything up, didn't you?*

Some part of me had secretly hoped there'd been some mistake. He'd been confused, seeing things, drunk—that he hadn't meant *me*, Katrina Kim.

But now I know. He'd expected to find me there that night on the bridge. He'd jumped off—or jumped forward and disappeared—and Leoni had later dropped his car off at the mechanic. But why? And how was Yocelyn involved in all of this?

My stomach churns again. It's possible the message isn't from Kurt at all. Handwriting can be faked.

What if it was Leoni, trying to frame Kurt? Given the message's chilling contents—*I'll get you, too*—it's not entirely impossible that one of them intended to murder me. *But why?*

And now Kurt's missing, I haven't seen Yocelyn since she went home "sick," and Leoni's disappeared into the wind.

I've got to get the fuck out of here.

I'm crossing the living room before I catch the closed bedroom door out of the corner of my eye. It pulls me straight toward it, like winding up a fishing reel.

Inside, there's another wire, though this one isn't plugged in. Which means someone—Kurt, I don't know why, I just *feel* like it's Kurt—must've taken turns moving the laptop or the wires back and forth. He could've been watching me sleep and dress and masturbate—

And go through the box. He's been watching me talk to myself, and draw endekagrams, and look at his postcard, and lay out my things on Leoni's bed.

The ghosts come back. Waver around my head. I feel like I'm going to be sick again, but I go back into the living area and flip on the main room lights, making everything around me dissipate in the harshness of their glare.

The laptop sharpens, details etching themselves in front of me. The top is blank—no apple or other logo, no stickers. A rectangular gadget about the size of a candy bar sits next to it, a small tail trailing away like a mouse's, ending in a USB plug. I pick it up. One side is glass. The other side has a logo with the word PORT-A-SCAN.

There's a pen underneath it, one I recognize. A phone number is embossed on the body, but it's only six digits long.

I have to take a breath. It's one of Leoni's misprint pens. Which means he's been *in* our apartment. Either that or Leoni—

No. I slid one of her pens into Kurt's desk on Friday, when Caressa was standing over me. It might be this one. This pen doesn't mean Leoni had anything to do with this apartment—although it doesn't mean she didn't, either.

I open the laptop and press the power button. Lights wink on like tiny stars as the fan whirs. The boot text scrolls across the display—but then it stops, leaving me with just a blinking white cursor on a black screen. The laptop is waiting for something, but I don't know what.

It doesn't even look like it fully loaded into an operating system—no Windows or Mac logo, nothing.

I can feel my mind getting stuck, wanting to grind away at this until it's solved—*whose laptop is this?*—but this is a bad place, and I've overstayed my welcome. I grab the laptop and charger, the portable scanner. I go to leave, counting my steps as I exit—but for once, I've calculated badly, am not used to the desk, and I reach the door on ten steps instead of eleven.

That doesn't work. Ten's an even number—not a prime, and too easily divisible into halves. It can't protect me from anything. And even though everything in me is screaming to flee, I feel like I can't leave without properly sealing away this room.

I turn around to take the eleventh step, but now I have a conundrum—I can't just take eleven more steps away and eleven back, because that will leave me with 33 total. It would be best, I think, if my steps added up to 121—not a prime number, but 121 is the square of eleven, which is strong, like a seal on top of a seal. A number that potent feels dangerous, as if the powers that be will punish you if you use it too frivolously, but this feels like the right time.

I trace a path back across the living room, then into the bedroom— I can circle it twice in 33 more steps, and then twice around the living room, and—

The door to the closet is cracked open, and there's a small, wooden box on the shelf. It's no wonder I missed it before. I can only see it now from the exact right angle, and only from far enough back in the room.

Leaving my step count in the middle makes my skin feel like it's going to peel off, but it's a *box*. A wooden box, just like mine, in this horribly empty apartment.

I take it out of the closet. It's plain, stained wood—not inlaid with blue—and, unlike mine, has a small metal lock in the front. But Kurt has a box. Another realization that makes the world swim.

I'm afraid to open it. I can't, not here, in this unsafe place. I take the box and the scanner and the laptop back up to my apartment, before realizing that the bedroom, the bathroom, maybe even the living room—none of it's safe, not really. Not when there are little holes in the floor, holes that once held cameras. I can't do anything without covering them up—but I need to open Kurt's box.

Where is safe? Where is safe?

And then I remember hiding in the closet, Leoni bringing me tea. It's a terrible memory, now, one that tastes like possible betrayal—but I take everything into the small closet. I trace my endekagram sigil on the door to ward everything out.

Only then do I open the laptop to give me some light. The box is still locked, but I know what to do. I slide in the small copper key from Kurt's key chain—the one that didn't fit into any of the mailboxes earlier—and it turns like butter.

I hold my breath and open the box.

I should have known.

The box is full of postcards: at least twenty in a dazzling range of art styles, everything from watercolor to blocky comics to collage. Some have words, but others are just images. I lay them out along the closet carpet, spacing them like cookies in a pan, trying to get as many as I can in the thin wash of the laptop's glow.

There is only one card I recognize—the one with the thieving hand. Everything else is new. I go from card to card, trying to hold each one in my mind, but it's like trying to remember a phone number: too much information to retain. These postcards are like an archaeological dig—a lifetime's work of cataloging, dissecting, note-taking, hypothesizing—and I don't have that kind of time.

I try another tack. I close my eyes and hover my hand over the cards like a Ouija planchette, waiting for a vibration, a twitch, a warmth—

Light flashes in my mind, a constellation of eleven-pointed stars in the dark. I open my eyes and look down.

The card under my hand makes my skin crawl. Most of the surface is covered by an ink drawing of a girl lying on her back. It's all black and white, save a seamlike wiggly blue line down her side: water. The disconcerting part, though, is the head: Kurt's cut—no, *torn*—the face off a full-color photo of a girl, pasted it on the drawing's head, and drawn dark *X*s over both of the eyes.

Beneath her, among little squiggles of seaweed and oddly shaped fish with teeth, is a short, handwritten poem all in caps:

LOVE IS PATIENT
LOVE IS KIND
MY LOVE IS THE SEA
IF YOU WON'T BE MINE

Could this be Kurt's poetry? It's stilted, almost churlish, and I don't know what it means.

I search through the rows, looking for a pattern, other similar cards with photo-faces. I find three more. The first is a man in black and white, the paper textured like newsprint. The drawing around the figure is so finely detailed, I have to hold it close to the laptop screen to make it out—but when I do, I feel sick.

It's a man, hanging from a noose. Kurt's written a word on the length of rope, block letters like a woodcut:

PROSPER

The second card is a photo from a color printer. I can even see little streaks in the ink wash, tiny imperfections where one line has bled into the next. This photo's an entire head and torso, a smiling man wearing what appears to be a suit, although Kurt has drawn a big tear in black ink on his cheek. Behind him is a picture cut out from a magazine, a crushed-up car with a deployed airbag and a crash dummy.

I only find one more photo card, but it's so terrible I have to cover my eyes for a moment, to take slow breaths and remind myself that I'm in my closet, that my protective sigil is over the door. That whatever magic the card might've held disappeared the moment Kurt jumped off the bridge.

The photo-face is scrambled, as if someone cut it into tiny squares and moved them around at random, like one of those dollar-store plastic puzzles with the sliding pieces. I can't even tell if it's meant to be a woman or a man, but Kurt's pasted the face on a dog's body. There's a little saddle on the dog's back, and the words around the border read:

LAP IT UP, BABY. LAP IT UP. LAP IT UP, BABY, LAP IT
UP. LAP—

I can't look at it anymore. I can feel lines of disdain and hate swimming off it, revulsion and rejection.

And I don't know what any of it means. I count the cards. There are twenty-one of them, which doesn't feel significant—until I remember that I have two more cards: his postcard professing to his fantasy world and his music-staff suicide note, which makes twenty-three.

Twenty-three is a prime number: a number of power, a number of protection. My vision swims again.

I need to stop. At least for now, I need to stop.

I scoop the cards up and put them in the box. I can barely see, so I feel my way—the hard line of the box's edges, the rough wood of the inside—but when my fingers touch the bottom, it feels off. Open.

Aching.

I take the cards out and stare at the inside of the box. Completely plain, though in the dim light, I could be missing some detail. I rotate it around in the laptop's glare, comparing the outside and the inside. The box seems awfully shallow.

This is important enough that it overrides my need to hide. I open the door and take the box into the kitchen, into better light, crushing mushrooms and disturbing dragonflies in my wake. I set the box on the stove beneath the oven light and flip that on, too, the click loud against the songs of the trees.

I see the crack as clear as day, the groove in the bottom of the box along one edge. For a moment, it reminds me of the wire, traveling along the wall baseboard, and I freeze—but then I open the drawer next to me and drag out a bread knife. It's the wrong size, all wrong, but I shove it into the groove and wiggle it back and forth.

I almost drop it when the bottom of the box flies open, a spring-loaded lid on hidden hinges. There's a second, smaller compartment here, a well-padded one, which accounts for the lack of rattling. It holds three objects.

The first is a USB stick, with one word, "tails," scrawled on the side in marker. Underneath is a white card with a small watermark on the back—another postcard? No, it looks like photo paper.

The third object is round and white, nestled against the side of the box, like a poker chip standing on its edge.

My stomach crawls as I pull it out. It's a round, wooden key chain. It's scraped and battered, and the year is different, sixth instead of twelfth, but the words are familiar. PLEASANCE SIXTH ANNUAL BAND FESTIVAL, FIRST PLACE.

It looks just like the one my father gave me, years ago.

My hands are shaking, my vision swimming so badly I struggle to extract the card from underneath and flip it over. The face is familiar, but younger—a photo of a teenaged Kurt, standing in front of a building I'd know anywhere.

The Pleasance Sunbeam Library.

The world goes dark, and the floor rises up to meet me.

CHAPTER 14

Finders Keepers

I've never fainted before.

The thought girds me as I blink awake. Even after a lifetime in this mind, in this body, I'm able to surprise myself.

I wasn't out long, but my brain's done some essential reorganizing: resetting breakers, replacing wires. Everything has to be Kurt's: Kurt's cards, Kurt's laptop, Kurt's apartment beneath me with its awful mirror message—but I'm sure Leoni is somehow enmeshed in all of this, too. Did she know about the surveillance and not tell me?

Another surprise. I never understood Leoni in my kitchen-door world at all. That shakes me right down to my bones.

I call her number again, listen to the disconnected message. I call it ten more times.

I send her an email. *Please,* I type. *I need to talk to you. It's urgent.* I almost, but do not, count the letters.

I get a reply immediately, which throws my pulse into overdrive, but it's just a mailer-daemon auto-reply: this email address no longer exists.

I go back to my clues. I don't understand how the key chain or the photo fit in; although I don't know the name of the sixth band festival winner, I'm sure it's not Kurt *or* Leoni—or Yocelyn, for that matter. When I won, they took a picture of me accepting my trophy and my key chain and put it into a huge display case in the band hall. I walked by that display case every day for years. Something tells me I would've remembered their faces.

At least, I hope that's true.

At some point, the laptop battery dies, so I move it onto the table and plug it in. Without light, I'm forced out of the closet.

I find the holes in the bathroom and bedroom and cover them both with stacks of heavy books, before filling two wineglasses with paperclips and precariously balancing one on the top edge of each stack. If someone pushes anything up through the holes, I should hear it, as long as I'm home—though it won't stop someone from putting in a *new* hole.

I lay the cards out on the floor, trying to divine their secrets.

The next time I surface from my meditations, it's dawn. I call in sick to work, both to Spectacular Staffing and to Advancex, grateful beyond measure when nobody picks up. I don't want to lie. I'm not even sure I can. It was hard to make my mouth simulate human speech for long enough to leave the messages, and that was a one-way conversation.

I go back to staring at the cards, shuffling their arrangement, begging them to reveal their occult meanings. I wonder if this is how it felt to discover the Voynich manuscript—which gives me a chill. The Voynich has never been deciphered, never solved. Worse, according to the Wikipedia page, many claim it's a hoax. And these horrible, chaotic cards feel so out of character from the Kurt I know, the man I've seen every day with his perfectly balanced meals of brown rice and stir-fried greens and grilled chicken and arugula salads, the man who dropped a 14 Dogs tape in the elevator—

Except. *Except.* If he'd been watching me, spying on my apartment with microphones and cameras shoved through holes in the floor, then all his normal routines at work, the dropped tape, the card in his desk—they could've just been a show for me. It wouldn't have been hard. I'd been so desperate, so eager to connect with him.

A hoax within a hoax within a hoax.

In between cycles of trying to reassemble the cards, I go back to the laptop. I turn it on a thousand times, only to get a blank screen. I inspect the USB stick with the word "tails" on it, but there's nothing special about it. When I plug it into my own computer, there are files, but none of them will open for me.

I type "tails" into Google and get a bunch of hits about Sonic the Hedgehog.

And then something shimmers in the back of my mind, so ethereal I have to take my time approaching it, come at it sideways, like the bathroom mirror.

I try another search: *tails + USB.*

The first result is from tails.boum.org, and right at the top of the screen is a picture of a computer and a USB drive.

Bees buzz in my ears. I blink and try to focus on the text.

Tails is a portable operating system that protects against surveillance and censorship.

Oh. *Oh.* That explains why there's nothing on the computer. Because there's *nothing on the computer.* It's all here, on the USB.

I grab a pen from inside Leoni's dresser and some paper. I click through the website, scrawling down notes as I go.

I learn that the Tails operating system doesn't leave traces on your computer. It never even touches your hard drive—instead, it loads directly from the USB stick. Using Tails means there is no record of websites you visited, files used or deleted, passwords you entered, or networks you connected to.

That gives me pause. If I'm understanding this correctly, it means that even if I do get the computer working, there won't be anything to find.

I follow the steps to boot from the USB. After a few odd moments of random text scrolling across the screen like the Matrix, I am suddenly dropped into a gray and white welcome screen that says, *Welcome to Tails!* It asks me to select my default keyboard and some other settings. At the bottom is a menu option that says, *Encrypted Persistent Storage.*

There's a blank for a password. I assemble everything I *think* I know about Kurt—but there's one word that leaps out.

Voynich.

I type it in. A moment later, the screen changes to a blue desktop. There are only four icons, neatly aligned on the left side of the screen—*Home, Report an Error, Tails Documentation,* and *Trash*—but there's a menu bar at the top that says *Applications,* so I click that.

I try all the applications, one by one. There's a browser called *Tor,* which has an empty history, an empty cache, and no saved favorites. There's an email client called *Thunderbird,* but there are no emails in it, and no accounts set up. Nothing else looks interesting.

I try the *Places* menu instead, and immediately hit pay dirt, because there's a menu item labeled *Persistent*: the same word that was used for the password-protected storage. I click on it. A folder opens with a single icon, just a small box around a question mark. Underneath the icon is the file name: *BUFFALO BILL'S OREGANO-STEGANO.* It sounds like a well-seasoned cowboy-dinosaur.

When I run it, a small black box launches into the center of my

screen, a white cursor blinking at the bottom left. I wait for the program to do something, but it seems to require some kind of input.

HELP, I type. The word disappears. The blinking cursor comes
back.

MENU.

START.

HOME.

VOYNICH.

I try a million words, but nothing works.

I mess around with the computer some more and find nothing. On
a hunch, I flip it over. There's no manufacturer sticker or serial number, which is strange. It's like someone built it from scratch.

I've known guys who built their own desktops—but laptops? I've never
heard of that before. Unless Kurt bought an old laptop and scrubbed it?

When it becomes clear I'm not going to get anything else out of the
computer, I go back to the postcards.

As the morning stretches into the afternoon, my world turns dreamy.
I keep closing my eyes and micro-sleeping, only to awaken when I tilt
forward on the couch. Once, I fall all the way to the floor, smacking
into it with a dull *thud* before jolting awake.

This is dangerous, going on like this. Nothing to stop me from
being snuck up on, and if I have to drive somewhere, I'll likely die. I
need some rest—but I don't want to be out too long or too deep. I don't
want to miss the *grind-grind-grind* of a manual hand drill slowly boring its way through my floor.

I set an alarm for forty minutes and crawl into my closet. I try to
draw the sigils, but as soon as I close the door behind me, the darkness
envelops me like a second skin. I don't make it past the medial hendecagram before I'm asleep.

I wake up. I study the cards. I fall asleep.

I wake up. I study the cards. I fall asleep.

I don't know how many times.

At some point, it occurs to me that I should call the police. I have evidence that somebody has been spying on my apartment. There's even a threat against me scrawled on the wall downstairs.

I get as far as searching for the local police station's number before I realize it's a bad idea. The mechanic could've told them about an Asian woman who broke into their lot. If the car was towed, someone could've pulled the registration and tried to contact Kurt—and found a missing person's report, or some mention of a girl who drove to the police station, only barely passing the Breathalyzer.

If the police come for me, they'll lock me away. I'm too messed up right now to pretend to be sane. At the very least, they'll take the laptop, the keys, the cards—and I can't give those up any more than I could've given up Kurt's first postcard, his earth-shattering reference to a fantasy world.

I set an alarm. Pass out. Set an alarm. Pass out. After a while, it feels like I'm playing chess with myself.

I'm in the middle of a dream about *my* box, with its blue turquoise inlay—only now, the box is the size of the entire room. The lid's open, and as soon as I see that, I realize my parents and I are inside, that the box is filled with thin, blue ink-squiggles of water.

My parents are wearing Hawaiian shirts, but the flowers are the long-stemmed purple doraji from my mother's garden. My father's nose is blotched with sunscreen. "Come on in," they call, though I'm right next to them. "The water's fine!"

My father stands up tall and waves a camera at my mom. She smiles and strikes a pose, a saucy turn in her waist like a beauty queen. Her hair is wrapped up tight to her head, like one of those old-fashioned movie stars. In the background, I hear the bouncy strains of teuroteu music, though the tune is sad. A song about the sound of a whistle, though I can't remember the name.

"Say gimchi!" He gives her a thumbs-up. There's a flash of the camera—

And then the alarm screams in my ear. I've set it to maximum volume, taken to falling asleep with it directly under my face. At this rate, I'll go deaf.

Spots swim in front of my eyes. It isn't enough, napping like this. I can feel each foray recharge me less and less, like I'm an old battery. When I open the closet door, the light is blinding—

Say gimchi!

Flash.

The sun through the trees.

Flash, flash, flash.

I suddenly know what I've been missing.

I crawl up onto my hands and knees, flip through the postcards again. I find the ones with the photographs and pull them out of the stack. I grab the portable scanner, but instead of plugging it into Kurt's laptop, I plug it into mine.

These faces had to have come from somewhere. At least one of them looks like it might've been printed directly off the internet. If I scan the cards and crop in close to the faces, I can drop them in a reverse-image search.

The first photograph I try, the one of the drowning girl, doesn't get me anything. The second, the scrambled face—this one doesn't, either, although I make a note to unscramble it. It shouldn't be too hard.

But the third one I try, the hanged man that says *PROSPER*, *this* one pulls up a plethora of matches right away—and almost all of them are news articles. I scan the headlines and the addresses, trying to find the easiest entry point to this vast web of information.

It takes me about twenty minutes to piece it all together. The man's name is Reginald Peters Sr., and he is—*was*—the CFO of a local financial management firm called Briar Stone Ventures, a name that sends bells ringing through my head. Briar Stone was in the middle of a giant scandal a while ago. Someone embezzled millions from their client accounts. The court trials are ongoing, and they're *still* sorting out the blame—but nobody knows where the money has gone.

And this man, Reginald Peters? Nobody knows where he is, either. He went missing a few days before the scandal hit the papers.

Is it possible that Kurt was in some way tied up with what happened? But if he'd taken the money, why was he working a shitty job at Advancex?

Unless—was he one of the people who'd been stolen from?

I spend the next half hour searching for pictures of people affiliated with Briar Stone, but there's nobody who looks like Kurt or Leoni. And there's nobody attached to the company or the scandal I can find who is named Kurt Smith, Curtis Smith, or any variation I can think of.

I bite my lip and try the last photograph, the man in the tuxedo, but I don't get anything that looks relevant.

My vision swims. At first, I think it's the kitchen-door world, but I close my eyes, hard, and a dull ache spreads through my head. I'm too exhausted for this.

I resolve to try one last thing before napping again. I blow the scrambled face up 200 percent. It's grainy, but not bad. I apply a sharpening filter and print it.

I cut out the pieces and lay them on the dresser. I start with the eyes and the nose, because they're the easiest—but as soon as I have those assembled, a chill goes down my spine. I already know what I'm going to find next, but I do it anyways—pluck out the lips, move them into place.

I keep working until there can be no mistake. A young Latina woman, with long, curly hair and warm brown eyes.

It's Yocelyn. Kurt cut out a picture of Yocelyn, scrambled her face, and stuck it on a dog's body. Even though I don't know what this means, I start crying again.

CHAPTER 15

Glass Ceilings

I wake up to my phone ringing.

My butt's in Leoni's chair, my face still on her dresser. I sit up, tiny pieces of Yocelyn's image fluttering down like butterflies. My heart pounds Leoni's name—but when I check the caller ID, it's Navya.

I consider not answering, but I do, because Navya has never deserved the way I've treated her. "Hello?"

She's crying, taking big, heaving breaths. "I *can't*...believe... you'd *lie* to me!"

For a moment, I want to laugh—my whole *life* is a lie—but it's Navya, and she's in pain. "What do you—" And then it hits me. "Is this because of the punch-in?"

She laughs, the way I almost did: cold and near-nonsensical. "*Yes,* it's because of the punch-in. You didn't *mention* you were going to leave the campus. You didn't *mention* that you'd be dumb enough to *swipe back into the parking structure with your badge.* They're *time-stamped.* They know you punched in almost fifteen minutes before you parked the car or rode up in the elevator."

She starts crying again, but quietly. Listening to her try to be strong feels like both a tragedy and a rebuke. "They fired me. I have four sons. The eldest is about to go away to college. *I cannot afford to lose my job right now.* I cannot afford to lose my insurance."

"I'm so sorry." I say it over and over, as if repeating it will undo this harm. As if a ritual has ever done me any good. "I'm so, so sorry—"

She hangs up. I pull the phone away from my ear and look at the screen.

It's eight thirty in the morning. I must've passed out without setting the alarm. And although this makes my stomach tighten, I feel better for having slept. Worse for ruining Navya's life.

But maybe I *haven't* ruined it. I check the date on the phone—it's Friday, the one-week anniversary of Kurt's jump. Everyone's in the office right now. Maybe there's something I can do, like lie. I can tell Caressa and management that Navya had nothing to do with what I did—no, that I was threatening her. I'll still get fired, but they *probably* won't send me to jail.

But I don't feel safe leaving Kurt's things here. I dig around in my closet until I find my JanSport backpack from college. I shake off the dust and the fluff before shoving in the laptop, the charger, the USB stick, and the box of postcards, and then I run down to my car. I don't draw the sigil, and I don't count my steps, no matter how much luck I need, no matter the consequences. Navya doesn't have the time.

I've forgotten my badge, so I find the closest meter I can and run away without paying. Yuto intercepts me as soon as I come in the door. From the way his lip curls as he looks me up and down, he's disgusted.

I don't blame him. I look like hell. "Sorry, Yuto, but I need to go up—"

"They're waiting for you." He talks over me so loudly, people turn to stop and stare. "On *twenty.*"

Holy. Shit. I've never heard of anybody going up to the twentieth floor who isn't upper management. It's...otherworldly. "But my
badge—"

He holds up his hand and rolls his eyes. "You have to take the
executive elevator up. I'll call it down. Go stand over there." He points
toward a corner away from the elevator bank, a corner I've never even
peeked around.

He waves me through the turnstile. I've never worn tennis shoes
in this building, and each step I take feels too grippy, like the floor is
clinging to me, and without the echo of my steps—

I take a deep, hard breath through my nose. I'm doing this for
Navya. I can't be myself right now. I need to lock it in.

The scene around the corner is disappointing. It looks the same as
the rest of the lobby, though the single elevator door is perhaps a *bit*
shinier, the floor less worn.

I get into the elevator. There are no buttons. This is so strange
that when the door shuts in front of me, I briefly picture plummeting
down, as if the elevator were one of those trapdoors in comedies about
Arthurian kings. *You've displeased me*, someone would say, and then
I'd be swimming in a pit full of sharks.

As I lurch upward, I count my breaths. Draw endekagrams on
my sweatpants. *Lock it in. Lock it in.* I fight the urge to repeat myself
eleven times.

When the doors open, a blinding light pours in, and I almost forget to exit.

Directly in front of me, a woman types on a computer at a huge,
ornate desk made of finely polished wood. It's covered in little knot-
holes that have been sanded smooth and stained before being smoth-
ered with a thick layer of clear epoxy. Shining from the midst of the
honey-colored wood, the effect is like an entire desk of tiny, dark eyes.

Despite the elevator's *ding* announcing my arrival, she doesn't notice me as I take her in. Her hair is perfect, her nails immaculate. I can tell her outfit is expensive—four hundred dollars? five?—although it also has little faded spots of wear and tear. She either really loves clothes she can't afford, or they're a job requirement.

I glance to either side. Twenty's footprint is smaller than eleven's, and everything is floor-to-ceiling windows, though I'm not close enough to see anything except sky. To my right is a small hallway with two doors. To my left is a single, open door, and from the pretty bronze sink inside, framed by an artful arrangement of flowers, it's some kind of executive bathroom.

I can hear each key the woman presses, every click of her mouse. It's quiet up here, no coworkers' murmurs or factory groans.

After another minute, I approach her desk. I glimpse just enough of her screen to tell she's looking at a wedding album. Judging by the dresses, though, each picture has a different bride.

I clear my throat.

"Oh!" she says, straightening as if startled. "I'm so—"

And then she takes me in, my sweats and mussy hair and what I'm assuming are under-eye bags deeper than the Mariana Trench. "Can I...help you?" It actually sounds like a question.

"Sorry," I say. "My name is Katrina Kim? Yuto said they wanted me up here?"

She squints at me, as dubious as Yuto, but with better manners.

Her eyes widen. She quickly composes herself. "Right, yes. I'll let them know you're here." She leans over and taps a button on her desk. "Katrina Kim," she says, sotto voce. She looks nervous.

My stomach turns. This seems like...a *lot* of pomp for forging a time stamp. And the way this woman reacted to figuring out who I was—

The bottom falls out from under me. Do they know about Kurt and the bridge?

I back up slowly, getting ready to run, searching for the emergency stairs.

One of the doors to my right swings open, revealing a conference room. Caressa steps out. Her eyes widen when she sees me, but she recovers even faster than the secretary did, sliding sideways and gesturing at the door. "Come in."

I can't move my feet at first, but then I remember Navya, red French hen Navya and her insurance and her sons, and I cross the small hallway into the room.

My eyes feel heavy as I enter, so I stare down at the carpet pile: *fancy* office carpet, but office carpet all the same. I inhale the vague smells of air freshener and citrus, no trace of the fart-and-hot-lunch scent of eleven.

Eventually though, I have to look up. The room's uninhabited. There's a massive conference table in the center with one of those weird triangle phones. Surrounding that are giant chrome and black leather chairs, and there's a pull-down projector screen in the back. Two of the walls are massive windows—and from this height and this angle, I glimpse a distant view of the river.

Caressa gestures at the table with a flat hand, palm-up. "Why don't you take a seat?"

I don't like sitting on a dead animal's skin, but this is for Navya, so I approach the table, and the city opens up below me. It's a dizzying view—like being on the bridge, but day instead of night, and without the safety of the guardrail.

I know my fear doesn't make sense. I watched Kurt go right over that rail, and this window would be much harder to breach. But looking down through the glass, to the water—water that would be so hard on impact, it'd be the same as concrete—it makes my knees shake.

Someone behind me clears their throat. "Beautiful, isn't it? I'll never get over this view."

A short Black woman in a navy pantsuit has let herself into the room. Her grooming reflects both expensive product and extensive practice, and although she's a bit older than I normally go for, something about the contrast between her meticulous appearance and the almost casual way she stands, as if she's perfectly comfortable in her environment—it's hellaciously sexy.

Or would be, if this weren't a soon-to-be inquisition.

"Yes," I say, although I've already forgotten her question.

"My name is Lauren."

"Katrina," I say, but of course, she already knows that. "Nice to meet you."

"Sure." Lauren indicates one of the seats in the corner. I'm not surprised to see that she has an immaculate French manicure, although the gold band on her pinkie finger is unexpected. I wonder what the story is: where she got it, why she wears it on that finger and not another.

I realize I'm still standing. I plop down into the leather chair and try not to think about the cow it came from. I'm directly across from her, though there's a good ten feet between us. I'm not exactly sure how we're supposed to conduct a meeting like this.

Then the door opens behind us, and two more people come in—a white man I recognize only vaguely, and a white woman with frizzy hair and an enormous, chunky necklace that reminds me of teeth. She closes the door behind her, but it's only when they get the nod from Lauren that they all sit down—first the man, then the white woman, and finally my boss, each taking seats next to Lauren on the other side of the table. I feel like a student about to defend my dissertation.

My stomach contents come to a boil. I have no idea what they want. Save Caressa, I've never met any of these people before: the lofty occupants of twenty never descend to eleven.

"Right," says Lauren. "Cynthia, why don't you go first?"

The white woman nods, and then she folds her hands in her lap and gives me a smile that I instantly hate: it appears effortless, is technically perfect, and comes across as utterly fake-looking. "I want to first make sure that we're all on the same page, and that you understand nobody is here to attack you or harass you."

She pauses, clearly expecting a response, so I nod.

"We're so glad you were able to make it in today—we were worried you might still be sick. My name is Cynthia, and I'm the director of Human Resources. The man to my left is Brian Kane from Legal. You know Caressa, and you've already met Lauren, who is our CEO."

I nod again. It's like I don't have a tongue anymore.

"Before we go any further, I want to make sure you understand that you're not technically an Advancex employee."

"Because I'm a temp."

"Right!" Cynthia says it excitedly, as if me understanding the basics of my employment status constitutes a major achievement. She gives me another machine-polished smile. "So, it would be easy to think that a lot of the policies and procedures that we have in place governing Advancex employees might not apply to you in the same way, but that would be wrong. It's okay, though—we'll get to that more in a moment."

Cynthia says this like it would be a natural thing for me to worry about. It's so surreal I want to laugh.

She pushes her hair from her forehead and opens her mouth as if to say something else, but then she shuts it and nods at Brian, whose smile is somehow even more practiced, though I can sense teeth underneath. I know without looking into the kitchen-door world that

Brian's analogue is a predator. Probably a shark—one of the ones in that Arthurian trapdoor situation.

"Kat-trina." I can tell I'm not going to like Brian from the way he pronounces the *t* twice, as if "Katrina" is a foreign word and not a name people just have in English sometimes. "We've recently learned some things that we *might* need to be concerned about. We want to make sure, first, that we understand what's going on. Okay?"

"Okay," I say, which is at least a word.

"It's important to remember that *no one here* is accusing you of anything. We're just trying to get to the bottom of things."

I suddenly need to use the restroom. I've read about people peeing their pants when they're afraid before—but I didn't think it was real. I have to shift in my seat to hold it in. "Okay."

"Why don't you tell us a little bit about your relationship with—" He glances down, as if to check his notes, but it's obviously just for show. "Kurt Smith?" His voice goes up, like it's a question. Another show.

So, I was right. This is about Kurt. But if they suspect me of being responsible for his disappearance, why not just call the police?

I need a clue.

I close my eyes and take a breath, and then I dig deeper, looking for the kitchen-door world. Maybe this man isn't really a shark, maybe he's something else, something I can use to my advantage—

The room falls away. Everything around me—the tables, the glass, the chairs—everything is gone, and instead, I'm sitting a hundred feet up, in the bough of a massive tree. The branch is just large enough to support me, but I'm far, far away from the trunk. It's so surprising, I can't hold on to the image, and I blink back into the room.

The four of them are staring at me. "I'm sorry," I say, my heart in my throat. "Kurt." I repeat his name a few times, trying to buy myself a minute.

I don't know what being in a tree meant—don't even remember it from the book, and there have been lots of instances lately where my kitchen-door world has steered me wrong—but something tells me there's a clue, here, if I can just find it. Being on that branch felt... precarious, but not imminently dangerous. A careful climber might get down without falling.

I decide not to give them more than they're giving me. "I guess... he was my coworker?"

Brian leans back in his chair. "What else?"

I shrug. "It would help if you told me what you're looking for."

They exchange glances. I can tell they're taken aback by the boldness of my response—especially Caressa, who just sits, her mouth open, her eyebrows up. I've never seen her make that expression.

I notice for the first time the wrinkles around the corners of her eyes. I realize I don't know if she's got a family at home, if she's from the area—I don't know anything about her.

How do you spend so much time with people every day and not know anything about them?

"Katrina." Brian glances over at Cynthia, then at Lauren—clearly, this meeting isn't going how he predicted. "We know you're not being entirely forthcoming, here."

And something about the way he says that line—the way his tone dips down, all the way until he makes that little smirk at the end—it makes me angry. He's talking to me like I'm not even a person.

That's how Advancex has treated me all along, isn't it? Not worthy of being a real *employee*, of their health insurance, of free parking? And I've been working for them for *three years*.

What a bum deal. "What *exactly* would you like me to be forthcoming about?" Even I'm surprised by how angry I sound.

Brian's eyes narrow. He doesn't like being challenged. He's imagining swatting me out of existence. "All right," he growls. "If *this* is how you want to play it. We know about your computer activity, all of the accounts and data you've been accessing despite not having proper clearance. We know *exactly* how much interest Kurt took in you before he quit—"

A flash of light, so bright I don't even hear the rest of his sentence.

They think Kurt *quit*. Not disappeared. Quit.

Another piece, sliding into place. The question pops out before I can stop it. "Did he give notice?"

"Did he...*what*?" Brian's face crumples with disgust—it's obvious he's been holding back this whole time, playing nice for the purposes of the investigation. He puts his mask back on, as deftly as shrugging into a coat. "This isn't the kind of interview where you ask the questions, Miss Kim."

There's something here. *Something.* I'm a *temp* employee, for chrissake. Not worth dragging up to twenty to fire. And Kurt—he's not important, either, so there's got to be a reason why so many high-level people are suddenly fascinated by his workplace activities—

Outside, somewhere in the hallway, I hear a faint *ding*, like an elevator. I don't know if it's real or imagined, but it gives me exactly what I need. I suddenly recall, in painful detail, the pressure of Yocelyn's fingers around my arm.

Stay away from him.

I'd thought she was jealous. But that postcard, the dog face, the sneering refrain—*LAP IT UP, BABY, LAP IT UP*—was Kurt.

He did something to her. She was trying to warn me.

As soon as I think this, I know it's right, even though I have no proof. Because Yocelyn's always been a white rat, a lab rat—and rats aren't mean. They're secretive, but not evil. I'd confused the animal with the things *done* to it—lab rats get experimented on.

Oh, Yocelyn, I'm so, so sorry.

Time for a bold move. I stand up from the conference table and scoot my chair behind me, before leaning over the desk and planting my palms, like I'm a TV cop running an interrogation, like I *really* mean business.

"You want to know about Kurt?" I'm all bravado. "I'll *tell* you about Kurt."

Even though I'm focused on Brian, out of the corner of my eye, I catch Cynthia turn toward Caressa and raise a hand, palm-up, as if to say, *What the hell?*

I'm sorry for Caressa, I really am—it's not like she has any idea what's running through my head right now.

Brian rallies fast. "Are you...have you been drinking? Are you *on* something?"

I lean farther into my power-pose. "I'm high on *life*, baby." And despite how horrifically embarrassed I feel, there's a little truth to it— this pose is really working.

Brian rubs his temples. I almost pity him; I doubt he gets many stress headaches at nine in the morning. He glances over at Lauren, who gives him the tiniest nod—I can tell from the way she's squinting ever so slightly that she, at least, is finding this entire charade interesting—and then he turns back toward me and sighs. "Yes. We want to know about Kurt."

"All right, here's the deal. I'll tell you all about our torrid love affair, about the *sexual harassment* he perpetrated on the women in our workplace—"

Around the table, everybody goes stiff, and I know I've hit the nail on the head.

"—but I have some terms."

Brian's mouth falls open. I have to admit, it feels good.

"What are the terms?" says Lauren. She's got the tip of one of her fingers against her chin. I realize she's enjoying this.

Right. Terms. "I want Navya's job back," I say, thinking fast. "It wasn't her fault she got forced to punch me in. She was, um, covering for me, because I had to go talk to Kurt. He was threatening me, and she was trying to protect me."

Brian looks over at Cynthia. "Navya? Who—"

"Done," says Lauren, without blinking.

"I want to know how Kurt quit."

A tiny vein pulses on the side of Brian's neck. I'm amazed this is the first time I'm seeing it. "I don't know what you mean—"

"I mean, was it a phone call? A note?"

Brian looks at Lauren. "As the head of Legal, I have to insist that—"

"It was an email," says Lauren.

An email. "When was it sent?"

Lauren glances at Caressa, who blinks, stunned. When she realizes Lauren is looking at her, she sits up straighter and clears her throat. "Um, it had to have been either Sunday night or Monday morning, because it wasn't there Sunday in the afternoon when I checked."

Oh. *Oh.* Kurt jumped on Friday night. There's no way he could've sent that email.

It was Leoni. It *had* to have been her. Add that to the car, and she's definitely covering up his death.

But why would she cover up his suicide? "It came from his work email?"

Caressa thinks for a second before inclining her head slightly. "I think so."

Which means it could've been Yocelyn, too—but I doubt it. I keep seeing her little white paws, her whiskers, her scaly tail. She's the victim. I'm sure.

"I think," says Brian, seething, "it's our turn to ask some questions."

I don't have anything else to ask, not yet, so I don't refuse.

"So," says Brian. "The nature of your relationship with Kurt was...?"

I pause, trying to think of an answer.

"Keep in mind, Miss Kim, that you were seen by the security guard going through Kurt's desk after hours, on a day that you were *supposedly* sent home sick. And this isn't the first time—you've been spotted by several coworkers and even your own supervisor. So, what were you doing in his desk? Keep in mind, we have the footage."

A security camera. Shit. I'm so stupid.

I swallow, grasping for a lie that would make sense with said footage. "I was leaving him a note."

Glances pass around the table. "What kind of note?" asks Brian.

"A note...asking him to leave me alone. I didn't want to be involved anymore. Not after...what happened to Yocelyn."

This time, nobody looks at each other—but it's too practiced, too deliberate, as if they were expecting it. "And what happened to Yocelyn?" asks Cynthia. She speaks very, very gently.

I'm back out on the limb of the tree, so far from the trunk that every move I make is dangerous—but I've already come this far. I've got to finish it. "He said that if she slept with him, he'd help her get promoted. I know he's not upper management or anything, but he"— I'm feeling my way along the branch, my feet curving over its wooden surface—"he said that he has powerful friends here at Advancex. But after they were together for a while, he started getting mean. Threatening her. Telling her she'd be fired."

Cynthia cleared her throat. "And what made you think this would happen to you?"

"He asked me out. At first, I was happy about it, but then Yocelyn came to warn me. Grabbed my arm in the elevator."

Brian leans over and mutters something in Lauren's ear. I catch the word "footage."

Cynthia nods. "And did this liaison occur on company property?"

"Yes. Kurt really liked getting away with stuff in the office."

Lauren pulls a face. Something in that expression—it makes me think she didn't like Kurt in the first place.

"And what about the computer usage?"

I have no idea what he's talking about, but there's something mean and eager behind the gleam in his eyes. I decide to play dumb. "I don't know what you mean."

"I think you *do* know, Miss Kim. I think the late-night logins and credential—"

Lauren makes a noise, just a soft clearing of her throat, but the sound flips Brian's switch. After a moment, he leans forward, steepling his fingers and resting them on the table surface like little finger-tents. "Here's the situation, Miss Kim. We need time to investigate these... circumstances, but if everything you've told us is true, then we should be able to help your friend Navya, assuming both you *and* Yocelyn would be willing to refrain from pressing charges. We'd like to close this out quickly. In writing."

I nod meekly.

"In the meantime, perhaps you should go home for a few days. You appear to be feeling unwell, and we'd like some time to consider our next steps."

"Yes," I say. When I close my eyes again, there's no rustle of leaves, no bark underfoot—no press of the kitchen-door world around me. And then, it's like my body moves of its own accord. I stand up and walk out of the room before I lose my nerve, shutting the door behind me.

A moment later, my legs dissolve into rubber, and I have to lean against the door to take a deep breath. But then I hear Brian inside, talking, the bass of his voice carrying in a way the women's voices don't, though I can't get anything more than snatches:

...story corroborates...Miss Hernandez...amenable to...settlement... keylogger—

"Ready to go down?" the receptionist asks.

I swivel carefully off the door. I walk all the way to the elevators before responding. "Yes, please."

She's back to her screen before the elevator even arrives, although she's traded in the wedding album for Discovery-Bang, my favorite YouTube channel about cryptid hunters. It feels fitting, though I don't know why.

CHAPTER 16

Coffee, Sorrow, Smoke

On my way to the car, there's something about that wedding website that sticks in my brain—some clue hidden in the shots of happy couples and doilied invitations and flower girls, something that will tell me more about Kurt, if only I could pull it out. I wrestle with it all the way back to my apartment.

I've got the key in the door when my phone rings. When I see it's Yocelyn, I almost drop it. "Hang on," I say, pushing my door open. "Okay, sorry."

There's a pause so long, it stretches my nerves into spiderwebs. "I need to speak with you," she finally says. "Can we meet somewhere?"

She wants to talk to me. I don't know if that's a good idea.

Maybe she realizes I'm anxious, because she adds, "It can be somewhere public, as long as we can talk quietly. Is there a coffee shop near you?"

"There's Bin-Bash." The answer was a reflex, one I regret. Bin-Bash has good coffee—but it's also where I met Leoni the first time, after the craigslist ad. We went there for coffee whenever she was home. It's just around the corner.

Then again, Yocelyn knows where I live. She dropped me off last year when my car battery died.

The thought repeats. The second iteration stops me cold. *She knows where I live.*

I don't *think* Yocelyn could be behind the apartment downstairs. The kitchen-door world says she's the one being taken advantage of here. But I'm wrong about things all the time, now. I could've easily assumed she was the victim, when she was the villain all along.

"Bin-Bash is perfect," she says. "I'm actually right down the street. I can be there in five."

She hangs up before I can come up with an excuse to say no.

I have to sit down. What was she doing so close to my apartment? Why does she want to meet?

I pick up the phone, but I don't call her back. The only thing worse than being afraid is not knowing what I'm afraid of.

Maybe the Mirror-Man's true power, all along, was in my refusal to look.

There isn't time to redraw my sigil on the door, but before I leave, I drop my phone in my box, as if I were going out to the bridge. One of the keys to ensure my safe return—because despite all that's happened, it worked, didn't it? I made it home safe?

And though I don't think Yocelyn is capable of violence, I take the stairs carefully, making sure to stick to the pattern.

Yocelyn wasn't kidding about being down the street. When I push in Bin-Bash's door and step into the warm smells of coffee and hot soy milk, she's already there, curled up in a booth in the back-right corner. She waves at me, her arm ascending rapidly, then pausing at its apex like a thrown ball. After sitting next to her for so long, I can tell she's nervous.

I wasn't expecting to see her yet, so I wave back and make an apologetic gesture at the coffee counter before getting in line. I don't know what to say, what she wants, why she couldn't explain what she needed over the phone.

Bin-Bash is normally pretty crowded, despite being a vegan café. Though there are lots of people in Grand Station who refuse to believe that a soy milk latte could be good, Bin-Bash has counterbalanced any loss of clientele with the installation of some screamingly fast internet, which makes it a favorite spot for computer programmers, website designers, and gamers. That's actually what it's named after—something to do with Linux operating systems.

But it's pulling up on eleven a.m. The lunch rush isn't here yet, and the morning rush is mostly out. The place is only half full—which makes it the emptiest I've ever seen it.

I almost order the special of the day, something called "Gingerbread Heaven," before realizing that this isn't the time to shake up my routine. I get my usual, a plain-Jane café latte, and wait as the barista makes the steamer roar.

When I can't delay any longer, I slink over to Yocelyn's booth.

"Thanks for coming," she says. "I owe you an apology. And my gratitude for what you did, coming clean about Kurt like that. They fired me when I reported it, even though they gave me another excuse. Now I might have a chance of getting my job back, or at least a settlement."

A lump forms in my throat. This isn't what I expected. I've been wrong so often lately; it feels strange and heady to have actually hit something so cleanly on the nose. Maybe I can trust my instincts after all.

I have to take a sip of my drink before I can answer, and my mouth fills with heat and sweetness. "There's no reason to thank me *or* apologize."

She waves my statement away. "You don't have to lie." Her face falls, and she looks down at her drink. I wonder how I never noticed the pain in her eyes, how I'd mistaken it for anger. "Janice called me."

"Janice?"

She nods, her dark curls bobbing up and down. "The secretary on twenty. She's actually a friend of my mother's, and she heard one of them mention me before the meeting, so she left the line open and eavesdropped. She heard everything. They think she's just a ditz, but Janice is savvy as hell. Nothing gets by Janice."

She glances around the room, leans forward, and lowers her voice until it's barely audible. "I would have reached out to you sooner, but I wasn't sure. When I caught you going through his desk, though, I got scared for you. That's why I came to warn you. By then, I knew what a monster he was, and I—" Her voice breaks.

I'm filled with such guilt: a horrid, drowning pool, threatening to engulf me like the wave crushing the mountain in the postcard. It would be so much easier to just go along with this. To let her think we were in this club together, that she wasn't alone.

It might even be kinder, but it wouldn't be the truth. After everything that's happened, she deserves the truth.

I take a slow breath and try not to think about the walls closing in on me. "I lied in the meeting."

"What?" It comes out sharp, and she glances around before continuing. "Lied about what?"

"He never propositioned me, or anything like that. I just had a feeling that he was doing something bad to you, and I guessed."

"Don't lie," she says, her voice trembling. "Don't lie. He was always *watching* you. Looking for you. Asking about you, even. Toward the end, before he quit, I started to think you were the only reason he'd even approached me in the first place—because we used to sit next to each other." She presses her lips together, but it doesn't stop them from quivering. "That's nuts, right?"

It's a chilling thought. How long had Kurt Smith been taking note of my movements? How long had the cameras been in my bedroom and my bathroom?

How long has Kurt Smith been the Mirror-Man?

It takes me forever to compose a reply. "I don't think it's nuts," I manage to squeak out. "I don't know *why* he was so interested in me, but I think it might involve something that happened a long time ago. Did you know he was from Pleasance Village?"

She blinks. I can tell I've surprised her. I realize, too late, that I've been talking about him in the past tense. "Your hometown?" She glances around the room again. "Did you know him before you moved here?"

I shake my head. "No. That's the thing I can't figure out." I bite my lip. I'm not sure how much I can tell her, but she used to *date* Kurt. She's spent time with him in his apartment, met his family, slept with him. She could give me some clue that solves all of this.

"You know I've been snooping through his things. I…found a photograph of him. He's maybe a teenager, standing in front of my old library."

I close my eyes, remembering the photo, and with it comes a flash of light. Bright and sunny, like early summer. "He's either lived there or has family there."

"But you don't remember him?"

I fight the knee-jerk response to say no and think hard—if stellations have taught me anything, it's that execution matters. Going over the same points with different rules, like skipping three points instead of two, draws an entirely different shape. "No," I say, finally. "I really don't think so. Can I…ask you some things about him?"

She bites her lip and leans forward, almost knocking into her mocha, hugging herself tightly. "You really didn't? With him, I mean?"

I shake my head. "I'm sorry."

"Then how did you know?"

I shrug. I can't explain the kitchen-door world or its logic, how it shows me the truth behind people's facades. "When I was sitting in that room on twenty, I realized they wouldn't be asking all those questions, unless it was something big. And you haven't been at work in a few days, and there was that weird moment in the elevator—"

She flinches, and I rush to explain. "I say *weird* because it wasn't like you. You were always nice to me, before you moved up to sit by him. I realized there had to be something going on."

But she's staring down into her drink. I feel awful, like I've broken some sacrament between us—and now I have to break another. "Yocelyn—I think Kurt's done something really bad. Something even worse than what he did to you."

She looks up at me. She doesn't seem surprised, just curious.

It makes my stomach turn. Even without knowing what the bad thing is, she knows he's capable of it.

"Like what?"

"I'm not sure, but I want to ask you some questions about him, if that's okay. I just have a hunch."

She scoffs. "Like the one you had upstairs?" When I nod, her expression softens. "You really—you just guessed?"

"I'm sorry." I really mean it. "I'm so, so sorry."

Her eyes well up with tears. I hear people typing behind us, superimposed on the soft strains of music I know is real and not from inside my head, because I never imagine gentle folk guitar.

But then she sits up straighter. "Okay," she says. "What do you want to know?"

"What he was, er, *is* like as a person." I close my eyes. Out of nowhere, the wedding album flashes through my mind again, a photo of a woman in a strapless mermaid dress, her long veil trailing behind. There's something there, if I could just put it together.

"I don't know. We dated for eight months. He was nice for two, and then his mask started to slip. By the end, he wasn't so nice. He was never *violent*. Just..." Yocelyn clenches her hands, struggling for words. "If I did something he didn't like, he'd find some way to *punish* me, but it was always something that could've easily been construed as benign. One time, I said something about him maybe changing haircuts, and he stopped answering my calls for a week. He claimed he dropped his phone in a puddle. And he *did* have a new phone after that, but even so..." She brushes some hair back from her face.

She doesn't want to finish the thought, but I can finish it for her. Oh, yes, I can. "Things didn't feel coincidental. The pattern was too much to ignore."

She nods.

This information about Kurt's need for control is valuable, but it doesn't explain how we're tied together. I file it away for later. "Did he ever mention Pleasance, or living somewhere before Grand Station? Or what he did before he came to Advancex?"

She laughs softly to herself. "No, he never did. Whenever I'd bring it up, he'd just steer the conversation back to asking about me. I didn't—I didn't take it as a problem, at first. He just acted so *interested* in me, like everything I said was fascinating. I was really flattered." She closes her eyes, drawing out a memory. "There was one time, we'd been drinking, and he mentioned something about working in a mail room, how annoying it was to push the cart around to all these big shots who treated him like dirt. He hated delivering the mail. He was like that—always putting on airs."

Big shots. The words make my skin tingle. "Did he say where that was?"

She purses her lips on one side of her mouth. "I don't think so—but I got the feeling it was somewhere fancy, like a law office?"

"Maybe a finance place?" Briar Stone Ventures. It has to be. The connection to the *PROSPER* postcard.

She shrugs. "Maybe. I have no idea, honestly. He never mentioned it again."

This time, when I see the wedding album, the image is of an invitation, though I can't make out any words. Just the picture of bells, the gold embossing. My mind tries to make sense of this new polygon, skipping different points to draw new stellations.

Invitation. Family.

"Did you ever meet his family?"

She looks sad then. "No. He was so *secretive*, you know. I got the feeling they had some kind of falling out."

I think about my parents and try not to react. "What kind of falling out?"

She shrugs helplessly.

I draw more points: *Connection. Ritual. Society.* "What about his friends?"

"No, I—" She puts her face down in her hands. "You have to understand. We were sneaking around because of the Advancex fraternization policy. I never—I never even wanted the promotion, really. I still don't know how he did it. I was just excited to be sitting next to him." She straightens and smooths a stray lock of hair behind her ear. "At first, I thought he was hiding me from his friends because of the job, but he never even let me see his apartment. I started to wonder if he was married. He was always checking that little flip phone in his drawer, although last week, I realized it was only when you weren't around, and I—" Her face contorts. "It's so embarrassing. I don't like to think I'm *that* kind of girl, someone who would date a married guy, but I honestly didn't know—"

"I don't think he was married." I say it with authority despite not having proof from either of my worlds. But there's something about him, how secretive he turned out to be—I can't believe he'd let someone else in like that and relinquish so much control.

She nods, relieved, before glancing at the clock behind me. She's going to bolt soon. This didn't turn out like she planned.

I close my eyes and see the wedding invitation. *Family. Connection. Society—*

What was it Sunder had said? Something about…how everybody has social media. "I just have one more question."

She freezes and settles back in her chair. I realize she'd been in the process of getting up.

"Did Kurt have any social media? Facebook or Twitter? Anything? Or like, even a website he visited a lot—"

She's shaking her head, but when I say "website," she perks up a bit. "Oh! There was that, what's it called? PostSecret? I caught him on it a few times."

"PostSecret?"

She nods. "Yeah, it's an art thing, I think." She stands up to leave, but then she sits down again, as if we're dancing. "Katrina, I have a lawyer. I'm going to take Kurt to court. I need you to consider testifying, because it could seriously help my case."

"I'm sorry, I can't. I really was lying about it." And Kurt's somewhere in the briny deep. They should find his body any day now.

I push that image away, picture shark-toothed Brian from twenty instead. He said something about…*amenable.* That they'd be amenable to a settlement. "Listen to me, Yocelyn. I overheard them chatting, right after I left the room. I think they're more scared than they're letting on. If you have a lawyer, you should push for a settlement, but fast, before they can change their mind."

She scowls. "You don't understand. This isn't just about me. This is about all the other women that Kurt's probably hurt. This is about making sure he can't hurt anybody else."

"He *can't.*"

There must be something in my voice that gives her pause, because when she speaks again, she's whispering. "How do you know?"

I don't want to tell her, but I owe it to her. She might lose her chance to get whatever good she can out of this situation, and I gambled with her job and career up on twenty. "Because he's probably dead. I saw him jump off a bridge. And they'll likely find the body soon, if they haven't already. When they do, who knows what will happen? There could be a huge investigation at Advancex, and with all of the chaos, you might lose your chance for a settlement. You need to get the money now, while you still can."

"Okay." Yocelyn's voice is quiet but heavy. I can't tell what she's feeling. "Okay."

Her hand shakes. Her face contorts through a range of expressions: confusion, shock, rage. She picks up her purse and clutches it tightly to her chest. "Well, thank you, I guess." Her voice is so flat it sounds tinny, like she's on a call with a bad connection and not standing in front of me at Bin-Bash.

"You're welcome," I say automatically. I don't know what else to say, though I imagine only psychopaths tell people *they're welcome* after announcing their sexual harasser is dead.

"I need to go." Her face shows no hint of the war just waged on it. "But you helped me, so I guess I should help you."

My mouth goes dry.

"On the phone, Janice mentioned they were upset with something involving the computer—your username had some high-level permissions assigned to it, some kind of access it shouldn't, and they're not sure how that happened. One of them wanted to report it, but it sounds like they decided to keep it quiet to stay out of hot water with their clients. Do you know anything about that?"

"No." The world is starting to feel wavery again. Could that have been Kurt or Leoni? What did they want with my username?

"Well, goodbye."

Before I can get myself under control, she turns and leaves. Her cup is still sitting in front of me, half-full, red lipstick imprinted along the rim.

She'll probably never speak to me again.

On my walk home from Bin-Bash, white flakes drift from the sky.

From the moment I see the first hint of snow, Debussy's "Clair de Lune" plays in my head. It's not what I would have chosen. It's somehow both trite and breathtakingly beautiful, but at least it doesn't overpower me. At least it gives me space to consider everything.

I thought I knew the people in my life—Kurt, Leoni, Yocelyn—but even when I was right, I was wrong.

I wonder what else I've been wrong about. Now that I've told Yocelyn about Kurt, I feel like I'm running out of time, as if voicing the truth somehow gave it life and forced me to look at something I've always managed to avoid.

Sometimes, *need* fills my entire life—things I have to do, things I can't, and it all has to happen right now, right here, or there will be consequences. I know these rituals aren't rational, but I exist on the knife-edge of believing and not-believing. Like a three-bladed propeller, my worlds spin around me: my childhood in Pleasance, my life in Grand Station, and the escape of Mi-Hee's kitchen-door world.

But this isn't just a ritual or an imaginary evil. They're going to drag Kurt's dead body out of the water. It could already be lying on a cold table, a medical examiner clicking their recorder on under the glare of a too-bright light, poised to begin the excavation that will put a name and a face to a John Doe.

At some point, the police will put it together. Advancex will find out Kurt somehow quit *after* he died. When that happens, my window into understanding Kurt Smith—why he was following me, what he wanted, how he relates to the kitchen-door world—will shut, possibly forever.

I have more clues than I have time. There's Leoni and her past. I could find the lease agreement for our place, and maybe Mr. Sacks ran a background check I can ask about. There's the phone, the car, the keys, the laptop, the apartment downstairs with its terrible message. There are the postcards, that website Yocelyn mentioned (*PostSecret?*), the photograph, the key chain. There's poor Yocelyn, Kurt's controlling nature, his anger about the mail room, his possible connection to Briar Stone Ventures.

Even with unlimited time and unlimited resources, I'll never solve it all. I have to pick and choose.

When I get home, I grab all the clues I have and lay them out on my bed. *My* bed, not Leoni's, because whatever magic it held was broken when she left. I let the pieces guide me, sink into that space between this world and the kitchen-door world.

Help me, Mi-Hee, I think. *Show me what I need.*

A new scent enters the room. Harsh, immediately identifiable: something burning.

I lean close to the bed, trying to find its source. It's not the laptop, the keys, the phone, the USB. It's not the cards, the key chain, or the photo.

The hair tingles on the back of my neck. I leave the bedroom, cross the living room. Go into the bathroom, press myself to the place where the camera used to be, sure it's coming from the room below, that I'm being smoked out by the Mirror-Man—

And for a brief, terrible second, the evening on the bridge flickers in front of me, and I can't tell if Kurt jumped down or forward, *down or forward—*

But the scent gets fainter. I go back to the bedroom and check again, and this time, I follow it to Leoni's dresser.

I pull the top drawer open, looking for a crack like the one I found in Kurt's box, a switch or a hidden panel. I move to the next drawer, my mind full of the things I missed: I should've known it was odd for her to leave her furniture behind, to bail in such a hurry.

Nothing in the second drawer. I try the bottom drawer, even though I already know what's there, because I opened it in my search for pens *after* she left. The pens go rolling back and forth, but there's nothing else, though it feels like the scent changes—sharper now, more metallic.

I lean down and inhale deeply, and I finally identify it: this drawer smells like cigarette smoke.

I remove the drawer and place it on Leoni's bed. I search it again, and when I don't find anything, I pull out the other drawers. The cigarette smell intensifies, as if it's coming from the dresser's frame.

It's possible the smell isn't real. It's possible this is some kitchen-door bullshit, that my discoveries over the last few days have actually driven me nuts.

I get down on my hands and knees and check under the dresser, feeling for missed holes in the carpet, signs of spying. When I don't find anything, I scramble to my feet, grabbing one of the dresser's ribs to haul myself up. Without the weight of the drawers to anchor it, the dresser wobbles and tips forward—

Something slides, faint and rustling, behind its back.

Fuck. Please don't be a mouse.

I grab the corner of the naked dresser and pull it away from the wall. There's another rustle, but this one ends in the faint slap of paper hitting carpet.

I kneel and jam my arm in the gap under the dresser, feeling around until I find something flat that slides under my fingers. I grab it and pull.

It's a water-stained envelope, a grainy photograph paper-clipped inside. Both are bent, and as soon as I bring them to my face, I smell cigarettes—but also the smell of mint. When I pull the photograph out, it sticks hard to the paper. The envelope must've fallen behind the dresser and gotten wedged the night I came in and knocked over Leoni's files and her cup of tea with my purse.

The photograph is of a black-haired girl with a skirt and scarf halfway through a crosswalk. Her face is obscured by the paperclip, but she's surrounded by skyscrapers covered with plastic light-up signs. The script makes my vision swim: the signs are all in hangeul—Korean letters—which means that this picture was either taken in Korea or in one of the handful of Korea Towns big enough for hangeul street signs: Flushing, New York, or maybe LA, but either of those would have English on the signs, too.

I pull the paperclip off her face, and for just a moment, I feel like I've slipped into the kitchen-door world, the impossible laid over the actual, and I don't know what's real anymore. It's a picture of me, taken in a place I've never been.

I study the photograph, looking for something, *anything*, that explains this impossibility. One of the signs by my hip is strangely curved, as if someone has—well, has made me fatter. The distortion implies the picture is digitally altered—which is good, because at least I haven't gone into a fugue state and lost time—but what *possible* use could Leoni have for this picture?

My fingers brush something rough on the back. I turn it over and find a sticky note, the text completely ruined by the tea, like one of those blotchy, coffee-filter tie-dye art projects they have kids do in elementary school. All that's legible is a smudge at the very end: *3-3-5.*

My blood goes cold. If I squint, the stain is the rough size and shape of an address, and the numbers—they're the same as the last three digits of the Pleasance Village zip code.

I have to sit down, so I perch on the edge of the bed, the photograph and the ruined envelope between my fingers. The smell of the smoke is already fading—though when I hold the photo to my nose, it deepens again.

Cigarettes. Smoking Sunder said the key to understanding why Kurt jumped was in his past, and now there's this odd connection between Pleasance and Leoni.

And a threat against me, scribbled on the wall in the apartment below, and holes in my floor where cameras used to spy.

This place will never be safe again.

My whole body constricts: a tight band around my chest, the hair on my arms tingling, my fingers suddenly numb. I've already lost the safety of the bridge. Before long, there won't be anywhere left to escape from myself.

I try to take a breath, but it's like I'm under concrete—and then there's a sudden stretching, like the moments right before I connect the last points of a stellation. I've got to finish this shape, no matter the cost, and there's only one way to draw the last line.

I've got to go back to Pleasance Village.

I close my eyes, and for just a moment, I can feel the weight of a rock in my hand.

FOURTH STELLATION

Fig 4. The Grand Hendecagram, or *gahn*, is created by taking the fourth stellation of a hendecagon and is the last of the regular 11-sided star polygons. It can be described by the notation {11/5}.

—The Magical World of Geometry

As her nemesis stepped through the mirror, Mi-Hee understood how wrong she'd been. Her spyglass had given her access to the kitchen-door world's hidden truths, but only where she pointed it, and only when she was willing to look.

For all her cleverness, Mi-Hee had never thought to point the spyglass at the Wizard. If she had, the lens would've revealed that under his wispy beard and his odd, colorful clothes, he was in fact no man at all, but instead a walking shell. A projection, connected to the Mirror-Man by lines of magic as obvious as the strings of any marionette—that he himself was a reflection, just another facet of the Mirror-Man.

There had been clues, of course, if only she'd paid attention. The power that had thrummed in the Heart, the power that came from any place where worlds overlapped—she'd sensed that power once, in the moments before she stepped through her kitchen door. And hadn't the Wizard himself been the one to give her the spell with the Mirror-Man's forgotten name?

(Why hadn't Mi-Hee realized that "Wizard" isn't a name, either?)

From the moment she'd stepped onto the sands of this world, the Wizard had helped her. She'd never once suspected that he'd been using her to let the Mirror-Man into this world—that her greatest ally could also be her greatest enemy.

CHAPTER 17

Crossed Stars

What do you take when your house is on fire?

Does it matter if the fire isn't real?

I don't own a suitcase, and I can't fit everything in my purse and backpack, so I grab one of the kitty trash bags from the kitchen. The moment feels permanent, somehow, enough that I take the time to say goodbye to the mushrooms and the dragonflies and the lullaby of the trees. Though I've wished a thousand times to never see them again, part of me hopes they'll follow me to my next home, wherever that turns out to be.

I'm desperate to leave, but I force myself to be meticulous. I can't afford mistakes. I draw my sigil on both sides of every door. I pack my ID, my documents, my box, some clothes, and my clues. I draw my sigil over the bathroom mirror with a capped eyelash pencil, an invisible ward to keep my destination a secret. I take 121 steps around the room as I leave.

Only then do I walk, counting steps in odd-even patterns, to my car. By now, there's a thin film of snow across the top, and the windshield is a block of ice—but when I open my trunk, the scraper is missing. I'm not sure what I did with it.

I start the car and get behind the wheel. Time is passing—it's a two-and-a-half-hour drive to Pleasance Village, if the traffic is right. It's already one p.m., and I need to get there before five, when the library shuts, because that's where Kurt's photo would've been taken, and I know from countless visits that they keep a shelf of yearbooks.

My stomach twists at the thought of revisiting the scene of my crime—but if Kurt's left some stamp on that place, I need to find it.

I can't leave, though, until the engine is warm and I can see out the windshield, so I decide to use the time to check out the PostSecret website that Yocelyn mentioned.

My phone is struggling. It takes forever to load the page: first the background, black, and then the top logo in scrawling script. Right when I'm about to give up, images start popping into view.

They're postcards.

My heart hammers as I scroll down the list. Postcard after postcard after postcard, most of them with a message somewhere on the face.

He doesn't know that I'm sleeping with his brother.

I've been stealing office supplies from work. I tried to stop, but I can't. I think I'm addicted.

I fell in love the moment we met, but you didn't remember me. I've spent the last year trying to get you to notice me. I staged our big date.

I click around. The website FAQ explains PostSecret is a place for people to anonymously spill their secrets.

It occurs to me how dumb I've been. I scanned the cards and did a reverse-image search for the faces, but I never did one for the cards *themselves.* It hadn't occurred to me that instead of sending them or saving them, Kurt could've been planning something else, like uploading them to a website.

I check the windshield. The air is blowing warm now, and there's a hole the size of my fist. Not quite safe to leave—or maybe I'm just telling myself that, because now that I've found this website, all of Mrs. Marple's demon cats couldn't stop me from image-searching the postcards.

I lean over and grab my backpack out of the footwell, before pulling out the *PROSPER* card. I snap a photo, crop the edges until it looks reasonably good, and stick it in a reverse image search.

I don't even have time to hold my breath. The match comes up immediately, but it's not PostSecret. Instead, it's another website, one called Better Secrets. It, too, is filled with postcards, but all the cards are Kurt's. Every single card of Kurt's, one after the other, posted for everyone to see.

I check for a menu or FAQ, but there's nothing. The site's just a black page, full of scanned postcards.

I'm stunned, but not sure what to do next, and I need to get to Pleasance before everything closes.

For a moment, I consider setting a route to Pleasance Village into my GPS—you never know if there's construction or an accident—but then I put it on the seat next to me. I don't need it any more than a migratory bird needs a map.

The many sides of Kurt swirl around in my head, but once I'm clear of Grand Station, automaticity takes over. I've spent so long in city traffic, I've forgotten how pleasant driving can be, though my enthusiasm is muted by the snow. Every so often, my car makes *the noise*, and there's an odd rattle from the back that occurs when I hit just the right speed. It takes me a while before I diagnose that it's coming from the loose seat.

If I get into an accident on the highway, that seat's going to fly forward and crush me. Potentially life-threatening, but there's nothing I can do about it now.

At the halfway point, I need to pee and stretch my legs. I keep my eye out for a mile marker, but then I see a turnoff sign. I pull off before realizing how familiar the exit looks. By the time I round the cloverleaf and a fake tiki-style roof comes into view, I'm already time-traveling to a decade ago, when Cindy Snelling and I snuck out of our houses. We'd each paid a senior twenty-five dollars we'd saved from our babysitting money to drive us to the GirlzKill concert. It was my first time coming to Grand Station alone, and I was so nervous and excited about the "big city" and the depths of our disobedience that I drank four cans of Coke in the first leg of the drive. By the time we'd pulled in here, at Happy Island Gas, I'd nearly peed my black and hot pink track pants.

It's my first hint of what awaits me as I approach Pleasance. The closer I get, the more I'll unbury the things I've tried so hard to push away, and although that scares me, I'm not about to turn around. Not when I've come this far.

I slow down as I approach the mostly deserted Happy Island parking lot before pulling right in front of the building, where I'll be able to see my car through the window, and slide out the passenger side. I don't lock the door. I don't even close it all the way, not when I might lose precious time trying to get back in.

When I return, I remember Kurt's burner phone, and try it on my charger. It fits—a good sign, one that makes me think I might get the clue I need to break into it soon.

I expect something horrible to happen on the drive, but it's like my trip is greased. The sun comes out from the clouds, making the snow sparkle, and it's finally warm enough that the road has started to melt, though the surrounding trees still wear their dusting proudly. Before long, the highway shrinks, four lanes down to two, and the speed limit drops from seventy to fifty-five as the interstate becomes a county highway.

I'd forgotten how beautiful the countryside can be. The way everything looks so fresh and clean—at some point, I can't help but crack the window, take in the cold, crisp air.

Everything turns from city to forest to farms, little tufts of woodsmoke and steam rising above the occasional distant houses. And in this moment, despite the *groan-groan-shriek* the engine sometimes makes, despite the occasional rattle of the could-be-projectile bench seat in the back, in this moment, I feel safe and happy, and it's such a foreign emotion that my heart breaks when I realize that I can't drive forever.

There is no exit for Pleasance Village, because by that point, you're not really driving on a highway. There's just an intersection with a two-way stop sign. It used to have big trees around it, massive pines as wide as they were tall, but someone's cut them down, and the intersection looks so unfamiliar, I almost miss it.

I brake too hard for the wet road and fishtail, but I get control of the car and pull off the county highway before somebody can plow into my vehicle from behind. Once I'm on the shoulder, I close my eyes and take long, shuddering breaths.

It feels like an omen, a sour welcoming home. I should've turned on the GPS. Then again, GPS never worked very well in Pleasance— the various map services had seen fit to ignore our small settlement.

Once I'm calmer, I ease back onto the road. After the turn, it's bumpier. I slow down and keep it to ten under—I don't have the budget for winter tires, or even *decent* tires, and the road here isn't clear.

After ten minutes, my mood improves. I realize I'm humming to myself, something bouncy and drifting that fits the afternoon light on the snow. It's not until my head echoes with pizzicato strings that I place it as Ravel's *Boléro*. As the sound swells, new instruments taking up the chorus, the flat planes of buried farmland start to transition— an occasional market here, a sign for a farm-stand, a gas station. When the clarinet enters, I tap the fingerings on my steering wheel.

Little by little, my surroundings turn denser, until I pass the LuxeDeluxe strip plaza, complete with a new microbrewery I don't recognize, and I'm suddenly in town. There's traffic again—heavy for Pleasance, but compared to what I'm used to in Grand Station, it feels like an easy stroll, and I'm able to zone out as I wind my way through the familiar streets, enjoying the benefit of a place where everyone follows the signs.

And even though I'm afraid of what I might find, it's like the air in the car is full of a soft, cool fog. Sunder was right—the core of the mystery is here, somewhere, in my hometown. I know this because I can feel myself getting closer to it, the way sharks sense blood in the water, or the way you sometimes know when the phone's about to ring.

Regardless of whether I was right about Kurt, whether I understood his deepest feelings or not, I was meant to do this, to come here. My stars and his stars were always spun together like two knotted strands of silk.

It was always going to be like this.

CHAPTER 18

Duck Psychology

I remember the Pleasance Sunbeam Library the way it is in Kurt's photograph: a small brick building, painted white, with a high, peaked roof. When I close my eyes, it sits in the middle of a giant field of grass, like a one-room schoolhouse from an old-timey movie about farmers.

As I approach, I can tell it's been expanded recently, the old and new portions not quite fitting together, but it isn't until I pull onto the blacktop in front that I realize how silly my memory is. This building always had a front parking lot, one I used every time I was a patron. The back lot, the one I slept in the night my parents shut their door in my face, was for staff only.

And yet, even after I'm parked in front, when I close my eyes, my memory doesn't correct itself. There's still a waving field of prairie grass around the old library, sun-soaked and inviting. I can almost smell it: pollen, water, earth.

Maybe I just don't *want* to remember—the lots, the cold weather, or the glass employee entrance, the way it shattered under the rock in my hand. Was there an investigation? Did someone get in trouble for what I did?

I roll down my window before I get out. I don't bother locking the door. This is Pleasance Village, and the lot is full of rust-bucket winter beaters and enormous, gleaming trucks that tower like giants. Nobody will mess with my car, and I have the backpack and my purse with all my documents, all of Kurt's clues. Everything else is just clothes.

The asphalt is so slick, I walk knees bent and butt curled under like a chimpanzee, but I make it across without wiping out. I open the library door and am greeted by a soft electronic chime. This, at least, has not changed.

The reception desk is newly renovated, no copy of *Mi-Hee and the Mirror-Man* turned toward the employee entrance in a little stand. I shake that image out of my head and focus on the clerk, who chats with a patron too softly for me to hear. I need to show her Kurt's photo, so I take a spot a respectful distance away, at least five feet back from where I'd stand in Grand Station, and try not to picture a grainy surveillance photo of me in the crime blotter of the *Pleasance Picayune*.

The librarian gives me a nod. I return it, but she's already gone back to her conversation. I look around, trying to get my bearings. The activity room to my right is empty—I think it's mostly for events—but colorful flyers and posters and kids' construction-paper art decorates the walls. There's a bank of six community computers to my left, though only one has a user, an old woman with horn-rimmed glasses and a loud sweater with a big cat appliqué, who appears to be googling myths about foxes.

The stacks are half obscured from my view by the reception desk. Occasional graying heads peek around the tall shelves in the adult section like groundhogs spotting spring, while a mom ambles through bins of brightly colored children's books with her three rambunctious kids.

It's been five minutes, but the conversation in front of me shows no sign of stopping. I clear my throat, which earns me a dirty look from one of the groundhogs.

"I'll be with you in just a moment. *Please* wait your turn." The librarian pushes her glasses back up her nose and returns to her patron, her frosty demeanor melting into a smile.

With each passing second, I get more nervous: fingers tapping, throat dry, my chest constricting. At first, I think it's because I'm afraid I'll be singled out for smashing the glass over three years ago, but when I prod at that idea, it caves in like rotten fruit.

It's not about the library. It's about what comes *after*: if I don't find what I need here, I'll have to go to the only other place I know is tied to Kurt, based on the key chain from the box—my old high school. The band's probably not in the full swing of winter yet, when after-school practices ramp up for holiday concerts, my father running back and forth, his white baton waving as he shouts out downbeats and changes in volume and *more air, support from the diaphragm*—

My eyes get hot and wet. "Can you come get me when you're ready?" I'm loud enough that a dozen heads in the room turn. Before the librarian answers, I push my way into the stacks. This is a small library. I can find the yearbooks myself.

This room should be known topography, but so much has changed. There are entire shelves devoted to items I don't remember being here, like DVDs and video games, a huge display of comic books. At least the shelf of moody teenage romances with werewolves and vampires and their ilk looks familiar—until I'm transfixed by a turned-out volume, the selkie on its cover giving the reader a dark stare. I can't figure out if it's *come hither* or *stay away*, but when I turn to launch myself out of the YA section, I'm drawing my sigil in the back of my mind, trying to convince myself the expression was not an omen.

I plunge into another section, and then another—*magazines, cookbooks, genealogy and local history*—before I hit pay dirt: a wall full of reference books: encyclopedias, dictionaries, state legal codes, bibles—

And yearbooks. Two entire shelves of them, but they're all out of order, 1968 right next to 1996, then 2006. They're also all startlingly different, a range of themes and colors that speaks volumes about the creators—like 1986, whose bright neon colors and Blade Runner font evoke a futuristic fever dream, or 1966, which is black and white, the cover marked with a pattern that echoes a mandala. 1978 has a stylized line drawing of the Death Star on it. Others are clearly meant to evoke *previous* eras, like 1970, which is black with an embossed gold title and twenties Art Deco line drawings.

There are at *least* fifty volumes here, if not more. I pull a few off the shelf at random, flipping to *S*, before I realize that Kurt's real last name might not be Smith. I have to check *all* the pictures—for Kurt's picture and Leoni's, and maybe Yocelyn's, though I no longer think she's embroiled in all this.

The key chain in Kurt's box said *sixth* annual band festival. From what I can remember, there's no special photo of the winner in the yearbook, but there should at least be a picture of the whole band. I think Kurt was about ten years older than me.

I take my graduation year and subtract ten: 2005. But I could be wrong about his age. To be on the safe side, I should check all the books from 2000 to, say, 2010. And that will include the band festival year, because if I won in my senior year, and it was the twelfth annual festival, then the *sixth* would have taken place in—I jot notes on the back of my hand—2009.

But, *but*, if Kurt *is* in one of these books, it might be as early as 1996 or so, because it takes someone four years to get through high school.

Okay. 1996 to 2010. I start scanning down the row for books in that date range. I'll grab them all at once so I don't miss one. And, lucky me, I already saw 2006, right next to 1996.

I pull them both out. 1996 is fairly plain, but 2006 has got a strange cover, one that looks familiar—one that makes me think of the selkie, though I can't figure out why until I squint at it *just* long enough for it to go blurry. It's a dead ringer for the cover of *Twilight*, the woman's hands holding the red apple.

Curious, I flip open the front cover. There's a small dedication from the senior class, with a note about how the apple "represents the learning passed from this year to the next." I smirk—that's a good job, getting it by whatever teacher supervised the yearbook that year.

I put it on the pile and keep looking, but when I reach the end of the first shelf, I haven't found a single book in my date range, and it's getting harder to breathe. On the second shelf, I find 1998, 1999, and 2000—but no 2001. Nothing else, actually, until 2010.

I find *my* senior yearbook—and though I long to open it, I'm too afraid to stumble upon some errant picture of my father, some errant picture of *myself*, and I put it back.

I check the shelves again, but there's nothing. All I've got is 1996, 1998, 1999, 2000, 2006, and 2010. Now, 1996 and 1998 feel too old. I set them aside.

It's strange that so many years are missing—strange enough that I'm starting to get nervous again. There's something important here I'm not picking up on, something I can sense I need my own spyglass for, my lens into the hidden parts of this world.

But this is a public place, and the steadiness that my last visit to the bridge gave me has evaporated in the midst of everything that's happened. It's a bad idea to go poking around in the kitchen-door world—except that failure here means going to the school.

Maybe I'll just take a peek.

I put both hands on the top of my small stack and close my eyes. I shuffle them: taking one book off the top, pushing it below. Taking one from the middle, placing it on top. I try to make it as random as possible—which is uncomfortable, I don't like random any more than

I like in-betweens or thresholds, but each book has to have an equal chance of being chosen.

After a little bit, my wrists and fingers tire from my careful grip and the aching slowness of my movements, but it's important to be deliberate if this is going to work. I shuffle and shuffle, until I really don't know which book is where, and then I let my mind go fuzzy and dip into the kitchen-door world.

The books are still there, but they've changed, now formed from something hard and crystalline instead of paper, and each is a different color. The shades I recognize right away because they're the same as the small pools on each side of the kitchen-door version of the Cayatoga, colors described in *Mi-Hee and the Mirror-Man* as *a verdant green, a brilliant gold, a fiery red, an unending blue*—and the colors of the four endekagrams that make up my protective sigil.

They're not in order, though. Green is on top, then blue, then gold, then red. It doesn't feel right to reorder them, so I leave them like that and start to feel my way through, one by one. It's like standing at a fork in the road, and not being able to remember which branch is the way home—I'm just navigating by instinct and feel.

Green feels like life and newness, like learning and hope. It's not the right fit for Kurt. I set that one aside, and as I do, I suddenly hear soft piano, sad and deliberate: Rachmaninoff's famous opus 3, no. 2, the Prelude in C-sharp Minor—though my father always preferred its other name, *The Bells of Moscow*, after the Kremlin's carillon: a giant, organ-like instrument, only instead of pipes, the baton-shaped keys pull wires to ring a series of giant bells. According to legend, Rachmaninoff was nineteen when he wrote it, after a dream in which he attended a funeral, only to open the coffin and find himself inside—

My chest hurts. I can't think about this, can't hear my father's voice. I go back to the books.

Blue feels peaceful, serene. There's a flicker of the wave painting from Kurt's card, of the vastness that can engulf us all—but it isn't the right fit for me or for Kurt, so I set that one aside, too.

Gold is passionate and brilliant. I almost—*almost*—open my eyes, but then I sense something below the veneer of its shine. It makes me think about gilding, about taking something ordinary like wood and tricking people into thinking it's something special, and although that *does* describe Kurt, it's also the opposite of what I'm looking for: something special hidden under something ordinary.

The last book is red. I lay my fingers on it and it feels like I've touched an oven burner—that flare of panic, the too-late burst of heat. I rub my thumb and fingers together, probing them gently, and I'm shocked to find that they're sore.

This book, then.

I open my eyes. It's 2006—I thought it would be, but this confirmation makes everything else in the world fade away. I turn the cover.

I begin, of course, with the Ss, looking for "Smith," for Kurt's face, but there's nothing. I start over. I don't waste time with the names—names are lies, ways of hiding a book that burns behind a different cover, a poison apple, a hoax within a hoax. I scan every single face, including the band pictures, but I make it through the whole book before confirming that none of them look like Kurt.

I take a deep breath. Try to figure out what that means. If his face isn't here, he wasn't a student in 2006. It's still *possible* he was one in 2009, the year of the band festival, but only if he'd transferred in from another school.

I want to tear the yearbook in half. I don't have enough information to draw any rational conclusions—but isn't that the way rational conclusions always go? One step forward, one step back? They're not like kitchen-door conclusions, like the conclusions of stellations, which can be misinterpreted, but always point clearly in one direction or another.

I lean into Mi-Hee's world, the part of me that defies the rational, but instead, I just see my father, braking for a line of ducks. My chest hurts again as I remember this, the time one of the ducks jumped out of line and hurried its way to the front.

My father leans out the window, yelling, "Wait your turn, duck. Wait your turn."

That's right. He doesn't like line-cutters. He doesn't let freshmen win the festival of the bands, only seniors or perhaps a particularly hardworking junior. Raw talent is always subservient to perseverance.

An ache opens deep in my stomach. Though I didn't tell them everything, it's no wonder my parents didn't embrace me when I failed out of school. My father doesn't even understand the essential nature of a duck.

I sit forever with the yearbooks, but I don't find anything. No faces I recognize, no mentions of Leoni or Kurt or even Harry, the terrible name scrawled on the wall in the apartment below mine.

And still, I don't want to let go of the yearbook. It feels like it could be helpful.

I slip it into my purse.

"*Excuse* me, young lady—"

A woman's voice, directly over my shoulder. I almost fall off my stool, but I take a deep breath and mash my most winning smile onto my face before turning. "Yes?"

It's the librarian. She looks *livid*, and for a moment I wonder again if she knows who I am, what I did to her door. "What, exactly, are you doing with that yearbook?"

I tell the most obvious lie. "I want to check it out. I was just getting ready to leave."

The librarian turns and taps the sign above the shelf. REFERENCE: DO NOT REMOVE FROM ROOM.

"Oh."

I slide the yearbook back out, but the librarian isn't appeased. "I've just about *had* it with you yearbook thieves—"

"Sorry?"

She narrows her eyes at me. "Don't act like you don't know. *What* is wrong with kids these days? Is this some inane internet challenge or something?"

I shake my head, trying to look contrite as the gears in my mind whir, like the factory at Advancex: roars of machinery, howls of steam. I can still salvage this. "A man at my office passed away, and uh, we don't have any photographs of him for the memorial. Photographs, from like, earlier in his life. And when we were talking about him, we realized we didn't know anything about him or even where he's from, but one of us found this in his desk."

I open my purse and slide out the photo of Kurt, push it across the table. She picks it up, and her eyes go wide—but then she slides it back to me. "I don't recognize him, but that's a lovely old photo of the library."

Disappointment crashes over me like the giant blue wave. I nod. "That's why I came. I'm from around here, originally, so when I recognized the library, I wanted to check the old yearbooks and see if we couldn't find some nice photos of him, but it seems like most of the ones from around when he would've been in school are missing."

She squints, her forehead twitching as she sizes me up, but sitting at the scene of my crime, it's easy to look rattled.

Finally, her shoulders fall. "I don't have them. They keep vanishing."

I blink. "People aren't returning them?"

"No, I told you, you can't check out a yearbook. But they keep disappearing from the stacks. I must've ordered four sets of books that fall into the same ten-year period. This last time, I decided to lock them up in the back, so it couldn't happen again, but when I got in touch with the yearbook distributor, they said they'd had some kind of emergency with their servers, and all the files before 2014 have been corrupted, so there was no chance of getting more."

My ears buzz. This can't be a coincidence.

"So that 2006, that's the only one I'm going to be able to get. It's a damn shame. And when I saw you on camera, futzing around with the yearbooks, well—"

"On camera?"

She slyly points at a little glass globe in the corner of the ceiling, next to a square sign that says, SMILE, YOU'RE ON CAMERA! with a happy face.

I hadn't noticed it before. Hadn't thought to look. I was coming back to a familiar place, and even though I could tell it'd changed, this had never entered my mind. "Ah," I say, wondering how long she was watching. If there's tape of me stacking the books and shuffling them with my eyes closed.

If there were cameras when I broke the library's side entrance.

She lifts her chin at the yearbook volume. "So, is he in your book?"

I shake my head. She plucks it up quickly, as if it's something precious, but she doesn't put it back on the shelf. "You know, I think I *will* keep this one behind the desk. Just in case. And if you *are* the one who keeps shuffling my books on the shelves, maybe you could stop? It's a real pain sorting them every time."

The look she gives me as she turns away is smug. I guess she didn't buy my story after all.

I sit a moment before checking the clock. It's four thirty. Not so late that if I showed up at the school it'd be completely deserted, what with all the after-school activities: chess club, 4-H, choir, sports...and band.

I don't want to go. *Don't* want to go.

But after a moment, I stand up and push my chair in, leaving the books where they are.

The librarian waves at me as I pass, still looking suspicious. "Hey, wait."

I stop and turn. The 2006 yearbook is sitting on the edge of the desk in front of her, two hands making an offering that can be interpreted three different ways: an apple of knowledge, the poison of a stepmother—or the *right* way, the secret way, which is a monument to the rebellion of teenage fantasy.

"Your name isn't Katrina, by any chance?"

For a moment, I'm confused—but I told her I was from around here. Pleasance is almost totally white *and* so small it's legally a village. There's probably one Asian kid every four years, if that—and it's also possible she remembers me from when I used to go to this library, even if I don't remember her.

"Sorry," I say, shaking my head.

"Do you know—" And then her phone rings. She turns away and picks it up, and it's clear from the way her voice rises that something has just *riveted* her. "What do you *mean*, 'water damage'?"

I bite my lip. The yearbook didn't help me at all. There's no reason to take it—but it's there, beckoning to me, three different meanings like three overlapping panes of colored glass. My fingers itch.

I shove it in my bag, and then I'm out the door.

CHAPTER 19

The Jagged Edge of the Familiar

The snow has started again by the time I exit the library, fat flakes that cling, wet and heavy, to the world around me. Instead of the beauty and wonder it filled me with this morning, everything now aches with a soft dread.

Snow is dangerous. It's easy to forget that when you're driving to work every day—when you know the route and the places likely to be slippery, when you're creeping along in gridlock traffic and the worst thing you envision is kissing someone's bumper.

But then you go back to the place where you're from, and you don't recognize your intersection until too late, hit the brakes too hard—and you're reminded that even the familiar can be dangerous. Even the familiar has teeth.

The school's the only other place in town that I know has yearbooks, but I don't want to go. I'd do anything to avoid seeing the disappointment on my father's face and feeling that rejection again—a shame so deep, it wasn't enough to flee to another city. I needed a whole new world.

I should've known everything was going to end at the school. Isn't that what I said to myself, pulling onto the highway?

It was always going to be like this.

Of course, I know the way.

My car protests several times on the journey: a warning, or just a complaint about the cold. At one point, I smell something sweet and pungent, like coolant, but my temperature gauge looks fine.

The snow is accumulating, sticking to the road, the lawns. My windshield wipers haven't been replaced in so long, they leave uneven streaks across the glass. I try pushing the button for washer fluid, but I'm out.

It occurs to me that I don't have a plan for the night. I don't have enough money for a hotel, not that there's one within twenty miles of Pleasance. If my investigations run too late, I'll either be spending the night in my car or driving back on a slick road with bad tires in the dark, hoping against hope my gas gauge has suddenly started under-estimating what's in the tank.

Panic rises in my throat, hot and bitter like bile. I breathe slowly through my nose, wiggle my toes in my shoes. It's hard to picture stel-lations while I'm driving, but I'm about to turn onto the corner that leads to the school—

A huge building swings into view. I'm stunned. This is *not* my school. It's four times the size it used to be, and there's a big fence around its border, a small entrance with a little parking guard station. Every surface shines in the winter sunlight, tons of glass that sparkles like the twentieth floor of Advancex.

There'd been some talk of expanding before I graduated. My father mentioned it to my mother more than once. He'd always sounded pleased, always taken the time to state what great things it would do for their home value, how despite the small size of the village, the school was one of the best in the state, worth the extra taxes.

And then my mother would always nod. "We made a good decision, moving here," she'd say, and I was never quite sure if she meant emigrating from Korea or just relocating to Pleasance. It's hard to know, when they've always been so secretive about their old lives.

I pull up to the parking guard, a white woman in an orange vest. She slides a bookmark into her romance novel and puts it down. I can see the front door right over her shoulder, so close I could probably reach it before her, if I was willing to get out and run.

She takes me in, and her eyebrow goes up like a signal flag. At first, I think it's my age, but then I see her gaze sweep over the boat. "Nice car."

Great. "Yep. It's, uh, my winter beater."

She nods. This is sensible—*if* you're rich enough to afford two cars. It always made me dizzy, the way half of us drove rusty trucks with bumpers dragging on the ground, while those whose parents had fancy jobs in town would swap their shiny BMWs for understated Camrys—except for the Jeep owners. My Buick LeSabre is old enough to drive itself, but in high school, I didn't *have* a car.

The parking guard holds out her hand.

I have no idea what she wants. I shake my head. "Sorry?"

She waves her other hand at the school, perhaps forgetting the book is still in it. The well-muscled, bare-torsoed pirate on its cover sails through the air. "You're not a student," she says, as if that explains anything.

"I am not," I confirm—perhaps a bit tersely, but after sticking the landing with that horrible meeting this morning at Advancex, I'll be damned if I'm going to let a high school parking guard unseat me.

"So, if you're here to *pick up* a student, I need your ID."

I shake my head. "Oh, I'm not. I, uh, need to use the library."

The corner of her mouth twitches. "The public library is just down the road. Just pull out and make a right—"

"I *know* where the library is."

"Then you should have no problem getting there." She picks up her book again, unruffled—of course she is, she deals with teenagers and crazy parents all day.

I can feel the yearbooks calling me, like the bright beam of a lighthouse. "Ma'am," I try, even though this woman looks just a few years older than me. "I apologize. I should've just told the truth. My dad—Mr. Kim—he's the band teacher here? I want to surprise him with a visit. A *surprise* visit," I say again, in case she didn't catch it the first time.

She squints at me before nodding—and honestly, I'm a bit pleased. She didn't just agree that I was his daughter because I'm Asian, like so many other people in this place would have. It was one reason I was so happy to leave: no more jokes about *can't tell them apart.*

Turns out, Grand Station was better, but not by much.

"Okay," she says. "You're his daughter."

"Right. So, about the *surprise* visit, do you think I could go in?"

She picks something up from beneath my view: a two-way radio.

"No, you don't have to—"

"I've got a woman here, says her father is Mr. Kim and she'd like to come in for a *surprise* visit?" She leans on the word, extra hard, and the smile she gives me is fake enough to chip.

I'm tempted to crawl through my window and drag her out into the snow.

The reply is slow in coming. After a moment, there's a crackle, and then a woman's voice answers. "Sure, send her to the visitor's office. He says he'll be right there."

She jerks her thumb behind her, already picking up her book.

I want to scream at her, but what's the point? I shift into reverse and start to back up—and somebody behind me lays on their horn. When I look in my rearview, there's a kid in a giant Lexus SUV, flipping me off.

Okay, *okay*, this is fine. I just have to pull forward enough to turn around. I make it five feet, ten, but the parking lot is almost empty, and the door is *right there*, which means there's nothing to obscure my view of the tall Korean man sprinting out the front door, moving faster than I could've believed possible.

My ears fill with the roar of ocean water.

I can see his glasses bouncing on his face, the neat V-neck collar of his knitted sweater. Memories come crashing in like a flood. *The whistle-howl of a teakettle, the citrus smell of the yuja-cha my mother always made when one of us was sick—*

His hair whips up and down, unruly. It already has flecks of snow in it—

My mom, teasing him about his hair. Always in Korean, one of the only things they never talk about in English in front of me, god, god, why were they so afraid I might pick up an accent? Would it really have been such a terrible thing?

He recognizes my car immediately—of course he does, it's *his* car. I spin the wheel, trying to avoid him, but the boat has a terrible turning radius, and he's already streaking across the parking lot.

He's yelling something, something that looks like my name, but *no, no, no*, I don't want to talk to him. I stomp on the gas pedal, and the engine roars—

And then there's a terrific *whoompf* as something inside the car breaks. The world smells like smoke. The Buick squeals, that horrible noise, amplified a thousandfold—and everything goes silent.

My father stops, shaken, but not so much that he doesn't rally a second later and run up to the open window, which I didn't have time to close.

"Katrina," he says, just loud enough for me to hear.

There's something about the way he says it—the crisp pressure behind the *t*, the little flip in the *r*, the soft openness of the final vowel. The way he always makes my name four syllables and not three. It's my dad's accent, my dad's voice.

It's my dad.

I can't say anything. I can't even breathe. I collapse over the steering wheel and start to weep, heaving sobs that consume my whole world. I'm only vaguely aware of him reaching in and gently extracting the keys from the ignition. Of him trying to open the door—he can't, *he can't*, it's glued shut—before he hits the unlock button instead.

He walks over to the passenger side. For once, the door opens on the first try. He slides in next to me, but I can't bring myself to look—what if it's like the Mirror-Man, but in reverse? What if I turn, and he's suddenly not there anymore?

What if he is, and he's still angry? Still disappointed?

And then he leans forward and gently encircles me with his arms, and I find I'm not the only one crying.

How long do we remain together, two bodies softly orbiting one another, the galaxy painted with our tears?

Long enough for the snow to cover the windshield, to go from melting to sticking as the glass cools.

Long enough for my spine to ache from being crunched over sideways, but I'm afraid to move. If I even let go to undo my seatbelt, that could end everything, and I am not ready.

I have so much to say—there are a thousand things passing through my head, a thousand crimes I want to call out, to demand justice and punishment and contrition, but *oh*, once I do that, it will hurt. It will hurt *so much*. It will hurt more than enough for both of my worlds, more than I can bear, and as long as we sit here, like this, cloaked by the quiet after the car's roar—I won't have to feel that hurt. I won't have to drive a wedge between myself and my father.

In this way, I am weak—but there's another way, too, because there's a part of me that wishes I could just let it go but knows I can't. I am the woman who can't let anything go—not Kurt's death, not the number eleven, not a children's book, not the meaning of a postcard. My entire life is hanging on.

Two kinds of weakness, and both bring only pain. As long as I sit here, holding on to my father, I can keep them both at bay.

It's the arrival of my mother that breaks the spell—not on a majestic steed or a sailing ship, as would befit the moment, but in a beat-up minivan, the lower half covered in bubbling paint that can only mean sloughing flakes of rust.

I'm surprised—by the car, which my parents have had forever—but also by the state of it. They always got their oil changed before the sticker date and fixed every crack and ding immediately. They were so invested in and prideful of the care they gave their things. It isn't like them to let a problem get so bad.

Or maybe I'm just focusing on it because I don't want to meet anyone's gaze. See something the wrong way, and bad things can happen. Sometimes it's so much better not to look.

When my mother pulls her minivan up alongside my car, my father gets out, clinging to my seatbelt, his hand the last part of him to exit, as if he's afraid that in the brief moment he lets go, I might flutter away—though that could just be my own fear, whispering in my ear.

"Her door is glued shut," he says, although I didn't tell him that and am not sure how he knows. "Her car just died in front of me."

"I don't care," says my mom. At first, I'm angry—but then she shoves him out of the way and bolts into the car herself. She clings to me so hard I can't breathe, so hard her fingers tear into my skin like a forest of terrible, grasping trees, desperate for my flesh.

And I let her. I'd let her consume me, if she wanted, right down to the bone, because the next words out of her mouth are ones I never thought I'd hear again. "Let's go home," she says, repeating it over and over as if it were a ritual, breathless as a prayer. "Let's go home."

I try to hold on to my anger, my rejection, my fear, but it's like the door that leads back to Mi-Hee's kitchen: let it out of your sight, and it's gone.

Let's go home.

CHAPTER 20

The Prodigal Returneth

We take my mother's minivan, of course. And I have to ride in the back, like I'm fourteen and not twenty-four, and every few seconds, she glances in the rearview, as if to make sure I'm still there.

I know my mother well enough to notice that her knuckles are white and her jaw is tense, and while neither of my parents are particularly talkative people, there's a new weight to this silence, the clinging heft of melting snow.

I try to focus on the differences between the last time I saw my parents and now. I am older. There's a spot on the apex of my dad's head that looks like it's balding. My mom has gotten a perm and a dye job. The car is deteriorating.

But my JanSport bag, my purse, and the kitty trash bag are all at my feet. My father insisted on helping me load them in, a well-worn ritual, as if nothing has changed, as if there had never been a night on their porch where the sleet was falling down around me, a night when he had shut their door in my face.

And the truth is that although I should be angry, there's nothing inside me but hurt. Three years of hurt, balled up and worried at, reinforced and tasted. How could they just cut me out of their life? Why did they wait until I showed up at the school?

They had my address this whole time. They could've called. Could've come.

Could've sent a postcard.

Pleasance Village is as tiny as its name implies, but it's been expanding over the last twenty years, pockets of people happy to exchange the traffic and prices of Springfield for a half-hour highway commute and well-regarded schools. A rash of businesses have taken advantage of the open land to set up shop: a brewery, a pharmaceuticals factory, a medical research facility.

With new businesses came new workers. With new workers came two cafés, a corner store, and a small grocery. Four new restaurants to fill in the holes that the preexisting burger joint, diner, and seasonal ice cream stand couldn't—and the more Pleasance expanded, the more people thought about moving in, until the village finally had to own up to the problem that's plagued it all along: it's never had quite enough housing.

Most of the rich people live outside of the village limits on huge lots in new construction, though some prefer once-farmhouses renovated at great expense. They were working on clearing land for a subdivision when I left, hundreds of acres of old forest and pristine grassland bulldozed for shiny new homes. There was a sign next to the planned site that raved about the forthcoming plots for purchase, though they all had the same three floor plans with four bedrooms and two and a half baths.

If you live in Pleasance, but you are not a rich person, or even a solidly middle-class person, you are likely *from* here—as from as you can be without being Native American—in which case, you also live in a farmhouse on a big plot of land, though there's a good chance actual farming is involved. If not, you probably live in one of the handful of small historic homes in the three blocks that form the minuscule downtown. I say historic, because they're all at least a hundred years old, but no mind is ever paid to that around here, not when half the houses are falling apart, although there's a sort of subtle charm in the thumbnail-sized lots and the odd configurations that result from a century of successive homeowners pasting on this room and that.

Or at least, there used to be. Looking at them now, they seem worse—like the entire world of my childhood has cracked, rusted, rotted, or faded. And as I notice that, I start to worry about my parents' house, the little saltbox with hunter-green plastic decorative shutters that cannot close, white vinyl siding that covers up any character it might've once had—though a careful eye could always spot the foundation. Fieldstone in this part, brick in that, and poured concrete under the newest bit, the kitchen.

I hold my breath as it comes into view in the distance, thinking of all the times I played in that yard while my mother scrubbed the shutters with vinegar and dish soap to get them clean. The times I rode my bike down the road to the library with an empty backpack, making mental lists of the books I was going to check out and haul back.

My parents were always proud of their little house, but when it comes into view, my stomach sinks. I barely recognize it. There are cheap plastic kids' toys everywhere, buried in drifts of snow and woody clumps of dead weeds. They've put up an eyesore of a fence—chicken wire over square wooden posts—and a hound runs howling back and forth as we approach. My mother's garden, with its brown stems left over from when her purple doraji flowers slumber for the winter, is nowhere in sight.

But my mother doesn't even slow, and when I glance forward, they're both sitting there, their postures perfectly straight. For once, my mother doesn't look in the rearview mirror.

We do stop before leaving the village, but just barely. We pull into the Pines on Front—what used to be Pleasance's only apartment complex, though they've surely built new ones by now. The Pines is short and squat and ugly, with paint that can't decide if it's gray or brown.

I don't understand what we're doing here, but then my mom parks, and both my parents get out. My father walks around to the side door and hauls it open, as if I'm a package about to be delivered.

My fingers feel numb. My face feels numb. I get out.

My mother turns and looks at my father. Her expression contorts— pain, real pain, and that alone is enough to make my head go dizzy. I've seen more emotion out of my parents in the last hour than in my entire life.

My father takes her by both shoulders. "I'm sorry," he says in Korean, one of the only phrases I know.

She nods slightly, and then he turns and gets my things out of the car, and I follow them into this strange apartment, this place where my parents must live.

I don't understand how any of this happened.

It's cramped inside, with carpeted floor, which I know my mother hates, because she says you can't ever know if it's really clean. To my left is a tiny kitchen, barely the size of my car, so narrow two people can't stand side by side, though there's a glass door that leads onto a small patio. To my right is a living room. I see no dining room, but there are two doors in the back—I'm guessing bedroom and bathroom.

This is their entire space. It's almost as small as my place in Grand Station.

I've heard of couples downsizing when their children leave, but my parents *loved* being homeowners. It was their favorite part of America, the way a once waitress mother and a band teacher father could somehow buy land. I can't believe they'd give it up, especially for a splotched ceiling and stained greige carpet.

My father sets my things on the table—all except my purse, which he gives to me before gesturing at the love seat. This, at least, is familiar—a piece of furniture from my childhood. But when I look around the room, it feels off, like someone else wearing my clothes, all the things I know, but in the wrong place, with the wrong proportions, so that they fill the room to bursting. I find the giant framed embroidery of a tiger they brought from Korea; it dominates the room now, instead of holding balanced space with the paintings of horses and mountains and magpies, the walls and walls of framed photos.

They still have the pine table, which is wedged up against the wall near the kitchen, though there are only two chairs, and they're both the metal folding kind, stowed away to save space. The love seats are here, but not the couch. It wouldn't fit, anyways.

Looking around this room, I get the feeling it's been ransacked. "What's going on?" I say it once, and when nobody answers, I ask again, a different way. "Didn't you like the house?"

My parents exchange a long look. I've never seen my father like this, his head hung like a bad dog's. And my mother is a small woman who's always felt big, only now, it's like she shrinks back into the shadows, like it's hard to spot her at all.

"Maybe we should go out on the patio." My father pulls a white package of cigarettes from his pocket, which makes no sense. He doesn't smoke.

"Yes," my mother says. "There's more room out there. Take a towel. I will make everybody a plate."

Even with the patio set, it's ludicrous to be out here—it's cold, and every surface is wet. My dad knocks the snow off the table and chairs and raises the umbrella before drying everything carefully with the towel, which he leaves balled up by the sliding door.

My mother comes out a moment later with a propane heater. She turns the button to light it and leaves it right next to me before disappearing again, and I suddenly don't feel so cold.

My father sits across from me before seemingly remembering his cigarette. "Do you mind?"

I shake my head. I don't know how to tell him I do.

He must pick up on it, though, because he creeps over to the far corner of the patio and checks the wind before lighting up. He takes a long drag, the tension falling away from him like the snow he just dislodged from the table.

After a moment, our gazes meet. I'm surprised by what I find in his eyes, because it's a feeling I know well: my dad is *ashamed*. I've often made that expression in the mirror; it's so strange to see it on his face.

My mom reemerges a second later, three plates balanced on her arm like the waitress she once was. She quit when I was born, but she can still balance almost anything.

She sets one down in front of each of us. A portion of rice, some tofu with green onions and soy sauce ladled on top. A side of gimchi, a small green salad, and a perfectly assembled gyeran-mari—a Korean rolled omelet, studded with small squares of mushroom and carrot, spiraled around a sheet of black seaweed.

"I don't eat eggs," I say, swallowing hard. My parents were

never okay with my decision to go vegan, were always so afraid I'd shrivel away without meat. I don't usually miss animal foods, but something about the tight, flattened pinwheels on the plate makes my mouth water.

"It's not eggs," she says, before miming pouring a bottle. "It's the egg thing—" She bites her lips together, the way she does when she can't remember the word she wants, and says something rapidly to my dad in Korean.

"Mung bean," he says. "It's mung bean. The JUST Egg stuff."

I blink. "How did you know I was coming?"

My mother's face crumples, but she recovers admirably. "We didn't know," she says, clearing her throat. "We hoped. We always have a fresh bottle, just in case."

I look down at the plate and try to understand. It's like the words— the *words* are working, but put them all together, and they repel the same as the like poles of magnets.

I've never been able to buy mung bean egg replacer with an expiration date further out than a month, and my mother would *never* serve anything expired. Which means they've made sure to have at least one new bottle, on hand, every month, for three years.

Thirty-six bottles of egg replacer.

I'm suddenly so livid, I can barely see. I can't control myself—one moment, I'm staring down at the plate, the rice, the gimchi, the not-eggs, and the next, I'm on my feet, and food is flying across the table, and I'm screaming at my mother for the first time in my life. "You didn't have to do this! You could've just replied to one of my letters! You could've just called! Don't you understand how hard it's been? How badly I wanted to hear from you? I just—"

My legs give out. I plop down in my seat and bury my face in my hands, and then I cry like I did over the steering wheel, an unending howl.

My parents don't move. They don't say anything. They let me cry and cry, and I'm sure I look ridiculous, like I've completely lost my mind, but I don't know what else to do with my grief.

It's my mother who finally leans over the table and puts her hand on mine—tentatively at first, but then firmer. She picks up my chin with her other hand—and I want to rip away from her touch, this woman who let me down when I needed her most, but I'm just not strong enough.

"Katrina," she says, four syllables, always four syllables. "Didn't your girlfriend tell you?"

And the question is so ludicrous, it breaks my brain. I sit there quietly, like a tantrum-throwing child distracted by some keys. "What?"

My parents exchange a glance—and this time, there is a flush in their cheeks, as if they've been drinking, but it's my father's turn to speak. "We *did* come," he says, his voice very low, and very firm. "A few days—no, maybe a week after you left. We tried to call you, but we couldn't get ahold of you."

I swallow, trying to remember. "I think my phone was shut off right around then."

His eyebrows go up, the way they do when he's concerned. "We got your address by calling one of your old friends in college, that girl—"

He glances over at my mother, who immediately supplies the name; I've always been in awe of the way they share a brain, each filling in for the other's deficits. "Kelsey."

My father nods. "Yes, Kelsey. She was the only one who had your new address."

I sniff. *Kelsey.* That's right. She was my RA in college and took pity on me. After I moved to Grand Station, she texted me, letting me know that she'd saved some of my things before the eviction and put them in a box. That she'd mail them to me if I gave her the address. "You called Kelsey?"

"Yes," my father says. "And when she told us you were in Grand Station, we got in the car, and we knocked on your door, but your girl-friend was the one who answered. She said that you were… that you were *unstable*, that you were in a hospital and weren't allowed to talk to anyone, even us." He reaches for my mother's hand, his voice qua-vering. "And she didn't know which hospital, but she took our number and our new address, and she said she'd call us as soon as she found out. And we waited and waited, and we called every hospital we could find in Grand Station, every hospital in the state, but everybody either confirmed you weren't a patient or said they couldn't discuss your personal information without your consent."

He's shaking, now. My father is shaking like a leaf. "And then your girlfriend called us a week later and told us that you were out of the hospital but were too angry to talk to us. That you needed some space, and that you were moving to Korea to teach English and learn about your roots. I told her that wasn't possible—it takes time to line up a teaching job, and you didn't even have a passport, but she said you'd been planning it for a long time, that it was why you left school. She even sent us a photo." He turns to my mother and says something, rapid fire, but I catch "sajin," which means "picture."

She jumps up and runs into the apartment. A moment later, she is back with a glossy photo, holding it by the very edges, like it's a CD.

I've seen this photo before. I have its duplicate. Me, walking through a crosswalk, the Korean signs all around.

So that's what Leoni was doing with it.

"It's a fake," I say, though it's hard to breathe.

My mother turns and says something to my father, and this time, her voice is *sharp.*

"Ah," he says gingerly. "Your mom thought so when we first got it.

I convinced her it wasn't." He hangs his head. "We called the embassy, our relatives in Korea. We had people looking for you. We used the last of our savings to fly there ourselves."

I furrow my brows. Half of what he said floats by me, as I get stuck on the end of his sentence. "The *last*? What do you mean, the last?" My parents have been meticulous savers their entire lives. It's one reason I didn't have a car in high school, even though we probably could've afforded some old beater.

"Ah." I can tell my father's struggling to speak. "We are here, then. It is time."

He takes my hands. This close, I can smell the cigarette on him. For an odd, hanging moment, I have the feeling that this man in front of me, he's my father, but he's not my *dad*, the man I grew up with— that he, too, is some kind of analogue, and my real father is at the grocery store right now or mowing his *real* lawn at his real house.

But if he is fake, and I am here, then what am I?

"The night that you came over, we were packing."

"To move here," I say, waving at the apartment behind me.

"Yes." He glances at my mother and sighs. "We lost our house."

"You *lost*—"

"There was a scandal," my mother breaks in—because between the two of them, she's always been the stronger one, the one able to deliver bad news. "A big financial scandal. We invested our savings with this company, and they embej . . . embej . . . they stole it all away."

It's like a noose around my neck, the word *PROSPER* written down the side. "Briar Stone Ventures."

She nods. "Yes. We lost everything. And—" She glances at my father.

He pats her hand. "Katrina—the day that you came, we were furiously packing, because we'd already received notice that they'd foreclosed on the house, and it'd taken us so long to get the apartment because of the foreclosure. They'd only let us rent here if we paid the entire year, up front, in cash. It was terrible. And in the middle of all of that, your mother discovered a lump."

My mouth goes dry. Even though I know she's okay, even though she's sitting in front of me, and her cheeks are pink and her plate is half empty, it's like death itself has reached in and touched my organs, has turned them all to stone. "You have cancer?"

She tilts her head to the side, chiding. "Cancer-free, two years now." And then she pats the back of her bun with one hand, as if she's just gotten her hair done and is showing off. "Hair is curly now, though."

I sag in my chair.

On top of the table, my dad clenches his hands into fists. "We were ashamed, Katrina. Of losing our house. We didn't know what to tell you, what to do. And I was so afraid your *mother*—"

He closes his eyes and swallows, and his next sentence is prim, almost formal. "I was very worried about her. And then you came, and you were so upset, because we couldn't pay what was left of your tuition—I was going to borrow the money, but everybody else had been taken in by them, too. Nobody had anything to give."

My mother pats his back, urging him to finish.

"I was weak. I'm so sorry, I was weak. Do you understand, though? It was just a few days. Just a few days when I was not a strong man, when I was not myself. And then nobody knew where you'd gone, and your girlfriend—" He crushes his forehead with the heel of one hand. His fingers are stained with nicotine. I don't know how I didn't see that before. "Your mother didn't even know you came. She was resting inside on the couch. And then we lost you for three years. We tried a private investigator, even, but after he spoke to your girlfriend, he said it wouldn't be possible to find you in another country without a lot more money than we could come up with."

I have to sit quietly for a long time. I draw stellations in my mind, trying to calm myself, but with each successive pass, everything turns tighter, like a string winding and winding around a nail. I'd assumed they'd been in agreement to send me away, because they always make their decisions together.

"You came to the apartment," I finally say.

"Yes," my parents say in unison, proving my point.

"Where you met my girlfriend. Who told you I'd left the country."

"Yes," they say again.

"If all this is true—then what about the insurance stickers? Why keep paying for the car? You didn't even know where it was."

My father hugs himself. There's so much sorrow in his face that when he speaks, my own throat catches. "We were hoping your girlfriend had lied. That you hated us for not taking you in, for letting you get kicked out of school. That you just didn't want to tell us where you were. We hoped that if you were still here, that you had mail forwarding, because then you'd get the stickers, and even though you didn't answer our letters or our voice mails, you'd still know we wanted you to be safe. That you could have the car. That we still loved you."

The car. The car I slept in. The car that took me to work.

The car that brought me back here.

I can almost feel the texture of the tags under my fingers—sticker after sticker, stacked up so high they became a mountain against the smooth metal of the license plate. My parents' last hope. My parents' love.

All at once, my sadness burns itself out, and in its place, there's so much rage I can't see, so much rage I have to close my eyes and force myself to breathe.

I already know the answer to the question I'm about to ask—because there's only one woman who's been in the middle of this, one woman who's been manipulating me all along, who's connected to every point of this mess.

But even so, rituals need to be completed. I can't stand here on the threshold of knowing something I haven't confirmed. "I didn't have a girlfriend," I say, my voice quavering with righteous anger. "I never knew you came."

My parents gasp and grab for each other's hands—as if we're in a falling elevator, in a car about to crash.

"So tell me: What did this woman look like?"

CHAPTER 21

Right Under Your Noses

The woman my mother describes is Leoni, because of course it is, and I have no idea *why* she kept us apart. My parents can only help me answer that question if I tell them the truth about everything. I'm not sure if I can.

It's getting dark, and despite the heater, none of us can stop shaking. Do I suggest going inside, or do they?

Does it even matter?

There are only two love seats, so my father pushes them against the wall while my mother pulls a small, square table out of the closet, unfolding its legs so they snap into place. When she sets it on the floor, it barely reaches my shins, though I remember it being so much taller, remember running into its sharp corners as I chased my toys.

She makes green tea and pours us all cups, and even though it'll make it hard to sleep, I accept one and warm my hands on it, trying to figure out how to explain what happened, how to tell them this story. It tastes bitter, not like what I normally drink—not mint and berries and gallons of sugar—but with each sip, it strips the sludge from my tongue, like steaming off old wallpaper.

Telling them my story is difficult, but I find a way. It helps that I have props: the postcards, the phone, the laptop. I don't take them out, not yet, but I put my hand into my purse and feel their edges under my fingers, a magic as sure and strong as the Cayatoga.

The whole time, I observe my parents carefully: watch as their faces pale, watch them grab each other's hands. It can't be easy to hear that your daughter has spent the last three years giving free rein to her obsessions and compulsions, that she's been following a man around at work, a man who killed himself right in front of her.

Harder still, to hear that someone has been spying on her apartment—and that everything she's been going through is somehow twisted up with the same company that cost you your life's savings.

But the hardest part of all must be hearing that for three years, she was within reach, if you only knew where to look. That while you called hospitals and cried at night and rehashed old fights and wondered if you ever really were a good parent, your daughter was right there, like a sewing needle you dropped in the carpet.

When I'm done, my father looks haggard, as if he's aged ten years. My mother could be made of brass for how little she moves. I wonder at the hurt in this room—if the walls of this sad place could ever contain it, if they will be indelibly marked by our collective grief.

My mother says Koreans have a word for a special kind of grief—han. Han is more than sadness: it's the aching loss of generations; the righteous, enduring anger of the once-occupied; the desperate yearning and unfathomable sorrow of a people who have had their families decimated and fractured by war.

Han is also uniquely tangible, like a stone on your chest, one that imprints itself so strongly it can be passed from parent to child, so enduring it can lodge itself into soil or brick or bone. It's han that's supposed to turn people into ghosts.

I've sometimes wondered if I'm really Korean, but now I believe it, because for the first time, I can taste this feeling, this han, and I know that although we've found each other again, this pain will never fully leave. At every argument, every unreturned call, we'll feel a flash of fear and worry that this is the start of another year, or three years, or forever, that we will never hear from our loved ones again.

We've been scarred, and it's all Leoni's fault.

My mother holds her fist to her chest. Tightly, as if guarding a jewel. "Katrina. Can we—can we see them? The cards and the—the other things?" A very "my mother" thing to ask: *show me.*

I lay everything out. My parents take turns poring over the clues I've collected. It feels so good to have access to fresh eyes, to not be carrying around this secret alone. For the first time in a long time, I feel settled in my world, though I know it won't last.

My father speaks first. "Leoni." Words that start with *L*s are particularly hard for him to pronounce—not so much that it slows him down, but they're one of the only sounds he consistently gets wrong. He always exerts maximal effort, trying to pronounce them perfectly, but now, he's glossed over Leoni's name, too wrapped up in thought to care.

It makes me happy to hear this mistake, as if it somehow robs the name of its power. As if, in my father's mouth, a name is just a name.

He stands up and ducks into the bedroom. When he emerges, he's flipping through a slim volume, muttering to himself. "Okay, yes. Harriet Piot…" He turns the book toward me and shows me the name, taps it with a finger, and I understand why it was so hard for him to pronounce.

I say it for him. "Piotrowicz."

He nods, looking sad. "That's who won the sixth annual band festival."

The back of my neck tingles, but I'm so close to solving this mystery. The "Harry" in that terrible message Kurt left on his bathroom wall—it must've been short for "Harriet." It must have been *her* key chain in Kurt's things.

Even though I know my parents spoke with Leoni, I ask, "Could Harriet be the woman you saw when you came to my apartment?"

He shakes his head before taking a sip of his tea. "No, Katrina."

I almost cry out. "Why not? You can change the way your face looks with contouring and makeup, and there's surgery, color contacts—"

"She's dead." He puts his cup down and rubs his face with his other hand. "She died right after she graduated. Drank too much at a college party on the beach and drowned. We had a memorial for her at the school. But there were invitations sent out and an announcement in the paper, and it was always with her full name. Harriet *Leoni* Piotro-wicz. It's a middle name, so I forgot."

I nod absently. I get what he means—Koreans don't use middle names. It's why I don't have one. My dad is terrible with names, and middle names he just ignores.

Something shimmers on the surface of my awareness like a water strider, but I can't quite grasp it, not yet.

"But here's the strange thing." He picks through the cards until he finds the one with the man in the suit, standing in front of the crashed car. "This photo is very grainy, but I think this is Mr. Fredericks. Her *dad*. He was a teacher here, but he left right after she died—and I think he was in a car accident right about then, too. I heard that he spent a long time in the hospital, and he never came back to school after that. Retired early."

My mouth goes dry. "Her *dad*? But the last names—"

He nods. "Stepdaughter." He glances at my mother. "I never thought about it. Koreans don't change their name, even when they get married. You can't just change your family."

Normally, I'd resent that—the way sometimes they talk about Koreans as "we," and sometimes as "Koreans," as if my membership in the group comes and goes—but the flash of irritation gets pushed aside, because I'm still scrambling with the postcards. If Harriet is dead, if her stepfather was Mr. Fredericks—then who is Leoni? Why did Leoni take Harriet's middle name?

I close my eyes and try to think. "Did Mr. Fredericks have any other children?"

My dad shrugs. "Maybe? If I taught a different subject, I'd be more sure—but I only know the kids who come through the band program, and I didn't know Mr. Fredericks very well. He was a lot older than me, and like I said, he retired not too long after I started. I don't think Harriet mentioned anybody, but she was a really quiet kid, and it's been years, now."

"What did he teach?"

"Computers—"

I don't hear the rest, because all at once, the thought I couldn't reach, it snaps like a rubber band: Harriet *drowned*. I sort through the postcards until I find the one of the girl lying in the water with the Xs over her eyes, the one with the terrible poem. "Is this her? Harriet, I mean."

My father picks up the card and stares at it for a long time. "It's hard to say, with the eyes crossed out like that, and I'm not good at hair." He rubs his thumb and first finger together. "Maybe. It could be—but I can't say for sure."

"Do you have Mr. Fredericks's phone number?"

He exchanges a glance with my mother, and they have another rapid-fire conversation in Korean. Most of the time, I don't mind it, because it's to help my mom with English words—but it feels like they're deliberately keeping something from me.

"Katrina," my dad says, his voice low. "If everything is like you say—don't you think we should go to the police? People have been watching you, threatening you." His face looks haggard, with wrinkles

I didn't notice before. Age? His new smoking habit? Or just the worry that his daughter might never come back?

My stomach clenches. He's right; there's enough evidence now that the police might actually do something—but I'm so close. What if they seal off the details of the investigation, and I never find out what happened?

I've come this far. I watched Kurt die, discovered he was the Mirror-Man, that both he and Leoni really were watching me. But until I know *exactly* what happened, I'm in an in-between state, a threshold, an unsafe place.

I can't live the rest of my life on the edge like that. It might kill me. I might kill *myself.* "The man who wrote that message is dead, Dad. I know this sounds crazy, but I just need a few more days. Please. You have to trust me." "Trust" is the wrong word, but it's the best I've got.

My parents look at each other, the same way they always have, because they've always been a perfect unit, like those documentaries about clown fish and anemones. My father says something, but my mother shakes her head. "I don't care," she says, switching to English. "You hear me? I don't care. I will not lose her again."

My parents never talk about the past—unless you get my dad drunk, which is how I know that once, when my mother was young, she led a student protest in Seoul against government corruption. And although he wouldn't get into the details, I know it wasn't peaceful. Molotov cocktails and tear gas were involved. A lot of people were beaten half to death. The police broke two of the fingers on my mom's right hand, and sometimes, they ache when it rains.

She turns toward me, and for the first time since I came home, I see her burn with some of her old fire.

"I will make you a deal. We are worried for your safety. We want to know what you're doing, where you're going. We won't stop you, but you have to promise us you will be careful. You don't do dangerous things. You stay in contact with us the whole time. In exchange, we will help you contact Mr. Fredericks, and depending on what he says, we decide *together* if we should call the police. Do we have a deal?"

She says it just like that, the way she used to when we were playing Monopoly and she was making an offer on Park Place. *Do we have a deal?*

What else can I say?

"Deal."

Mr. Fredericks picks up on the very first ring. I can only overhear my father's half of the conversation, his statement that I want to talk about Harriet—but every so often, he interrupts with, "What? Come again?" After a moment, he pulls the phone away from his face.

"The call dropped," he says apologetically. "Bad reception. Let me try again."

Before he does, his phone lights up in his hand. "It's a text message from Mr. Fredericks." He passes it over.

I'm fishing at my cabin. I was planning on heading home tomorrow morning, as I've got some important errands to run. If you want, I can call you as soon as I get in, and we can figure out a place to meet. It's always nice to see an old student.

"Oh," I say, confused. "But I wasn't his student."

"I don't think he could hear me. The connection was really, really bad." He looks up at my mom, and then back at me, and the barest impression of a smile sneaks onto his face. "Maybe you should stay here tonight. We have an air mattress, or you can take our bed."

I look around the room. At first, I can't imagine sleeping here. It's worse than my apartment, and it feels like sadness.

But then I close my eyes and slip into the kitchen-door world. My mother gasps—I told them about this thing I do, and I'm sure they've been looking for signs of it.

I'm standing on a mountain, a pine forest blooming around me. I can see far, far into the valley below, though surrounding everything at the bottom is a terrible barrier of thorns. I know that down there, the trees have leering faces, their expressions so hateful that just thinking of them makes it hard to breathe.

But then I look over, and there are my parents. Shining and regal, a magpie king and queen. Releasing feathered messengers into the air, once a year, desperate to keep me safe.

I blink, and I'm here again, their drawn faces staring at me, afraid of what I might say next.

"I'd love to stay," I say, and they take each other's hands.

I don't think I can sleep. I've never been able to relax fully in an unfamiliar place, as if every creak and groan, every pocket of cold air, suddenly gets amplified, until it's all I can do to lie there quietly. And there's too much to turn over in my mind. It feels like I'm floating on rapids, being tossed in every direction as I get sprayed by white foam.

But my parents aren't sleeping, either. I can hear snatches of conversation I don't understand, murmurs of Korean. I close my eyes and listen to the sound, the way their intonations are so distinct—my parents are from different provinces, which is one reason my dad's inflections, though deep, always *feel* lighter, whereas my mother's tones are always falling, landing hard at the end of each sentence. When they have a conversation like this, fast and furious, it feels like music, like the contrapuntal dance of the second Brandenburg concerto. Each new voice, each reiteration, is familiar, and yet shockingly different.

It makes me feel safe. And although I don't know if it happens early or late, if we're in the day I arrived or the one that follows, I drift off to their music.

I awaken like I've been submerged, breaking the surface and gasping.

My mother is by my side at once: holding me, murmuring. She smells like food, like onions and garlic, like soap and laundry softener and like *my mother*, and I can suddenly breathe.

"It's okay," she says, alternating between English and Korean, as if trying to make sure I'll understand no matter what. *It's okay, gwaenchana, it's okay.*

My bearings are slow to arrive. I am in their apartment. There's food cooking. The sun says it's morning. I have my dad's cell phone in my hand—at some point during the night, I must have pulled it too hard and unplugged it, because the battery is mostly dead.

I plug it back in. "Where's Dad?"

My mom takes a long look at me, as if making sure I'm really here and really okay, and then she goes back to the stove to whisk the onions. They smell like they've started to burn. "I dropped him off at the school right after you fell asleep. He's been there all night with his tools, trying to fix your car."

I blink. "Dad doesn't know how to fix cars."

My mother laughs—bitter at first, but then something changes, and the room fills with her mirth. "Daddy *didn't* know how to fix cars. But after we lost all our money, we learned lots of new things." She holds the wooden spoon up, brown pieces of caramelized onion stuck to the rim. "I've never told him this, but he looks so handsome when he's all dirty with the rust and the grease. And he's not very *good* at fixing cars, but he's getting better. Like last year, he learned that if you don't"— she looks for a word she can't find, even glances around the room as if my father will suddenly appear, before giving up—"if you don't do a thing after fixing brakes, they don't work. He turned the car on, and it drove into the garage door. *Slowly*, though. Nobody noticed." And then she's laughing again.

And I have to admit, after a second, I'm laughing, too.

Mr. Fredericks hasn't called yet, though my mother tells me to be patient.

At seven thirteen in the morning, my father returns to the apartment, driving my car. I see him coming through the patio glass—and although I *think* I can also spot wisps of oddly colored smoke coming out of the engine, it's running, which I never thought it would do again.

He parks in a space by the patio and strolls in, and just like my mother and the glint in her eye, my father looks more like my father again—prouder, his posture straighter, despite the dark bags under his eyes. Seeing him like that, I want to break the car all over again, as many times as he needs.

"Okay," he says, before I can say anything. "I want you to understand—this car is *not* fixed. I did what I could to get it here, but it's probably going to take me a few more nights before it's safe to go anywhere in it. I need to get parts and rent some special tools. Once it's fixed, we should probably follow behind you for a while, just to make sure it doesn't die on you."

I nod, my chest tight. I'd been right to be so attached to the car. Seeing it now, it's just a pile of rust and oil—but one my father brought back to life. I don't even know what to say.

"Thank you."

He glances at my mother. "Did Mr. Fredericks call?"

She shakes her head and goes back to making what looks like a mung bean scramble. She pours in two entire bottles, enough to serve an army. I know they probably don't eat like this when I'm not here—especially given how expensive the egg replacer is—but it means something that they do it, right now, for me.

"Okay." He looks down at his clothes. "I need to shower. I called the school to see if I could take the day off—"

"But it's Saturday," I say, before I remember. "Oh. You're getting ready for the winter concert." There were always a few weekend days where the band had to meet to rehearse. I'd forgotten about those.

He nods. "They won't let me out, not for anything less than a war, but it's just a few hours. Your mother and I talked, and she's going to drop me off at work, and then she can take you if he calls before I get back, okay?"

He looks at me, nervous again, and I realize that if I told him it wasn't enough, he'd quit his job, right now, and it's such a huge, crushing burden that I almost sway under the weight of it. "That sounds great, Dad," I finally manage.

Both of my parents brighten. My father smiles and heads into the bathroom, and I hear the hiss and drum of the shower coming on. My mother serves me a plate of garden scramble, and it's good, so good, as if she's got access to a secret ingredient that I've never been quite able to figure out—although on second thought, it's probably just gimchi: salty, spicy pickled cabbage.

We eat, and she fills an old Greek yogurt container with scramble and rice for my dad. Before they leave, they stand in the door, suddenly small again, hand clasped in hand.

"Would you like to ride with us?" my dad asks meekly.

I understand then. They're afraid to let me out of their sight. And I want to go with them, I really do, but when I look down at the phone in my hand, the battery has trailed into the red.

My heart starts to beat. "This—this isn't charging."

My mother blinks at me, the non sequitur throwing her off—but then she realizes the problem. She walks across the room and flips the light switch closest to me. The lamp turns on, and a little lightning bolt appears on the battery indicator. "This outlet doesn't work if the switch is off," she says apologetically.

I bite my lip. "I didn't realize. The phone's almost dead—do you have a car charger?" There's one in my car, but it's the wrong size for their phone.

They look at each other. My father shakes his head.

I want to go with them, but I can't run the risk of missing Mr. Fredericks's call. "I'll wait here."

They exchange a brief volley of Korean, and then my mother runs to the refrigerator and pulls down an index card with a bunch of phone numbers on it, labeled in a mixture of English and Korean.

She takes a pen and circles the top one before giving it to me. "This is your dad's number at the school. If you have an emergency, you need to call it."

I frown. "Why can't I just call the other cell?"

My mom bites her lip. "We only have one phone. Your dad is always at the school, and when he's not, he's with me. We didn't see the need to keep both phones."

My stomach clenches. Maybe that's the truth—my dad has *always* despised cell phones, been vocal about how much he hates carrying one—but I can't help but think that money's the real reason. I glance down at the phone, unplugging it for a second, hoping against hope that the battery indicator has somehow magically filled, but it's still mostly dead. "I don't want to leave it. I can't miss this call, Mom."

She nods. "Then I will drop him off now. Stay here. Don't go anywhere. Okay? Whatever happens, we don't want you to go alone."

"Okay," I say, and then I hug them both.

My mother's only been gone a minute when the phone rings. I almost go running down the driveway to see if I can catch them on the street, but I answer the call instead. "Hello?"

"Hello," says a man's voice. It's soft and reminds me of when you cook beans too long, the way they get silky and fall apart. "I'm looking for Mr. Kim?"

My heart is pounding so hard I feel nauseated. "Is this Mr. Fredericks?"

A brief pause. "Oh! You must be Katrina. You wanted to speak with me?"

"Yes," I say, a bit too desperately, realizing too late that I am not prepared for this call. I don't have anything to take notes with. "I was hoping you might have some information for me. I've been looking into some strange occurrences at my workplace, and I think they might have something to do with your…"

Despite rehearsing it half the night, I can't manage to say the word "daughter."

"You think I did something at your workplace?" He sounds bewildered.

"No, sorry—I think the person who did it might be connected to you and your past. Is there any way we could meet? I could explain better."

I still can't find a pen; my mother's living room is, of course, perfectly clean. She even straightened my belongings sometime before I got up.

I might have one in my backpack. I pull the yearbook out to get a better view, before I realize Mr. Fredericks has been silent for a while.

"Sure," he finally says. "Let me give you my address."

That gives me pause. I don't want to go to a stranger's house, not even a former teacher my dad knows. "I'm so sorry to ask this, but is there somewhere public we can meet? Maybe that new café on Main?"

"Oh." He says it heavy, like the single syllable weighs a ton. "Your father didn't tell you?"

I swallow. "Tell me what?"

"I was in an accident. A bad one. I sustained a severe head injury."

"I'm sorry." I'm not sure how this relates, but it feels like the right thing to say.

"I'm blind. I can't drive anywhere. If you want to go to the café, you can come and pick me up, but I use a wheelchair, so you need a vehicle big enough to fit that. And we have to hurry—"

"I thought you were fishing." I blurt it out before I realize what I'm saying. I close my eyes and cringe, but it's too late.

"I can still fish," he says frostily.

"Of course. Please excuse me, that was really rude. And dumb." I'm so embarrassed, I could just die. I still have the yearbook in my other hand. I set it down—and it's only then that it hits me: Harriet's last name might be Piotrowicz, but if she had a stepsister, then that woman's last name might actually be "Fredericks."

I hold the phone to my ear with my shoulder as I flip through to the *F*s, and there it is: Lydia Fredericks. I pull her photo closer to my face.

It's Leoni, though I never would have recognized her. The colors are all wrong: her hair is long and black instead of short and bleached blond, her eyes blue instead of walnut brown. Her features aren't even the same—she's thin, so thin her cheekbones look completely different, her eyebrows bushy instead of the barely there arches she was always raising in my direction.

It's Leoni, though. I'm sure of it.

Mr. Fredericks just said something. I clear my throat. "Sorry, I didn't catch that last bit. Bad connection, I think."

"I'm texting you my address." He says it loudly and slowly this time, making up for a network issue that doesn't exist. "If you want to come by, you can. I'll be here for a little bit. I needed some supplies, so I stopped back into town—but I'm going to be leaving again soon."

"How soon?" I ask, checking the clock. My mother's only been gone a few minutes. The school isn't far, but it's far enough, and if she's hit any traffic or gotten stuck behind a tractor...

It almost hurts to breathe. I promised my parents that I'd wait, that I wouldn't go alone—but I can't lose this opportunity, not when I'm so close, not when I'm holding Leoni's—no, *Lydia's*—picture in my hand, when her father could give me the key to everything.

"Send me the address."

CHAPTER 22

And When the Postman Rings Again

I jot down a profusely apologetic note for my mother, detailing the conversation, the situation, and the address. I leave my clothes here, in the kitty trash bag, to prove I haven't left for good. Kurt's things won't all fit in my purse, so I dump the contents of my backpack on the table and split my clues between the two.

My GPS says the address isn't far—about ten minutes outside of town, somewhere on County Highway 55. I catch myself speeding before remembering my father's warning not to drive my car and the mechanic's admonition to play nice with the engine. If this car dies with me minutes away from answers, I'll likely die, too.

But when the GPS tells me I've arrived, there's nothing here: just a patch of farmland with a cornfield on one side of the road, the brown, snow-dusted stalks cropped about ten inches from the ground. The other side of the road is mowed closer, so that it's almost buried— likely soybeans—but there's no house.

My insides are shaking when I pull out my mother's cell phone and open it. The battery is back to the red danger zone, so I key Mr. Fredericks's number into my phone instead.

Mr. Fredericks answers immediately. "Hello?"

I'm so relieved I lean over the steering wheel. "Yes, this is Katrina? I drove out to the address you gave me, but there's no house—"

"Ah. You're using GPS?"

I nod, before realizing he can't see me. "Yes."

"It's not a problem—you're at the right address, you just have to keep going. Are you driving east or west?"

I'd forgotten this, this small-town direction bullshit. When all the distances are far and markers are sparse, everybody navigates with an innate understanding of the sun.

I never managed to get the hang of it. I flail for a moment, before realizing he can probably help me. "I'm on the side with the corn," I say. "The sun's mostly behind me?"

"Okay. Just keep driving straight. Before long, you'll see a little trail turn off to the left. Follow that, and there should be a house in the back."

"Thank you." I look down at my mother's phone in my other hand. "I was on another phone before, but it's mostly dead. Can I give you my number, just in case?"

"Sure."

I rattle it off. I hear clicking in the background. It takes me a moment before I place it as computer keys.

"Okay," he says. "One moment, and I'll recite it back to you."

Someone speaks in the background. *"Two-six—"*

The hair goes up on the back of my neck. "Is someone there?"

A pause. "What?"

"I heard a voice."

He chuckles, then, lighthearted and happy. "Oh, I'm sorry. That's Nellie."

I hear fabric shuffle and slide over the receiver—and then my phone number, spoken extra-fast, tinny and mechanical. "It's how I use a computer. I type things, and Nellie reads them back."

I'm not sure how many times I can utterly, completely embarrass myself in one day, but I'm nearing my all-time record. "I'm sorry."

"No problem," he says. "But I'd hurry. Think I'll be leaving soon."

"Okay," I say, hanging up, and then I pull forward, looking for any sign of his house.

I zing right by the entrance Mr. Fredericks called a "little trail," hidden by a clump of trees. It's in the middle of a looping stretch of road that starts and ends with two separate blind curves, and the narrow shoulder on both sides pitches almost immediately into a ditch.

There's nowhere to turn around—but I don't want to keep going and risk getting lost, not with the time quickly ticking away. I pull over and make a ten-point turn, praying the entire time that nobody barrels into me—and that my mother never finds out.

It's a gravel driveway, not a trail, and as soon as I turn onto it, I barely miss hitting a mailbox obscured by a long pine bough.

I inch around it and check the mailbox number—11513, which matches the address he gave me. As I creep down the driveway, it bends almost ninety degrees to the left. My skin tingles at how tight these trees are—no places for the light to flash through. This forest is mostly pine and spruce, and something tells me it's likely older than the downtown historic district, though that's probably just my imagination.

When the house comes into view, my stomach drops. It's dilapidated, even worse than my parents' apartment or their old house downtown. The siding's wood shingle is rotting in several places, the soffits punched through with holes. I imagine there's at least one family of bats hiding out in the rafters.

One of the front windows is broken, the insides covered with plastic, and from the way the screen door sags in the frame, I doubt it latches completely. The driveway's empty, but leading up to the front door, there's—it's not a ramp, exactly. It looks too rickety, too slopped together to be called a permanent structure.

In fact, when I'm right up to it, I realize it's just some boards nailed on top of a log. The angle is steep enough that I know it's not safe, especially for a blind person in a wheelchair. Leoni's rants over the phone have taught me at least that much—although, now that I think of it, if this is her father, why didn't she have this fixed?

Was she really even an occupational therapist? If not, where was she getting her money?

I swallow and grab the outer door. As I swing it open, the black screen flops out of the frame and drapes itself over my hand, making my skin crawl.

I knock.

"Come in. Door's open!" calls Mr. Fredericks.

I square my shoulders and turn the knob. The door swings in, revealing a shadowy room.

Mr. Fredericks is blind, I remind myself. *He probably doesn't need the lights.* I do, though. "It's a bit dark," I say, trying to sound casual.

"Oh!" He laughs. I hear something creak inside, the swish of wheels turning, like a bicycle. The overhead lights come on. They're dim, but combined with the illumination from the windows, I can see fine. The room that meets the eye is surprisingly cozy—a sofa in the middle with a glass coffee table. Rustic wood floors, like a log cabin.

Mr. Fredericks is in his wheelchair. He deftly backs up until he's on the other side of the coffee table. "Am I facing the right way?" he jokes, his voice infectiously warm.

"You're good enough," I say, happy to play along. "May I sit?"

"Please." He waves at the sofa.

I sit down in front of him, buoyed by his good humor, but my stomach is still twisting all the same. Looking at him now—the curve of his bald head, the prominent nose—I can tell it's the same man on Kurt's card, the suit-man with a crash dummy and a crushed car. And while Mr. Fredericks seems healthy enough, I can't help but feel sad at the state of his house, the rickety not-ramp.

"So," he says, breaking the silence. "What is it you wanted to talk about?"

I am not certain how to tell this story without the magic of my props. "Well," I start, foundering. "There's...a man at my job. He, um, jumped off a bridge."

Mr. Fredericks has kept his eyes closed this whole time, but his eyebrows still go up. "Oh," he says softly. "That's terrible."

"Yes. After he died, I came into possession of some postcards he made, a laptop, and a USB stick. And the thing is, your picture—it's on one of the postcards."

He frowns. "I don't know why—"

"—and the postcard also has a crashed car on it. And there was another thing...do you mind holding out your hand?"

He doesn't seem happy about it, but he does. I take the key chain I found in Kurt's box and place it in his palm. He rolls it around for a moment. "I'm sorry—what is this?"

"It's a key chain," I say, my heart pounding. "It was awarded to—" I swallow. "To Harriet. For winning the band festival."

His gasp is sharp, telling me I've reopened an old wound when I had no right. I pray he can forgive me, that both of my universes can forgive me, because I know I can't stop. "So, when I found this and the postcard, and my dad identified you, I knew I needed to speak with you. I can't explain, but I believe it's all linked together."

He's silent for a long moment. I feel compelled to glance at my phone and check the time. How is it possible that less than two min-utes have gone by since I set foot in this house?

He clears his throat. "I'm assuming from your tone that your father told you Harriet is dead."

I don't want to speak, but he won't see me nod. "Yes. He said she drowned at a party."

He scowls. "That's what the police said."

This feels wrong, this moment—like he should be crying, rending his clothes and tearing out his hair, but instead, he's almost perfectly calm, his voice emotionless, as if we were comparing gallon prices at Pleasance's two gas stations.

Instead, it's me who's biting my lip, me who's digging my finger-tips into my leg to keep my voice from shaking, because I can feel the answers waiting to well out like blood from a fresh cut. "Do you not agree with the police?"

"Harriet, she had this... stalker, I guess is what you'd call him."

Any other word wouldn't have hit as hard. For a moment, I smell smoke.

"I actually knew him. He was one of my students when he was a kid, and he came to me one day with a question about a simple pro-gram, one that would automatically scrape web pages for information. You have to understand that back in those days, that was really quite clever, so I sat down and helped him work through a solution. After that, he'd visit me all the time to ask programming questions. I taught him what I knew, but he surpassed me very quickly. He wound up leaving early for college on a scholarship, but he'd come home for the summers to see his folks. But his senior year, he got kicked out for hacking into the university database and changing test scores. That was all long before, though."

I swallow. Was Kurt the man Mr. Fredericks was describing? "What was his name?"

Mr. Fredericks sighs again, so big he shifts up and down in his chair. "William. William Coscarelli."

"William," I say, trying to fit the name to Kurt. I can't tell if it works.

"Yes. And my daughter Harriet, she went to college, and she had this part-time job as a receptionist at an accountant's office—"

"Briar Stone?"

His face hardens into steel. "No. This was years and years before those bastards. It was just some little CPA that did taxes and whatnot. Anyways, this man Bill—that was William—he was working there. He'd managed to convince them he'd be good at doing their books—"

"But what about his record?"

Mr. Fredericks shrugged. "Didn't have one. They kicked him out of school, but they didn't take it any farther. Knowing how good he was with computers, I wouldn't be surprised if he found something salacious on an administrator's laptop and convinced them it was in their interest to let it go. You have to remember—this was almost fifteen years ago. Not quite when you could hack a modem with a whistle, but security wasn't like it is now—though you'd be surprised how many really important companies are running insecure, decades-old software and technology."

He rubs his chin, lost in thought. I glance around the room, taking in more details. There's something strange, an absence that throws me, but it's not until I'm staring at the blank space next to the window that I realize his walls are bare—no art, no photos. Makes sense, I guess.

From the front of the house comes a noisy series of *pops*. It takes me a second to place it as the crunch of gravel under car tires. "Are you expecting someone?"

"People use my driveway to turn around all the time." He lifts his hand and points at the door, as if either one of us can see through it.

"There's a little intersection right down there with a turn that's pretty much hidden by some trees. If you miss it, this is the first safe place to turn around—the shoulder's too narrow."

"Right," I say, hoping he didn't somehow hear my struggles in front of his house.

Mr. Fredericks clears his throat. "At some point, Bill took an interest in Harriet. It got so bad that she left that job, and still, he kept calling. She threatened to go to the police. The calls stopped, but she couldn't get over the feeling she was being watched. That's when she phoned me, and when she described him, I realized it was my old student. I don't know why he picked my daughter—if it was some deliberate father-figure situation, or just terrible luck. I felt guilty, but I called and told him I'd come down there and beat his ass myself if he didn't leave her alone. He apologized profusely."

His Adam's apple jumps. "I thought that was the end of it, but a week later, the police came to tell me that Harriet had drowned at a frat party. I knew it wasn't true—my daughter didn't drink, never lost control. But I didn't have any proof. When I convinced them to question Bill, he was gone. Every trace of him had been erased."

For a moment, I'm not in this cabin-like house in the woods, set back from the gravel driveway, a block past the long-cut fields of soy and corn. I'm Harriet in college, my emails showing up read, the feeling of eyes over my shoulder, afraid of the bathroom mirror—

I'm suddenly so, so glad he can't see my face, because I'm crying. It takes everything I have to cry silently, but I manage.

"A week later, I'm driving down the road, and my brakes give out. When I wake up, I'm blind. It takes months before I can get home, but when I do, my phone rings, and I pick it up, and it's Bill. And he says—" His voice cracks. "He calls my daughter a dyke. He says he hopes I learned my lesson. And then he hangs up, and I never hear from him again."

He turns toward me, and even though his eyes are closed and he can't see me, a chill travels down my spine. "If it *was* Bill who jumped off that bridge—well, I can't say I'm sorry he's dead. You know he killed her right before her birthday? That sick bastard deserved far worse."

"I'm sorry." I close my eyes. I can't think about that, because I'll start screaming. I try, too, not to think about flashes of light or stellations or smoke or the kitchen-door world. There's something he's said, some key, if only I could find it, something in the laptop, the USB, PostSecret and Better Secrets. "Is there a way to use a computer to hide something? Online? Like on a website?"

Mr. Fredericks dips his head down. "You mean like steganography?"

My throat catches as another piece slots into place. The program on the USB, *BUFFALO BILL'S OREGANO-STEGANO.* "What's that?"

"It's the science of hiding something secret inside of something public, like a coded message in a newspaper, or a series of symbols in a painting." As he speaks, his voice gets richer, faster, the old teacher in him warming up. "People have been doing it since the dawn of time: coded manuscripts, books, newspapers, art."

"What about computers?"

He shrugs. "Modern techniques involve hiding encrypted messages inside of other files. Computers can perceive subtle variations in color or sound that are indistinguishable to the naked eye, so one way to hide a message is to create some noise in an exact color or pitch that isn't used anywhere else in an image, sound file, or video. You won't necessarily be able to pick out those blocks with *your* senses, but to a computer, they're all little zeros and ones, on and off switches that can be used to store messages."

This is it. I know it is. I'm slowly starting to unravel my ex-coworker, from what he did to Mr. Fredericks to his treatment of poor Yocelyn, the fear in her voice. The creeping way he worked his way up from William Coscarelli, a kid who conned a small accounting office into taking him on as a bookkeeper, to Kurt Smith, a villain working on encrypted, homemade laptops who was in some way involved in the biggest financial scandal Grand Station, at least, had ever seen.

A narcissist who felt he was above the law. The kind of man who'd make a record of his exploits, put it on a public website where anybody could find it, if only they were smart enough to notice.

My skin feels cold, but my insides are electric. "Is there a way to check? For stegano…steganog…" I feel like my mom, trying to say "embezzled."

He nods. "There are some programs that check for patterns, though if the image is encrypted with a key or a pass-phrase, it won't mean anything without the key. Can I ask where this is all coming from?"

I pull the postcards out of my purse. "Kurt had a website called Better Secrets where he made scans of all these postcards. If I pull it up, can you try to see if one of the images has been altered like that?"

He nods again. "Follow me." He pushes his chair toward a room in the back.

I pause by the door. From the big medical bed in the middle, I'm guessing this is where he sleeps, and I'm not comfortable going in— but then I spy the desk on one side, the massive computer sitting on top. There are a number of boxy electronics around it, things I've never seen before.

He positions himself in front of the computer and wiggles the mouse to wake it up. He hits keys, navigating through a series of menus. The computer narrates what he's doing in a soft voice I can barely hear, the words so fast they blur together.

"What was the address of the website?"

I clear my throat. I've moved into the room, but there's nowhere to sit, so I pick the only spot that gives me a view of the computer and is sufficiently far from anything breakable, right in front of a closet door in the back of the room. Something about the door itself is off-putting—like some dimension of the crack underneath doesn't match the conformation of the room, as if it were a portal to somewhere else—but I know this feeling's just me, a manifestation of my discomfort being in his bedroom, my jumpiness from the earlier noise. "Better Secrets dot com."

He navigates to the website. "Which image?"

I scan through them. So many—and if I know Kurt, the order matters—but my mom will be getting home soon, and I'm sure the first thing she'll do when she reads my note is drive straight here.

I decide to start with the *PROSPER* card. "It's—the one with the noose…"

"Which number is the photo, counting from the top?"

"I can't see them all."

He hits a key and points at the keyboard. "It'll scroll with the arrow keys. Just push up and down."

I do as he says, keeping careful count. "The tenth one," I finally say. "And then the second one."

The second one down is the drowning girl. If there's something hidden here, he has a right to know.

He types a million words a minute, navigating through a series of menus with his keyboard, his computer's speech like the world's most pleasant robot auctioneer. He launches a program called Steghide and drops in the first photo. "I need a pass-phrase to try to decrypt it," he says. "Any guesses?"

It comes to me, easy as breathing. "Try Voynich."

"Like the manuscript?" He cocks his head, but he types it in. A moment later, the computer starts to read. *"Oh-oh-oh-six-one-two-nine-nine-four-six-seven-eight-four-five-period. Oh-oh-six—"*

He hits a button, and the computer is suddenly silent. "You've got the key, but it sounds like it's just numbers."

I swallow. It's account numbers—it has to be. Which means that if

Kurt—no, Bill—stole the money from Briar Stone, then maybe it's not really lost. "What about the other image?"

He taps a bunch of keys, and the computer starts to read again, this time from the picture of the drowning girl, a series of words so blisteringly fast, entire sentences happen before Mr. Fredericks can gasp, before he can lean forward and make it stop—

"I-was-the-best-thing-that-ever-happened-to-Harry-period-she deserved-what-she-got-period-it-felt-so-good-to-wrap-my-fingers-in-her-hair-and-hold-her-under-the water—"

And finally, finally, Mr. Fredericks gets the computer to stop, and then he leans forward and howls into his hands. Despite being proven right, I wonder if this is worth it. If it's worth what has to come next.

"Mr. Fredericks?"

He doesn't hear me. I don't know what to do, if I should approach him, try to hug him—but the idea of being so close, of touching this stranger...it makes me so anxious my chest hurts. And yet, I can't just back out of the room and leave him to his grief. Not when so much hangs in the balance.

I glance around, as if I'm going to find the answer written on one of the walls—and that's when I realize what bugged me about the door earlier. If it opened to a closet, it would've been completely dark underneath, but instead, there's a small sliver of natural light, as if from a window.

A bathroom, then. I can get him some tissues to blow his nose, maybe a drink of water. I grab the knob and look back—Mr. Fredericks is still crying—and then I give it a slow turn.

The hair goes up on the back of my neck, but I don't stop, because I don't trust my own instincts, because I don't yet understand. And then the door's open, and standing in the soft light of the window is Leoni, the lines of a walk-in glass shower glistening behind her.

For a moment, we're both shocked. We face each other, silent, waiting—but then she reaches into her purse. When she pulls her hand back out, she's gripping a small, silver revolver.

Before I can say anything, she holds a finger up to her mouth, the universal sign for *be quiet*, and waves the gun at the door.

I almost cry out, but there's something in her eyes, a hardness that confirms what I knew all along: that Leoni—no, *Lydia*—is a creature of vengeance and blood.

"Katrina." Mr. Fredericks stops crying, though his voice is thick. "I'm sorry you had to hear that."

I don't answer, because Lydia's still got a finger over her lips. She waves at the door again, the meaning crystal clear.

Get out.

Your old roommate steals out of a bathroom and points a gun at you. What do you do?

If you were a smarter person, a better person—the kind of person who never entered the kitchen-door world in the first place—you'd cry out and take your chances. Your roommate would shoot you and escape, and you'd bleed out on the floor while a confused Mr. Fredericks called the police.

But you aren't that person. You wanted to go to never-never land. You wanted to find out the identity of the Mirror-Man. You didn't stay home, even when your mother warned you, even though you promised. You don't have all the pieces yet—*so close, but not all of them*—because the biggest piece of all, the woman who lied to you for three years about who she is and what she wanted, is standing right in front of you, and she's waving a gun.

And so you leave Mr. Fredericks behind. You walk past the living room and out the front door, the barrel digging into your spine.

CHAPTER 23

You Can't Always Get What You Want

My vision swims as I make it onto the porch. There's a new vehicle in the driveway, a big white van that I'm sure is Mr. Fredericks's. Through the windshield, I spy a brown grocery bag filled with brightly colored Mylar packages of chips and pouches of beef jerky, the kind of snacks you might take on a fishing trip—and then it wavers, and the van disappears as the pine forest transforms into a tangle of enchanted thorns.

Leoni gestures her gun forward, and I start walking.

I knew she wasn't who she'd said. That she'd lied to me, that she was likely responsible for Kurt's death, that she was capable of violence—and yet, somehow I'm still surprised.

Maybe it's the fact that for so long, Leoni, *no, Lydia*—

For the first time, I wonder if changing a name really can change a person, if I would've been someone different with a middle name or a Korean name or a boy's name. If Leoni and Lydia *are* two different people, and the one I'd grown to love—the one who had cleaned the apartment and made sure the bills were paid and given me a soft place to land in the hardest months of my life—is the same woman as the one who has a gun trained on me now, who kept me from my family with an altered picture, the same woman who guided me away from Kurt and somehow prompted him to write my name in a threatening message on the wall—

It's only after the front door closes behind us that Lydia deigns to speak.

"You really screwed me here, Kat," she says, her voice strangely calm. "All you had to do was leave the bathroom door alone, get back in your car, and drive away. Why didn't you do that, Katrina? Why can't you ever leave *anything* alone?"

And even though I'm afraid of her gun, afraid of this moment, her criticism stings, because it's true. I really can't. "I don't know." My voice is high-pitched and yet somehow coarse, like I'm a kid who's been crying for hours. "I'm sorry."

"You're *sorry*." She scoffs. "Well, here's what's going to happen: You're going to take us for a little drive in your car. Once we reach our destination, you'll get in the trunk. As long as you don't do anything stupid, nobody gets hurt." Her voice softens, almost pleading. "I just need a few hours' head start, and then I'll call the police so they can come let you out, okay? Just a few hours. I don't think that's too much to ask."

"You can just leave me here. I won't do anything. I promise."

Her eyes narrow. "Can't risk it, Kat. One call to the police, *one call about Kurt*, and you'll blow a plan that's been a long time in the making. Now *go*."

I know from a thousand detective shows that you *never* leave with a kidnapper for a second location. My mother's certainly found the note I left for her by now. I have my dad's phone, so she may have driven back to the school to get my father—

But *oh*, my mother will arrive. *Here*. And if she sees Leoni with a gun, nothing will stop her. She'll do anything she can to protect me, and then Leoni will shoot her, just when she's beat cancer, just when I've got her back—

The forest of thorns around me gets sharper, denser. I see the snare of the Mirror-Man's dark magic, the curse that has woven its way so completely into my life, into my parents' life, into this moment. I cannot let Lydia take my parents. Cannot let her hurt my mother.

I walk over to my car. *Forgive me, Mom,* I think, as if my message will carry to her as surely as her yearly envelopes came to me.

"Not the passenger side. You're driving."

I shake my head, the movement making me feel even more like throwing up. "The driver's door doesn't work. It's glued shut. I have to go in this way."

She wants to argue, but then she nods, and I go in through the passenger side, before sliding over. The gun's in my face the whole time, and how I wish she would just *hurry the fuck up,* because my mother will be here any second—

"Unlock the doors."

I push the button. She gets into the back seat and presses the gun against the nape of my neck. "Now, pull forward, slowly. No funny business."

I turn the car on. I pull forward—not too slowly, though, not when every second brings my mother closer—until we're all the way down the driveway, and out onto the road.

Leoni directs me away from town.

It takes me a moment to work up the nerve to say anything. "Where are we going?"

Leoni jabs the gun into my neck, a warning against running my mouth—but I am the woman who walked through the kitchen door, the one who can't stop herself from jumping fences and breaking into places she doesn't belong.

I never had a chance. "Does your dad know what you're doing right now? That you kidnapped me?"

The pressure of the gun barrel lightens, but only for a second. Then, Leoni grabs my hair and yanks it so hard I cry out. The car swerves for a moment before I manage to right it, the road straightening out in the bottom of my vision, my head still tightly pinned by her fist.

"Don't. Fucking. Talk about him. I could've left him, and he would've been fine, but you just had to involve him and *fuck everything up.* You're lucky I don't just kill you now—do you understand how *royally* you've screwed me?"

It sounds familiar. It's not until she lets go of my hair, though, that I realize it's because the accusation reminds me of Kurt's final words on the bridge.

At least Mr. Fredericks is safe. I was so worried she would hurt him, and he's so helpless—

I suddenly remember the crunching gravel in the driveway, his easy explanation that it was someone turning around.

He must have been expecting her to come, but he'd kept that to himself.

Had he lied then? Or was she lying now? Either way, I feel like I'm going to throw up. But I've got to keep her talking. "Leoni, I—"

She digs the barrel in so hard I see stars. "I told you to shut up."

I wish I could. "I just—why are you doing this? Is this because of Harriet?"

She inhales sharply through her nose.

"Because Kurt killed her, I mean. He…he was a bad man," I say, and it's so ludicrous, such a complete understatement, that I almost start laughing.

It's the right thing to say, though, because the pressure of the gun barrel finally lightens. "Yes, he was."

I've got to ask. "Did you kill him?"

She inhales again, this time slowly. Not surprised, just bracing. "Does it matter?"

I glance in my rearview. She's not looking at me, not directly—her gaze is trained ahead, out the windshield, though she glances up briefly when she senses my attention.

Does it matter?

Before this moment, I don't know if anything in my life has ever mattered more. Finding out the answer to the mystery of Kurt's death has been the only thing I could think about, the only propulsion that gave my life meaning.

But it's too easy to see how alike Lydia, Kurt, and I really are. All three of us, thieves, burning like wax to fuel our obsessions, our dreams, our lies. Lydia could've been my own future, if I hadn't found my parents again. Now, I'll gladly drive this car to the bottom of the ocean if it means keeping them safe.

"I . . . I just need to know. I think you understand that," I say, intuition suddenly taking hold. My kitchen-door observations of Leoni were right all along. She was seeking justice. Even now, that's what she thinks she's doing—meting out punishments deserved. "After everything that's happened, I have a right to know."

I've only spent three years trailing Kurt around, only tasted the tip of obsession. But Leoni? Leoni gave up her entire *life*. It's perverse, but if anybody understands, it's her.

"You know what I don't get? If Kurt had the Briar Stone money, why not just leave? It'd be enough to hole up on a beach somewhere, right?"

She doesn't answer, but her breath is ragged. I need something else, something to push her over the edge. "If Kurt was this terrible guy, why couldn't you just tell me? I could've helped you—"

Her laugh is bitterly cold. "You? *You*, help me? Kat, have you *seen* yourself? You're fucking insane. You *see things* in our kitchen. You're a goddamn stalker. You can't even take out the *garbage* without fucking up."

I can't breathe. I can barely see. She's armed and literally kidnapping me, and *I'm* the crazy one? "Fine." I don't mean to snap at her, but I do. "Just tell me why you involved *me* in all this. Don't I deserve that?" I hazard a guess. "Advancex has surveillance. They know you were using my credentials, that you gave me all these system privileges—"

"That was Kurt, actually." She sighs, and when I glance in the rearview mirror, guilt twists on her face. "I mean, yes, I used them—but only after he hacked into them first."

"But why—"

"Don't you get it? Briar Stone was a pretty small investment firm, all things considered. Springfield only has a little over a hundred thousand people in it, and then you add the little outlying towns—it's not like he managed to drain every single account dry. Sure, he's a millionaire—but is that enough, long term, for the kind of lifestyle Kurt thought he deserved?"

The gun twitches. I tense, but I manage to keep driving straight.

"Do you have any idea how much more money he could've stolen from Advancex, how much cash flows through those hospital and insurance accounts? And they keep *such* shitty track of things, claims and payments bouncing around, being misapplied for months if not years. He just needed time and access to set up a little virus and let it run—and someone else to take the blame."

My stomach drops. *Me.* He was going to pin a multimillion-dollar theft on *me.*

"And you, you did this to yourself. You put in the craigslist ad that you were from Pleasance. I'd just figured out that he was working at Advancex. I thought you might even *be* him, because that's the kind of thing he liked to do, tease you right in the open. When I got to BinBash, and it was just you—I was disappointed, but then I realized this was an opportunity to get closer to him without being recognized. I could use *your* badge, track your phone and emails. I let myself in one evening about a year ago and slipped a mobile phone into his desk, because I knew, *knew* there was proof of what he was planning somewhere. I just needed to freak him out, so he'd make a mistake. I was so close to finding the account numbers—I knew as soon as Briar Stone happened that he'd had something to do with it." She shifts. "And maybe I wanted to fuck with him. He *deserved* to be fucked with."

I spot a deer on the side of the road and brace myself to take advantage of the confusion of it leaping out—but it turns and bolts back into the woods.

"But you had to fuck it up. I asked you about him *one time* in some photographs, *three years ago*, and then you found that tape, and just like that, you would *not* stop following him around. At some point, he must've figured out that you were from Pleasance, that you were watching him, and *he* became obsessed with *you*. He slipped a note under our door when you weren't home." She shakes her head, her short hair moving in the corner of my eye. "For *months* I'd been taunting him, threatening him, trying to get him to crack—and just like that, he had a convenient person to blame his planned theft from Advancex on, a mentally ill woman from Pleasance whose parents had been taken for everything they were worth. No matter what I said, I couldn't convince him I was someone else."

I'm shaking so much, it's hard to drive.

Her voice trembles. "I used to sit outside the building and try to follow him home, but it's like he always knew I was there. I never managed to find it—his address in the employment records, in the DMV, on his insurance. It's all fake. Even his name is fake."

I refrain from pointing out the irony of the situation, the fact that she's as fake as he is. Even so, a tiny part of me is relieved that my failures to discover Kurt's address were, in fact, not my fault.

My body's cold, and yet, I feel like laughing hysterically. "Did you know? About downstairs?"

Her voice is like lead. "What?"

"He had an apartment. Downstairs. He was spying on us through little cameras."

"You're insane," she says, though it's clear I've rattled her. "And lucky I was there to look out for you. Last week, he texted and told me he was going to kill me—kill *you*, that is. I couldn't let that happen."

"That doesn't make sense. Why wait for so long? Why even tell you in the first place?"

"I think he needed to wait until he was ready to move the money. And if he just killed you without threatening you, he wouldn't have had a chance to enjoy your fear." She cackles. "It must have *fucked him up*, how utterly unafraid of him you seemed."

I bite my lip. My eyes are moist. I fantasize about snapping around and going for the gun, but she's got it pressed so tightly to my neck. I can tell from the way she's tensing up and glancing out the window that we're getting close to our destination. "Why the bridge?"

"I remembered what you said."

"What I—"

"We were drinking once, and I asked you why you'd picked Grand Station to live in, and you said it was because of the bridge, that it was a place of power. I liked that idea, of killing him at a place of power." She sighs. "I texted him and told him to meet me—well, *you*—on the bridge. I hadn't figured on him arriving right after me, though—much less him recognizing me and ramming his car into mine. And then he saw you, and—oh, I *wish* I could've teased him about that. Do you have *any* idea how confused he must have been in those final moments, thinking we were working together all along? And Scout's honor, I didn't expect that fucking megalomaniac to jump. I hope it *hurt*—" Her voice chokes off. She must be thinking of her sister, the computer narrating how Kurt held her under the water.

I'm scrambling for something to say when she taps the gun on my neck. "Slow down a bit—see that building?"

I slow down. It's more cornfields around me, cropped down to about ten inches and covered with snow, though there's a barn in the distance. "The barn?"

Lydia pushes the gun into my neck so hard it hurts. "Pull in behind it."

I obey. There's a car behind the barn, obscured from the road: a small, white four-door. It looks like it could be the one I saw in front on the bridge. The back is full—bags, suitcases, a few cardboard containers.

She'd been packing to flee. Without her father—because otherwise, she would've taken his van. Or maybe she was going to bring the van here and grab everything, abandon the car where it likely wouldn't be found until next spring.

"Park next to it," she says, and I do. "Now, get out."

I don't get out. I can see exactly how this plays out—the bullet in my forehead, my body lost among the corn. Nobody will find it for days, until some farmer notices the vultures or a dog leaps out of a truck bed to lead a driver to my bones.

"Get out, or I'm going to shoot you right now. I don't have time for this."

She sounds like she means it, so I get out.

"Leave the purse and pop the trunk."

I swallow, but I put my purse back on the seat and hit the trunk release.

"Get in."

A semi horn suddenly blasts from across the road, making us both jump—but it's enough to turn her head the smallest fraction, and I spin and grab at the gun. She recovers fast and fights me, hard. It goes off, deafeningly loud at this close range, and fire grazes my right cheek.

Ears ringing, I let go of the gun and punch her in the nose. Her hands fly up, and the gun falls soundlessly to our feet. I kick at it before she can snatch it, and I dive for the passenger seat of my car.

She clutches my ankle and jerks me backward, and I slam into the dirt, my face erupting in pain. I kick frantically and stomp my free foot down on her head and shoulders, until she finally lets go.

I scramble halfway up. I've got my fingers on the seat, the frame—

She kicks me in the stomach, the blow so hard it sends me rolling onto the ground. I feel my ribs snap as she kicks again, and then I'm suddenly vomiting out my insides.

She doesn't even pause. She grabs me by my hair and hauls me to my feet. I'm too stunned, too dizzy to fight as she drags me toward the trunk. Everything is doubled and wavering, real world or kitchen door, I can't tell.

"I'm sorry," she says, her voice underwater—or am *I* underwater? Am I Harriet? Was it me who dove from the bridge that night? "And thank you for the account numbers."

I don't know where I am. I don't know *who* I am—but as she shoves me forward, I hear the bouncing strings of "Libiamo, ne' lieti calici," the famous duet from Verdi's *La Traviata*. It's such a mafioso movie cliché that I start laughing, explosions of pain ricocheting through my broken ribs—and then I'm throwing up again, blood spewing from me as I collapse like a rag doll onto my junk: the jack, the bottles of empty water and antifreeze, the spare tire, each an exquisite starburst of pain.

Somehow, in the fall, I rotate around just enough to see her. My last view is not of Leoni or Lydia, but of a unicorn, white and sparkling, her mane flowing majestically.

She shuts the lid.

It's dark at first, but after some time—*a minute? an hour?*—my eyes adjust.

Dim light leaks in from behind me. I slowly roll onto my side, shifting trash around. Every movement makes my eyes water.

There's a crack of light, glowing at the bottom of the seat where I broke off the clip.

I'm suddenly so, so tired. I can see myself slipping down into something soft and billowing, like a cloud—but then the image shifts, becoming instead a field of purple flowers.

My mom. If Leoni's going back to Mr. Fredericks's house, my mom and possibly Mr. Fredericks are both in danger. I don't have time to wait.

I kick hard. The pain's so intense I almost pass out, but the loose back seat launches forward. I find my hands and knees, and then I crawl toward the hole.

The opening between the trunk and the rest of the car is ringed by sharp, rusty metal, unfit for human transit. Good thing I don't really feel human anymore.

I try to go carefully, but it's impossible with such an awkward, tight fit. My eye has swollen until I'm half blind, and I've got to crush myself down against the metal to squeeze through. My arms, my hands, my shins, they all flash with pain, torn by the sharp fangs of the metal I was too fucking lazy to just cover with some duct tape—

And then I make it through, into the back seat. In the light, I can see my legs are wet with my own blood. A lot of blood, enough that my stomach churns, and I focus instead on what I came for.

My dad's phone is gone. My purse in the front seat is gone, too, and my phone with it, as are Kurt's postcards and his box and the key chain.

I scream and bang my fist against the edge of the steering wheel, my hand lighting up with pain. But my mom is still there in the front of my mind, Leoni approaching swiftly with her gun.

I don't remember seeing any houses since Mr. Fredericks's. The road wasn't busy, save the lone honking horn from before, some trucker no doubt flushing out a deer. Who knows how much time might pass before someone drives by?

My head is swimming. There isn't time for any of this, isn't time for—

A light flicks on in my mind. I look over, into the footwell by the passenger seat, and the backpack is still there, jammed underneath. I'm trying to remember how I divided the items. Was the laptop in my purse? The burner phone?

Most phones have an emergency call function that works even when the screen is locked.

I grab the backpack. It doesn't want to come out at first, though that could be because of how bloody my hand is, too slippery to get a good grip. And then it pops out from under the seat like a cork, though there's a crunch—Kurt's laptop, I bet.

I don't waste time looking through it. I turn it over and dump everything right onto the seat. The laptop falls out and bounces, hits the ground. Out comes the key chain, the photo of me in Korea, and the yearbook. Nothing else, although it's heavy enough that there's more in it, I think.

I give it a shake. My arm feels weak, but the burner phone bounces out.

My fingers are sticky with my own blood. It smears all over the cheap plastic. I flip the phone open and hit the HOME button, still some juice, thank god, but no signal.

I dial 911. The call doesn't connect.

I try again, and again. It doesn't even ring. I have to get out of this car, out of this field, closer to the road.

My whole body screams as I pull myself out the passenger side. With each step, my legs light up with fire, though it comes too late, from a distance, like I'm out of sync with my senses. My heart is beating so fast I'm not sure if it's real or if I'm imagining it, a flutter like a hummingbird.

I take a step and my leg buckles, though I catch myself. I look down. The cut in my right calf is worse than I thought, right through the clothes, right through the muscle—I think I even see bone, though it's hard to tell, with the way my pant leg and sock are soaked in blood.

I try again. 911.

Nothing. I stumble toward the road, half dragging my right leg behind me. The road's close now, closer than it should be, as if I've lost time or teleported.

I try again. 911.

I try again. 911.

And just when the world around me is going fuzzy, I hear a *click*—and then a ring.

"Hello, 911 operator, what's your emergency?"

I tell her there's an armed woman possibly going to Mr. Fredericks's house, that my mom is on her way there, that the woman abducted me, that I'm cut and bleeding and near a barn. I describe my location the best I can. Everything is melting together like watercolors, and I have to sit down.

"Apply pressure," the woman is saying, so I do. I take off my shirt and sit down, right next to the road, the snow crunching under my body. I'm freezing. I tell myself it's good that I can still feel cold as I press my hands into the wound. My other leg is bleeding, too. I hadn't noticed.

"Help is on the way."

I look back. My blood is all over the snow. "Save my mom, please. Don't let Leoni hurt her," I say, right as the call drops. Too late, I realize it's the wrong name. Leoni wouldn't hurt my mom—only Lydia would. Lydia, who knows my mother's face.

I try to redial, but my arm is heavier than it should be, my fingers numb like they're on ice. The phone slips out of my hand and goes skittering into the road like a skipped stone. I reach for it, but I'm suddenly so tired. I don't care anymore.

I lie down, settling into the road as if it were my bed. No, it's Leoni's bed—I can even smell the flowers. I hear a screech that I think could be brakes. The *thud-thud* of car doors opening and closing. A woman's voice, "God, Ted, call 911—"

I want to see what happens next, but I'm so tired, and the thorns are so close, and the snow's falling.

Everything goes quiet and dark.

And in that dark, terrible moment, as all but one of the glass mirrors in the Heart shattered around her, Mi-Hee suddenly knew what to do. Her travels had taught her many things, but none were more important than what she had learned in the Vicious Valley—that she, for all her faults, was strong enough to hold something as heavy as the truth.

It didn't have to be anybody else's truth. It could just be her own.

CHAPTER 24

Coda

If you're going to have massive blood loss, it's best to do it in the wintertime. The cold drives the blood away from your extremities and into your core, which slows down the rate at which you bleed out.

If you are going to have massive blood loss in the middle of a rural area, I strongly recommend doing it next to—not *in*, mind you, but next to—a road, where a passing veterinarian can drive by and notice your body. She'll elevate and apply pressure so that you survive until emergency services get there—although by that point, you probably won't know what's happening. You're in shock, and you have a nasty concussion.

If you don't die, the part that follows will not be pleasant—the interrogations by police, the media furor, the crawling progress in physical therapy. Neither most nor least will be the pain: unrelenting, breathtaking, and yet welcome, because it means you're still alive.

None of it matters, though. For the first time in a long time, you're absolutely free, and you're back with your family, and you just don't give a shit about anything else.

The first time I come to full consciousness in the hospital, it's night, and the lights are all dimmed. When I open my eyes, I see a copy of *Mi-Hee and the Mirror-Man* on the bedside table, the sticker on the cover winking in the glow of one of the machines next to my bed.

I make a noise—not quite a gasp, not quite a groan—and even with all the drugs that are being shunted through the IVs in my arms, my ribs hurt like I'm being kicked again.

Before I understand what's happening, my parents are by my side.

"Katrina, are you all right?" My father. I love the way he says my name so much, I tear up.

"Katrina. Katrina, don't cry, Mommy's here, you shouldn't have gone by yourself, we were so worried, *Katrina*—"

Now my mother is crying. I know this, I understand this, but everything is happening in slow motion, like my brain and body are bundled up in cotton. "Mom?"

My parents both nod. For a moment, no one speaks.

I turn my head, trying to make sense of this strange place—and there's the book again. There's even a little dog-ear in the corner, a bend in the cover near the bottom of the mirror from when I fell asleep on it, years and years ago. "Mom...is that my book?"

My mother looks startled. She exchanges a glance with my dad, one in which they're definitely debating brain damage. "Yes, I—"

"How did my book get here?"

She bites her lip. "I borrowed it. When you went to college."

I picture my mom reading my book and feel giggly. "Why would you do that?"

"I thought—" She rubs her hands together. "I thought if I held on to it, maybe you'd find your way back to me safe. I know that's silly."

"It's not," I say. "I understand."

And I do. I really, really do.

Another thought bursts through the fog in my brain. "What about Lydia? And Mr. Fredericks?"

My parents exchange a glance. "They're gone," my dad says, jaw clenched, his eyes telegraphing murder. My brain understands I've never seen my dad like this, but with all the drugs, I can't really feel it.

"What about . . . what about Kurt?"

They give each other another long look. "They found . . . something. In the water."

"Something?"

My mom hugs herself. "It's not a body, exactly. They think maybe it was cut up by a boat—" She glances at my father.

"Propeller." He swallows. "It's just part of a torso and legs—no fingers or teeth, so they're not sure on the identification yet, but they think it may be that awful Kurt man. And Katrina, there's a *bullet* in the leg."

Time passes in slow motion. I'm on the bridge, hearing that crash—was there a shot first?

I'm not sure. There could have been.

In all my obsessing, I never stopped to figure out why Kurt crashed his car in the first place. I'd assumed he'd lost control, or been trying to run Leoni off the road—but what if it was because Leoni had *shot* him? He must've known she would've killed him as he was climbing that rail. He had no choice but to take his chances and jump.

I bet he even thought he'd survive it.

I realize my mom's still talking. "Your daddy thinks they're going to do DNA, but that takes a while."

"What a jerk." I'm suddenly tired again.

My mom blinks. "What?"

"Dead or alive. He should just pick one. Anything else is rude."

And then I'm out again.

In case you're wondering, here's how it all plays out in the end:

The next time you wake up, the police are there. Your parents have given them *some* information, broad strokes only, but for the most part, they've waited for you to decide exactly how much you want to say. They've also procured you a relatively new and therefore earnest lawyer who has not yet been ground down by the system. A lawyer whose own parents were taken advantage of in the Briar Stone theft and is therefore *hell-bent* on defending you, once you explain everything that happened.

Though said lawyer is smart enough to have you emerge from this experience smelling like a rose, you decide to tell the truth. You'll never lie about your truth again, no matter how weird or fucked up or impossible it is.

The police have talked to your coworkers. They've crawled through your bloody car, your apartment, the apartment below. They have your box of postcards, which you've mentally relinquished with an ease you previously imagined would be impossible. They've broken into the burner phone, discovered Lydia's taunting texts about Harriet's death and Briar Stone and Advancex, texts in which Kurt's replies identify you by name before threatening to kill you—which have made them very, very suspicious.

On the counsel of your lawyer, you tell them about the encounter with Lydia in Mr. Fredericks's house. For reasons you don't understand, you don't want to mention the gun, but you do, because as I said before—you're done lying. You'll try to show them the Better Secrets website, but it's gone, every last trace scrubbed from search engines with a finesse that the police's cyber security guy calls "frankly scary."

You'll cry, then, at the thought of all that stolen money—money that belonged to your parents, your teachers, the people you grew up with—all of it vanished as if it'd never existed.

The police insinuate that Kurt was responsible for the missing yearbooks, the destroyed backup files that had so perplexed the librarian, but you're not sure. Hacking is more than computer savvy: it's calling places and pretending to be an admin; it's fishing someone's ID out of their laundry basket and stealing into their job after hours. The point is, both Kurt and Leoni were living lives other than the ones they'd been born with. Both had reasons for making the past disappear and the skills to do it.

As the weeks go on, any case they might have against you will start to collapse. They'll determine that some of the postcards Kurt made were not just created with ink and paint and pencil, but with things like blood and the burnt hair of a girl he drowned, a college student who died when you were still in grade school. They'll find the missing Reginald Peters, the hanged man on the *PROSPER* card, encased in cement, with a bullet in his chest.

Advancex will claim that you hacked into their servers, that you'd been seen with the burner phone by numerous coworkers—but the company's own cameras will exonerate you. Half of the messages were sent from outside the office when the footage clearly shows you typing away at your computer.

By then, speculation about the story is going viral, both in the news and in Reddit crime forums, which seem to make connections *way* faster than humanly possible. In one, you'll read someone's theory that Kurt's plan to frame you for stealing from Advancex was likely foiled by his treatment of Yocelyn, who was brave enough to report her harassment to management, thereby starting the internal investigation that would lead Advancex to discover the suspicious activity before Kurt had the chance to move the money.

In your opinion, it's a pretty good theory.

In the end, the police will add all of this to the texts between Mr. Fredericks—*It's not too late to just call the police*—and Lydia—*No. She wouldn't have reached out if she didn't know something. Just get her talking. I've almost got everything ready.* Your lawyer will helpfully point out that you went to the police that very first night and reported what you saw—and that nobody believed you, so why would you want to go back? Little by little, any investigation into your own actions will peter out.

The sweetest part of all this will be what happens to Advancex. As it turns out, there are a *lot* of laws governing how companies that handle medical and insurance data are supposed to deal with security breaches. When it gets out that there were several known, unauthorized accesses by malicious entities in an attempt to steal a bunch of money, and that Advancex had kept it quiet—well, everything hasn't run its course yet, but you're betting it's not going to end well for them.

Actually, that's not right—the sweetest thing is what happens last. Just as the frenzy is starting to look like it's going to blow over, a number of people call the police to report the *opposite* of a crime. In each case, their money, once embezzled and lost, has been returned to their accounts—save a small fraction. When added altogether, the fractions are just enough for Lydia and her father to hide out under the radar somewhere tropical—or perhaps somewhere cold. Somewhere without extradition, maybe, although I doubt falsifying a few documents and records would be beyond either of them.

Then again, on the day Lydia disappeared, her considerable bank accounts were drained—as it turns out, working full time as a travel therapist really *is* good money, especially when you're writing code on the side. Not steal-a-bunch-of-people's-retirement level money, but she's now better off than you'll ever be—not to mention a folk hero. Lydia-Leoni, whose stepsister was killed by the man who stole her father's retirement money and left him blind. Lydia-Leoni, who tracked the perpetrator for a decade, until she finally managed to corner him on the bridge.

There's even a song written about her, by a local band that includes one of the founding members of 14 Dogs. You think about listening to it but decide against it. You're not sure if you hate her or if you're grateful, but you know that however inventive the song's lyrics may be, they probably don't mention the way she lied to your parents and kept them from you for years, all so she could continue to access your Advancex credentials and ID badge.

You wonder where she and her father are sometimes, but not too hard. You're busy. You've called two coworkers from your old job and explained what happened, that you're sorry, that you want to be friends, and one of them even came to visit you—and considering the shit you pulled, getting one friend out of this is way better than you deserved.

And you have your parents. Your dad, who says your name just the way you like it. Your mom, who has curly hair, but is healthy.

The truth is you got everything you wanted. You did the impossible and crawled your way through the mirror. You found your way home.

"All right, Katrina. I think it's time for the worksheets."

I find Vicky really boring, which actually makes her a pretty good therapist for me. Her focus on worksheets is annoying—especially when I see it working—and her steadfast refusal to render a diagnosis in anything more than the vaguest terms "so the insurance will let me treat you" defies my need for classification.

Therapy is also really fucking uncomfortable. Do you know what the treatment for a compulsion is? It's to sit there with a *timer*, to sit there with your skin peeling off and your heart thumping and your world going wavery—and to push it off for five minutes, then six minutes, then ten. To know that if you *don't* draw your sigil on the door something awful will happen—and then to set a timer and try to watch a terrible movie or exercise or make dinner, knowing all the time the sigil is there, waiting to be drawn, but that you can't do anything about it until the timer goes off.

It's hell.

But Vicky also doesn't bullshit me. She doesn't fight me on the kitchen-door world, either—instead her approach is mostly *So what?* She tells me, over and over, that just because something exists doesn't mean I have to engage with it—and the fact that I do sometimes engage with it doesn't have to cause me distress. I may never be normal. I will almost certainly never have a brain like other people, a brain that doesn't want to draw sigils and obsess about the number eleven—and I will always be in danger of losing control. Too much stress, and things will get harder for me, make it easier to fall into that trap.

And to be honest, some things don't have rational explanations. That's the point, isn't it? That not every mystery has an answer, that even trying to define reality is control I don't get to have. I still haven't figured out if the photoshopped picture of me actually smelled like smoke, or if the yearbook in the Sunbeam Library really was hot to the touch. If my mom's possession of *Mi-Hee and the Mirror-Man* kept me safe.

I don't know if Lydia-Leoni really was trying to keep Kurt from killing me—and if so, if it was because of her conscience, because she didn't want to be implicated in my murder, or something else. Part of me thinks she planned on shooting him all along, and I *really was* the one who messed everything up.

When it comes to my rituals, though, I have to admit things are getting better. Achingly slowly, little by little, the timer interval is getting longer. Every once in a while, I'll be so absorbed in my distraction activity that it's a surprise when the timer goes off. Sometimes, the urge to make the sigil, the stellations, to count my steps—sometimes it even ebbs, melting away like a headache, and I realize that I'm too tired or bored or busy to be bothered.

It doesn't happen often, and it won't happen forever, but for now, it gives me hope.

A few months after I move in with my parents, but before I help them celebrate the return of their life's savings by going with them to pick out a house, I get a phone call from Sunder.

"I want to talk to you about a job," she says, her voice gravelly. I can almost smell her cigarettes—almost, because my dad is working on quitting again, although his success is spotty.

I don't know how to answer her. "A job?"

"Yeah. I need a receptionist."

I start laughing, because I live in my parents' apartment and sleep on an air mattress. Because I have no experience, because I never managed to finish college. Because I can't be trusted to just go into an office and do basic tasks every day. "Sorry," I say, "but I don't think I'd be very good at that."

"It wouldn't be forever, the receptionist thing." She takes a drag of her cigarette. "Just until you get your feet wet. Then you could start doing gopher activities, fetching paperwork, et cetera. Once you get some experience under your belt, I'd like to see about getting you licensed as a PI. I kept tabs on you, you know, after our call. My friends in the force told me you solved the Briar Stone case. That's pretty admirable. I think you'd be pretty good at it."

"I solved the *case*?" My voice goes up, but I can't help it. "Sunder, I know you don't know me, but you don't *want* me as an employee. I almost got *murdered*. I can't show up on time, I can't keep a schedule, I'm a disorganized mess—"

"And you're tenacious, and you have good instincts," she says, taking another drag. "And you're energetic, and honestly, I'm getting old and kind of tired of doing all the grunt work. Just think it over. Remember, you owe me a favor."

I'm shaking my head. "Look—I've got *problems*. Like, you know, mental problems. Sometimes I see things that aren't there. It's probably not a good idea."

She snorts. "Did Navya tell you anything about me?"

"No," I say, thinking of Navya. I hope she's okay. My parents gave me a small portion of their returned retirement savings as a kind of finder's fee, and I sent it to Navya for her kids' college.

"I'm a sixty-year-old Indian-American lesbian woman who assumed a man's name and decided to open a private investigation office instead of getting married and having babies. As far as my *parents* are concerned, my mental illnesses could eat your mental illnesses for breakfast—they'd *much* prefer I just saw things. More importantly, we have good health insurance, and I guarantee you'll make more than you were making at Advancex. Just tell me you'll think it over."

"I will," I say, although I won't... probably.

"Besides, I like crazy people. And oh, Katrina?"

The hair stands up on the back of my neck. Whatever she's about to say, I don't want to hear it—except that I do, because that's who I am. I want to know things, even when I don't. "Yes?"

"Do you know what a keylogger is?"

The word is vaguely familiar, though I'm not sure where from. "No."

"It's a program. You use it to secretly track what keys people hit, so you know what they're doing on their computer." She takes a drag of her cigarette. "The *interesting* thing about keyloggers is—let's say your job installs one, and then someone *else* who is *also* tracking you decides to install one on the same computer. Do you know what might happen then?"

"No," I say, although I do, because she's talking about *my* computer at work. That must have been the program on the sticky note, the one that ended in "KL.exe." A keylogger. My computer kept freezing because more than one person was tracking my movements on it.

"Find out," she says, and she hangs up before I can answer, because that's the kind of woman Sunder is.

And although I don't call her back that night, when I curl up on the air bed in the middle of my parents' living room, I start to see a new life for myself, one where I can make good use of my need to always know the answer.

EPILOGUE

I can't leave things incomplete—and they have to be complete the *right way*, finished in the same way they started. My therapist would call that a compulsion, my new boss "a personality quirk," my mom something I "get from her."

But here are the hidden truths that my spyglass eventually revealed:

The Mirror-Man was real, and his name was William Coscarelli.

The unicorn was real, but her name doesn't actually matter. What matters is that she was full of vengeance.

The Cayatoga Bridge is a magical place. And after the unicorn shot William there, he crashed his car and climbed the bridge's railing, just like the Mirror-Man, trying to burrow his way into the *Heart*.

Maybe the unicorn's gift was truth, but it was a gift that William would never accept. He thought he was a man above death, too good to be killed by anyone else, and that's why he jumped.

Sometimes, I think it never happened at all.

But then I visit the bridge and look down, and I can see him standing on the bottom, screaming into the deep.

ACKNOWLEDGMENTS

When publication takes twenty-plus years and twenty-plus manuscripts, there are a lot of people to thank—and if you're me, the joy of writing your acknowledgments section quickly turns into the dread of leaving someone important out. If that's you, I'm *really*, really sorry.

In true Katrina Kim fashion, I've tried (and failed) to do these chronologically:

Thank you to the English teachers who taught me to write and read—and Mrs. Stieve, I'll never forget your kindness. Thank you to my band teachers, who threw me a much-needed lifeline. (Especially Leo Hazen and Dave Papenhagen.)

Thank you to my parents and my sister for always supporting my writing endeavors, and to Justin for his unwavering faith in me despite my many stumbles and struggles. To Rachell, a font of constant optimism and perseverance, who has dragged me up by the scruff of my neck more times than I can count. To the Monsters, whose witty banter and keen eye have guided me through many a tough revision—Samantha Rajaram, Kola Heyward-Rotimi, Lucas Cober, Ava Reid, and most of all, my partner in crime, Steve Westenra, who always understands what I'm trying to do with my work and how to make it better. To Ashley Winstead, Tami Olsen, Jeff Wooten, Keeley Madison, and every other writer that's contributed a kind word or a keen set of eyes along the way.

Thank you to the many, many people who have taken me under their wing over the years—the editors at so many incredible magazines, the entire Pitch Wars organization, and particularly R. F. Kuang and Victoria Lee, who saw fit to mentor me through the basics of plot and characterization, once upon a time.

Thank you to my agent, the indomitable Amy Bishop, who has proved her worth as a partner time and time again, and to my editor, Rachael Kelly, for whipping out her own amazing spyglass and revealing what this book could be. Thank you to my amazing team at Grand Central, including Luria Rittenberg, Justine Gardner, Theresa DeLucci, Kamrun Nesa, and Ivy Cheng, as well as Shreya Gupta for her amazing artwork.

And most of all, thank you, dear reader. Without you, this book would've never been possible.

ABOUT THE AUTHOR

Maria Dong's short fiction, articles, and poetry have been published in over a dozen venues, including *Best American Science Fiction and Fantasy, Apex, Apparition Literary Magazine, Augur, Fantasy Magazine, Fusion Fragment, Kaleidotrope, Khōréō, Lightspeed*, and *Nightmare*, among others. Currently a computer programmer, she has had a diverse career as a property manager, English teacher, and occupational therapist. She lives with her partner in southwest Michigan, in a centenarian saltbox house that is almost certainly haunted, and loves watching K-dramas and drinking Bell's beer.

MariaDong.com
Twitter @mariadongwrites
Instagram @maria_dong_writes